UNSPEAKABLE

SANDRA BROWN

UNSPEAKABLE

WARNER BOOKS

A Time Warner Company

Copyright © 1998 by Sandra Brown Management, Ltd.
All rights reserved.
Warner Books, Inc., 1271 Avenue of the Americas,
New York, NY 10020
Visit our Web site at http://warnerbooks.com

A Time Warner Company

Printed in the United States of America

ISBN 0-446-51979-0

Acknowledgment

While writing this novel, I was challenged to express the thoughts of an individual who was born profoundly deaf and whose first means of communication was sign language. My experience being limited, I sought help from the deaf community. One young woman in particular helped enormously . . . and not for the first time.

Jenni, thank you again.

As instructive as she and her family were, I'm sure I made mistakes. Because of language limitations on my part, it was necessary in some passages to take creative license. Please forgive any errors. They are entirely my own and not the responsibility of those who so willingly and generously shared their time and knowledge with me.

—Sandra Brown

UNSPEAKABLE

Chapter One

"*M*yron, are you listening to me?" Carl Herbold glowered at his fellow convict, impatiently shook his head, and muttered, "Stupid, stupid."

Impervious to the insult, Myron Hutts's vacant grin remained in place.

Carl thrust his face closer. "Lose the grin, okay, Myron? This is serious stuff I'm talking here. Has anything sunk into that lump of shit riding on top of your shoulders? Have you heard a fucking word I've said?"

Myron chomped down on his PayDay candy bar. "Sure, Carl, I heard you. You said for me to listen good and pay attention."

"Okay then."

Carl relaxed somewhat, but he wasn't convinced that even a fraction of what he told Myron would register. Myron wasn't what you'd call brainy. In fact, stretching, Myron's IQ might range in the single digits.

He was physically strong and eager to please, but his shortage in the smarts department made him a risk to Carl's carefully laid plans. Having someone with Myron's limitations as an accomplice wasn't without its drawbacks.

On the plus side, Carl needed a Myron Hutts. He needed a nonthinker who did what he was told, when he was told to do it, without question or argument or scruple. That's why Myron was a perfect choice. Even if he'd been a fucking Einstein with gray matter to spare, Myron was missing a conscience.

A conscience was "internal dialogue." Now wasn't that a catchy phrase? Carl had picked it up from an article in a magazine. He'd committed it to memory, then pulled it out and used it on the parole board the last time he came up for review. For five minutes he had waxed eloquent on how he had been having internal dialogues with himself about his past misdeeds and the havoc he'd wreaked on his life and the lives of others. These dialogues had shown him the error of his ways and pointed him toward the light of self-discovery and accountability. He was remorseful and wished to atone.

The board members weren't impressed by the big words he'd thrown in. They'd seen his speech for the string of bullshit it was and rejected his petition for parole.

But supposing the conscience *was* internal dialogue. That entailed abstract ideas and concepts, which Myron was just too plain stupid to grasp. Actually Carl didn't give a damn whether Myron had a conscience or not. He would act on his impulses of the moment, period. Which was precisely why Carl had chosen him. Myron wouldn't go squeamish on him if things got ugly.

And speaking of ugly, Myron was one butt-ugly dude. His skin had only a trace of pigmentation. Most of his coloration was concentrated in his lips. They were large and unnaturally red. By contrast, the irises of his eyes were virtually colorless. Pale, sparse eyebrows and lashes made his vacuous gaze appear even emptier. His hair was thin, but coarsely textured, radiating from his head like crinkled wire. It was almost white.

He was particularly unattractive with the half-masticated nougat center of a PayDay oozing from the corners of his fleshy lips. As his tongue swabbed up the drool, Carl looked away.

Many would wonder why he and Myron were pals, as the contrast between them was so striking. Carl was tall, dark, and handsome. He worked out with weights when the mood struck him, but he religiously did push-ups and sit-ups in his cell to keep his torso hard. He had a killer smile that was reminiscent of a young Warren Beatty. At least that's what he'd been told. Personally, he thought he was better looking than the actor, whom Carl had always thought of as a fruit. Beatty had a great-looking wife, though. A real sweet piece was Mrs. Beatty.

Carl was certainly superior to Myron Hutts in the brains department. The quantity Myron lacked, Carl had as extra. He was a great planner. Brilliant ideas just seemed to come to him naturally. He also had a real talent for taking a loosely woven idea and pulling all the strings tight until it became a grand scheme.

If he'd been in the military, he would have been a general. But even the highest-ranking officers needed soldiers to carry out their strategies. Thus, Myron.

He could have picked his partner from any man in the joint. Myron spooked most people, even hardened criminals. They steered clear of him. But Carl's leadership qualities drew people like a magnet. Seniority had given him a lot of clout among the convict population. That and his innate charisma. He could have anointed any number of inmates as his partner, all of them smarter and meaner than Myron—because for all his violent tendencies, Myron was sweet-tempered. But anybody brainier also could have caused Carl problems.

He didn't need anybody with a conflicting opinion giving him lip along the way. Disharmony led to distraction, and distraction led to disaster, namely getting recaptured. All he needed for this escape plan was an extra pair of eyes and ears, and someone who could shoot and wasn't afraid to when necessary. Myron Hutts filled the bill. Myron didn't need any cunning. Carl had enough for both of them.

Besides, he was going to catch enough guff from Cecil. Cecil thought *too* much. He overanalyzed every goddamn thing. While he was weighing the odds, he missed opportunities. Like that funny postcard Carl had seen one time of a man holding a camera to his face and taking a picture of the Eiffel Tower while a naked French lady was strolling past—that was Cecil.

But Carl didn't want to think about his older brother now. Later, when he was alone, he'd think about Cecil.

As he leaned back against the chain-link fence, his gaze roved over the exercise yard. The vigilance was second nature. Twenty years of incarceration had taught him always to be on the alert for the first sign of trouble from an enemy, declared or otherwise. He wielded a lot of influence and had a wide circle of friends, but he wasn't a favorite of everyone.

Across the yard a gang of weight-lifting blacks were flexing their well-oiled muscles and glaring at him with undiluted hatred for no other reason than that he wasn't one of them. Society was all hepped up about rival gangs, street warfare, vendettas. Laughable. Until you'd been inside, you didn't know shit about gangs. The society inside was the most demarcated, polarized, segregated, in the universe.

He'd had differences of opinion with the black prisoners, which had caused exchanges of insults, which had eventually led to fights, which had resulted in disciplinary actions.

But he wasn't going to get anything started with anybody today or in the near future. Until the day he and Myron had their turn to work on the road crew, Carl Herbold was going to be an ideal prisoner. It was a new program, part of prison reform designed to make convicts feel like contributing members of society again. He didn't give a crap about the social implications. All he cared about was how it affected him. When his turn came to leave these walls and work outside, he would be first on the bus.

So he was keeping a low profile, doing nothing that might call the screws' attention to him. No rule-breaking, no fights, not even a bad attitude. If he heard a mumbled insult directed at him, he ignored it. What he didn't like, he pretended not to see. A few nights back, he'd had to stand by and watch Myron suck a guy off. The other prisoner, a white trash wife-killer two years into a life sentence, had bribed Myron with a prize, so Myron had obliged him.

Frequently the more aggressive prisoners tried to take advantage of Myron's mental incapacity. Carl usually intervened. But this close to their break, it hadn't been worth the risk of a confrontation. Besides, Myron hadn't minded too much. In exchange for the blow job he'd been given a live mouse, which he'd later disemboweled with his long pinkie fingernail.

"Now, remember what I told you, Myron," Carl said to him now, realizing that rec time was almost up and they would have little privacy for the rest of the day. When our turn comes up to work the road crew, you can't seem too excited about it."

"Okay," Myron said, becoming distracted by the bleeding cuticle around his thumb.

"It might even be good if we could look sorta pissed that we gotta pull that detail. Think you can manage that? To look pissed?"

"Sure, Carl." He was gnawing the pulverized cuticle with all the relish he'd shown the PayDay.

"Because if they think we're eager to go, then—"

He never saw it coming. The blow literally knocked him off the bleacher on which he'd been sitting. One second he was looking into Myron's slack-jawed, candy-encrusted grin. The next he was lying on his side in the dirt, his ears ringing, his vision blurring, his gut heaving, and his kidney getting the piss kicked out of it.

He forgot about his resolve not to cause or continue any trouble. Survival instinct asserted itself. Rolling to his back, he brought his foot up and thrust it into his attacker's crotch. The black weight lifter, who obviously depended strictly on muscle instead of fighting finesse, hadn't anticipated a counterattack. He fell to his knees, yowling and clutching his testicles. Of course the other blacks sought reprisal by piling onto Carl and hammering him with their fists.

The screws came running, swinging their clubs. Other prisoners began either to try to break up the fight or to cheer it on, depending. The struggle was quickly contained. When order had been restored and the damage assessed, it was found to be minimal. Only two prisoners were sent to the infirmary with injuries.

One of them was Carl Herbold.

Chapter Two

I thought it was a very nice occasion."

His wife's comment caused Ezzy Hardge to snort with disdain. "That was the toughest piece of meat I've ever tried to eat, and the air conditioner was working at half capacity. Thought I was going to melt inside that black suit."

"Well, you wouldn't have been happy with the dinner no matter what. You were bound and determined to be a grouch about it."

Ezzy had been married to Cora two years longer than he had served as sheriff of Blewer County—fifty-two years. He'd first spotted her at a tent revival, which he and a group of friends had attended just for laughs. Almost in defiance of the hellfire being preached from the pulpit, Cora had been wearing a sassy red bow in her hair and lipstick to match. During the hymn singing, her eyes had drifted away from the songbook and across the aisle to land on Ezzy, who was staring at her with unabashed interest and speculation. The light in her eyes was not religious fervor but devilish mischief. She had winked at him.

In all these years, none of her sass had worn off, and he still liked it.

"The people of this county went to a lot of trouble and expense to host that dinner for you. The least you could do is show a little gratitude." Peeling off her housecoat, she joined him in bed. "If I'd had a dinner held in my honor, I think I could find it within myself to be gracious about it."

"I didn't ask for a testimonial dinner. I felt like a goddamn fool."

"You're not mad about the dinner. You're mad because you're having to retire."

Cora rarely minced words. Tonight was no exception. Sullenly, Ezzy pulled the sheet up over them.

"Don't think for a minute that I look forward to your retirement, either," she said, unnecessarily pounding her pillow into shape. "You think I want you home all day, underfoot, sulking around and getting in my way as I go about my business? No, sir."

"Would you rather I'd've got shot one night by some rabble-rouser with one too many Lone Stars under his belt, spared you all the headaches of having me around?"

Cora simmered for several seconds. "You've been trying to provoke me all evening, and you've finally succeeded. It's that kind of talk that makes me furious, Ezra Hardge."

She yanked on the small chain on the nightstand lamp and plunged the bedroom into darkness, then rolled to her side, giving him her back. Ordinarily they went to sleep lying face to face.

She knew him well. He *had* deliberately said something that was guaranteed to get her dander up. The irony of it was that every day of his tenure as sheriff he had prayed that he wouldn't get killed on the job and leave Cora a bloody corpse to deal with.

But from a practical standpoint, he should have died in the line of duty. It would have been cleaner, neater, simpler for all concerned. The community leaders would have been spared the embarrassment of *suggesting* that he not seek office again. They would have saved the expense of tonight's shindig at the Community Center, or at least put the funds to better use. If he had died sooner, he wouldn't be facing a future where he was going to feel about as useful as snowshoes in the Sahara.

Seventy-two years old, going on seventy-three. Arthritis in every joint. Felt like it anyway. And his mind probably wasn't as sharp as it used to be. No, he hadn't noticed any slippage, but others probably had and laughed at his encroaching senility behind his back.

What hurt most was knowing everybody was right. He was old and decrepit and had no business heading up a law enforcement office. Okay, he could see that. Even if he didn't like it or wish it, he could accept retirement because the people of his county would be better served by having a younger man in office.

He just wished to hell that he hadn't had to quit before his job was finished. And it would never be finished until he knew what had happened to Patsy McCorkle.

For twenty-two years that girl had been sleeping between him and Cora. In a manner of speaking, of course. Feeling guilty about that intrusion now, especially in light of their quarrel, he rolled to his side and placed his hand on Cora's hip. He patted it lovingly. "Cora?"

"Forget it," she grumbled. "I'm too mad."

* * *

When Ezzy walked into the sheriff's office a few hours later, the dispatcher on duty lifted his head sleepily, then bounded from his chair. "Hey, Ezzy, what the hell you doin' here?"

"Sorry I interrupted your nap, Frank. Don't mind me. I've got some files that need clearing out."

The deputy glanced at the large wall clock. "This time o' morning?"

"Couldn't sleep. Now that I'm officially out, I figured I just as well get all my things. Sheriff Foster will be wanting to move in tomorrow."

"I reckon. What do you think about him?"

"He's a good man. He'll make a good sheriff," Ezzy replied sincerely.

"Maybe so, but he's no Ezzy Hardge."

"Thanks for that."

"Sorry I didn't get to go to the banquet last evenin'. How was it?"

"You didn't miss a thing. Most boring time I've ever had." Ezzy entered his private office and switched on the light, probably for the last time. "Never heard so many speeches in all my life. What is it about turning a microphone over to somebody, they automatically become long-winded?"

"Folks got a lot to say about a living legend."

Ezzy harrumphed. "I'm no longer your boss, Frank, but I'll get physical with you if you keep talking like that. Got a spare cup of coffee? I'd sure appreciate it."

"Comin' right up."

Unable to sleep after such an emotionally strenuous evening, not to mention Cora's rebuff of his affection, he'd gotten up, dressed, and crept from the house. Cora had a radar system as good as a vampire bat's, picking up any sound and motion he made. He hadn't wanted a confrontation with her about the stupidity of going out in the wee hours to do a job that the county had granted him a week to get done.

But since they'd retired him, he reasoned they didn't want him lurking around, no matter how many times they assured him that he would always be welcome in the sheriff's office of Blewer County. Last thing he wanted to do was make a pest of himself, or become a pathetic old man who clung to the glory days and couldn't accept that he was no longer needed or wanted.

He didn't want to start having regular self-pity parties, either, but that's what this was, wasn't it?

He thanked the deputy when he set a steaming mug of coffee on his desk. "Close the door behind you, please, Frank. I don't want to disturb you."

"Won't bother me any. It's been a quiet night."

All the same, Frank pulled the door closed. Ezzy wasn't worried about disturbing the dispatcher. Fact was, he didn't want any chitchat while he went about this chore. The official files were, of course, a matter of public record, shared with the city police, the Texas Department of Public Safety, the Texas Rangers, and any other law enforcement agency with which his office cooperated and coordinated investigations.

But the file cabinets in his office contained Ezzy's personal notes—lists of questions to pose to a suspect, times and dates and names of individuals connected to a case, information imparted by reliable informants or witnesses who wished to remain anonymous. For the most part, these notes had been handwritten by him in a shorthand he had developed and that only he could decipher, usually jotted down with a number-two pencil on any scrap of paper available to him at the time. Ezzy considered them as private as a diary. More than those damn flowery speeches he'd had to endure at the Community Center last night, these personal files documented his career.

He took a sip of coffee, rolled his chair over to the metal filing cabinet, and pulled open the bottom drawer. The files were more or less categorized by year. He removed a few of the earliest ones, leafed through them, found them not worth saving, and tossed them into the ugly, dented, brown metal wastebasket that had been there as long as he had.

He went about the clean-out methodically and efficiently, but he was inexorably working his way toward 1976. By the time he got to that year's files, the coffee had gone sour in his stomach and he was belching it.

One file was different from the rest chiefly because it was larger and had seen the most use. It was comprised of several manila folders held together by a wide rubber band. The edges of each folder were soiled, frayed, and curled, testifying to the many times they'd been reopened, fingered as Ezzy reviewed the contents, spilled on, wedged into the cabinet between less significant folders, only to be removed again and put through the same cycle.

He rolled the rubber band off the folders and onto his thick wrist. He wore a copper bracelet because Cora said copper was good for arthritis, but you couldn't tell it by him.

Stacking the folders on his desk, he sipped the fresh coffee that the deputy had refilled without any acknowledgment from Ezzy, then opened the top one. First item in it was a page from the Blewer Bucks yearbook. Ezzy remembered the day he'd torn out this page of the high school annual to use for reference. Senior section, third row down, second picture from the left. Patricia Joyce McCorkle.

She was looking directly into the camera's lens, wearing an expression that said she knew a secret the photographer would love to know. Activities listed at the end of the row beneath her name were Chorus, Spanish Club, and Future Homemakers. Her advice to lowerclassmen: "Party, party, party, and party hearty."

Cap-and-gown photos were rarely flattering, but Patsy's was downright unattractive, mainly because she wasn't pretty to begin with. Her eyes were small, her nose wide and flat, her lips thin, and she had hardly any chin at all.

Her lack of beauty hadn't kept Patsy from being popular, however. It hadn't taken long for Ezzy to learn that Patsy McCorkle had had more dates than just about any other senior girl that year, including the homecoming princess and the class beauty.

Because, as one of her classmates—who now owned and operated the Texaco station on Crockett Street—had told him, stammering with embarrassment, "Patsy put out for everybody, Sheriff Hardge. Know what I mean?"

Ezzy knew. Even when he was in high school there had been girls who put out for everybody, and every boy knew who they were.

Nevertheless, Patsy's soiled reputation hadn't made it any easier for him to go to her home that hot August morning and deliver the news that no parent ever wants to hear.

McCorkle managed the public-service office downtown. Ezzy knew him to speak to, but they weren't close acquaintances. McCorkle intercepted him even before he reached the front porch. He pushed open the screened door and the first words out of his mouth were, "What's she done, Sheriff?"

Ezzy had asked if he could come in. As they made their way through the tidy, livable rooms of the house to the kitchen, where McCorkle already had coffee percolating, he told the sheriff that lately his girl had been wild as a March hare.

"We can't do anything with her. She's half-wrecked her car by driving it too fast and reckless. She stays out till all hours every night, drinking till she gets drunk, then puking it up every morning. She's smoking cigarettes and I'm afraid to know what else. She breaks all our rules and makes no secret of it. She won't ever tell me or her mother who she's with when she's out, but I hear she's been messing around with those Herbold brothers. When I confronted her about running with delinquents like that, she told me to mind my own goddamn business. Her words. She said she could date anybody she damn well pleased, and that included married men if she took a mind to. The way she's behaving, Sheriff Hardge, it wouldn't surprise me if she has."

He handed the sheriff a cup of fresh coffee. "It was only a matter of time before she broke the law, I guess. Since she didn't come home last night, I've been more or less expecting you. What's she done?" he repeated.

"Is Mrs. McCorkle here?"

"Upstairs. Still asleep."

Ezzy nodded, looked down at the toes of his black uniform boots, up at the white ruffled curtain in the kitchen window, over at the red cat stretching itself against the leg of the table, onto which he set his coffee. "Your girl was found dead this morning, Mr. McCorkle."

He hated this part of his job. Thank God this particular duty didn't come around too often or he might have opted for some other line of work. It was damned hard to meet a person eye-to-eye when you had just informed him that a family member wasn't coming home. But it was doubly hard when moments before he'd been talking trash about the deceased.

All the muscles in the man's face seemed to drop as though they'd been snipped off at the bone. After that day, McCorkle had never looked the same. Townsfolk commented on the change. Ezzy could pinpoint the instant that transformation in his face had taken place.

"Car wreck?" he wheezed.

Ezzy wished that were the case. He shook his head sadly. "No, sir. She, uh, she was found just after dawn, out in the woods, down by the river."

"Sheriff Hardge?"

He turned, and there in the kitchen doorway stood Mrs. McCorkle wearing a summer-weight housecoat spattered with daisies. Her hair was in curlers and her eyes were puffy from just waking up.

"Sheriff Hardge? Pardon me, Ezzy?"

Ezzy looked toward the office door and blinked the deputy into focus. He'd forgotten where he was. His recollection had carried him back twenty-two years. He was in the McCorkles' kitchen, hearing not Frank, but Mrs. McCorkle speaking his name with a question mark—and a suggestion of dread—behind it. Ezzy rubbed his gritty eyes. "Uh, yeah, Frank. What is it?"

"Hate to interrupt, but Cora's on the phone, wanting to know if you're here." He winked. "Are you?"

"Yeah. Thanks, Frank."

The moment he said hello, Cora lit into him. "I don't appreciate you sneaking out while I'm asleep and not telling me where you're going."

"I left you a note."

"You said you were going to work. And since you officially retired last night, I couldn't guess where you are presently employed."

He smiled, thinking about how she looked right now. He could see her, all sixty-one inches of her drawn up ramrod straight, hands on hips, eyes flashing. It was a cliché, but it fit: Cora was prettier when she was angry. "I was thinking 'bout taking you out to breakfast at the IHOP, but since you're in such a pissy mood, I might ask me some other girl."

"As if any other girl would put up with you." After a huffy pause, she added, "I'll be ready in ten minutes. Don't keep me waiting."

He tidied up before leaving the office and gathered what he'd salvaged into some boxes the county had thoughtfully provided. Frank helped him carry the boxes to his car. After they were loaded into the trunk, they shook hands. "See you 'round, Ezzy."

"Take care, Frank."

Only after the dispatcher had returned inside did Ezzy lay the McCorkle file on top of the others. He wouldn't unload the trunk while Cora was around. If she saw that file, she would know that was what had got him up in the middle of the night and had kept him occupied these last few hours. Then she really would be pissed.

Chapter Three

*C*arl whispered to Myron, "It's tomorrow now, remember?"

"Sure, Carl. I remember."

"So don't do anything that might keep you from getting into that road-crew van."

"I won't, Carl."

Dumber than dirt, Carl was thinking as he gazed into the cerebral desert behind Myron's clear eyes.

Although it wasn't quite fair to question Myron's behavior when he himself had come close to screwing up their plan. All he'd done was try to protect himself from a sound beating. But if he had it to do over again, he wouldn't fight back.

After that nigger attacked him, he'd gone plumb berserk with rage. It had taken four men to get him into the infirmary and strapped onto the bed. Even then he'd managed to bite a chunk of flesh from the forearm of a male nurse. They couldn't give him a sedative because they hadn't yet examined his head to determine the extent of his injury.

Uncaring about the blasted headache, he had ranted and raved the rest of that day and the livelong night. He had screamed like a banshee, railing against God, and the devil and the niggers, who might have cost him his one chance for escape.

In hindsight he realized he should have lain there in the dirt and let that weight lifter keep on kicking him till the bulls got there and pulled him off. How much damage could have been done in a matter of a few more seconds?

He'd been diagnosed with a mild concussion. He had vomited a few times. His vision was slightly blurry, but it had completely cleared by late the following day. He'd had a headache that no amount of medication had alleviated; it had finally just worn off. His kidney was bruised and sore, but the doc said no permanent damage had been done.

He'd suffered a few days of discomfort, but he had been grateful for the injuries. They demonstrated to the warden that he was the injured party and that he had only been trying to protect himself when he kicked the other prisoner in his privates.

Carl had derived tremendous satisfaction from leaving the infirmary intact, able to walk out under his own power, while the nigger's balls were still swollen. Their grotesque size was a source of amusement for everyone in the infirmary. He had a tube stuck in his dick, peeing for him, which also generated all sorts of ridicule. He cried like a baby every time he moved.

So in the long run, it had worked out all right. The doc had declared him fit to go back to work on the grounds maintenance crew, making him eligible to pull road-crew duty as well. Squeaking by once, he was taking no more chances on getting disqualified for that special detail.

Since leaving the infirmary, he had kept his distance from the rest of the prison population, except for Myron. He hadn't engaged anyone in conversation. He hadn't looked askance at anybody, especially the blacks. He hated like hell to leave without killing one of them in retaliation for all the grief they'd given him over the years, but in the grand scheme of things, it just wasn't worth it. He might have a few fleeting moments of enjoyment from seeing their blood run, but then his ass would be hash. He would never see the light of day again. And he had a real hankering to see just how bright the sunshine was in Mexico and to taste all the exotic pleasures that country had to afford.

But he had to get out of here first.

Today his and Myron's names had appeared on the list. Tomorrow was the day. He had waited for it. Planned it. A few hours from now he would be a free man. If everything went his way. There was a lot that could go wrong. That's why his stomach was so nervous he could barely choke down the beanie-wienies and sauerkraut on the dinner tray.

But he ate the food anyway to keep from drawing the screws' attention and arousing their suspicion. "Myron, tonight before you go to sleep, you might try going over the plan in your mind."

A spoonful of sauerkraut disappeared into Myron's mouth. "What plan, Carl?"

"Jesus," Carl muttered. This was hopeless. How many times had they been over it? If the idiot fucked this up for him, he would kill him with his bare hands. Taking a deep sigh of resignation, he said, "Never mind, Myron. You just stick to me like a fly to shit tomorrow, okay?"

"Okay, Carl."

"When I tell you to do something, I want you to do it, okay?"

"Okay."

"No arguments, no discussion, just do it, okay?"

"Okay."

Go stick your dick in a meat grinder, Myron, okay? Okay, Carl.

On the verge of screaming with frustration, Carl reminded himself that this was the kind of blind obedience he wanted and needed. He was the top gun, the leader, the head honcho. He was the dashing, good-looking, shrewd, ladies' man, strategist stud. In an operation like this, there couldn't be more than one boss. It needed mules, too.

So actually it was better that Myron was dumb and obedient to a fault. Because when Carl told him to do something—like, say, slit the bastard guard's throat—that's what Myron would do.

Without shame or remorse, Myron had told Carl stories about his childhood. Young Myron Hutts had been one twisted fuck. He'd been a one-man extermination brigade in his town, ridding the community and outlying areas of pets and small animals before the authorities finally caught him and sent him away for psychiatric analysis. Members of his family had petitioned the state authorities until they finally released him from the head hospital. They lived—not for long, however—to regret it.

Myron had spoken matter-of-factly about their slaughter. "Grandma's head went *plop,* and her wig come right off. It fell into the gravy bowl."

Myron was particularly fond of telling that part because on occasion Grandma had used Myron's head as a wig form while she was putting curlers in it. The rest of the family always laughed hysterically upon seeing their tall, gawky Myron in Grandma's gray wig all wound up in pink sponge curlers.

His head had also been used as a punching bag when his old man got drunk and disorderly. One particularly bad drinking binge had resulted in Myron's retardation. His daddy had repeatedly slammed the head of his two-year-old son into the room radiator. It had been summer and the radiator was cold, but it had done its damage just the same.

From that day on, Myron was an easy target for verbal and physical potshots. He was made fun of at school, routinely abused by the bullies. But it was his family—Dad, Mom, sister, and Granny—who tortured and humiliated the boy for their amusement.

They didn't laugh the evening Myron came to the supper table with a hatchet and a shotgun.

He'd made one hell of a mess of his family. A killing like that, it was a wonder he hadn't been deemed criminally insane and confined to a psychiatric hospital for analysis and healing. Most likely a fire-breathing prosecutor had argued that Myron was bright enough to go to the big house, and that if he were confined to a hospital rather than sentenced to a maximum-security prison, the state would be running the risk of some bleeding-heart shrink eventually declaring him "cured" and unleashing him on an unsuspecting public. And, in fact, he showed no compunction against killing. Bugs, animals, people—you name it. Carl had watched Myron torture small creatures for hours before killing them.

Oh, yes, Carl needed a Myron. A case could be made that he was taking advantage of Myron just as ruthlessly as had the bullies in his grade school. But, as with all twinges of conscience, Carl ignored this one.

Feeling a sudden rush of affection for the man who obviously idolized him, Carl leaned across the table and smiled at his confederate. "Have I told you the two things I'm gonna do when I get outta here, Myron?"

"Find some sweet Mexican pussy."

Carl laughed. "You remember that one, don't you, Myron?"

"Yeah, I remember that one." Myron smiled through a mouthful of beanie-wienies.

"That and what else?" Carl asked. "What else am I gonna do?"

Myron pushed the food down his throat with a hard, noisy swallow. "Kill the motherfuckers who got you put in prison."

Chapter Four

*J*ack Sawyer stepped down from the cab of his pickup. "Need some help there?"

His footsteps crunched across the loose gravel of the driveway, sending up small clouds of dust that resettled on his scuffed snakeskin boots, boots handcrafted by a Mexican saddle maker more than a decade ago. The old guy had been fond of taking frequent tequila shots, so Jack's left boot was a fraction of an inch longer than the right. He'd never asked the cobbler to correct it. Instead, his foot had adjusted to the slight imperfection.

The boy to whom he had addressed the question seemed particularly interested in his boots as he watched Jack's approach with unconcealed curiosity, his tongue tucked securely in his cheek. Jack had no experience with children, but he estimated the boy to be about five years old. He nudged his mother's thigh to get her attention, but she brushed his hand aside while her head and shoulders remained beneath the hood of the car, where she was examining an engine that was obviously giving her trouble.

The boy started toward him. They met about halfway between Jack's pickup and the stalled car. The kid tilted his head back to look up at Jack and squinted against the bright noon sun. Jack said, "Hi."

"Did you know I have a book about dinosaurs?"

"No kidding?"

"A video, too."

"Hmm."

"Velociraptors are my favorite."

"You don't say? Mine too," Jack told him.

"Really?"

"Yep."

"Cool. What about pterodactyls?"

"Pretty scary, those pterodactyls."

The boy gave him an approving grin, which revealed a space recently vacated by a front tooth. The new one had pushed through his gums to form a jagged little mountain range in the gap.

He was a cute kid, dressed in shorts and sneakers and a T-shirt bearing the likeness of a TV cartoon character whom Jack recognized but couldn't name. The boy had rosy cheeks and a healthy sprinkling of freckles. A few strands of dark hair were sweat-stuck to his forehead.

"What's your name?"

"Jack. What's yours?"

"David."

"Pleased to meet you, David." He hitched his chin toward the car. "What seems to be the problem?"

The boy shrugged, pulling both shoulders up beneath his ears and extending his arms at his sides, palms up. "I dunno. My mom and me were going into town, but when we got in the car it went like this." He made a choking sound and gyrated like somebody with a terrible palsy. "Then it stopped and my mom can't start it again."

Jack nodded and started moving toward the car and the woman, who wasn't nearly as friendly as her son. Either that or she didn't welcome the interference of a stranger. Or she was scared of him and thought that maybe if she just ignored him he would go away. "Uh, ma'am? Can I be of help?"

The boy went to his mother, placed the heel of his hand on the outside of her thigh, and gave it several urgent pushes. This time she straightened up and turned toward him with exasperation. That's when she must've caught sight of Jack out the corner of her eye, because she did a double take, then jumped like she'd been scalded.

"My mom's deaf," the boy informed him. "She didn't hear you coming. I think you scared her."

Jack thought so too. Her eyes were bouncing around like twin Ping-Pong balls in a heated tournament, moving from him to his pickup and back again, trying to gauge whether or not he was dangerous.

The boy said, "When you sneak up on her she gets mad."

"I didn't know I was sneaking up on her." Jack extended one hand in apology. She reacted by flattening herself against the grill of the car and yanking the kid up against her.

"Mo-om." David stretched the protest into two syllables as he wiggled free. He signed and spoke at the same time. "Don't be scared. He's nice. His name's Jack. He—"

She held her hand up in a silent command that he stop.

"Tell her I'm sorry. I didn't—"

"She can read your lips," the boy said, interrupting. "I'll try to sign what you say, but she's good at reading lips."

Looking directly at her, Jack overenunciated, "Can you understand me?"

Her eyes narrowed a fraction. From irritation was Jack's guess. Although he couldn't imagine what he'd said to tick her off. Then he received a curt bob of her head that shook loose a hank of hair from a summertime topknot. It was the same dark color as the boy's, but the sun had found threads of copper in it.

"I didn't mean to startle you, ma'am. I'm here to see Mr. Corbett, but long as I'm here, I'd be happy to try and start your car for you."

The boy nudged her to get her attention. "Can he, Mom?"

She shook her head no.

Forlornly the boy said to Jack, "I don't think she's gonna let you."

"I don't mean any harm, ma'am," Jack said to her.

She continued to eye Jack warily as she signed for the boy to interpret. "She says thank you, but we'll call a garage."

"Yeah, you could do that, all right. But it might not be necessary." Jack motioned toward the car. "It could be something real simple."

Her fingers moved furiously fast. Her lips formed words, too, although no sound came out. The gist of what she was saying was conveyed by her animated facial expressions, but Jack looked to David for interpretation.

"She says if it was something real simple, she could fix it herself. She says she's deaf, not—I missed that, Mom. What's that sign mean?" He tapped his first two fingers against the center of his forehead.

She spelled out the word alphabetically. David recited the letters as she signed them. "What's that spell, Jack?"

"Stupid," he said.

"Oh," David said. "It makes her mad for people to think she's dumb just 'cause she's deaf."

"No offense intended." Jack rubbed his chin, becoming a little irritated himself. "You want me to take a look at your busted car or not? Because if not, it's hotter than *h-e*-double-ell out here and I'd just as soon be trying to find some shade if there's any to be found."

David's plump fingers were spelling out *h-e*-double-ell in the sign language alphabet. "Jack, what does that spell? Is it hell?"

Refraining to answer, Jack said, "How 'bout it, ma'am?"

David interpreted her reply. *"Thank you, but Mr. Corbett will see to it."*

"Is he around?"

"Some steers broke down a section of fence. That way." David pointed out the direction. "My grandpa's fixing it."

"Your grandpa?"

"Yeah."

"Where's your dad?"

"He died."

"Died?"

"Before I was borned."

Jack looked at the woman, who in turn shot her son a look that could kill, then got his attention and began to sign. "She says I'm talking too much."

"The offer is still good. How bad did you need to get to town?"

Maybe his persistence finally wore her down, although she didn't look like a person who would capitulate easily. Maybe she'd decided he wasn't a threat after all. Or maybe the suggestion of finding some shade appealed to her. For whatever reason, she was on the brink of acquiescing when her eyes dropped to his waist.

Following his mother's gaze, David remarked, "It might be your knife that's scaring her."

"Oh. Is that all?" Jack unsnapped the leather scabbard. The woman stiffened. He eased the knife from the sheath and laid it on his palm. Crouching down in front of David, he gave the boy a closer look.

"An Indian brave made this, David. A Comanche warrior. Long time ago."

"Wow," the boy exclaimed in a reverent and hushed voice. He extended his hand to touch the weapon, but timidly withdrew it before making contact.

"It's okay. You can touch it."

"How come it's bumpy?"

"That's the way the Indians made their knives back then."

David ran his finger along the bluish, rippled blade. "Cool," he said in the same reverential tone.

Slowly Jack came to his feet. Keeping his eyes on the woman's face, he replaced the knife in its scabbard. He then raised both hands in surrender.

She didn't take kindly to the mockery, but, giving him a retiring look, she stepped aside and signaled that it was okay if he looked at the engine.

He removed his straw cowboy hat and sunglasses, placed the sunglasses in the crown of his hat, and set it on the fender. Poking his head beneath the raised hood, he bent over the motor. A bead of sweat rolled off his forehead and splashed onto the hot casing, making a small sizzling sound as it evaporated.

Hell of a new experience, this was. He'd never run across a deaf woman before.

Or one who had such an enormous burr up her ass.

Turning, he asked her to start the engine and rev it, which she did. Jack's knowledge of cars wasn't extensive, but this diagnosis was elementary. Something was blocking the fuel line. He set to work.

David took up a post just beneath his elbow. Obviously wishing to impress Jack, he boasted, "We have a whole ranch."

"I see that."

"Just the three of us. Mom, Grandpa, and me. I'd like to have a brother or sister, but Mom says I'm a handful all by myself and anyway you can't have a baby without a daddy, she says. Do you like peach pie, Jack? My mom makes good peach pie and Grandpa makes vanilla ice cream and I get to sit on the tub while he's turning the crank, and the ice cream's good on peach pie or just plain. Can you swim? Grandpa says when he has time he's gonna teach me to swim, 'cept Mom's afraid of cottonmouths in the river. We've got a river, and I've caught fish before, and after Grandpa and me took their guts out Mom cooked 'em and we had 'em for supper. I can already do a face float and that's the first step to swimming, a face float. Maybe you could see my room. I've got a Dallas Cowboys poster on my closet door. Do you have a little boy?"

"No, I never had a little boy. Or a little girl either." As he removed a filter from the fuel line, he smiled down at the boy.

The woman was hovering nearby. She signed something. Looking chagrined, David reported, "She says I'm probably wearing out your ears with so much—I didn't get the last."

"Chatter?" Jack ventured.

"Maybe," David said. "Sometimes Grandpa calls me a chatterbox."

"I don't mind if you talk. I like having company."

"We never have company."

"How come?" Jack addressed the question to David, although he was looking at the woman.

"I think it's 'cause my mom's deaf or something."

"Hmm." Jack put the filter to his mouth and blew into it hard. Then he replaced it and motioned for her to try the ignition again. She got in and turned the key. After she pumped the accelerator several times, the car started.

Jack lowered the hood and dusted off his hands. "There you go." He replaced his sunglasses and hat. "Shouldn't give you any more problem. You had a piece of grit stuck in your filter."

"You sure are smart."

"Not too smart, David. It happened on my truck once. Cost me fifty bucks for a mechanic to blow out the speck." Turning to the boy's mother, he said, "I'd like to see Mr. Corbett now, please."

"Can I show him where Grandpa's at, Mom?"

She shook her head no, and motioned for David to get into the car.

"Point me in the right direction and I'll find him," Jack said.

"It's that way, past those trees," David told him. "But I'll take you. It's not far."

David's mother stamped her foot to get his attention. Her fingers moving with the speed of light, she issued a parental order. "Aw, Mom. Please. Why can't I stay here with Grandpa and Jack? I hate going to the dumb grocery store."

With her arm held shoulder high and straight as an arrow, she pointed an imperious index finger at the passenger door of the car.

Jack patted David's shoulder. "Better mind her."

"Will you still be here when we get back?"

"We'll see."

"I hope so. Well, bye, Jack."

"Bye."

David trudged around the rear of the car. As he passed his mother, he ducked his head so that she couldn't read his lips and muttered, "You're a mean ol' mom."

It was all Jack could do to contain his grin, but he soberly tipped the brim of his hat. "Ma'am."

She climbed behind the wheel and closed the door. After securing her seat belt and making sure that David had done the same, she turned to Jack. Through the open car window she signed something that he supposed was *"Thank you."*

He watched them drive away. When they reached the main road, they turned toward town. The wrought-iron letters bridging the main drive spelled out CORBETT CATTLE RANCH. Not very elaborate or imaginative, Jack thought, but certainly informative.

He turned to gaze at the house. It was a neat two-story, white frame structure with dark green shutters accenting the windows. Ferns on stands stood sentinel on either side of the front door. Pots of blooming flowers sat on the edge of each of three steps leading down from the deep porch. Functional columns supported the roof above it. It was a pleasant-looking place, but nothing distinguished it from thousands of other such ranch houses scattered across the south central states.

Jack crossed the yard and went through a gate, walked past a large barn and a corral where several horses were eating hay from a trough and whisking flies with their tails. Beyond the corral, he opened the gate into a pasture, where he kept on the lookout for cow chips as he moved through the grass.

He thought of a countless number of reasons why he should retrace his steps to his truck and drive away.

He had heard the news of the prison break all the way down in Corpus Christi. Even though it had taken place in Arkansas, it was big news across the region. Though most viewers had probably listened with half an ear and readily dismissed it, the story had galvanized him. Almost before he realized it, he was speeding toward Blewer. He had arrived at midnight and checked into a local motel.

He wasn't particular when it came to lodging, and the room was comfortable enough, but he'd lain awake the remainder of the night, watching the John Wayne Flick Festival on a cable station and arguing with himself about the compulsion that had caused him to abandon a good job and come here.

Of course he'd been doing that all his adult life—moving at the drop of a hat. He was a loner, an adventurer, a drifter, having no ties to anything or anybody. All his worldly possessions he could carry in his truck. He went where he wanted and stopped when he took a notion. If he liked the place, he stayed. When he tired of it, he left. He had a driver's license and a Social Security number, but no bank account or credit card. He lived on cash earned by doing what interested him at the time.

At dawn, just as *Rio Bravo* was ending, he'd gotten up, showered, shaved, and climbed into his truck. While sipping a cup of good coffee at the doughnut shop across the highway from the motel, he reached a compromise decision: It was a bad idea, and risky to boot, but he was going to do it anyhow.

He had to do it.

Over the years he had come this way many times, just passing through, taking a curious look around but never stopping. Whenever in the area, he drove past the Corbett place and wondered about the people who lived inside the wrought-iron gate. But his wonder had never been so urgent that he stopped to inquire.

When this was the last place on the planet he should be, why did he feel it necessary to be here?

Carl Herbold's prison break, sure. But that had only been the catalyst. There was something inside himself that kept bringing him back here at intervals over the years. He had tried to forget the connection, tried to outrun it, but it always overtook him. More specifically, he carried it with him wherever he went.

His travels had exposed him to different religions. He had sampled peyote with a shaman from one of the tribes in Arizona who believed the gods spoke through drug-induced visions. He had caddied one summer for a golfing rabbi who had talked to him about God's covenants and the promised Messiah. He had discussed the gospel with a group of Christian seminary students at an outdoor rock concert.

All had believed wholeheartedly that something greater than themselves was directing their destiny. Something greater than themselves was at least helping them choose the right path.

Jack didn't know which religion was valid, or if any of them were. He couldn't imagine a God who was omniscient enough to create the cosmos only to direct the lives of men with such petulance and caprice. The reason for natural disasters escaped him. He didn't comprehend why bad things happened to good folk, or why mankind was forced to suffer pestilence and famine and war. He wasn't so sure about the whole concept of redemption, either.

But he knew that sin was real enough. And so was the guilt that went with it.

Call it providence, or fate, or God, or just plain conscience. *Something*—a will greater than his own—had compelled him to leave his present circumstances and come here when he heard the news that Carl Herbold was on the loose.

What would happen next was anybody's guess. Jack himself didn't know. Even as he'd driven beneath the iron arch he hadn't known what he was going to say or do when he got here. He had no concrete plan. He certainly hadn't counted on meeting a woman and child in the driveway of Delray Corbett's place. From this point forward, he would roll with the punches, react to events as they occurred.

In any event, the die would be cast seconds from now.

Spotting the rancher down on one knee struggling with a contrary strand of barbed wire, Jack hesitated only a moment before cupping his hands and calling out, "Mr. Corbett?"

Chapter Five

*S*tartled to hear his name, Delray Corbett turned and saw Jack walking toward him. Reluctantly, he came to his feet. He stood about five feet ten inches, a man in his midsixties, with a comfortable middle-aged softness around his waist, stocky legs, and a stern countenance. His displeasure upon seeing a stranger in his pasture was evident. Jack tried not to let the man's frown discourage him.

"Mr. Corbett," he said again, extending his hand. "Jack Sawyer."

Markedly unrushed, Corbett removed his right glove and shook Jack's hand in an obligatory way. From beneath the bill of his dozer cap he regarded Jack with unfriendly eyes.

Jack tipped his head toward the fence. "Heard some steers knocked down a section of your fence."

"Where'd you hear that?"

"From your grandson." He pointed to Corbett's forearm, where a long nasty scratch was still bleeding slightly. "Catch some barbed wire?"

Corbett made a disinterested swipe at the scratch. "It's nothing. Where did you run into my grandson?"

"Up at the house."

"You tried to talk to them?" he asked angrily. "Damn it. I already told you people I don't know anything. Leave us alone."

"Pardon? Look, Mr. Corbett, I don't know who you're mistaking me for."

That was a white lie. Delray Corbett would be among the first to be contacted about Carl Herbold's prison break. Apparently law enforcement agencies had already been in touch with him. He was resentful of the intrusion. Or worried about the repercussions. Both were valid reactions.

"Whatever you're thinking, you're wrong," Jack assured him. "I only talked to your family because your daughter-in-law was having some trouble with her car."

Corbett glanced toward the house with concern.

Jack said, "It didn't amount to anything. Just some grit in the fuel-line filter. She's on her way now."

Corbett's eyes moved back to him. "Nobody sent you?"

"No."

"Sorry."

"It's okay."

Still wary, Corbett removed a handkerchief from the rear pocket of his jeans and took off his cap long enough to mop perspiration from his face. He had very dark hair, barely threaded with gray. "Did Anna give you something?"

Anna. Her name was Anna. Busy assimilating that information, Jack didn't catch the rest of what Corbett had said. "Come again?"

"Did you come out here to get some money from me? For the time and trouble you spent fixing her car," he added, when it became obvious that his meaning hadn't clicked.

Jack replied with a terse "No, sir. I was glad to help her out. I came here to speak with you."

Corbett's guard went up again. "You selling something?"

"You could say so."

"Well then you've wasted your time. I can't think of a thing I need."

"How about me?"

"Huh?"

"I need a job. You need a hand. My services are for sale."

Corbett looked as though he were waiting for the punch line. Finally he said, "You're serious?"

"As death and taxes. I could start right now by helping you string that fence."

The rancher moved a few inches to his right, placing himself between Jack and the coiled strands of barbed wire, either to block them from Jack's view or to protect them from his interference; Jack couldn't tell. What was all too apparent was that Corbett didn't take his proposal at face value.

He responded with chilly politeness. "I don't think so, Mr. Sawyer. But thanks all the same." He returned his handkerchief to his pocket and his cap to his head and his attention to his chore.

"You haven't heard me out."

"I don't have a hand."

"That's obvious." The remark brought him around again, as Jack had hoped it would. "No offense, Mr. Corbett, but your place needs some work. Looks to me like this whole fence needs replacing, not just this section. That entails digging holes, setting posts—"

"I know what it entails," Corbett snapped.

"So you know it's too much work for one man, especially when daily chores have to be done, too. Your barn door is loose. That trough in the horse corral is about to collapse, and two of the horses need shoeing. That's just for starters. A place this size, it's more than even two men could do efficiently."

"My son and I held it together."

"But he's no longer around, right?" Corbett glared at him hard. Quietly Jack added, "The boy told me his daddy had died."

"That's right." Corbett assumed a tight-lipped, stoic expression. "Now if you'll excuse me, Mr. Sawyer, I'd like to get back to my work. I'm not hiring. You or anybody."

Stalling, Jack looked down at the ground and dug a little trench in the dirt with the riding heel of his boot. He hadn't known how he was going to approach Corbett. The idea of asking the man for a job hadn't occurred to him until he heard himself proposing it. Now it seemed the logical course. Good thing he had observed and made subconscious mental notes of the needed repairs. If the ranch had been in tiptop shape, this would have been a tougher sale.

"I'd be willing to give you a hand with that fence anyway," he offered. "No obligation."

Corbett looked at him with irritation and seemed ready to order him off his property.

"I'm a good worker," Jack said.

It was Corbett who finally relented with a shrug. "Suit yourself. Got some gloves?"

Jack removed a pair of leather work gloves from his hip pocket and approached the fence. "Want me to hold the post or wind the wire?"

Pride wouldn't let Corbett do the easier job. "I'll handle the wire."

They worked in silence. Jack held the post in place while Corbett pulled and stretched the barbed wire taut around it, then nailed it into place. They moved to the next post. Then the next.

"How many acres have you got?"

"Six fifty. Just over a section."

Jack whistled. "How long have you had the property?"

"All my life. I inherited it from my father."

"How many head you run?"

"Several hundred."

"Where are they now?"

"In another pasture. Across the river."

"Herefords?"

"And a few Angus. Prime beef. The hell of it is . . ." He grunted with the effort of stretching the wire.

"Want me to do that?"

"I can get it."

Jack noticed that the older man's face was turning red from the effort, but he let it pass. "Hell of it is?" he prompted.

"Too many vegetarians these days." He hammered the last nail into place.

"The scourge of a beef cattle rancher." Jack let go of the cedar post, removed his hat, and fanned his face with it.

Corbett reached for a thermal jug that he'd previously stowed in the notch of a cottonwood tree. Before taking a drink himself, he offered it to Jack. "Go ahead," Jack told him. Corbett drank directly from the spout, then handed the Thermos to Jack.

"Where'd you get your experience?" Corbett asked, once again using his handkerchief to blot his face.

Jack recapped the Thermos and put it back in the tree. "Everywhere."

"You've worked ranches?"

"I've done a little of everything."

"Then you must come with plenty of references."

"No, sir. None."

Corbett came as close to a smile as he ever got, Jack thought. "You've got gall, Mr. Sawyer. I'll hand you that."

"Call me Jack. Why do you say that?"

"You ask me for a job, but you have no references."

"Guess you'll just have to trust me."

"Guess again," Corbett returned curtly as he bent down to gather his tools. After neatly replacing them in a metal box, he came to his full height, retrieved his Thermos, then faced Jack. "I appreciate you helping Anna with her car if it was giving her trouble. And thanks for your help with the fence. But I won't be hiring you."

As he headed across the pasture, Jack fell into step with him. "Mind if I ask why not?"

"No, I don't mind you asking. And I don't mind telling you. I don't know you from Adam. You could rob me blind."

"That would be pretty stupid. If I was going to do that, I wouldn't have introduced myself first."

"I've got David and Anna's safety to think about."

"Hiring me isn't going to endanger you or them."

"I don't know that, do I?"

Jack placed his hand on the other man's arm, halting him. Corbett glanced down at his hand and Jack immediately removed it. "All right, you don't know me. I'm a stranger that dropped out of nowhere. Yesterday I left a job in Corpus. If you want a reference you can call my boss there."

"How come you left?"

"I got ready to."

"Just like that?"

"That's the way I live."

"Doesn't make you sound very reliable, does it, Mr. Sawyer?"

He started moving again. Jack, undeterred, went with him. "As long as I'm here, I'll give you a full day's effort, every day. I have experience in all types of work because I've paid my way doing just about anything that was legal.

"I've been a short-order cook and a fishing guide. I've worked in oil fields and assembly plants. I've broken horses, milked goats, washed dishes, cleaned toilets, and once, when I was real hungry, I pimped for a five-dollar whore."

Corbett stopped walking and turned to him.

"That's right, Mr. Corbett, I've done a lot of things I'm not too proud of. Show me a man who hasn't. But I swear to God there's one thing I'm not, and that's a thief. I won't steal from you. And I would never hurt you, your daughter-in-law, or her boy. In fact, it might give you some peace of mind to have another man around, keeping an eye on the place."

That was the ace that Jack had been waiting to play, and it worked. He had Corbett's attention and could sense his resolve weakening. So it came as a mild surprise and a huge disappointment when Corbett shook his head no. "I'm sorry, Mr. Sawyer. The answer is still no."

"What can I say that'll change your mind?"

"Nothing. Fact is, I can't afford you."

Jack grinned. "Probably not. I'm fairly expensive. But I think we can work something out."

"Like what?"

"I need a place to live."

Corbett actually uttered a sound that could pass for a laugh. "You must think I'm crazy."

"I'm not suggesting that you take me into your home. But what about that old trailer parked on the north side of the barn? I could bunk in it."

Corbett glanced in that direction. "It hasn't been used in years. My wife and I lived in it while we were building the house. We tore down the original, but wanted to build on the same site. That was almost forty years ago. I should've sold it to a salvage yard, but never could bring myself to. It's probably falling apart."

"Does it have water and electricity?"

"Hookups. The stove works on butane."

"I'll clean it out. It'll suit me fine." Corbett tested him with another long, measure-taking stare. Jack's eyes didn't flicker. He'd developed that knack by dealing blackjack in a Reno gambling hall. "Well, Mr. Corbett, what do you say?"

Chapter Six

Cecil Herbold had gnawed his index fingernail down to a nub by the time the Arkansas state policemen strolled into the office of the garage and body shop where he worked. There were two of them. Mean bastards, by the looks of them.

It had only been a matter of time before they showed up. They had let him sweat out the morning in anxious anticipation of the inevitable. Now here it was well after lunch on a sweltering afternoon, and even though he had been expecting the visit, his sphincter was tested when one of the duo upended a wastepaper basket and sat down on it, facing him, not more than six inches away from the tip of his nose.

"Now, Cecil," he began, "we asked Mr. Reynolds if he would lend us this nice office of his so we could talk to you private, away from your coworkers and all. He was most obliging. So I'd hate to test his hospitality and wear out our welcome. We pride ourselves on not taking advantage of law-abiding citizens. Let's make this short and sweet, okay?"

These guys were nothing but hillbillies with shiny badges, starched uniforms, and fast cars. Cecil didn't know these two personally, but he'd known their type all his life, and hated them. Their faces were shaved so close their skin was chapped. There wasn't a wrinkle between them. Hot as it was, there weren't even sweat rings under their arms.

But they looked as stupid as the day is long. Take away the uniforms and badges, the fast cars and good guns, and he and Carl would make mincemeat out of them in no time flat.

Soon. But later. This wasn't the time. For now, he had to play dumb and scared. Which was good. He could be convincing. Not that he was dumb. But he was a little scared.

"If you've come here to talk to me about that stunt my brother pulled yesterday, I'll tell you right off that I don't know anything about it."

The guy sitting on the trash can glanced over at his partner, who was leaning against the wall, arms folded, ankles crossed. He rolled a matchstick from one side of his mouth to the other and said, "He must think we've got shee-ut for brains."

"Swear to God," Cecil cried earnestly. "I'm telling you the truth." The worst that could happen would be that they would throw him in jail on some trumped-up charge just to keep an eye on him. He must convince them that they had his full cooperation.

"First I knew of that prison break, I heard it on the evenin' news when I got home from work. I settled down with a Diet Pepsi in front of the TV and there was my brother's face, filling up the goddamn screen. Nearly messed my pants." He paused to gauge their reactions, but they were revealing none.

Doggedly he continued, "All I know is the same as what everybody knows. I learned about it from the TV."

Matchstick hitched up his pistol holster. The one on the trash can pursed his lips and continued to stare at Cecil, who squirmed uncomfortably in his seat until he could stand the tense silence no longer. *"What?"*

"You think we're stupid, Cecil?"

"No, sir."

"You know Myron Hutts?"

"No, sir."

"You never met him?"

"No, sir. Him and my brother linked up at Tucker. I was never in Tucker."

"No, you were in Cummins."

Because the Cummins Unit was a medium maximum-security facility, Cecil felt that a little righteous indignation was called for here. "That's right, I was."

"You served for armed robbery, right?"

"Right. I never killed anybody."

"Oh, right, right. Almost forgot that. You left the actual killing to your little brother Carl, didn't you? That's why your sentence was so much lighter than his."

This was a sore subject. Cecil couldn't argue the trooper's point or he would be confessing to a murder that, technically and truthfully, Carl had committed. But he didn't want to admit to a character flaw, either. That flaw being that, while Carl seemed unaffected, even exhilarated, by shedding someone's blood, the thought of taking another human life made Cecil slightly queasy.

Disturbed by this introspection, he blurted out, "I went to prison and paid my debt to society. I found Jesus and got rehabilitated."

Matchstick nearly choked before removing the shredded wood from his mouth so he could laugh.

"I'm on parole," Cecil declared. "You think I'm going to do something as damn-fool stupid as my brother did? No way. Cummins was no picnic, you know. I got out and I'm staying out."

"Uh-huh." The seated officer wasn't impressed by his sincerity. "Hear about those guards at Tucker?"

"Heard they, uh . . . they died."

The trooper came closer, until he was almost touching noses with Cecil. "They didn't *die*, asshole. They were assassinated. Your brother got one of them in the heart with a shank. Stabbed him through the eyeball while he was at it. Hutts slit another one's throat, nearly cut his head clean off."

He leaned back and tugged at his earlobe as though reflecting on the prison break, which had mobilized every law enforcement agency in Arkansas and neighboring states. A manhunt had been organized for the apprehension of Carl Herbold and Myron Hutts, who were to be regarded as armed and dangerous. Citizens were warned to exercise extreme caution if they sighted the pair.

"Have to hand it to old Carl. He planned it good," the state officer remarked. "That Myron character, he's a certifiable idiot. Hasn't got the sense God gave a rubber duck. But your brother is one smart sum'bitch. He had even figured a way to get those tracking devices off them. They were found, but Carl and Myron weren't attached to them. No, sir. All that's been found is their prison uniforms, their dog tags, and those high-tech devices, which turned out to be good for nothing. 'Cause those boys are long gone."

The convicts had outfoxed the authorities and outrun the tracking dogs. Helicopter patrols, search parties on foot, and roadblocks hadn't turned up a trace of them during the night.

Damn, Cecil was proud of his little brother!

It was all he could do to keep from smiling proudly as the trooper enumerated Carl's crimes, which Cecil considered accomplishments on a par with those of his heroes Jesse James, John Dillinger, and Clyde Barrow.

To conceal his pride, he worked his face into an emotional grimace. "I just hope y'all don't kill him. Our whole lives it's just been me and him."

"Now, that ain't quite the truth is it, Cecil? Y'all had a mama. She married a nice man, who tried to do right by y'all. I got the records, see? So don't be lying to me, Cecil."

"Our stepdaddy was a hard-ass. He hated us right off, and we hated him. He didn't raise a peep of protest when they sent us to that school for wayward boys when Carl was barely fifteen."

"Prob'ly 'cause that's what y'all were. Wayward, I mean."

"When Mama died, he came down on us even harder. Didn't faze me much," he added as a precaution. "But Carl, being the baby, it tarnished him. Getting no love from anybody, he grew up angry and mean. He's rotten to the core. You think I don't know he's meaner than sin? He refuses to see the light. He won't accept Jesus and get saved for nothing." For emphasis, he whisked a tear from his eye. "But he's my kin, my blood, all that's left of my family. I don't want him dead."

"See," the trooper said, shifting to a more comfortable position on the bottom of the trash can, "that's what we're counting on, Cecil. If Carl and his friend Myron showed up at your place one night, you'd probably feel such brotherly love you'd aid and abet those boys."

"No, sir," Cecil said, shaking his head adamantly. "I'd call y'all right off."

"Is that right?"

"That's right."

The trooper turned to his partner. "Do you think he's lying or what?"

Matchstick yawned. "He's lying. All Herbolds is born liars. Everybody knows that."

"Swear on Jesus' holy name—"

"Shut the fuck up about Jesus, Cecil!" The state officer came to his feet so suddenly he knocked over the trash can. "You ain't fit to speak the Lord's name around decent folks. Oh, you sound real sincere, but you're a convicted felon. You and your brother practically shared the same skin till y'all were sent to separate prisons. So here's the way it's gonna be." Placing his hands on his knees, he bent down low, placing his face once again on a level with Cecil's. "We're gonna be on you like white on rice. You hear me?"

Indignantly Cecil drew himself up. "Think what you want to, Officer. I'm telling y'all that I'd turn Carl in. I swear I would, to keep him from getting his crazy self killed."

"See that you do, Cecil."

"Yeah, Cecil," Matchstick said, "see that you do."

The two sauntered out, spoke briefly with Mr. Reynolds who owned the garage, then got into their shiny, well-equipped car and sped off.

Cecil slunk back to the bay where he had been working on a pickup truck when the laws showed up. Reynolds wasted no time joining him.

"Were you telling them the truth?" he growled. "If you even look like you're about to get into trouble again, you're gone. Understand?"

"Yes, sir, Mr. Reynolds. I need this job. I don't want anything to do with that sorry brother of mine. I've learned my lesson."

Reynolds glared threateningly, then stamped into his office and slammed the door behind him.

That uptight asshole wasn't worth wasting epithets on, Cecil thought as he curbed his impulse to shoot his boss the finger. Besides, other workers were around. Some of them sucked up to Reynolds. Cecil trusted none of them. Cowards and ass-kissers is what they were.

He bent back over the open hood of the pickup and resumed his work. It was a no-brainer repair job, enabling him to concentrate on other matters.

He had known the law would come to him. They would expect Carl to run to family first. Carl had taken that into account, of course, and had warned Cecil about it on their last visitation day together. "They'll have your place and the garage staked out. You probably won't see them, but the bastards'll be around, so watch yourself." The phone lines would probably be tapped, too, Carl had said. His warnings were unnecessary. Cecil knew how to be careful.

Of course the laws were right. The brothers would rendezvous. When they did, it wouldn't be covert. The authorities would know about the reunion immediately. What a day that was going to be!

Cecil could hardly contain his excitement. He didn't know how he was going to survive the wait without giving away his anticipation. Parole was little better than prison. He was subject to regular visits from a parole officer who pried into every aspect of his life. He reported to work every day only to take verbal abuse from a son of a bitch like Reynolds. This was no life for him. He was too smart and too talented to waste himself on a life that any asshole could lead.

Besides, he and Carl belonged together. Soon they would be together again, doing what they did best, doing what they'd done together since they were boys—raising hell.

Cecil spent the remainder of the afternoon reviewing their plan, going over it time and again in his mind, making certain he hadn't overlooked a single detail. It rankled a little that Carl was still the chief instigator and overseer. Even from prison he was the leader, as he'd always been, although the leadership role rightfully should have belonged to Cecil since he was the elder. But, never one to stand on ceremony, Carl had assumed that position early on and never had relinquished it.

One thing they had to get straight: From here on out, Cecil was going to have equal say. He would make that clear to his brother from the get-go. Carl shouldn't have a problem with a more democratic approach. They weren't kids any longer. Cecil didn't need coaching. He had been to prison too. The experience had toughened him. Although he'd played the sniveling weakling for the troopers, he was stronger than his brother remembered him.

This time there would be no mistakes. All the arrangements were in place. He had devised a fail-safe job and an even better getaway plan. Hell, he even had a secret weapon that Carl didn't know about.

Bending to his repair task, he chuckled just thinking of how surprised Carl was going to be when he sprang that surprise on him.

Chapter Seven

*J*ack said an Indian brave made his knife. A Comanche, Grandpa."
David interrupted his chatter about Jack Sawyer only long enough
to cram a forkful of mashed potatoes into his mouth. "He sure knows a
lot of neat stuff."

Jack Sawyer was David's current favorite topic. When they returned
from town and David had spotted his pickup truck still parked in the
driveway, he had barely allowed the car to come to a stop before getting
out.

Delray met them at the gate that separated the landscaped yard from
the pasture. "Did you meet Jack, Grandpa?" Breathless with excitement,
David asked so many questions so fast that Anna missed most of them.
Delray ordered the boy to calm down.

That was not unusual. Delray loved his grandson, but David's high
energy level frequently got on Delray's nerves. What struck Anna
immediately was the change in Delray himself. He was a man of strong
convictions. He held tightly to his opinions. Once he had made up his
mind about something, he never wavered. Whatever he did, he did decisively and without apology.

So it wasn't like him to appear unsure and tentative when he
informed her that he had hired Jack Sawyer as a ranch hand.

Trying not to show her shock, she signed, *That quickly? What do
you know about him?*

"He's okay. I think he'll be a hard worker." He wasn't looking
directly at her when he added, "He'll be living in the old trailer."

That was even more surprising, but before she could sign a comment,
he pressed on.

"He's fixing it up himself, so you don't have to worry about it. In fact, you shouldn't even know he's around. I've already put him to work inside the barn. I just wanted you to know that he would be working here for a while. Now, I've got to get back to work. See you at supper."

With no more explanation than that, he had turned and walked away.

In the years since Dean died, she had been responsible for the house, but Delray had done all the ranching himself. He had stubbornly refused to consider hiring permanent help, although she often had suggested that he should.

He was getting too old to work so hard, and that was part of the problem. Pride kept him from taking on a hand. He didn't want to admit, even to himself, that he was no longer up to handling the job that had been his life's work.

Perhaps he also felt that hiring another man would be disloyal to the son he had lost. No one could take Dean's place in Delray's heart. He didn't want anyone trying to take Dean's place beside him at work, either.

As Anna ate her dinner, she wondered why this sudden reversal in Delray's policy. Was it a true change of heart? Had he finally admitted that he needed help? Or was Sawyer just a good salesman? Maybe. But there was another possibility—one that made her terribly uneasy.

Last evening's news.

To settle her own mind, she tapped the table to get her father-in-law's attention. *"Are you afraid he'll come here?"* she signed.

"No."

She read the terse reply on his lips. He added a stern shake of his head. Even so, Anna didn't quite believe him. *"Is that why you hired this man? To have someone else around just in case—"*

"One has nothing to do with the other. This Sawyer showed up, needing work. I had been giving thought to taking a man on. That's it." Agitated, he took a few bites of food. She continued to watch him. Finally he laid down his fork and addressed her without shifting his eyes. "He won't come here, Anna. It would be too risky for him. Besides, they'll catch him before he gets too far."

"Catch who, Grandpa?" David asked.

"Nobody. And don't talk with your mouth full." Returning to Anna, he said, "The state police called today. They asked if I wanted somebody out here to watch the house. Just as a precaution. I told them no."

She lowered her eyes to her plate. Delray tapped the table. Sensing the vibration, she looked up at him again. "I honestly don't think there's any danger. But if you want me to, I'll call them back and accept their offer."

To have someone guarding his family would be to acknowledge his own apprehension over Carl Herbold's escape. Delray would consider it a weakness to take such drastic precautions. He would make the concession if she asked him to, but he wouldn't like it.

She shook her head no; Delray looked relieved.

His decision was made, and the subject was now closed. But whether he admitted it or not, Anna doubted Delray would have hired Jack Sawyer if there had been no prison escape the day before.

"I wonder what Jack's having for supper." David leaned forward so he could see the trailer through the window.

Their days were so predictable that any variation in routine was remarkable, especially to a five-year-old with boundless curiosity. Her son had learned sign language along with English, so from the time he could use his stubby fingers to communicate, he had asked countless questions like any other child. At the end of each day Anna's hands would be cramping from answering them.

"Maybe Jack doesn't have any supper. What's he gonna eat? Does he know how to cook, Grandpa?"

"It's none of our business what he eats," Delray told him. "He just works here, is all."

"Maybe sometimes he can play with me."

"You stay away from him, David, and I mean it."

Crestfallen, David said, "But he's nice. He likes dinosaurs, too."

"He's here to work, not entertain you."

Anna signed, *Did he say where he is from?*

"He's sort of a drifter."

She gave her father-in-law an inquisitive look, indicating that she didn't quite understand. *Like a hobo? A tramp?*

"No, he works. He just moves around a lot. Never stays too long in one place. He could be gone tomorrow."

Stricken by that possibility, David asked, "Do you think he'll leave tomorrow, Grandpa? Mom, will he?"

She signed that she didn't think he would be leaving that soon. Delray told David to finish his supper, which he did without further conversation. Secretly she wished that David would ask a few more questions of Delray. She wanted to know more about Jack Sawyer herself, but for the time being she kept her curiosity to herself.

Following the evening meal their routine was for David to clear the dishes from the table and carry them to the sink while she and Delray relaxed over a last cup of coffee and discussed the day's events.

Delray wasn't a talkative man, and for that reason he didn't mind her silence. But tonight he seemed especially quiet. After a time, she asked, *"Did you read in the newspaper about Ezzy Hardge's retirement dinner?"*

"Long overdue if you ask me," he said. "He's got to be near eighty."

Anna smiled into her coffee cup. The retired sheriff wasn't that much older than Delray. *"You should have gone to the dinner. There was a large crowd. You would have known a lot of people there."*

"I wouldn't have been caught dead there. The tickets were twenty bucks apiece."

It wasn't the cost of the ticket that had kept him from going. He wouldn't have attended the community function if the tickets had been free. Of course it never would have occurred to him that she might like to go. Ezzy Hardge had been sheriff all her life. She felt he deserved a good send-off. But if she had suggested they go, Delray would have said no.

The first time Dean brought her home to meet his father, he had warned her beforehand that Delray wasn't the outgoing type. She discovered that to be an understatement. Dean's mother Mary had been Delray's second wife. Before finding happiness with his new family, Delray had lived through terrible times. Those troubled years had left their mark on him.

What little social life he had had died along with Mary and Dean. Gradually his small number of friends stopped notifying him of their get-togethers. He seemed not to notice or mind.

At first Anna had thought that he was embarrassed by her handicap and that he felt awkward using sign language in public places. Or that he was sensitive to her being a young widow and was reluctant to leave her at home alone in the evenings, especially after David was born.

Eventually she had come to realize that his solitude had little to do with her. He didn't like people in general. He resented their curiosity and gossip. He rebuffed any act of friendliness or kindness because he mistrusted the motive behind it. He preferred living in semi-isolation. Her impairment gave him a good excuse and made it convenient for him.

"Get all your errands run today?"

His question roused her from her thoughts. Suddenly remembering something, she held up her finger to indicate that she would be right back. She fetched a business card from her handbag and brought it back to Delray.

"Emory Lomax." His lips formed the name, then a curse, which she hoped he spoke beneath his breath so David couldn't hear.

"I went into the bank," she told him. *"Mr. Lomax made a point of crossing the lobby just to come over to say hello."*

"Oily bastard."

Although the word was strangely out of context, she understood what Delray meant. "Oily" was a perfect word to describe the loan officer. Whenever he touched her, which was each time she saw him, she felt the need to wash right away. *"He asked that teller who knows sign to interpret for him."*

"What did he have to say for himself?"

"He reminded me that an interest payment is past due—"

"I mailed it yesterday."

"That's what I told him. He said the two of you need to meet and discuss how and when you'll start reducing the principal of the loan. He offered to come here for the meeting."

"I bet he did."

"To save you a trip into town, he said."

"More to the point, to give him a chance to look the place over." Delray took a toothpick from the glass holder in the center of the table and clamped it between his teeth as he stood up. "I'm going to watch TV. Maybe there's some good news tonight."

He was angry over the loan officer's conversation with her. Possibly a little afraid about the news from Arkansas. As he left the kitchen, Delray resembled an aging bear, one who had lost his claws and feared he could no longer protect himself.

"Is Grandpa mad at me?" David asked.

Anna reached out and drew her son close, hugging him tightly. *"Why would he be mad at you?"*

"'Cause I talk too much."

"He's not mad. He's worried about grown-up stuff."

"That man at the bank?"

She nodded.

David made a face of distaste. "I don't like him. He smells like mouthwash."

Laughing, she signed, *"Grandpa doesn't like him either."*

"Do you?"

She shuddered. *"No!"*

Emory Lomax couldn't carry on a conversation without rubbing his hand up and down her arm, or holding her hand too long after shaking it. Certainly she had never encouraged his attention. She had been nothing except polite. But Lomax's ego couldn't separate common manners from a flirtation. The next time he touched her she should call him what he was—an asshole—and tell him to keep his hands to himself.

Could she get the teller to interpret that? she wondered.

"*Bath time,*" she told David, shooing him up the stairs.

As he splashed in the tub with his fleet of plastic ships, she went through her face-cleansing routine. Usually she approached it as a necessary, no-fuss procedure, which she performed without thinking too much about it.

Tonight, however, she took a few extra moments to study her face closely in the mirror above the sink. The hated dusting of freckles was responding to the summer sun. She must remember to apply sunscreen before going out. Her deep blue eyes were her father's. Her small nose was her mother's. Luckily she had inherited the best of both of them.

Unluckily, she had lost her parents far too early. They had died, months apart, shortly after she married Dean—her mother of liver cancer, her father of heart disease.

She wished they had lived long enough to see her healthy, hearing son. Of course she wished Dean had, too.

Impatient with herself for dwelling on sad things, she pulled David from the tub. He took forever to dry off, put on his pajamas, and brush his teeth, delaying bedtime until she had to scold him mildly. When finally his head was on the pillow, she sat down on the edge of the bed for his prayers.

He closed his eyes and folded his hands beneath his chin. She watched his lips form the familiar words. "God bless Daddy who's already in heaven. God bless Grandpa. God bless Mom. And God bless Jack."

Anna wasn't sure she had read his lips correctly. David seldom changed his prayer. Since the nighttime ritual had begun, there had been very few extra "God bless"es. Once for a raccoon. They had treated the scavenger like a pet, scattering Lucky Charms on the porch for him every evening, then watching from inside when he came to feast. One morning Delray found him dead in the road just outside their gate. He'd been run over. David had prayed for him for several nights.

Another time he had asked God's blessing on a teddy bear he'd accidentally left at McDonald's. By the time they discovered the toy missing and went back for it, it was gone. The teddy had been remembered for about a week.

Those were the only two exceptions she could recall.

But was it really all that surprising that David should include Jack Sawyer in his prayers? His arrival was the most exciting thing to happen to David in a long time.

To a boy David's age, Sawyer must seem like a character from an adventure story. He wasn't as old as Delray, not by twenty years or more. He wasn't soft and pale like the pediatrician who had treated David since he was born. He didn't have the gentle mannerisms of the minister who sometimes came to visit them even though the last sermon they'd heard from him was Dean's burial service. Jack Sawyer wasn't like any other man within her son's small world.

With his boots, his Indian-made knife, his knowledge of dinosaurs, and his battered pickup truck—a faded orange Chevy that bore its scars as proudly as a war veteran—it was little wonder that he had made such a striking impression.

After saying a final amen, David opened his eyes. "Do you think he liked me, Mom?"

It was pointless to play dumb and pretend that she didn't know he was referring to Jack Sawyer. *"I'm sure he did. Who wouldn't like you?"* She reached out and tickled his belly.

Usually he enjoyed the tickling sessions and wanted them to continue even when Anna was ready to call it quits. But tonight he didn't respond with his customary giggles. Instead, he rolled to his side and stacked his hands beneath his cheek.

"When I grow up, will I be as tall as Jack?"

"You may even be taller."

"I wish I could show him my dinosaur book." Then he yawned hugely and closed his eyes.

Anna remained seated on the edge of his bed, stroking his hair, her heart and throat feeling tight as she gazed down at him and wished Dean could have known him. Dean would have made a wonderful father. David had been cheated out of that.

Delray was the only adult male in his life. Delray was a good man. Although outwardly stern, underneath he was kindhearted. But he wasn't a daddy to David. It was difficult for him to show affection. He couldn't be silly for silliness' sake. He seldom laughed. David's constant activity annoyed him. Worse, he let his annoyance show.

He never spoke of his first marriage, or of the problems it had created, or of that summer when all the difficulties came to a head. It was as though his life had begun in 1976 and the years prior to that had belonged to another man. Wishing to forget that life, he had buried the bad memories deep within himself. No doubt there were days when he actually did forget them.

Unfortunately, Carl Herbold's escape from prison yesterday had brought them to the surface.

Chapter Eight

"Not many biting, Ezzy. Too damn hot." Burl Mundy flapped open a brown paper sack and dropped a bag of Fritos and a Peanut Pattie into it.

"You're probably right, but I needed something to do."

"Ain't you adjusted to retirement yet?"

"Don't think I ever will."

"I know what you mean. I've been running this bait shop here at the point practically all my life. They'll carry me out of here feetfirst."

"I'll need some of those crickets," Ezzy said. "And put a couple of soda pops in here." He set a portable cooler on the cloudy glass countertop.

"How 'bout a coupla beers instead?"

"No way. I gotta go home tonight."

Mundy chuckled. "Cora's still against drinking, huh?"

"Baptist to the bone." Ezzy paid in cash. "That ought to cover the gas, too." He'd pumped fuel into the motor of his small bass boat before coming inside. He picked up his sack of snacks, the carton of crickets he'd bought for bait, and the cooler, which now contained two Dr Peppers. "Thanks, Burl."

"Happy fishing, Ezzy." Before Ezzy got through the door, Burl had readjusted his oscillating fan and returned to his recliner and a well-thumbed Louis L'Amour paperback.

Ezzy set his purchases in the bottom of his boat, where he had already stowed his fishing gear. It wasn't expensive or sophisticated equipment; he was an indifferent fisherman. Because emergencies arose on every day of the year and at all hours, scheduling leisure activities was impossible for a county sheriff in a poor county. Ezzy's office had always been understaffed and over budget. Consequently, for fifty years he'd been overworked and on call twenty-four, seven, three-hundred-sixty-five.

Even if his demanding schedule had allowed him more time for recreation, he doubted he would have indulged in fishing, golfing, hunting, or any of the hobbies that other men lived for. He just flat wasn't interested. Nothing had engrossed him more than his work. He had loved it. His life had revolved around it. Even when asleep, he had thought about it.

Today, as he trolled the river, he yearned to be working still.

The spring had been uncustomarily dry, so the water level was low, the current sluggish. The river seemed in no hurry to empty into the Gulf waters a few hundred miles south. Sunlight turned the still surface into a glaring mirror that put his RayBans to the test.

Where the river narrowed, tree branches formed a shady canopy. Those patches of momentary coolness were welcome. There was no breeze. Not a leaf stirred. Plants along the banks had wilted in the oppressive heat, making the landscape look forlorn. Turtles and water snakes were detectable only by their heads barely breaking the surface of the murky waters near the shore. They were too listless to swim. Even the cicadas were halfhearted in their music-making.

Ezzy's shirt was soaked with perspiration by the time he angled his craft toward the riverbank. Stepping from the boat, he pulled it into the tall, dry reeds. He hadn't even had to search for the spot. It was as familiar to him as his own face. Actually, he had spent much more time exploring this terrain than he'd ever spent looking at himself.

Over the past twenty-two years, he had lost count of the number of times he had come here alone. Like a pilgrim to a shrine, he faithfully returned. He didn't examine this compulsion of his too closely, afraid that he would see that it was a sick preoccupation and that only a man possessed would continue it.

But he came anyway, begging the goddamn place to give up its secret.

Many times while here he had even got down on his knees. Not to pray, but to crawl along the ground, inspecting it a fraction of an inch at a time, imploring it to divulge even the slightest hint of what had happened to Patricia McCorkle.

This insignificant plot on the planet had become the center of Sheriff Ezra Hardge's universe.

That's why Cora had hated the McCorkle case so much. She cursed it for the toll it had taken on him, first in terms of the time he devoted to it. He had pursued every avenue of jurisprudence to bring to justice those he believed were responsible for the girl's death. Then, when it became obvious that that goal would elude him, he had lapsed into a depression that had almost destroyed their marriage.

Cora threatened to leave him and take the kids if he didn't snap out of it. He snapped out of it. Or pretended to. The daily grind of his job kept him occupied most of the time. But when he should have been free to relax and enjoy his family, he continued to brood over the unresolved case.

The case had kept him from being a good father to his children. Cora had reared them with little influence or interference from him. He barely remembered their childhoods, and then only the troubled times. The worst was when their son had experimented with drugs. Thank God his usage had been discovered in time to save it from becoming a life-altering problem. Now married with two daughters, he was a high school principal, a pillar of his community.

Their daughter, two years younger than her brother, got out of Blewer as soon as she graduated high school. She went to college to find a husband she considered worthy of her, and did. She married a stockbroker from Dallas. Childless and glad to be, she was president of half a dozen societies and clubs and spent her days organizing luncheons and fundraising galas. Ezzy hated the life she had made for herself with that stuffy, snobby butthole she was married to. But she seemed happy, and Ezzy supposed that was what counted.

He claimed no credit for how well the children had turned out. It belonged to Cora. Left to him, they would have been human disasters.

His obsession with Patsy McCorkle's death had been a strain on his home life for the past twenty-two years, and it still was. Cora was giddy about the freedom his retirement allowed them. But Ezzy knew that he would never be free as long as this case remained open. To most folks it was ancient history. No one remembered or cared. But he did. Even if he had deluded himself into believing he could let it go, the news of Carl Herbold's escape two days ago had shattered that delusion.

He'd never lied to his wife, and he didn't intend to start now. Many times lying would have made things easier and more harmonious, but Ezzy felt that deception had no place in a marriage. Besides, Cora could see straight through the most innocent fib.

She probably knew he wasn't coming out on this stifling afternoon to fish.

Leaving the gear and the box of live crickets in the hull, he lifted the cooler and the sack from the boat and carried them with him to the deadfall. God only knew how long it had been here or what natural occurrence had caused the tree to fall. The trunk was covered in lichen and vines. Insects had hollowed it out, but it still supported Ezzy's weight as he sat down. He opened one of the Dr Peppers and took a long drink. He began to eat the corn chips with the same level of detachment.

Because every time he stared at the spot where Patsy McCorkle had taken her last breath, he recalled the shock of seeing her body the morning after she died.

"Has anybody touched her?"

That was all he could think to say to the young, pale, and shaken deputy who had been the first law enforcement officer on the scene after a fisherman had made the gruesome discovery.

"No, sir, Ezzy."

"Not even the guy who found her?"

"You kiddin'? He was scared shitless. Didn't even come ashore. His boat was drifting past. He saw her lying here and beat it back to Mundy's Point to call us. I know better than to contaminate a crime scene. I've secured the area."

The deputy must have picked up the lingo on a TV cop show, because Ezzy was certain he had never used that terminology. Not too many of their crime scenes had to be cordoned off to prevent evidence contamination.

Mostly they did routine patrols and maintained general law and order. They were called to stop fights that broke out in the beer joints, or to settle a dispute between feuding family members, or to lock up a drunk who had become disorderly and potentially destructive.

There were few outbreaks of violence that left victims dead, but on those rare occasions, the motivation was clear-cut. Armed robbery. Assault with a deadly weapon. Wife beating. The perpetrator usually had motivation that, if not justifiable or legal, was at least apparent.

Senseless crimes that were committed for no other reason except outright meanness occurred somewhere else. In big cities. In urban ghettos. They were unheard of in Blewer County, Texas. So neither the deputy nor Ezzy, who was already a seasoned officer of the law, had ever seen anything as disturbing as this.

In an area of trampled grass, she was lying facedown. Literally. Her head wasn't even turned to one side. One arm was folded beneath her. The other lay along her side, palm up, fingers curled slightly inward. Her legs were spread. She was wearing a pair of sandals. Nothing else. It was summertime, so she was tanned except for a strip of white across the middle of her back, and her buttocks.

To Ezzy it seemed indecent for them to be staring down at her naked body. They were acting in an official capacity, but even so, they were as guilty as her murderer—Ezzy had immediately assumed that she had met with foul play—of stripping this young woman of all dignity and respect.

"It's bad for us that it rained so hard last night," the deputy remarked, noting, as Ezzy had, the pool of rainwater that had collected in the small of the girl's back. "That probably washed away a lot of evidence."

"We'll have to work with what we've got."

"Yes, sir." The deputy blotted his moist upper lip with a folded handkerchief. "You think she was murdered?"

"It doesn't look like natural causes, does it, Deputy?"

A blue jay squawked angrily in the tree overhead, bringing Ezzy back into the present. He stuffed the empty Fritos package into the sack and chased their saltiness with the teeth-aching sweetness of the Peanut Pattie. Nibbling the pink, sugary candy, he stood and walked over to the spot where Patsy McCorkle had lain.

"Lord o' mercy. What've we got here, Ezzy?"

Startled, Ezzy glanced around, almost expecting old Harvey Stroud to materialize out of the surrounding forest. The coroner had been dead for fifteen years, and retired two years before that, but his voice was as real to Ezzy this morning as it had been when Stroud had knelt down beside Patsy McCorkle's corpse and slipped on his eyeglasses for a better look.

Ezzy asked, "Did you bring your camera?"

"That fellow from the *Banner* is coming out right behind me."

Ezzy had hoped to contain news of this until he'd had time to ask some preliminary questions of Patsy's close friends. He also wanted to allow the McCorkles time to absorb their shock and prepare for the onslaught of speculation their daughter's death would generate. But since Stroud had called in the newspaper's photographer, it would be the topic of conversation all over town by lunchtime.

"Can you tell anything yet, Harvey?"

"Don't rush me. I just got here." Without touching the body, he studied it from several angles, intent on his task. Finally he made a verbal observation. "There's a bruise on her neck." He pointed to the purplish mark with the tip of a Bic.

"Strangulation?"

"Maybe."

"Was she raped?"

"Possibly. That residue there on her thighs looks like semen."

"Jesus."

"Yeah."

The photographer arrived, eager as a beaver to take his pictures until confronted with the grim reality of the girl's corpse. He lost his breakfast Honeybun in the bushes, then, sitting with his head between his knees, repeatedly assured them that this wasn't the first time he'd seen a naked woman—only the first time he'd seen one dead. It took a while before he had recovered sufficiently to take Stroud's required photos.

Parked a short distance away from the body was a car registered to Patsy. Near it Ezzy found a pile of clothes. Using a pair of tweezers to pick up each article, he examined it before carefully placing it in a labeled plastic bag. There were a blouse and skirt, a brassiere, and a pair of panties. They were rain-soaked, but from what Ezzy could tell there were no rips in the cloth or missing buttons, which would indicate that the garments had been forcibly removed. They warranted further examination, of course.

Both the driver and passenger doors of the car were standing open. From that he deduced that someone had accompanied her here. The empty liquor bottles, one on the floorboard of the car, one lying in the mud nearby, suggested a party atmosphere.

"How're her fingernails, Harvey?"

"Polished red. None broken, torn, or bleeding. Doesn't appear to be any tissue under them. 'Course I'll clean them in the lab." The coroner also pointed out that there was no bruising on her wrists or ankles, nothing to indicate that she had been bound or gagged, or that a struggle had taken place.

Clearly Patsy McCorkle had felt comfortable about coming here with her companion and hadn't expected to die.

Hearing his radio activate, Ezzy immediately returned to his patrol car and spoke into the hand mike. "Yeah, Jim?"

"The McCorkle girl was at the Wagon Wheel last night," Deputy Jim Clark reported.

Cora and her group of teetotalers had been trying to vote the county dry for years, but that was one election that brought out the drinkers. Their proposed ordinance always failed miserably. They had, however, succeeded in prohibiting the sale of liquor within the township proper. Consequently, package stores and taverns lined both sides of the state highway just outside the city limits. The Wagon Wheel was one such club.

"Who'd you talk to there?"

"The guy who owns it, name of Parker Gee. He was tending bar last night. Says Patsy McCorkle was there for several hours and left around midnight."

"Alone?"

"With the Herbold brothers."

Chapter Nine

$\mathcal{E}$mory Lomax's desk phone rang. Vexed over the interruption, he depressed the intercom button. "Who is it, Mrs. Presley?"

"EastPark Development."

That quickly changed his attitude. "I'll take it."

He was buried in paperwork, but it could wait. His future wasn't dependent on this job at the bank. This bank was laughably small-time when compared to the business deals EPD out of Houston pulled together. They could buy this chickenshit operation a hundred times over and it would still be pocket change to them.

"Hello, Glen," he said smoothly. "How're things in—"

"Hold for Mr. Connaught."

Emory frowned, disliking the secretary's brusque dismissal and the fact that his call had been relegated to an underling and hadn't come directly from Connaught himself.

He was left on hold with Kenny G. music for almost three minutes before Connaught came on the line. Without any preliminary statements or pleasantries, he asked, "Lomax, did you receive the syllabus we sent you?"

"Yesterday. It looks fantasti—"

"What was Corbett's reaction?"

"I . . . well, I haven't shared it with him yet. As I said, I just received it myself yesterday. I haven't had time to study it." The silence on the other end of the line sent chills up Emory's spine. "But I spoke with his daughter-in-law. She's agreed to a meeting. I intend to go over all the printed material tonight. Memorize it if I have to. All forty-six pages."

If they thought he was going to spend an evening of his time plodding through all that shit about projections and phases, cost analyses and construction diagrams, they were wrong. He could swing this deal for them without having to know all the boring particulars.

"You understand where I'm coming from, Glen," he said in his most persuasive tone. "I don't want to leave Corbett any room to maneuver. Before I approach him, I want to know the material forward and backward. That way I can counter any argument he raises with a fact that'll dazzle him."

"If you're not up to this job, we'd like to know now."

Emory's heart lurched. "But I am!"

"You were a convenient choice for us because you handle Corbett's banking. You were already familiar with his finances. In other words, by using you we saved a step. But if you don't deliver you'll be replaced."

"Please, Glen. This is as important to me as it is to you."

"I doubt that. When will I hear from you?"

"Soon." Not good enough. "Very soon." Still not good enough. "Immediately after I've talked to Corbett."

"I'll be waiting."

Emory was left holding a telephone receiver as dead as a limp dick.

Uncomfortable with the analogy, he dropped the receiver back into place and spun his chair around to stare through the window that overlooked Blewer's Main Street.

The bank had a second floor, but he was glad his office was on the street level. The windows were tinted so that he could see out onto the sidewalk but no one could see in. As he watched the pedestrian traffic, he amused himself by making obscene gestures to people he disliked and staring his fill at attractive women. Rarely could one walk past without checking her reflection in the darkened glass. He liked to pretend that when a cute working girl or shopper turned her head toward the glass, she was looking at him.

Yesterday, he'd seen Anna Corbett coming from a block away. As she and her kid made their way down the sidewalk, they paused to gaze into various display windows. When she talked to the kid with her hands, he'd smiled.

Emory had watched them cross the street and head toward the bank's doors, making it easy for him to ambush her in the lobby. She was a looker. Tidy, compact figure. Tight ass. Not much in the tit department, but the air-conditioning inside the bank had brought her nipples up.

And to think that all that was being wasted on the old man. Everybody knew he fucked her. They had lived out there together for six years. Of course he fucked her.

From Corbett's perspective, it made sense. But why would she settle for that grouchy old codger? Probably because she was deaf, Emory reasoned. That must be it. She thought her daddy-in-law was as good as she could expect. Emory meant to show her different.

The thought made him smile.

But the smile didn't last long. The deaf broad was a secondary conquest. First he had to deliver to EastPark Development what he had promised. He couldn't do it by being nice. He had tried that approach. His attempts to be Corbett's financial adviser and confidant had met with no success.

Connaught and the others were getting impatient. Time was running out. But as long as Corbett met the scheduled payments on his loan, he could last for years. Emory feared that EastPark would hand this opportunity to someone else, or give up the project altogether and withdraw their offer. Then he would be screwed. He would be stuck in the loan department of this bank for the rest of his life working for wages.

Since it was one of few banks still family-owned and -operated, his chances of advancement were nil. The president had two sons, each as humorless as he. All were tight-asses, sticklers about time and money and customer service. None of them liked him overly much. They could just as well fire him as not.

Bottom line: He had to make that EastPark deal. He must convince Corbett to sell his ranch. But all inroads had failed. The old man wouldn't even discuss it, wouldn't even *listen*.

What he needed was a new plan of attack. Yes. Something bold.

Bold. What a great word. When people talked about it later—and Emory was certain they would—they would say, "It never would have come about if Lomax hadn't made that bold move." "Brass balls. That's what Lomax had or he never would have done something that bold."

Absently gazing through the tinted window, he willed himself to be inspired.

But all he noted was a battered pickup truck cruising slowly down Main Street.

Chapter Ten

"**H**e seemed okay," Delray said into the telephone. "But you can't be too careful these days."

"Especially in your situation, Mr. Corbett. I mean now that—"

"I know what you mean," Delray said, interrupting curtly.

The man on the other end of the line must have realized that he had put his foot in his mouth, because he rushed to say, "Just remember that I did this as a personal favor to you. This sort of detective work isn't my company's specialty."

"I understand."

"What I'd like to propose is for you to let me send out an armed guard. Just until this, uh, incident blows over."

"No thank you." Delray didn't equivocate. "I appreciate what you did for me. Especially since it's not really your line. But that's all I need. Good-bye."

He hung up, his face flushed with anger. He had asked the owner of a local security company, son of one of his former domino buddies, now deceased, to run a background check on Jack Sawyer.

That was all. But, sticking to tradition, the guy couldn't resist connecting him to Carl Herbold.

He took several deep breaths, forcing himself to calm down. The guy's remarks weren't worth a rise in his blood pressure. He talked it down to a safer level and focused on the good news. The report on Sawyer had come back clean.

The security company had entered his name, Social Security number, driver's license, and car tag into the system. They hadn't cross-matched any bankruptcies, bad credit, or bounced checks. He owed no back child support. No arrests were on record. Not even a traffic ticket.

Assimilating the information, Delray moved to the living room window and looked out across the yard. Sawyer had promised David that he would hang a swing from one of the large pecan trees. He'd gone into town yesterday to buy the supplies. Then last night, after hours and on his own time, he had sawed, sanded, and varnished the board for the seat. He'd found the chain in the toolshed and asked Delray's permission to use it.

Now he was adjusting the length of the chain so that the swing would be suspended the proper distance from the ground to accommodate the boy. With the swing about to be finished, David was hopping around and chattering with more animation than usual.

Naturally, Delray was relieved to learn that he hadn't hired a criminal or a deadbeat. It spoke well of his judgment that the report on Sawyer turned up nothing unfavorable.

So why did he feel a little let down? Had he secretly wanted to hear that David's new hero had an arrest record as long as his arm, that he was wanted by the FBI, the IRS, and several other government entities? Had he been looking for a good excuse to send Sawyer packing?

On the one hand he would hate to. After only three days, he would feel the loss. It was too early to make a sound determination, of course, but so far he couldn't complain about Sawyer's work ethic. Just as he'd promised, the man put in a full day and then some. And it was damned easier to get through the workday with an extra pair of hands and a strong back helping out. He could no longer argue that he didn't need a hand. Having Sawyer had convinced him that he did.

But he disliked Sawyer's being around all the time, and in such close proximity. He didn't welcome having other people on the place. Particularly other men. Even more particularly, men he knew virtually nothing about.

He, Anna, and David had lived here alone for a long time. They were creatures of habit. One day varied little from another. He liked knowing when he got up in the morning what he could expect of the day. The three of them had developed a well-suited, comfortable routine. Their life had structure, and Delray liked it that way. His peace of mind depended on it.

Jack Sawyer would disturb the ordered pattern of their life. Any fourth party would. Having him around was certain to have an effect. It was the nature of that effect that concerned Delray.

Plainly, David had developed a bad case of hero worship. But he was a child and easily impressed. His interests were mercurial, switching constantly and rapidly. Today it was dinosaurs. Tomorrow it could be rockets, or volcanoes, or jungles. Delray wasn't that worried about David's infatuation with Sawyer.

But what about Anna?

He glanced over his shoulder at her now. She was sitting in an uphol-stered easy chair, her feet tucked beneath her, a glass of iced tea at her elbow, a novel in her lap. Only she wasn't reading. She was gazing through another window at the tree, the swing, the boy, and the man. Feeling Delray's stare, she looked at him, then quickly returned her eyes to her book.

Her guilty reaction needled him and played upon his worst fear.

Feeling in need of a chaw to help him relax, he made his way to the front door. No sooner had he cleared the threshold and stepped onto the porch than David shouted at him to come push him in his new swing.

"Jack says I can't go too high till I get the hang of it. Do you think I'll get the hang of it by tomorrow, Jack?"

As he crossed the yard, Delray tucked a plug of tobacco into his cheek. Then, stepping behind the swing, he gave it a push. "I can go higher than that, Grandpa," David complained. "I'm not a baby."

Jack leaned against the trunk of the tree. "Better warn you, Delray. He'll wear you out in no time."

David started making airplane noises. Delray gave the seat of the swing gentle shoves each time it arced back toward him. He glanced across at Sawyer. "Did you find your way around yesterday? In town, I mean."

"I followed my nose and managed not to get lost."

Delray nodded. He pushed the swing a few more times. "You don't have to stick around in the evenings, you know. You're free to come and go after hours, so long as you lock the gate behind you when you come in."

"Thanks, but I've got nowhere to go."

"Blewer's got a new multiscreen movie house the chamber of commerce is mighty proud of."

"Can't afford the picture show. What they want for a ticket, much less a bag of popcorn, is highway robbery."

"I hear some of the nightclubs are pretty lively."

Sawyer laughed softly. "More lively than me, I'm sure."

"Well, there are other places to meet folks. My daughter-in-law and I stick close to home, but a single man like you, stuck way out here, might get lonesome for . . . companionship."

"I might," Sawyer said, scratching the back of his neck. "But I've got little energy to go looking for it. By the end of the workday, I'm worn to a frazzle."

"There used to be a Bible study group for singles. I don't know if they still meet, but you could check around."

"I'm not *that* frazzled."

Delray laughed, but his heart wasn't in it, and apparently Sawyer noticed that he was beating around the bush. He asked, "Something on your mind tonight, Delray?"

Sawyer had started calling him by his first name right off. He'd seen no reason to make an issue of it. "Why do you ask?"

Sawyer shrugged. "Seems like there might be."

Perceptive of him, Delray thought. But then they had been working side by side for the last three days. You sweat with a man, you come to know him. Like him and Dean. He had shared an uncommon bond with his son. It had been forged by the perspiration each had put into this place. Despite sports and other activities, Dean had worked with him after school and during the summers all the way through junior college and right up until he joined the army.

Abruptly he said, "I've got some people who want to buy the ranch."

He sensed a tension in Sawyer's posture, although he didn't actually move. "I didn't know you were selling."

"I'm not. That's the hell of it. This guy has been pestering me. He represents some people. I've told him I won't sell to anybody. He's not taking no for an answer."

"Higher, Grandpa!"

"Let me take over for a while." Jack motioned Delray aside and moved in behind the swing. "Hold on tight now, David."

"I will, Jack. Push me high."

Sawyer gave the swing a push. "What people, Delray?"

Delray spat a string of tobacco juice. "Developers. An outfit out of Houston. This guy—Lomax is his name—put a fancy notebook full of charts and graphs in my mailbox last night. I thumbed through it after supper."

"And?"

"Basically they want to chop up my ranch into acre lots for rich people to put weekend houses on. Build a golf course, clubhouse, swimming pool, the works."

"I've seen it happening everywhere," Jack said. "There's an empty space, next week somebody's filled it with a fast-food restaurant or a convenience store. Some people think just because there's a space, something's got to go there."

"This Lomax is coming out in a few days to talk it over."

"What's his angle?"

"I don't know. It doesn't matter. My answer won't change. It's final. This meeting will be a waste of my time and his, but he insisted on coming, so I guess I owe him an audience."

"You don't owe him a damn thing."

Delray looked at him sharply. Sawyer's face was in shadow, so he couldn't easily read his expression. His tone of voice, however, spoke volumes. Sawyer wouldn't back down from a fight. Maybe his new hired hand wasn't as easygoing as he had first seemed.

Delray said, "At the very least I'll have a chance to tell Lomax to his face to take a flying you-know-what."

"A flying what, Grandpa?"

Jack grinned at Delray, man-to-man.

He wanted to return the smile but felt it might compromise their relationship. He was this man's boss, not his newfound friend. Not his anything, really. In fact, he now regretted sharing with Sawyer his thoughts on the sale of his property. It bestowed on Sawyer a rank he hadn't earned.

Spitting out his tobacco, he said, "I'm turning in. See you in the morning, Sawyer. Come along, David."

"I just started swinging, Grandpa," the boy whined. "Just a little longer? Please?"

"I'll see that he gets in," Jack offered.

The boy was having a grand time on the swing, and Delray really had no reason to insist that he go indoors. "Okay. Anna will be coming for him soon anyway."

Happy again, David chirped, "G'night, Grandpa."

"Good night, David."

At the door, Delray paused to take one last look at the swing. David was talking. Sawyer was listening patiently. He looked comfortable in the role of baby-sitter.

Jack Sawyer's security check had come back clean. He hadn't displayed a temper. He was intelligent and well read. Delray hadn't found a topic yet that Sawyer couldn't talk about. Except himself. He hadn't talked a whit about himself. Mostly he listened. He was a good listener, knowing when to comment as well as when to say nothing.

He was a good wrangler and had an encyclopedic knowledge of cattle. What he didn't know, he asked about. He worked hard. He never sloughed off. He initiated projects for himself. He took good care of the equipment. He put implements away after using them. He was a damned good ranch hand.

So why was a smart, congenial guy like him drifting from here to there in an old pickup truck, working odd jobs, without any family or friends or tether of any kind?

Furthermore, he seemed to have dropped out of the sky directly following Carl's escape from prison.

But if there were a connection between Jack Sawyer and Carl, it would have shown up in the security check.

Delray mistrusted coincidences. He didn't really believe in them. By nature he was suspicious and careful to a fault. He liked the younger man, but he didn't entirely trust him.

Delray liked for things to add up.

Jack Sawyer didn't.

Chapter Eleven

his is a *j*. You just draw it in the air with your little finger."

Jack followed David's instruction, but the boy shook his head. "No, you gotta make an *i* first. See? Then . . ."

"Oh, okay, got it." Jack tried again.

"That's it, Jack. That's good. You're good at sign language."

"I've got a good teacher. How 'bout *a*?"

David secured his tongue in the corner of his mouth and with his chubby fist formed the sign for the letter. Jack imitated it. "Like this?"

"Um-huh. That's it. What comes next?"

"*C*."

"*C*'s look easy. It looks just like it does when you print it. I can print, too. My mom taught me when I was only three."

"Pretty smart."

"That's what my mom says."

"Okay. *J-a-c*." Jack formed the letters with his right hand as he spelled them out. "*K* comes next."

"That's kinda hard. It's like this."

"This?"

"No, you gotta . . . Wait! My mom can show you. Hi, Mom. I was just showing Jack how to spell his name in sign language."

Jack, who'd been sitting on his haunches in front of the swing, came to his feet, turned around, and smiled sheepishly. "Hi."

Anna Corbett gave him such a cool once-over he wondered what he'd done to piss her off this time. He thought he'd been forgiven for his unintentional slight when they met. After all, he had fixed her car and saved her a repair bill. She had signed a *"Thank you"* to him.

Maybe he had misinterpreted. Could she have signed something else? *"Fuck you,"* maybe.

Since moving into the trailer, he had caught only fleeting glimpses of her; once when she was watering the flowerpots on the front steps, another time when she walked with David down to the road to get the mail, and earlier today, when he was shoeing one of the horses, he glanced up and saw her standing in the back door. But she'd been gone in a blink, so he wasn't sure she'd even noticed him in the corral.

She certainly hadn't gone out of her way to make him feel welcome. He got the impression that she was avoiding him. He could also be reading a lot more into her avoidance than it signified.

She signed something to David, which he immediately protested. "There aren't any mosquitoes out here, Mom. I haven't got bit. Not once."

She said more. Whatever it was, David felt it prudent to obey. He slid off the seat of the swing and said to Jack, "I gotta go take my bath."

"Well, we guys gotta do what we gotta do. The sooner you do it, the sooner you get to bed, the sooner you can get up and swing again."

"Will you push me higher tomorrow?"

"We'll see." He gave David a high five.

His mother turned him about by the shoulders and gave the seat of his shorts an affectionate swat to direct him toward the porch. Then, to Jack's surprise, she motioned him in the same direction.

He pointed to his own chest. "Me? Come inside?"

She gave a curt nod and, without waiting to see whether or not he would follow, she started in after her son. Curious, Jack fell into step behind her. "Yes, ma'am," he said out loud.

Inside the entry, she pointed David upstairs. "What're you and Jack gonna do? Can I stay down here with y'all?"

She held up her index finger and mouthed *one*. A couple seconds later, she raised the second finger. *Two.*

"When she starts counting, I'm in trouble," David said.

"Better scoot then."

The boy turned and trudged up the staircase, calling down, "Good night, Jack."

"'Night."

Anna motioned Jack down the central hallway. Rooms opened into the hall from both sides, but she gave him no time to stop and look into them as they went toward the back of the house, where she showed him into a small room tucked beneath the sloped ceiling behind the stairwell.

One wall had a window with louvered shutters. Two other walls were

lined with bookshelves. Against the third stood a desk, on which were
set two keyboards, one belonging to the special telephone for Anna's
use. The state provided a telephone network where the hearing-impaired
could type information to an operator, who in turn would vocally relay
the message to the hearing person on the other end. For messages sent
to a deaf individual, the system worked in reverse.

The second keyboard belonged to a computer. The screen saver was
on. Planets and meteors streaked across a starry sky.

She pointed him into a wide leather chair. He sat down and looked up
at her expectantly. "Now what?" She held out her hand like a traffic cop.
"Halt? Stop? Stay?"

She nodded.

"Stay." He repeated the word and she repeated her nod, then she
turned and left him alone. "Just call me Rover," he muttered, listening
to her footfalls on the stairs and reasoning that she was going up to
check on David and the progress of his bath. Delray, he assumed, was
already in bed.

He left the chair and began a slow circuit of the room, acknowledging his nosiness. But if she hadn't wanted him to look around, she
shouldn't have invited him to come inside.

The furniture wasn't new, but it was well polished. The leaves on the
thriving ivies were glossy. Everything was in its proper place. The room
was homey but uncluttered. Anna Corbett was a good housekeeper.

The book collection on the shelves showed an eclectic reading taste.
There were numerous biographies and nonfiction books covering a wide
range of topics, in addition to leather-bound volumes of classic litera-
ture and recent best-selling fiction paperbacks.

On a lower shelf, he found a comprehensive sign language dictionary. Curious, he took it out and scanned the introductory pages. He was
fascinated to learn that there was a difference between American Sign
Language and Signed English. He had always thought that sign language was sign language. Apparently not.

According to the foreword of this dictionary, Signed English was
based on using one sign for one word. Other signs, called word mark-
ers, designated plurality, tense, prefixes and suffixes, and other elements
of English.

American Sign Language didn't equate to English either written or
spoken. It was a language unto itself. One sign could translate to several
English words with synonymous meanings. Some of the signs used in
Signed English were taken from ASL so that users of Signed English
could communicate with users of ASL. But the two were entirely dif-

ferent, and the advantages of one over the other was a topic of heated debate among deaf educators.

Jack read just enough to become confused. But he smiled when he glanced through a diagram of the manual alphabet and discovered that David had shown him correctly how to form the letters of his name.

There were also several pages of diagrams depicting common phrases. He tried out a few, and smiled again when he saw that Anna *had* signed *"Thank you"* and not an obscenity.

He was practicing a few of the rudimentary signs when Anna rejoined him. She moved straight to him, took the book out of his hands, closed it emphatically, and replaced it on the shelf.

More puzzled by her rudeness than miffed by it, he watched her sit down in the desk chair and work the computer mouse until she had a blank screen. She then typed what was apparently a message for him. He dragged a wooden ladder-back chair closer to the computer table, positioning it so that he could see the screen and she could see his face to read his lips. He straddled the seat backward.

On the screen she had typed, "Why were you having David teach you sign?"

He shrugged. "I wanted to learn."

Her fingers moving faster than his eyes could follow, she typed, "Why?"

The answer seemed obvious. He raised his shoulders in a second shrug. "What's the big deal?"

"You don't need to learn sign. If you have something to say to me, you can say it through David and Delray."

His eyes shifted from the computer screen to her. "Oh, I get it. This is your way of letting me know that we really don't have anything to say to each other."

She made a slight affirmative motion with her head.

"How come? When did you decide I wouldn't be a good conversationalist?" He could tell she'd missed the last word, so he made an adjustment. "When did you decide I wouldn't be good at conversation?"

Slender fingers tapped the keys with lightning efficiency. "Don't talk to me like I'm dumb. I'm deaf, not—"

Jack reached out and stopped her hands. Then he made the sign he had seen David question her about. *Stupid.* "I remember."

There was a lot of turbulence going on behind the spectacular blue irises of her eyes. He knew enough psychology to figure out that Anna Corbett liked to sting before she could be stung. It was an understandable defense mechanism. Human nature being what it is, Anna must have been teased by classmates in school. Even well-meaning adults could be thoughtless and tactless. She had developed her own method of self-preservation. She fought ignorance and cruelty by striking first.

"No one could think you're stupid," he told her. "What you are is a . . ." Reaching over the back of the chair, he used the hunt-and-peck system to type the word *snob*.

She pushed his hand aside and reached for the computer's power button. "No way," he said, stopping her hands again. "That's too easy. You're going to listen . . . I mean you're going to hear what . . . Hell, you know what I mean."

He paused to take a breath and arrange his thoughts. She was regarding him with open hostility, but he didn't believe deafness gave her an excuse to be rude. Why should she have open season on him just because she couldn't hear?

"You've got this bug up your butt about being deaf—"

She frowned with misapprehension. The idiom had escaped her. He started over. "You've got this chip on your shoulder . . ." He paused and she nodded curtly, indicating that she understood. "From the minute we met, I've been nice to you. You've treated me like shit. Now why is that? Because I can hear and you can't?"

Furiously she shook her head no.

"Then why?"

She typed, "Because I'm afraid of you."

Jack was taken aback by the words that appeared on the screen. She couldn't have said anything that would have surprised or wounded him more. "Afraid of me?"

Her eyes moved from his lips, up to his eyes, then she faced the computer screen again. "I'm afraid that it will hurt David when you leave. And Delray."

Jack smiled wryly. "I just got here. I'm not thinking about leaving."

"But you <u>will</u>," she typed, underlining the last word.

Her intent gaze was unnerving, but he answered her honestly. "Yeah. I will."

She typed a short sentence. "When you go, they'll be sad."

"Why should they be sad?" he asked.

Her fingers hovered above the keys for a few seconds before she typed, "You fill a . . ." She struggled with the next word. Finally she consulted the well-used thesaurus that was sitting next to the keyboard. She typed "void," then looked at him, her eyes inquiring.

"That fits," he said. "What I mean is, that's the correct word. I'm not sure it's what you mean to say."

Nodding, she mouthed *It is,* then began to type again. "Delray was an unhappy man before he met Mary, my husband's mother. Mary was his second wife. His first wife had two sons when he married her. His stepsons were bad boys. They gave him a lot of trouble. Really bad trouble. After his wife died, he . . ." Again she paused to search for a word. Looking at Jack, she made an imperious motion with her hand.

"Pushed them away? Had nothing to do with them? Disowned them?"

Nodding, she continued, "That was a long time ago. Delray pretends it never happened. He had a second life with Mary. He loved her very much. But she died. Then Dean. When Dean died, Delray withdraw."

"Withdrew," Jack corrected absently. He asked, "How did he die?"

Jack read the words as they appeared on the screen. Dean Corbett was a soldier. He joined the army to supplement his education, never guessing that the U.S. would go to war during his active duty. He was sent from Fort Hood, Texas, to Iraq during Desert Storm. After the surrender, his unit remained behind to assist in the clean-up of Kuwait. He returned uninjured, but a casualty nevertheless.

"There was infection in his lungs because of the oil-well fires," she wrote. "One after another until he became very sick and died."

She stopped typing and Jack looked at her. "I'm sorry."

She gazed at him a moment, then down at her fingers, which were still resting on the keyboard. The grandfather clock in the central hallway struck the hour. Jack reacted. She did not. She dealt with her handicap so facilely it was easy to forget that her world was silent.

Getting her attention, he asked, "David wasn't even born yet?"

She smiled wistfully, then typed, "Three months after Dean died."

Jack rubbed his knuckle across his lips. He supposed there were worse things than living alone all your adult life, as he had done. One of them had to be losing the father of your child before the child was even born. He wanted to ask if she would have reconsidered having David had she known she would be an early widow. But he didn't. He knew the answer. She would have wanted David no matter what.

She began typing again. "Delray has built his life a second time. I don't want him to hurt again."

"You are giving me more importance than I deserve, Anna. I won't hurt anybody."

She was shaking her head even before he finished. "It won't be your fault. David wants a father. Delray misses his son." She looked at him and shrugged, the conclusion being obvious. Jack refrained from pointing out that when Dean died she had also lost a husband. He wondered if there was a man filling that void in her life.

Instead he asked, "Does David look like Dean?"

She stuck out her hand, palm down, and waggled it back and forth. She then got up and retrieved a leather-bound photo album from a shelf and brought it back to him.

The first picture in the album was of Anna and Dean on their wedding day. She was garbed in the traditional gown and veil, looking positively radiant. Dean had been a stocky, physically fit young man with an honest face like Delray's, but showing much more humor. It shone in his lively eyes. He wore a broad smile. Probably because he had been head-over-heels in love with his bride.

"The two of you looked real good together," Jack told her as he continued to turn the pages of the album. "Happy."

She nodded vigorously.

One group of pictures had been taken at a beach. "Honeymoon?" he asked. Again she nodded. There were shots of them together, sipping drinks with paper umbrellas in them. Dean, preening like a bodybuilder. Anna in a bikini, striking a cheesecake pose.

Jack studied the picture of her, tilting his head as though giving it an objective appraisal. When he glanced up at her, he grinned and bobbed his eyebrows. She blushed and kept her eyes lowered. He laughed.

Then he turned another page in the album and was arrested by the marked difference in the last collection of photos. They weren't the standard professionally posed wedding portraits, or the candid honeymoon snapshots. They were a series of black-and-white eight-by-tens.

The first photo was of Dean Corbett. He was sitting almost in silhouette in an open window, staring out. The mood conveyed by the photo was noticeably different from the one taken of him on his wedding day. Gone were the smile and the liveliness. In this picture he looked aged, pensive, and very sad.

Anna typed, "He was sick. We were just about to leave for the hospital." Then she added, "For the last time."

What the portrait expressed so eloquently was that Dean Corbett had known he was dying, leaving behind his beautiful wife and unborn child.

Poor bastard, Jack thought. He had had a taste of what he would be missing by dying young. Jack didn't know if it was a curse or a blessing to have something you love and lose it, or whether it was better never to have had it. Shakespeare had penned an opinion, but Jack wasn't sure he agreed with it. If the Bard had seen this picture of Dean Corbett, he might have written a different couplet.

Anna was watching him for a reaction to the photograph. "It's sad," he said. "But it's a great picture. You can tell exactly what he's feeling."

He turned the page. The second photo had an even greater impact on him than the one of Dean. Reacting to it like a sock in the gut, he took a sharp breath.

The film had been overexposed, creating extreme degrees of light and dark, but it was that contrast that made the picture so captivating. That and the subject matter.

The background was a solid white sky. The foreground was inky black. On the horizon where the two came together stretched a wire fence, much like the one he'd helped Delray repair his first day. The rough cedar posts were uneven, some listing slightly. One of the strands of barbed wire had sprung, creating a cruel-looking curl. These imperfections didn't detract, however. They gave the fence character and told its story. They said that it had withstood years of hard use.

But the fence was only a backdrop. The focal point of the photo was the woman leaning against one of the posts, her hands sandwiched between it and the small of her back. Her face was turned away from the camera, exposing her neck and throat to the harsh light, which formed deep shadows between the slender tendons and in the notch in the center of her collarbone.

The wind had swept her hair across her face. The same strong wind—it had to be strong to have done such a good job—had molded her dress to the front of her body, delineating her shape so precisely and perfectly that she might just as well not have been wearing the dress.

Against that sheet of sky, her breasts were high and small and provocative. The dimple of her navel held an innocent allure, while the vee at the top of her thighs was darkly shadowed and not at all innocent. The cloth seemed to have been liquefied and poured over her.

It was an incredibly seductive photograph. Jack responded with a whispered curse and a dry swallow.

Anna grabbed the album from him and got up to put it away. "Hey, wait. Who was that? Was that you?" Realizing he was talking to her back, he waited until she came back around. He repeated the questions, but she ignored him and began working backward out of her software program and shutting down the computer.

Determined, he touched her arm to get her attention. "Was that you?"

She pointed to her wristwatch, put her palms together, then rested her tilted head on her hands. "Bedtime," he said with chagrin. "A convenient retreat. To keep me from asking about the woman in the picture. Who I hope to God I have real dirty dreams about tonight."

Of course she missed all that, as he intended for her to. They left the study together and she led him to the front door, where she stepped aside, waiting to lock up behind him.

Jack stepped across the threshold, but before she could close the door, he said, "I almost forgot the reason for that meeting. You don't want David to teach me any more sign language, right?"

She nodded.

"Because that's your secret language. If people can't understand what you're saying, you have control. You feel superior. And you like to lord it over people that you're deaf. That sets you apart from us common hearing folk."

She angrily shook her head no and began signing a rebuttal that he figured must be chock-full of epithets.

"Yeah, that's what I thought," he said obtusely. "Well, I won't ask David to teach me sign because I don't want him to get into trouble on account of me."

She bobbed her head in agreement, believing she had won the argument.

But just as she was about to close the door, Jack tapped the porch lightly with the heel of his boot. Signing it perfectly, he said, *"Good night, Anna."*

Chapter Twelve

*E*zzy awakened at four thirty, his usual time to get up. Retirement hadn't reset his body clock or altered his sleep patterns. But where work had once consumed his days, now the hours of wakefulness were barren and seemed to last forever. Most folks toiled for decades to reach this point in life. Ezzy couldn't figure why. It baffled him that anyone would strive for uselessness.

Cora had it in her head that they should buy a Winnebago and strike out to see the country. There were a few spots on the national map that might be worth the trip. The Grand Canyon. The Tetons. Niagara Falls. New England in the fall. But he couldn't work up much enthusiasm for the endless driving that kind of trip would entail.

She also had mentioned a cruise. He couldn't think of anything worse than being stranded on a ship with a bunch of strangers and a hyperactive crew determined to see that he had a good time doing things he didn't want to do. He had patently ignored the colorful brochures Cora kept poking under his nose.

Eventually she would wear him down. Guilt would compel him to give in. Vacations weren't important to him, so he hadn't missed taking them. Cora had. Sooner or later he would have to accompany her on one of her fantasy holidays.

But he hoped to delay it for as long as possible. He felt—and this was the silly part—that he shouldn't leave town just yet. Although he had been formally retired and there was a new man already on the job, and things at the Blewer County S.O. seemed to be chugging along just fine without him, he had an almost eerie notion that his work wasn't finished.

Of course, he was deluding himself. He was hunting for signs and omens that he could whittle down to fit his present situation. "I'm a god-damn crazy old man, is what I am," he muttered scornfully as he shuffled into the kitchen.

The preset timer on the coffeemaker assured him a hot, fresh cup. He carried it outside onto the redwood deck, a Christmas present from their kids a few years back. Even at this time of morning, well before the sun was up, the needle on the outdoor thermometer was nudging the eighty-degree mark. The moon was low on the western horizon. There wasn't a cloud in sight. Today would be another scorcher.

It had been exceptionally hot that summer, too.

Especially that August morning when Patsy's body had been discovered. The heat probably had contributed to the brash newspaper photographer's nausea. Responding to Deputy Jim Clark's summons, Ezzy had left him and the coroner Harvey Stroud at the crime scene and had sped to the lounge where Patsy had last been seen alive.

Clark and another deputy had already rounded up people who had been there the night before. By the time Ezzy arrived, they'd been questioned, but he conducted his own interrogations, taking notes on cocktail napkins imprinted with a wagon wheel.

"That's right, Sheriff. Cecil and Carl were here with Patsy most of the evening. They were having themselves a real good time."

"Patsy, she'd dance one song with Carl, then the next with Cecil. And when I say dance, I mean, you know, she plastered herself against 'em. Had 'em both heated up real good. I was kinda heated up myself, just watching."

"By 'provocative' do you mean she was leading them on? Yes, sir, Sheriff Hardge. She surely was. I think she enjoyed having an audience while she did it, too."

"I don't mean to speak bad of the dead, you understand, but Patsy . . . well, sir, she was making herself available, if you know what I mean."

"She and Cecil, they were giving everybody a real good show out on the dance floor. He had his hands on her ass—pardon the French—and his tongue down her throat."

"I thought she and Carl were gonna go at it right over yonder on the pool table. 'N front o' God and everybody."

"Jealous? No, Sheriff, the brothers didn't act jealous toward each other. They was sharing her and that seemed to suit them fine. 'Course they's trash."

The only witness who didn't cooperate was the owner of the club, Parker Gee. He resented having his nightclub invaded by "cops" and his clientele interrogated like criminals. All questions posed to him were answered with a surly "I was busy last night. I don't remember."

Leaving deputies to take official statements, Ezzy put out an APB on the Herbolds, stressing that at this point they were wanted only for questioning. He drove straight from the tavern to the mobile-home park where they lived together in a ratty trailer. Their car was gone and they didn't answer his knock. He resisted the urge to search the trailer without a warrant. On this case, everything must be done by the book. If the brothers were charged with murder, he didn't want the case dismissed because of a technicality.

When he questioned their neighbors, they looked scornfully at the trailer and told the sheriff they hoped he arrested Carl and Cecil and locked them up for good. They were nuisances, coming and going at all hours of the night, speeding through the park and endangering the youngsters playing outdoors, terrorizing young women with crude remarks and catcalls. Their trailer was an eyesore in an otherwise neat community. Unanimously their neighbors would like to be rid of them.

He then drove to the oil-drilling rig where the Herbolds were employed. "They didn't show up for work this morning," the foreman told Ezzy. "I knew they'd done time, but everybody deserves a second chance. Now I'm two hands short. So much for being a nice guy. What'd they do, anyhow?"

Ezzy had declined to answer. But even if he had, he wouldn't have known where to begin. The answer would have been long and complicated. The Herbolds had been getting into trouble since they were just kids still living with their stepfather.

Delray Corbett had married their widowed mother when the boys were in primary school. She was a pretty woman, shy and quiet, who was obviously intimidated by her boisterous sons. She never had exerted parental control over them. This made them all the more resentful of and rebellious against their new stepfather's stern discipline. After their mother died, leaving Delray their guardian, their hostility toward him had intensified. When he remarried, they became full-fledged incorrigibles, making life hell for him and Mary.

The boys' first malfeasance was a suspected shoplifting of a six-pack of beer. "They weren't caught with the goods, Delray, so we can't prove it."

Ezzy remembered Delray Corbett's mortification when he delivered the two tipsy boys to his doorstep. "I'll tend to it, Sheriff Hardge. Thank you for bringing them home. You have my word that this will be the last time."

Delray was unable to keep his promise. The boys grew more unruly with each passing year, especially after Dean Corbett was born. He was the apple of his daddy's eye. Cecil and Carl seemed determined to be just the opposite.

Their misdeeds increased in seriousness until, in Cecil's sophomore year of high school—Carl was a grade younger—a girl accused them of exposing themselves to her on the school bus and forcing her to fondle them. The boys claimed that she was lying, that the incident had never happened, that it was wishful thinking on her part. Since it was her word against theirs, they went unpunished. The girl's parents were outraged and publicly blamed Delray for his stepsons' behavior.

There followed a string of petty thefts, vandalism, and DUIs, but the boys were clever. None of the charges stuck. Then one night they were caught red-handed stealing auto parts from a salvage yard. They were sentenced to eighteen months in a juvenile detention facility. They were released after serving a year and returned to parental custody.

Delray had laid down the law: One misstep and they were out. Two nights later they got drunk, stole a car off a used-car lot, and drove it to Dallas, where they ran head-on into a van, seriously injuring the driver. They were tried as adults and sent to Huntsville. Delray washed his hands of them.

When they were released on parole, they didn't return to Blewer. Not until the spring of 1976.

Earlier that year a drilling outfit had struck oil and in quick succession brought in three new wells. This incited a flurry of drilling, creating a demand for workers. Roughnecks looking for jobs flocked to the area. The Herbolds were among them.

One night a fight broke out in a local motel that catered to the transients. When Ezzy arrived on the scene, he was surprised to see the Herbold brothers in the thick of the fracas.

They had always been good-looking boys, and prison had done nothing to detract from their handsomeness. The bleeding cut above Carl's eyebrow made him even more dashing and enhanced his natural charm.

"Well, I'll be goddamned. Sheriff Hardge." Carl grinned at Ezzy as he pulled him off a guy he'd been pummeling. "Long time no see."

"Still making mischief, Carl? Didn't you learn your lesson up at Huntsville?"

"We sure did, Sheriff." Cecil elbowed his brother aside to address Ezzy. They were both rotten to the core, but Cecil was the least offensive. Ezzy doubted Cecil was any more righteous than his little brother, just more cautious. "This here was an accident."

"Accident. Your brother was beating the hell out of that guy."

A deputy was trying to bring the unconscious man around by smartly slapping his cheeks. "My brother was only protecting himself," Cecil argued. "We're no more to blame for the fight than any man here. If you arrest us, you have to arrest everybody. I don't think your jail is big enough."

He was right, of course. If Ezzy questioned these men all night, he would hear dozens of conflicting versions of how the fight started. Trying to get to the truth would be a waste of time and manpower. Instead, he imposed a curfew, ordering everyone to clear the area and return to their rooms to sleep it off.

Cecil tried pulling Carl toward their room, but Carl resisted. "Hey, Sheriff, you ever see our stepdaddy?"

"Sometimes."

"Next time you do, tell him to go fuck himself." Carl jabbed his finger for emphasis. "You tell that cocksucker I said that."

"Shut up, Carl." Smiling apologetically, Cecil dragged his brother across the parking lot.

The next day Ezzy had called Delray. He didn't relay Carl's message, but he asked if Delray knew his stepsons were back in the area.

"I'd heard, but I haven't seen them. They know where they stand with me. I want no part of them."

Ezzy had seen them on only one other occasion, and, again, they'd been at the epicenter of a disturbance. It had taken place at the Wrangler, one of the few remaining drive-in movie theaters in East Texas. Alcohol was prohibited anywhere on the premises, but enough alcohol to float a battleship was consumed there just about every night during the summer.

Admittance was a dollar a carload. At that price, the drive-in was cheap entertainment for teenagers from Blewer and surrounding towns. It didn't matter what movie was playing; kids by the hundreds flocked there, moving from car to car to visit, neck, drink.

On that particular night, for reasons that were never determined, the crowd at the drive-in became polarized. Those parked on the north end went to war with those parked on the south end. The graveled acreage was split right down the middle in the manner of the Mason-Dixon Line.

By the time it was all over, some blood had been shed, several cars had been vandalized, a fire had been started in the projection room, and the sheriff's office had dispatched all five patrol cars to the scene.

Ezzy spotted Carl stanching a bloody nose while trying to pack a hopelessly inebriated woman into the front seat of a station wagon. "You just can't stay out of trouble, can you, Carl?"

Immediately defensive, he sneered, "Hey, I didn't start it."

"That's the God's truth. He was just defending his girl's honor. You can't arrest him for that."

Ezzy turned toward Cecil, who once again had come to his brother's defense. "He's in violation of parole," Ezzy remarked. "I can arrest him for that."

"Give him a break, Sheriff Hardge. What was he supposed to do? Some asshole called his girlfriend a fucking whore."

Ezzy recognized the woman slumped in the front seat. She was in fact a well-known whore whom he'd had to jail a few times for boldly soliciting on the parking lot of the Piggly Wiggly store. "Get on out of here, you two. But this makes twice. From here on, I've got my eye on you."

Carl retorted, "Yeah, which one?"

Later Ezzy castigated himself for not cuffing them that night and taking them in. He should have reported them to their parole officer. He should have used the slightest infraction as an excuse to put them in jail. If he had, Patsy McCorkle might have lived.

Those two encounters with the Herbolds would haunt Ezzy for many years to come, but never more so than three days after Patsy's body was discovered. Harvey Stroud had been wearing a linen suit the color of sweet cream when he huffed into Ezzy's office and tossed a manila envelope onto his desk. "That's it."

"'Bout time," Ezzy grumbled as he lowered his boots from the corner of his desk and opened the envelope.

"Couldn't rush something like this, Ezzy." The coroner removed his hat and fanned himself with it. "You got a cold Co'Cola you could spare?"

A deputy brought the county official the requested soft drink. He had drunk half of it before Ezzy raised his head from the reading material. "She died of a broken neck?"

"Snapped like a twig. Clean in two. Death was instantaneous."

"What do you think happened?"

Stroud said, "Well, for starters, she had sexual intercourse with at least two partners."

"Forced?"

"I prepared a rape kit just in case. It's included there. But rape would be tough to prove because there's no forensic evidence to support it. Besides, from what I hear about this girl, a young man wouldn't have to force himself on her."

"I'm concerned with her mortality, not her morality. That statement is unworthy of you, Harvey."

"Maybe," the coroner replied without taking umbrage. "But don't you know it to be true?"

He did, and for that reason he didn't pursue the argument. "What about the bruise on her neck?"

"It was a hickey. There was one to match it on her left breast. Caused by deep kissing, but nothing violent."

"It says here you found semen in her vagina as well as her, uh . . ."

"Rectum. Only one donor there. I ran the tests several times on the specimen I took from there. Only one man ejaculated into her rectum." Stroud belched and set his empty soda bottle on the edge of Ezzy's desk. "There were abrasions and tearing around the anus. Light bleeding. So she was alive when she was penetrated there. My guess . . . If you're interested in my guess, Ezzy."

He motioned for Stroud to continue, although each word out of the coroner's mouth was making him a little sick to his stomach.

"My guess is that she went willingly with the boys. They had themselves an orgy."

"And then one of them raped her anally."

The coroner frowned and thoughtfully tugged on his earlobe. "Again, that's an iffy call. She could have been game. It could have been something new and untried for her. For all we know she even initiated it."

Ezzy thought about Mrs. McCorkle in her daisy-patterned housecoat and hoped to hell she never had to hear this about her only child.

"What happened from there is anybody's guess," Stroud continued. "She might have balked and said no, and the boy held her down. But, again, there's no significant bruising or scratching to suggest an all-out fight."

"That's what you'd testify to in court?"

"If it came to that, yeah, Ezzy. Under oath that's what I would have to testify. Maybe she said yes initially, then changed her mind when it began to hurt. She put up a struggle; he killed her. Simple as that.

"But it is just as likely that the girl was enjoying it. Even people who engage in that particular sexual activity on a somewhat regular basis can experience irritation and bleeding."

Ezzy rubbed his temple. Head down, he asked, "Then how did she wind up with a broken neck?"

"My theory? It happened in the throes of passion. The young man got a little carried away and unintentionally broke her neck."

"You can't be certain it was an accident."

"True. But I can't be certain that it was deliberate either. The only thing I know with certainty is that he completed the act."

Ezzy stood and stretched his back. He wandered over to the window and needlessly adjusted the blinds. "Say it was an accident; why didn't he report it?"

"And own up to the fact that he screwed her to death?" The coroner snorted skeptically. "Anyway, motivation is your department, Ezzy. I've done my part." Stroud replaced his hat and heaved himself out of the chair. "I heard through the grapevine that the Herbold brothers are your prime suspects."

"She was last seen in their company."

"Hmm. Well, I'd say it could be either way, then. Unreported accidental death. Or rape and manslaughter."

"Or murder."

"Could be. What do the boys say?"

"They've run to ground."

"Disappeared?"

"They were last seen leaving the Wagon Wheel with Patsy."

"You don't say? Hell of a thing for Delray, huh? Well, happy hunting. Thanks for the Coke."

One of the reasons Ezzy hadn't arrested the Herbolds when he'd had the opportunity was to spare Delray Corbett the embarrassment. As it turned out, he had done Delray no favors. The next time he saw him, Ezzy had to inform him that he was looking for his stepsons in connection with Patsy McCorkle's death.

"Do you know where they are, Delray?"

"If I did I'd hand them over to you," he had said, and Ezzy had believed him.

"It's going to kill you, you know."

Ezzy had been so lost in thought he hadn't heard Cora's approach. Her voice didn't jolt him back into the present. His reemergence was a struggle, like working himself out of a spiderweb. Guilty memories clung to him with sticky tenacity.

When finally free of them, he smiled up at his wife. "Good morning to you, too."

Apparently Cora didn't consider it a good morning at all. Maintaining a stony silence, she filled his coffee cup from the carafe she'd carried out to the deck with her, then poured herself a cup and sat down in the lounger next to his. He could smell her talcum powder. She had dusted with it after every bath for as long as they'd been married.

"What's going to kill me?" he asked.

"This obsession."

"I'm not obsessed with anything except you." He reached across the narrow space separating the chaises and covered her knee with his hand.

She promptly removed it. "That girl's been dead more than twenty years."

Dropping all pretense, he sighed. For several moments he stared out across the lawn and sipped his coffee. "I know how long she's been dead, Cora."

"Her daddy's gone. For all we know Mrs. McCorkle is, too."

McCorkle had followed his daughter to the grave five summers later. He had simply dropped dead one day at his desk at the Public Service Office while running an audit on someone's electric bill. His widow had moved to Oklahoma. She hadn't returned to Blewer, not even to decorate the graves of her daughter and husband. Ezzy couldn't blame her. The town hadn't left her with too many good memories.

"The only person blaming you for what happened to them is you," Cora said, emphasizing the last word. "When are you going to let it go, Ezzy? When are you going to stop thinking about it?"

"How do you know that's what I'm thinking about?"

"Don't insult me on top of making me mad," she snapped. "I know you snuck out the other night so you could go through those old files. And I saw through that fishing lie before you were out the back door."

"I went fishing," he argued lamely.

"You went to the place on the river where she died." Setting her coffee cup on the small table between the chaises, she clasped her hands in her lap. "I could fight another woman, Ezzy. I would know what to do about that. But this . . . I don't know how to fight this. And . . ." She paused and drew a deep breath. "And I'm tired of trying."

He looked at her, saw the stubborn angle of her chin, and all of a sudden his heart felt like a lump of lead inside his chest.

"I'm leaving you, Ezzy. I'm leaving you to the damn ghosts I've had to share you with." She began to cry.

"Cora—"

"No, don't say anything. We've talked about it a thousand times. Those talks don't do any good. We've fought about it too, but fighting hasn't solved anything either."

"It's this prison escape. Carl's in the news and that's brought it all back. Soon as he's caught—"

"No, Ezzy. When he was sentenced to prison in Arkansas, you told me that was the end of it. But it wasn't. For years you've been promising me that you would give it up, that you would forget about it. Yet here you are, retired and free to enjoy yourself. Free to enjoy *me*," she said, her voice cracking. "But you're not enjoying anything. You're miserable. You're mired in the past, and that's your choice. But it's not mine. So, as the kids nowadays say, I'm outta here."

He tried to keep his voice calm. "You can't mean that."

"Oh, yes I can." She wiped her eyes on the sleeve of her housecoat and stood up. "I've loved you since the night we met. I'll love you as I draw my last breath. But I'm not going to live with you any longer, Ezzy. I refuse to stand by while this thing eats away at you until there's nothing left. I've watched it haunt you, but damned if I'll watch it kill you."

Chapter Thirteen

elray hadn't spoken a word since discovering the dead cows. He came slowly to his feet. He removed his dozer cap and used it to dust off the knee of his pants leg, on which he had been kneeling. He swiped his shirtsleeve across his sweating forehead, then stared out across the pasture, lost in thought, silent.

Finally Jack asked, "What do you make of it, Delray?"

"Well, they're dead," he replied, stating the obvious.

"I mean, any ideas on what killed them?"

Corbett replaced his cap, then turned and looked across at Jack. "A few. None of them good."

Jack shifted from one foot to the other, feeling uncomfortable. It was hard to look innocent under such an accusatory stare. "Coyote, you think? Or bobcat?" Jack was groping to find a feasible explanation for the three carcasses growing stiff in the morning heat. But he didn't believe this was an animal attack. There wasn't a mark on the cattle, no bites or wounds. A hungry predator would have killed one cow and eaten his fill, leaving behind a bloody mess for the buzzards to pick clean. Instead the remains of the Herefords were seemingly untouched.

As though reading his thoughts, Delray said, "It wasn't a four-legged animal that got them."

His point, clearly, was that a two-legged animal was responsible. Jack wanted to disclaim the subtle accusation but decided it would be better if he said nothing. To declare his innocence before he was even accused would make him look all the more guilty. He ventured another guess. "Disease?"

"Maybe," Corbett said. "I won't know till the vet takes a look."

"If it is disease, shouldn't we be moving the rest of the herd into another pasture?"

Corbett nodded in his laconic fashion. "I'll start on that. You go up to the house and call the vet. Ask Anna to give you the phone number."

"I'll be glad to stay here and start moving—"

"Do as I ask, please," Corbett said, interrupting his protest and brooking no argument.

"All right. I'll leave the truck with you and go on foot."

Jack made his way across the uneven ground to Corbett's pickup, which they'd left parked just inside the pasture gate. He conscientiously latched the gate behind himself. When he reached the road, he broke into a jog. By the time he had covered the half mile to the house, he was drenched with sweat.

But he barely noticed. His mind was still on the dead cows and Corbett's hard, suspicious stare. He had sworn to Corbett that he wouldn't steal from him, or harm his family. He hadn't made a specific promise that he wouldn't endanger his herd. Maybe he should have.

At the front door of the house, he depressed the button that not only rang chimes but also lit several lights in the house to alert Anna that someone was there. Sixty seconds elapsed, but no one came. He tested the door. It was unlocked. He let himself in. "David?"

Getting no response but hearing the TV, he followed the sound into a large living area, which he had glimpsed from the center hallway two nights before. The decor was bright, cheery, and inviting. Magazines were neatly stacked on end tables. Cushy pillows accented every chair. A bowl of green apples was on the coffee table. On the TV screen Gomer Pyle smiled sappily while getting a stern dressing-down from the Sarge. The dialogue was captioned at the bottom of the picture.

David was asleep on the sofa.

Jack didn't see or hear Anna.

He was about to wake David up and ask him to go get his mother when he reconsidered. Did the boy really need to hear about dead cows?

Retreating into the hallway, Jack moved from room to room on the lower floor, checking first the office where Anna's computer was, then the kitchen, and finally the utility room, where the washing machine was in a spin cycle.

He retraced his steps back to the entry. At the foot of the stairs, he paused. Maybe he should try the bell again. She might see the light this time. Or maybe he should awaken David after all.

Yes, he should.

But he didn't. He started upstairs.

Until now it hadn't occurred to him how dangerous it was for Anna to be alone in the house. How would she know if someone broke in? She wouldn't. Not until it was too late.

He passed a bathroom. The door was open and the room was unoccupied. Farther along the hall, he poked his head into a bedroom that was obviously David's. He spotted the mentioned Dallas Cowboys poster on the closet door and the book about dinosaurs on the nightstand.

The next open door he came to led into a narrow staircase, which obviously went up the attic. "Anna?" He called her name before he could stop himself. Habits die hard.

He went up the stairs, pausing one step short of the top one. She was there in the attic, sitting cross-legged on the floor, her back to him, fiddling with something in her lap. The as yet unidentified object had her undivided attention.

She thought she was alone, and that made Jack uneasy. It was unfair of him to creep up on her like this. It was even more unfair to look at her when she was unaware of being watched.

But she was a sight worth looking at. Her tank top hugged her torso, which was slender enough to show ribs. Strands of hair lay against the back of her neck where her skin was a couple shades lighter than her arms and shoulders, which had been exposed to the sun. There was a narrow strip of exposed skin across the small of her back between the hem of her top and the waistband of her shorts. Jack looked at that patch of skin for longer than his conscience was comfortable with.

Removing his straw cowboy hat, he loudly cleared his throat before once again remembering that no sound would alert her to his presence. David had told him that she didn't like people sneaking up on her, but Jack saw no way to avoid it. She would get some warning if he took the last step up, making sure that his tread was firm enough to create a vibration she would feel.

But he must have stepped a little too firmly.

Because she nearly jumped out of her skin.

The sudden flash of light blinded him.

He recoiled, staggered backward, and would have tumbled ass over elbows down the enclosed staircase if he hadn't put out his hand just in time to grab the door frame and break his fall.

She had shot him!

That was his first thought. He ran a quick mental check of all his parts. But he experienced no searing pain, no sting, no sensation of a dull blow, which is what those who knew had told him getting shot felt like. Blinking his eyes clear, he glanced down his front but didn't see any blood.

"What the . . . ?"

He looked up at her. She was standing now, facing him, holding a camera in one hand and a flash attachment in the other. "What the hell do you think you're doing?" he shouted. "You scared the shit out of me with that thing!"

She set the photography equipment on the floor and started signing. While he couldn't tell what she was saying, he got the gist of it from her angry facial expressions.

"Wait a minute, wait a minute!" he said, holding up both hands. She stopped signing, but her chest rose and fell in supreme agitation. In all fairness, she'd been just as startled by his appearance as he had been by the flash of light.

"I didn't mean to sneak up on you."

She signed something that he couldn't interpret, but he recognized David's name on her moving lips. "David is downstairs asleep." She continued to eye him warily. "Look, if I scared you, I'm sorry, but you scared me, too. I'm still seeing purple flying saucers."

Not quite catching the last, she tilted her head quizzically.

"Never mind," he muttered. Speaking more distinctly, he said, "Delray sent me. I need the vet's phone number. Vet," he repeated, spelling it out with his fingers, glad that he'd been practicing the manual alphabet. Then he held his hand to the side of his head, thumb near his ear, little finger at his mouth, the sign for *telephone* used and understood anywhere in the world.

Again her expression conveyed more than her signing.

"What's wrong?" he said, guessing. She nodded. "We found three dead cows in the pasture this morning. Delray needs to know what killed them."

The urgency of the situation didn't escape her. She brushed past him and rushed down the staircase. He followed, pausing only long enough to retrieve his hat, which he'd dropped when he stumbled backward. By the time he caught up with her, she was already on the ground floor, in the kitchen, thumbing through a personal telephone directory.

"Thanks," he said as she extended it to him and pointed at an entry. He dialed the number. While the telephone on the other end was ringing, he and Anna watched each other. His scrutiny must have made her nervous. Self-consciously, she tugged on the bottom of her tank top. Her hand made a pass against her hair, tucking a strand behind her ear. Then she seemed not to know what to do with her arms and hands, finally deciding to let them hang at her sides.

"Animal clinic."

"Uh, yeah, hi. I'm calling for Mr. Corbett."

"Delray?"

"That's right. Is Dr. Andersen in? We've got some dead cows out here."

The receptionist put him on hold while she summoned the veterinarian.

Jack said to Anna, "I knew it was you who took those pictures. And I knew it was you in the one with the fence."

She shook her head slightly, pretending not to understand what he said.

But he knew differently.

Late in the evening, Anna climbed the stairs to the attic for the second time. Before today, it had been months since she had been up there, and then only to exchange seasonal clothes.

She liked tidiness, but Delray demanded it. Consequently, the attic was as orderly as the rest of the house. Christmas decorations were boxed and labeled. Woolens were zipped into moth-proof bags. Dean Corbett's athletic equipment—several footballs and a scarred helmet, gloves and bats, a deflated basketball, a tennis racket—were neatly arranged on metal shelving. Tarnished trophies dating back to his grade-school days were lined up as precisely as toy soldiers. His jerseys from various teams had been washed and folded and placed in boxes. Keepsakes belonging to Mary were likewise stored in boxes with the contents listed on the airtight lids.

There were no keepsakes of Delray's first wife and her two sons.

Anna wasn't a pack rat. After her parents died, she had kept only a few personal items. The majority of their things she had divided among several charities. Her wedding dress was stored in a special box, but only one other crate in the attic belonged to her. It contained her photographic equipment.

Her camera and the flash attachment were lying on the floor where she had left them when Jack Sawyer had surprised her this morning. The black bag beside them contained optional, interchangeable lenses and other accessories.

Since showing her photographs to Jack Sawyer, she'd been unable to get them off her mind. After years of pretending that she was no longer interested in photography and of divorcing herself from the photos she had taken, the moment she'd looked at those pictures a feeling not unlike homesickness had come over her. She hadn't realized how much she missed her avocation until she was reminded of it. Now she was filled with a yearning to handle the camera equipment again.

So this morning, when she'd discovered David napping in front of the television, she had gone to the attic for a few precious moments alone. That stolen time had been abruptly cut short by the emergency in the pasture.

For the remainder of the day, she hadn't had a spare moment to herself. After speaking to the veterinarian by telephone, Jack Sawyer had left to rejoin Delray. Although he had made the taunting remarks about photographs, she could sense his preoccupation with the dead cattle. When Delray failed to show up for his noon meal, she'd packed enough lunch for two and drove it out to the pasture.

She was unsure how David would react to seeing the carcasses, but he appeared more curious than upset. It wasn't like having one of the horses die. He saw them every day, sometimes fed them by hand. They had names. He had no personal relationship with the herd.

But Delray had been very upset. He thanked her for the lunch, but his manner was brusque. If she hadn't offered a sandwich to Jack Sawyer, he would have gone without food. Delray was unaware of everyone and everything except Dr. Andersen, who was busy examining the carcasses.

She'd taken David home before the trailer arrived to haul off the dead cattle. Delray didn't return to the house until suppertime. He seemed very tired. He was irritable and curt. She took the hint and didn't try to draw him into conversation. She also advised David to leave Grandpa alone. As soon as they finished the meal, Delray went upstairs to his bedroom.

Now that David was down for the night and she had some time to herself, she had come back to the attic on the pretext of returning her camera to the shelf where it had resided for six years.

She picked it up off the floor, thinking that it felt heavier in her hands than she remembered. She examined it, turning it this way and that. She blew a speck of dust off the lens, then raised the viewfinder to her eye.

It was too dark in the attic to see much, but she fiddled with the aperture and focus rings. She set the ASA as though the camera had film in it, then raised it to her eye again and depressed the shutter.

It felt so good, so right. She depressed it again.

Should she—*could* she—resume her photography? Once her passion, she hadn't indulged it since before Dean died. When he was sick, she had little time to do anything except nurse him. She hadn't resented him for the demands his illness had made on her. She had chosen to care for him and wouldn't trade anything for the time they had spent together.

But unquestionably her photography had been sacrificed, first to caring for him, then to parenting David. By the time David was more self-sufficient, she was out of the habit and out of practice. Now so much time had passed that she probably had forgotten everything she ever knew about the art and science of photography. The technology had changed. To resume, she would be starting from scratch as a rank amateur.

But acknowledging the challenge didn't dampen her excitement. Merely holding the camera between her hands made her heart beat faster. It wouldn't be easy, but she could study the new technology. She could learn about new products and techniques. Being deaf limited her, but only as much as she would let it. Deafness could be her motivator, not her hindrance.

If nothing else, she should be taking more than just random snapshots of David. Her son would make a wonderful subject. She could experiment with different lenses and lighting. She could perfect the style she had been cultivating when she left off.

With practice, she might branch out beyond David and start photographing other subjects. Other people. Not pretty people, necessarily. Interesting people. People with flaws and imperfections. People whose faces had character.

Jack Sawyer's, for instance. His face would make a good photographic subject. Made of tissue and bone, it was a landscape all the same, shaped by plains and ridges and crevices. Weather-beaten and windswept. Aged yet ageless. Telling stories without speaking a word.

Words that were wasted because they couldn't be heard anyway.

Anna had learned the meanings of words. She had an unusually broad vocabulary and was very good at translating her thoughts into the written and spoken language she had been taught by loving parents and excellent teachers. Her communication skills were exemplary for a person with profound deafness.

But she didn't think in a language. Like a silent movie, she relied on visual images for her impressions of situations and places and people. For that reason, when she thought about Jack Sawyer's face, it conjured up a vivid image in her mind.

Feeling slightly uncomfortable with the intensity of that image, she quickly repacked the camera equipment in its customized carrying case. But she didn't replace it on the shelf. She took it with her when she left the attic.

It was stifling hot in the barn. Even with the doors open at both ends of the building, there was no air moving inside. Jack had taken this unpleasant chore upon himself, partially because the air-conditioning unit in the trailer was louder than a propeller airplane. He could only tolerate it when he was dead tired and on the verge of sleep. So he'd just as soon be outside.

Second, he was mucking out the horse stalls in the hope of staying in Delray's good graces.

He hadn't seen much of Corbett after the vet removed the carcasses. Corbett had spent the long afternoon on the tractor mowing the pasture that would later be harvested for hay. Jack had kept himself busy doing other chores.

They had spoken only once. Late in the afternoon, as Corbett was parking the tractor behind the barn, Jack approached him. "When do you expect to hear from the vet?"

"He said tomorrow at the earliest."

"Hmm. Well, there's not much we can do before we know what killed them, is there?"

"Nope."

That had been the extent of their conversation. Since finding the dead cattle this morning, Delray had said very little to him and had given him a wide berth. Call him paranoid, but he took that avoidance as a bad sign.

He didn't see Anna until he turned. She was standing at the entrance to the stall in which he was working. Startled, he almost dropped the pitchfork, exclaiming softly, "Shit." Then, "Sorry about that. The cussing, I mean. I didn't hear you." Then, realizing he had made yet another blunder, he rolled his eyes. "Every time I open my mouth, I put my foot in it."

To alleviate the heat, he had removed his shirt and hung it on a nail. He reached for it now and put it on. It was little more than a rag. The sleeves had been ripped out ages ago. From countless washings, the armholes were ragged with soft fringe. The cloth was faded, the plaid pattern was blurred. Only three of the pearl snaps remained on the placket. He fastened the center one.

He regarded her cautiously, reasoning that her appearance in the barn could herald only bad news. "What can I do for you?"

She held out a bottle of cold beer to him.

It was so unexpected that he stared at it like he didn't recognize what it was. He looked at her quizzically. A bit impatiently, she thrust the longneck bottle toward him. "Uh, thanks."

He removed his yellow leather work gloves, reached for the beer and twisted off the cap, then took a long drink. Nothing had ever tasted as good. He smiled at her as he wiped his mouth with the back of his hand. "That's great."

While he had been drinking, she had been writing on a small pad. She turned it toward him. "When I locked the back door, I saw the light in the barn and realized you were still working. I thought you might be thirsty."

"I was. Thanks. Aren't you having one?"

She shook her head, making a face. He laughed. "Don't like it, huh?"

Rather than writing, she signed. *"No."*

"That's no?" When she nodded, Jack set the beer bottle and gloves on a grain barrel, anchored the handle of the pitchfork beneath his arm to free his hands, then mimicked the sign. "Like this?"

"Yes."

"And that's yes?"

She nodded. He tried out the signs a few more times, committing them to memory, and she nodded approval as they smiled at each other. Then her gaze moved beyond him to look pointedly at the fresh straw he'd been scattering in the clean stall.

When she looked back at him Jack shrugged self-consciously. "I got the feeling that Delray thought I killed those cows."

He knew he had hit the nail on the head when she lowered her eyes. He tapped her arm. "Does he think I killed them?"

She wrote on the pad, "He doesn't know yet."

"But he suspects me, right?"

She glanced away evasively. "Never mind," Jack said. "I know he does."

He drained the beer bottle and tossed it into an empty metal trash barrel. It clattered noisily. He winced, "Sorry."

She motioned toward her ears and raised her shoulders in a shrug.

Chagrined, he said, "It's the damnedest thing. I know you can't hear, but I keep forgetting."

Nodding understanding, she wrote on her pad. "Everyone does. My parents. Dean. Delray. Even people I live with forget."

He read the message, and absently acknowledged it. He was curious about her deafness but didn't want to offend her by asking. "Anna," he said hesitantly, "it's none of my business. I'm just curious, is all. And if you don't want to talk about it, believe me, I'll understand."

She signaled for him to continue.

"Well, I just wondered if you have been, you know, deaf all your life. Were you born deaf?"

"Yes."

"I see."

Ducking his head, he scratched the vertical frown line between his eyebrows with his thumbnail. It didn't itch. He just needed something to do so he wouldn't feel so awkward about his question and her answer.

Finally he raised his head and grinned weakly. "I'm sorry, I'm at a loss. I don't know what to say next. God knows I don't pity you, and I don't want to be a jerk. I just wanted to know."

She wrote, "I know when a person looks at me and thinks, Poor little deaf girl. I know when a person thinks I'm dumb. You don't act like that, like stupid people."

He laughed softly. "That's a relief. I wouldn't want to make an ass of myself."

Grinning back, she shook her head no.

He looked at her a moment, then down at the toes of his boots. "The other night . . ." Realizing he was talking to the floor, he raised his head and began again. "The other night, why were you against me learning sign?"

She chose her words carefully before writing them down. When she was finished she turned the pad toward him. "I was surprised that you wanted to learn. I acted hateful because I didn't know how to act. No one else besides Dean has learned my language."

It wasn't necessary for Jack to reread the message, but he did so because what she had said was inaccurate. Delray had learned sign, and so had David. Yet she had distinguished Dean Corbett and Jack Sawyer, and he couldn't help but wonder what he had in common with the man she had married. Why had she linked the two of them in her mind?

It was a question that begged rumination, but not now, when they were standing face-to-face, ankle deep in fresh straw and she was close enough for him to count her eyelashes.

Apparently her thoughts were moving along the same track, because she looked flustered and began backing away. Certain that she was on the verge of telling him good night, he raised his hand and forestalled her. "Wait. Watch this." After propping the pitchfork against the wall of the stall, he proudly spelled out his name with the manual alphabet.

She was smiling until he formed the last sign, when she made a small negative motion with her head. Signing the letter *k*, she held her hand up so he could see it better.

He tried again. "Like this?"

Still frowning slightly, she reached for his right hand. Meticulously, she moved his fingers into place, folding his little and ring fingers toward his palm, angling his middle finger, positioning his raised index finger, then placing his thumb against his middle finger, just so. Loosely clasping his wrist, she studied her handiwork, deemed it right, and smiled up at him.

Except that Jack wasn't smiling.

Quickly she dropped her hands from his and stepped back.

He snatched his hands away and slid them into the rear pockets of his jeans.

The air suddenly seemed thicker, harder to inhale. In any event, it was insufficient. His voice sounded as dry as a husk when he said, "I think I've got it now."

She signed good night, then turned and beat a hasty retreat down the center aisle of the barn. Jack followed her as far as the wide door and stood there watching her as she crossed the yard like the devil was after her and disappeared into the house.

He propped himself against the doorjamb and prayed for a breath of breeze to cool him down. A bead of sweat trickled down his temple into his eyebrow. His heart was beating fast behind his ribs. Even though he'd just finished a cold beer, his throat was hot and dry. He couldn't have worked up a spit if his life had depended on it.

His hands and fingers were so callused from years of manual labor that it wouldn't have surprised him if the nerve endings in them were dead. But they were telegraphing sensations to his brain and doing a damn good job of recalling her touch and making him regret that there were only twenty-six letters in the alphabet. She could have dallied with his hand all night and you wouldn't have heard him complaining. Was his head just full of grain and strawdust, or had having her fiddling with his fingers truly been as erotic as hell?

He was aroused and breathing hard, and it was Delray Corbett's daughter-in-law who'd got him that way. This time last week he hadn't known she existed. Tonight she seemed the most desirable woman in the world. Anna Corbett. Delray Corbett's daughter-in-law.

Closing his eyes, he expelled a long, deep breath, letting a curse word or two glide out along with it. Leaning back against the door frame, he thumped his head on the old wood.

Fate had fucked Jack Sawyer again.

When he finally opened his eyes and was about to turn back into the barn, he happened to glance up at the second-story bedroom window of the house.

He stood very still and stared for a moment. Then he whispered, "Aw shit."

Chapter Fourteen

The mailbox read MR. AND MRS. G. R. BAILEY. The house was set well off the road in a grove of trees. It was a large house with two chimneys, a lightning rod, and a satellite dish extending from the roof. There were several outbuildings, including a barn and a pump house. Although it was dark, it seemed to Carl Herbold that everything looked neat and tidy and bespoke rural prosperity.

He glanced across at Myron. "What do you think?"

"'Bout what?"

"Jesus," Carl muttered. Making the decision on his own, he turned the car into the private drive.

He had to hand it to Cecil: The getaway car had been right where he had said it would be. He found it in prime condition, full of gasoline, ready to go. In the trunk were a suitcase of clothes, forty dollars in cash, several guns with ample ammunition, and a few bottles of whiskey, with which he and Myron had celebrated their successful escape.

For a few days they had camped beside a lake, nursing their hangovers, sleeping in the car, sunning themselves during the daytime. At least he had. Myron's skin couldn't tolerate the sun, so he'd dozed beneath the shade trees.

After spending years inside walls with only limited periods in the exercise yard, the great outdoors had felt wonderful. But there was a limit, and Carl had reached his this morning when he woke up to find an armadillo rooting beneath their car and a tick burrowing through his pubic hair.

It was time to find shelter. They set out in search of an appropriate place and had been cruising all day, sticking to the back roads, avoiding major highways, which were more likely to be patrolled by law officers on the lookout for the escaped convicts.

It tickled Carl each time he heard his name on the car radio.

He wished his mother were alive to hear it. She would sob. She would cry her eyes out. That's what she had done best. His earliest impression of her was one of red-rimmed eyes and a runny nose, saying over and over again into a soggy Kleenex that she didn't know what she was going to do with them—him and Cecil.

He had no recollection of his father. He had died when Cecil was a toddler and Carl was still in diapers. If he had ever known his daddy's cause of death, he had forgotten it. He assumed that his old man willed himself into an early grave so he wouldn't have to listen to her bawling any longer.

She'd worked in a beauty parlor. Carl remembered the ammonia smell of permanent waves that clung to her when she came home in the evenings. He also remembered her whining about how tired she was and begging him and Cecil to be quiet and not fuss and not misbehave so she could rest. But when they didn't, she was powerless to do anything about it.

Then he and Cecil had begun noticing a change in her. She perked up, and started fixing her hair prettier and wearing lipstick, high heels, and stockings. On Saturday nights she went out on dates. One of his most vivid memories was of the day she brought a man into the house and introduced him as Delray Corbett and told them that he was going to be their new daddy and wasn't that swell.

Carl took his foot off the accelerator and let the car coast the rest of the way to the house. He turned off the headlights before he even cut the engine. As he tucked a pistol into his belt, he said, "Myron, you stay here out of sight until I get inside, okay?"

"Okay."

Carl opened the driver's door and stepped out. Immediately he smelled manure and hay. The odors brought back memories of the forced move out of town to the country. For years his and Cecil's turf had been the streets and alleyways of Blewer. Each day after school they had met their buddies at a designated spot and gone looking for adventure. There was always something to be tried that hadn't been experienced before, a new dare to be met.

From older boys they learned to smoke and drink and steal. They were naturals when it came to fistfights. They emulated bullies and scorned wimps. About girls they learned that what they had between their legs was better than candy, and that when charm didn't work to get you some, intimidation usually did. Carl was a quicker study than Cecil, but Cecil got his share.

Then suddenly they had been yanked from everything familiar: their friends and their environment and the freedom they'd enjoyed. Carl had hated the ranch. He hated the stink and the daily chores, the rules and table manners and Bible readings, hated the punishment Corbett doled out when he or Cecil balked at one of his rigid commands.

The feelings he had for his stepfather had raised hatred to a new level. He despised his mother for inflicting Corbett on them. He had celebrated the blood clot that traveled from her leg to her lung and killed her. The day they buried her, he and Cecil had held a private little party because they no longer had to listen to her sniveling pleas that they be good boys, that they try to get along with Delray, who could be such a good father to them if only they would let him.

Memories of her whining and Corbett's harsh censure could still twist Carl's guts into knots.

He raised his fist and knocked on the door, harder than he intended. A few moments later the porch light came on. Knowing he was probably being observed through the peephole, he flinched comically and shaded his eyes against the glare. The front door came open.

"Hey there, Mrs. Bailey," he said in a friendly tone. "That's a mighty bright bulb you've got in that porch light. Gotta be a thousand-watt."

"Can I help you, young man?"

She was a slight, bespectacled woman in her seventies, with pale blue hair and a sweet smile. In other words, a piece of cake.

"Sister, who is it?"

A near duplicate joined her in the open doorway, this one plumper, prettier, and even more pleasant.

Carl's disarming grin stretched wider.

Chapter Fifteen

*J*ack figured that somewhere between the ranch and the feed store, Delray was going to fire him.

Early that morning, the rancher had handed him a list of chores to do, then he had left in his pickup. He hadn't said where he was going, but Jack assumed he would check the herd to see if he had lost any more head during the night. Jack did the jobs on Delray's list, and when he was finished with those he created others to keep him busy.

He saw Delray return in time for lunch, but he went into the house without speaking. It was almost three o'clock before Delray sought him out where he was repairing a bridle in the tack room. "We're going to the feed store."

When Jack emerged from the small toilet in the barn after washing his hands, Delray was already in his pickup truck with the engine running. He didn't acknowledge Jack when he got in. They didn't make even idle conversation.

Jack was itching to know if Delray had spoken to the vet and what he had learned from the postmortem on the cattle, but he felt the less he said now, the better. So they drove toward town in stony silence. Jack guessed he should be glad Delray wasn't talking. As long as Delray wasn't talking, he wasn't being dismissed.

The hell of it was, he didn't want to leave.

It was his rule never to form an attachment that he couldn't walk away from at a moment's notice. He hadn't wanted to live like that. That kind of solitary life had chosen him, not the other way around. But he was used to it by now. He went into every situation knowing that it was temporary. He had developed a knack for knowing when the time was right to say good-bye and move on. Ordinarily he did so without a backward glance and let his nose lead him to his next destination.

But this was no ordinary situation. He hadn't picked the Corbett Cattle Ranch at random. Nor had he selected the timing of his arrival. That had been determined when Carl Herbold escaped from prison.

He'd broken his pattern. His standard operating procedure didn't apply. He couldn't just drive away when he felt it was advisable. If he was basing his decisions on what was advisable, he wouldn't have come here to start with. But he was here. And until Carl Herbold was recaptured, he wanted to stay.

Of course if Delray told him to clear out, there wouldn't be much he could do about it except pack up and go.

At the feed store, Delray placed his order with the cashier. His economy of words bordered on rudeness. It was Jack who thanked the man when he handed Delray his receipt. The vendor didn't offer to help them load the heavy sacks of grain into the pickup and, because of Delray's brusqueness, Jack couldn't say he blamed him.

But Jack couldn't help but notice how hard Delray was exerting himself. "This heat is a bitch. Start the motor and turn on the air. I'll finish up."

"Don't you think I can handle a man's job?"

Soundly rebuked, Jack let the matter drop. Delray was pissed, and it wasn't because Jack had offered to do the heavy work for him. It wasn't entirely because of the dead cows, either. Jack's money was on Anna and the beer in the barn.

Delray secured the tailgate and they got back into the truck. His face was red and congested. "I could stand something to drink."

Jack was surprised that the older man owned up to a weakness of any kind, but he said, "Sounds good."

Delray drove to the Dairy Queen. They went inside to enjoy the airconditioning, placed their order with the adolescent girl tending the counter, then chose a booth and sat down across from each other. Glancing over his shoulder, Delray frowned disdainfully at the girl. Every feature of her face had been pierced with a hoop or a stud. Even her tongue had been harpooned, and on it sat a black pearl.

"Why'd she do that to herself?"

"Probably to rile old farts like us."

Delray looked at Jack, then came as close to laughing as he ever had. "You're probably right."

For the next few minutes they enjoyed their slushy frozen lemonades. Delray finished his drink first and pushed aside his cup. Staring out the window at a bed of dusty sunflowers, he made no attempt at conversation. Jack wondered if he was choosing the words he was going to use to fire him. Rather than sweat it out, he decided to seize the bull by the horns. "So what did he say?"

Delray didn't even pretend to misunderstand. His gaze switched from the sunflowers to Jack. "Poison."

Jack's heart sank. He had hoped that the cows died from some rare bovine virus, or by some other means that in no way implicated him. This was as bad as it could get. "What does this mean for the rest of the herd?"

"I found two more dead this morning. The poison was on the salt lick. Of course it might be days before we know how many more got to it before it was removed." He snorted with contempt. "Wasn't a very smart son of a bitch. He could've hurt me a lot worse if he'd dumped poison in the pond."

"Maybe it was a warning shot."

"Maybe."

"I didn't do it."

"I didn't say you did."

"But that's what you think."

Delray's face turned redder, and Jack thought the man should be commended for holding his temper so well, especially if he believed Jack had tried to ruin his livelihood. Leaning across the table, Jack asked, "Why would I do it?"

"Why would you drop out of the blue and ask for a job?"

"I needed the work."

"Bullshit. I called that last guy you worked for. In Corpus. He gave you a glowing reference. Hated to lose you, he said. Wished he had a hundred like you. You had a good job but you walked off to come to work for me for half the money." Shaking his head, he scoffed. "Doesn't make sense. Never has."

"It makes sense to me. I wanted a change."

"A change." Delray simmered for a moment, then pointed his blunt index finger at Jack. "I don't trust you."

"Then why did you hire me?"

"So I could keep an eye on you till I figured out your angle."

"Have you?"

"I think so."

Jack spread his hands wide, inviting Delray to share his conclusions.

"You're working for that Houston outfit. That EastPark."

Jack stared at him for several seconds, then laughed out loud. "Me? A corporate saboteur?"

"Okay, you don't look the type. But that makes you the perfect man for the job."

"In another lifetime, maybe," Jack said, still chuckling with incredulity. "I told you my opinion of those greedy bastards."

"Because you knew that's what I wanted to hear. You were blowing smoke."

Jack stared at him for several moments, shaking his head. "Okay, say I am connected, how do you explain the job in Corpus?"

"You were doing the same thing there. EastPark is just a slice of a big pie. Those guys are into everything. Oil and gas, real estate, computers. They even have a government contract with NASA. All that's in the propaganda Emory Lomax gave me. That's another thing that should have tipped me off. He started pressuring me just when you showed up. You work the inside track. They send you where they need you, when they need you. And you dress the part," he added, glancing up at Jack's straw cowboy hat.

Sighing, Jack eased away until he was settled against the back of the booth. He raised his shoulders in a gesture of helplessness. "You're wrong, Delray. Dead wrong."

"I don't think so."

"If I'm a corporate whiz kid, don't you think I'd be more subtle than to poison your herd just a few days after I got here? And let me tell you this: If I were out to destroy you in the hope of acquiring your ranch, I wouldn't have fucked around like this bozo did. I would have done it right. I *would* have poisoned the water supply."

Delray studied him for a long time, taking his measure, weighing his words, searching his eyes for deception. Jack held his stare. That's why neither of them noticed the other man's approach until he spoke.

"Hey, Delray."

Taken unaware, Delray turned his head quickly. "Oh, hey, Sheriff Hardge. Didn't see you come in."

"How are you?"

"Can't complain. You?"

"All right, I guess. Not sheriff anymore, though."

"Right, right," Delray said absently. "How's retirement?"

"Can't get used to having all this free time." He frowned down at the gooey banana split he had ordered. "Keep this up, I'm likely to get fat." He gave Delray a wry smile, then glanced curiously at Jack.

Delray gestured across the table. "I decided to hire on some help. He's my new hand."

"Jack," he said, extending his right hand.

"Ezzy."

"Pleasure."

"Same."

The hand Jack was shaking felt as rough as tree bark. The man was tall and rangy, with wide shoulders that curved inward toward a chest that had once been broad but had gone slightly concave with age. Gray hair curled from beneath a hat similar to his own. Both had seen equal amounts of wear and tear. Hardge's face was as long as that of a basset hound, his expression as bleak.

Courtesies dispensed with, the retired sheriff turned back to Delray. "You heard anything out of Arkansas?"

"Nothing. I don't expect to."

"No, I don't reckon you will. That boy has got more sense than to come this way."

Delray clasped his hands on the tabletop. "All that happened a long time ago, Ezzy."

"Way long. Lots of water under the bridge since then." After a short but awkward silence, Hardge changed the subject. "Awful hot weather we're having."

Delray unclasped his hands and some of the tension eased from his shoulders. "We could stand some rain, all right."

The tall man looked down into the melting confection in the little plastic boat. "Well, gotta get this thing eaten before it becomes ice cream soup. Y'all take care."

With interest Jack watched the old man leave the restaurant and climb into a decade-old Lincoln. "He looks like a sheriff." Then his eyes moved back to Delray. "You think I poisoned your cows. Why didn't you turn me in?"

"He's not sheriff any longer."

"That's no answer."

Delray scooted to the end of the booth and stood up. "I'm going to take some ice cream home to David and Anna."

He walked over to the counter and placed another order. Jack waited for him at the door. Togther they got back into the truck and headed toward the ranch.

Was that it? Jack thought. Did he stand accused but not yet convicted? Or had he argued his case so well that Delray dropped the charge?

Jack glanced at Delray's stern profile. He drove with his hands positioned at ten and two o'clock, eyes straight ahead, keeping well within the speed limit. A man as strictly disciplined as Delray Corbett wouldn't change his mind so easily. Jack figured the jury was still out.

For the time being he was still here. He would do well to leave well enough alone. But they needed to clear the air on another matter, too. "I was talking to Anna last night," he remarked casually.

"The two of you made conversation?"

"Of a fashion. Mostly I asked questions and she signed yes or no. She wrote some things down on a notepad."

Delray's fingers flexed once before closing around the steering wheel again. "So what'd you talk about?"

"Her deafness. She told me she'd been deaf since birth."

"That's my understanding. It was a genetic defect."

"Awful tough on a kid and her parents."

"I didn't know her folks. Didn't meet Anna till Dean brought her home."

Jack assumed a listening posture. Delray glanced at him but he didn't start speaking again until his eyes were back on the road. "I can't say I was too happy about it. My boy came home all excited about this deaf girl he'd met at the junior college. Sure, I admired her for attending school. College isn't easy on kids who aren't handicapped. Must be a real struggle for someone like Anna. She had an interpreter, but it's gotta take guts."

Jack stretched one arm along the back of the seat. "Kids who have to work harder at it probably appreciate it more, and might even do better because of it."

"I know Anna did. She worked hard and got good grades. But admiring somebody for what they've accomplished and inviting them into your family are two different things. I admit that I was against Dean and her being together. At first. But then I got to know her and saw how crazy Dean was about her, and—"

"And if Dean was the man he should have been—and I figure he was—your opinion wasn't going to matter."

Delray turned his head, looking ready to challenge Jack's comment. Then his features softened and he shook his head with chagrin. "My opinion *didn't* matter. They got married and for a while were as happy as any two people I've ever seen. Then he decided to join the army."

Jack let Delray tell him the rest of the story, even though he'd already heard it from Anna.

"While Dean was overseas, Anna continued her schooling. Her parents had left her enough of a legacy to pay for her education. After she finished at the junior college, she drove forty miles one way to take her upper-division courses. She was studying photography.

"But when Dean came home and got sick, she gave up school to take care of him. After he died and David came along, there wasn't much point in her continuing her studies, I guess."

Jack disagreed, but it wasn't his place to say so.

"That's when she stopped talking, too."

Jack had been mentally arguing all the reasons why Anna should have completed her education and earned her degree. It took several seconds for him to process Delray's last statement. When he did, he lowered his arm from the back of the seat. "Come again? Did you say that Anna used to speak?"

"She was shy about it, especially around strangers, but Dean had encouraged her to keep up her speech classes."

Jack was still struggling with his disbelief. "She could speak?"

"Not like you and me, but pretty good. You could understand her. Actually it's amazing when you think about it. That she could say out loud sounds she had never heard."

This revelation left Jack shell-shocked. Whenever Anna signed, she mouthed the words. Her moving lips were an intrinsic part of her very expressive face. But she had never put her voice behind the words. "Why'd she stop? Why doesn't she speak now?"

Delray's shrug looked defensive. He shifted in his seat like it had suddenly become prickly. "She doesn't need to. Fact is, some deaf people don't want to speak and resent those who think they should learn. They rely strictly on sign language."

"But don't others—like Anna did—combine them?"

"Sometimes, yeah."

"They sign, read lips, *and* speak, right?"

"I'm not an expert on deaf education."

Jack persisted. "It must have taken years for her to develop those skills. Why did she stop using them?"

"I don't know." Delray's tone was testy and his volume bordered on a shout. "Why don't you ask Anna? Next time you two get together for a chat."

Jack had been right. Delray was angry about what he had spied from his bedroom window the night before. Jack had seen him standing there, outlined against a faint interior light.

Darkness and distance prevented their eyes from connecting, but Jack had known beyond a doubt that Delray was looking directly at him. He also got the impression that Delray had been standing there a long time and had seen Anna leaving the barn.

Neither had moved for several seconds. Finally Delray had turned into his room and disappeared from the window.

Now he was hunched over the steering wheel, gripping it tightly, staring at the road ahead as though it were the enemy and he had resolved to conquer it. His jaw looked set in concrete. If Jack were to guess, he would say the man was angry and in emotional pain.

Quietly he asked, "How long have you loved her, Delray?"

Chapter Sixteen

Naturally the Mexicans had demanded to be paid immediately.

Emory Lomax was out fifty bucks, but if it had cost him twice that to sabotage Delray Corbett's livelihood, it would have been well worth it. Jesse Garcia and his ever-changing band of assorted kin had rumbled down Main Street just when Emory needed them. If he hadn't happened to be looking out his office window at the same time Garcia's pickup truck rolled past, he still would be trying to formulate a plan to ensure acquisition of the Corbett ranch.

Fortune had smiled on him in the form of Jesse Garcia.

He was known around town as a fix-it man. Screen doors, sprinkler systems, septic tanks. And situations. You needed a storm-door lock replaced, Garcia was your man. Your trees needed the deadwood trimmed, Garcia and his cousins could take care of it in an afternoon and haul off the brush. You wanted to see your asshole of a neighbor run into some real bad luck with his brand-new van, fifty bucks in Garcia's hand, and you had the pleasure of watching the man next door have a hissy fit in his driveway.

When it came to payback, Garcia was a good man to know. He didn't mind getting his hands dirty, literally and figuratively. All those things people said they would like to do to their enemy, Garcia did for them. He drew the line at maiming or killing, but he had a creative imagination. If you didn't have an idea for a befitting revenge, he had a menu of selections.

He didn't discriminate. He would work for anybody willing to pay his fee. You might be his client one night, his victim the next. But that was Garcia's system. Nobody argued with it because nobody wanted *him* as their enemy, and it is an established fact that all Mexicans carry knives.

He had told Garcia to create a little havoc with the Corbett herd. "Nothing too catastrophic. Do you *comprende* catastrophic, Jesse?"

He had *comprended*, and the following day it was all over town that Corbett had lost several head of cattle under mysterious circumstances, the scourge of every cattleman. Bad for business. Stigmatizing. That kind of scare would have any rancher shivering in his shoes. Look what mad cow disease had done to beef sales in England.

Emory's step had been jaunty with confidence as he left the bank for his scheduled appointment with Corbett, believing that he would be in a bargaining mood. But Emory had an unpleasant surprise waiting on him when he arrived at the ranch. Incredibly, Corbett was no more ready to entertain his offer than before.

"Did you look through the material?" he asked out of frustration after half an hour of seesawing.

"I did."

"Wouldn't you say their track record is impressive?"

"I suppose."

How could the old coot not be dazzled by that glossy brochure and the information it contained? Or was he just being stubborn in the hope of jacking up the asking price? "They're making a mighty generous offer on your place, Mr. Corbett. Mighty generous."

Not nearly as complacent as he pretended, Emory sat back in the easy chair and propped one ankle on his opposite knee. "EastPark Development wants this property in the worst way. Their offer is much higher than the appraised value. But it's their money, right?" He glanced across the living room at Anna and winked.

She had politely served him a glass of iced tea when he arrived, but she had looked at him like he had tracked in dog shit. Where did she get off being so hoity-toity?

He had been charming and mannerly, making eye contact with her so she wouldn't feel excluded from the discussion, even though Delray had been signing their conversation for her benefit. He never failed to go out of his way to be nice to her when she came into the bank, but she wasn't what he would call friendly in return.

Right now an ice cube wouldn't melt on her ass. But he would still like to get his hands on it. He bet he could readjust her attitude easily enough.

Delray closed the syllabus and tossed it onto the coffee table. "Let me understand this, Lomax. They want me to part with a square mile of land that I already own, and settle for a little chunk of it?"

Emory smiled expansively. "That's oversimplifying, of course, but yes, as an incentive for you to accept the deal, they're willing to let you have first choice of the lots, plus they would waive all homeowner fees and give you a lifetime club membership."

"A lifetime club membership."

"That's right," Emory replied in a spider-to-the-fly tone. "How's that sound?"

"No deal."

Corbett stood. Lomax shot to his feet. "Mr. Corbett, we put the proposal in layman's terms for you, but I think you're still failing to grasp—"

"I can read, Mr. Lomax."

"I didn't mean to imply . . . Please don't think that . . ." He was sunk if Corbett thought he thought he was stupid. He must tread lightly. "It's just that unless you conduct this kind of transaction on a regular basis, the complexities are liable to escape you."

"That may be. But there's no complexity to my answer. I'm not interested."

His voice going shrill, Emory said, "They're willing to pay you more than the property is worth."

"Then they're a bunch of damn fools, aren't they?"

Emory lowered his voice to a more reasonable tone. "You would have a great deal of money. You could build any kind of house you wanted on your lot."

"I like this house and this lot."

Emory was hanging on by a thread and he could feel it unraveling in his fist. His pager beeped. Impatiently he turned it off and desperately tried another tack with Corbett. "It shouldn't be your decision alone. What about Anna here? What does she think of our proposal?"

Before he had fully completed the question, she was signing an answer. "She says the ranch is mine," Delray told him. "It's her son's legacy. She backs my decision."

"I'm glad she brought up her son. Take him into account. His education. By the time he gets to college—"

"We already have funds set aside for that."

"But—"

Delray held up his hand. "I listened to your sales pitch, Mr. Lomax. It was a waste of breath on your part, and a waste of my time, but I showed you the courtesy of a meeting. Which is now over. Good-bye."

When Delray turned, ready to leave the room, Lomax grappled for his final handhold. "There's the matter of your loan."

Corbett stopped dead in his tracks, then came around slowly and glared at him. His face was turning red. "What about it?"

Emory drew his lips into a pucker of regret. He gave his head a small, sorrowful shake that said he hated to bring this up and only did so because he'd been left no choice. "This quarter's interest payment was late, Mr. Corbett."

"Only by a few days."

"What about next quarter? And the one after that?"

"I have never failed to meet my financial obligations."

"I'm sure that's true. But you've never had as rough a time as you're having these days. And, frankly, I don't see any end to it in the near future. The beef market is soft. You're a beef cattle rancher. You see my point?" He spread his arms wide. "Because you've always been a good customer, the bank was willing to extend you a sizable loan. But we can't let it just sit there forever."

"You're making money on it, Lomax. As long as I pay the interest—"

"But we're at the mercy of the bank examiners. They're the ones who're getting nervous, not me." To demonstrate his earnestness, he folded his hands over his chest. "Because of pressure from them, I'm placed in the position of demanding that you begin reducing the principal in addition to making the interest payments."

"Fine. I'll manage."

"How? As overseer of your accounts, I know that your present cash flow is practically nil. Your overhead hasn't decreased, in fact just the opposite. Do the arithmetic. Your balance sheet is looking less and less optimistic. And now with this other . . . difficulty."

That got Corbett's attention. His head snapped back as though Emory had socked him on the chin. Actually, this was better. A verbal attack was eminently more satisfying to Emory than physically beating the old codger.

"No sooner had you called Dr. Andersen than the tom-toms started telegraphing word of a possible cattle-killing epidemic. Every rancher for miles around heard about your misfortune."

"There was no disease in my herd. It was an isolated incident."

"It appears so, yes, but it was an expensive loss for you. Especially now, when every pound of beef translates into dollars and cents."

"I only lost five head. It won't happen again."

"But you can't be sure, can you? There might be repercussions even after your stepson is captured."

That verbal volley was even better than the last round. It seemed to strike Corbett in the belly. It was all Emory could do not to smile. Jesus, this was great! He was in top form. Why weren't Connaught and the other muckety-mucks of EastPark here to see this? If Connaught could see how effectively he was manipulating Delray Corbett, he would probably boost him into a vice-president's position.

"What does Carl Herbold's escape have to do with . . ." Corbett paused, wheezed. "With anything?"

Emory shot a rueful glance in Anna's direction. She'd gone pale, but if her expression was a fair indicator of her feelings, he'd slipped from being a tracker-in of dog shit to a Nazi death-camp guard.

"I'm sorry, Mr. Corbett. I thought you knew how . . . how folks feel about . . . all that. You're guilty by association. You know how people are, always looking for a scapegoat. I guess some feel that you're to blame for those boys' meanness. This incident with your cattle, well, I think that proves what people around here think of you. They forgot about it for a while, but this prison escape has got folks all stirred up again. It's all anybody is talking about."

"Excuse me, who're you?"

Emory spun around. He had been painting such a bleak picture, and doing such a damn good job of it, that he resented the rude interruption. He was also surprised by it. He had believed Anna and Delray Corbett to be alone on the ranch except for the kid, who, upon his arrival, had been banished to another room to play.

The man standing in the wide opening connecting the central hall to the living room was about six feet tall and lean to the point of being borderline skinny. He was dressed like a cowboy in faded blue jeans and boots. He was tapping a beat-up straw hat against his thigh. The hat had mashed down sand-colored hair, darkened a little by perspiration. The armholes of his chambray work shirt looked like they'd been chewed on by a rottweiler. His arms were all muscle and sinew and as brown as a pecan hull. It was hard to detect the color of his eyes because they were squinting, as though he were studying the focus of them very hard. And Emory was the focus.

Emory resisted the impulse to squirm beneath that stare and instead demanded, "Who wants to know?" His retort didn't sound nearly as condescending spoken out loud as it had inside his head. In fact it sounded petulant and childish.

The cowboy laughed. "Let me guess. You're Lomax. Delray told me he was meeting with you this afternoon."

Emory was subjected to a slow once-over. When his eyes landed on the cell phone in Emory's hand, he chuckled again, then dismissed him and turned to Delray. "I need a part before I can repair the water pump. I've located what I need, but it's at a supply house in Nacogdoches. I'll probably be gone the rest of the afternoon."

Corbett nodded. "Fine."

The cowboy replaced his hat and, after throwing another ridiculing glance in Emory's direction, he went out.

"Who was that? Does he work for you?"

"Yeah."

"Since when?"

"I hired him a few days ago."

Emory saw an opportunity to distance himself further from the poisoning of the cattle. "Have you checked him out? Could he have poisoned your cows?"

"Lomax, I think we've said all that needs to be said. Lay your mind at rest about the loan. The bank is in no danger of losing its money. The collateral is worth a lot more than I borrowed."

Emory put on his best smile. "Neither of us would have any worries if you accepted EastPark's offer."

Corbett's face turned redder. "Anna, please show him out."

"I would be derelict in my duties as a financial adviser if I didn't warn you that you're making a big mistake, Mr. Corbett."

"I'll consider myself dutifully warned. Good-bye, Lomax. Tell your pals at EDP—"

"EPD."

"Whatever. Tell them my ranch is not for sale. Don't bother me again."

He left the room and climbed the stairs to the second floor. Emory cursed every step Corbett took until he disappeared at the landing. He turned to Anna. "He'll eventually change his mind."

She shook her head no.

Tilting his head to one side, he smiled at her as he sauntered forward. "If it was your choice, what would *you* do?" On the emphasized word, he poked her lightly in the chest with his index finger.

Quickly she turned her back on him and made her way to the front door. He followed, but at the door he ignored that she was holding it open for him in a blatant invitation for him to leave.

Not much headway had been made with the old man. Corbett was still unshakable. Something else must be tried.

It would be terribly risky to engage Jesse Garcia again. Garcia wouldn't have stayed in business this long if he were untrustworthy. Your fifty dollars bought you not only his services, but also his silence. But Garcia had never been caught, either. He usually contracted the job out to a needy transient relative who got paid a pittance for doing the actual deed while Garcia, safe at home with a dozen alibis, retained a huge commission for himself.

There was a first time for everything, however. One of his relatives might get sloppy. If he were caught, he would point the finger at Garcia, and Garcia struck Emory as a man who would rat out his own mother if it came down to freedom versus going to jail. Emory didn't want the distinction of being Jesse Garcia's first fuckup. He wouldn't be using the Mexican again.

Nor did he know the strength of that bullshit about Carl Herbold. He hadn't even known that the escaped con and Corbett were connected until this morning, when his secretary reminded him of the appointment. Not that he had needed the reminder. He had been about to tell Mrs. Presley that when she'd added, "Poor old Delray. He'll never live down being those mean boys' stepdaddy."

And for the next half hour she had provided Emory with all the juicy details about Cecil and Carl Herbold. He had pulled a sad face. He had furrowed his brow. Every once in a while he had murmured a "Jeez Louise," or a "Hmm-hmm-hmm. Rotten kids," when mentally he'd been rubbing his hands together and salivating. He had added the information to his arsenal of weapons to use against the obstinate rancher.

When he dropped the convict's name into his argument, it had seemed an ingenious ad-lib, another sockeroo to Delray's stubborn chin. But if Herbold was recaptured soon, that argument would no longer have punch, and he would be right back where he started, which was exactly nowhere.

The key to his success could be Anna Corbett.

He moved in closer. "Anna, you can read my lips, right?"

She nodded.

He smiled. "Good. Because I want you to understand how important this deal could be to your future. Think of what that money would mean to your son. If I were you," he said, placing his hand on her arm, "being a woman, and deaf, I'd want to secure a solid future for myself and my kid when I had the chance." He gave her arm a stroke.

"An opportunity like this might not come along again. I'm just glad I'm the one who can give it to you." He massaged her triceps. "Why don't you and I get together soon and talk about it?"

Sometimes he was so smart he scared himself. Just as he guessed, the woman was starved for affection. He'd nailed it the first time he met her. Under that stiff exterior, she was mushy with the need for male attention. For *young* male attention. Her father-in-law wasn't enough for her. What an exciting prospect. Accustomed to stodgy ol' Delray, a young cock would probably make her go wild and crazy in bed.

At his touch, her haughtiness disappeared. Looking innocent and frightened, sweet and shy and sexy all at the same time, she tugged on her lower lip with her teeth. She glanced up the stairs like a teenager afraid of being caught by a vigilant parent. She lowered her eyelashes. When she tried to catch her breath, she shuddered delicately.

Then she pulled her arm free and, smiling up at him, signed something.

Emory leaned in closer. "I don't know what you said, but it looked mighty good to me." He pressed her arm once more and winked. "I'll be in touch."

Chapter Seventeen

*J*ack didn't return from his errand until after dark. Surprisingly, Delray and David were out on the front porch in spite of the heat. He had no intention of intruding. He was amazed that he was still employed.

Yesterday afternoon he had really overstepped his bounds. He had plunged headfirst into the turbulent waters of a moral conflict, ostensibly to save a drowning man who hadn't asked to be saved. Now, more than twenty-four hours later, he was still berating himself for asking Delray how long he had loved his daughter-in-law.

What the hell business was it of his? None. Except that Delray was upset because he and Anna had been alone together in the barn. And Delray suspected him of poisoning his herd of beef cattle. Jack supposed that gave him some license to speak his mind. Even so, it had been an inappropriate question and he had known that when he asked it.

Delray's reaction had been justifiably irate. He had turned his head so quickly that he'd inadvertently turned the steering wheel of his pickup too. It had swerved off the road and onto the shoulder. Delray had applied the brakes in time to keep them from plunging into the ditch, but inertia caused the truck to strain forward before rocking back and coming to a jarring stop.

When Delray turned to Jack, the veins in his forehead were bulging with anger. "I don't know what gutter you crawled out of, but you and your dirty mind . . ." He had been breathing so hard, he'd had to pause to catch his breath. "Let me set you straight on one thing. I have never laid a hand on Anna. Nothing, *nothing,* improper has ever passed between her and me."

"I believe you," Jack told him. "I didn't ask you how long you'd been sleeping with her; I asked how long you'd loved her."

Delray had continued to glare at him for several moments, but Jack hadn't backed down. He had known he was right. Delray's reaction had rid him of all doubt that he was mistaken.

Finally Delray slumped back in his seat and pressed his fingers into his eye sockets. He stayed that way for a full minute. Jack scarcely moved, hardly breathed. It was a long sixty seconds.

When at last Delray lowered his hand, it seemed to weigh a thousand pounds. It flopped lifelessly into his lap. He stared disconsolately through the windshield, looking old, defeated, and incredibly sad.

"Does she know?"

Delray shook his head. "No. No."

Jack had said nothing else, knowing he had said more than enough.

After a time Delray had steered the truck back onto the road and they returned to the ranch. It wouldn't have surprised Jack if Delray had ordered him then to pack and leave. He had two very good reasons to fire him.

But Delray hadn't mentioned dismissal then, or this morning when Jack reported to work. He was still employed this afternoon when he left to get the part for the broken pump. Apparently, he was still on the payroll.

But he certainly didn't expect an invitation to join the family tonight, so he hesitated even when David waved to him from the porch. He shouted, "Hey, Jack! Come here! We're making ice cream."

Couldn't hurt to stop and say hello, he thought. He stopped his truck and got out.

"Hi, Jack."

"Hey, David." As Jack climbed the porch steps he nodded at the antiquated machine. "I thought all ice cream freezers were electric these days. Didn't know they still made the wooden ones."

"They don't." Delray was sweating from the exertion, but he actually seemed to be enjoying himself. "We've got an electric one, but, I don't know, it just doesn't seem to taste as good as when you crank it yourself."

Delray was having to apply himself to turn the hand crank. David was sitting on top of the gear mechanism, a folded towel cushioning it for him. The freezer, a barrel made of vertical wooden slats, was standing in a plastic tub so the brine draining from a hole in the side of it wouldn't run into the flower beds at the edge of the porch.

"It freezes faster if I'm sitting on it," David told him.

"That's why you're such an important fellow around here."

The boy flashed his snaggle-toothed grin.

"Get the part?" Delray asked.

"Yeah, I'll start on that pump first thing tomorrow morning. Unless you want me to do it tonight."

"Hell no. Sit down."

Surprised by the invitation, he sat down on the top step.

"You're not s'posed to say hell, Grandpa."

"You're right, David, I'm not. Did you have some supper?" he asked Jack.

"I stopped for a burger."

"This should be ready in a few more minutes."

As though on cue, Anna came through the door carrying a tray of bowls, napkins, and spoons. Jack jumped up and relieved her of the tray, which seemed to fluster her. Or maybe she was flustered because she didn't have enough utensils for him and had to go back inside to get them. When she returned, Delray pronounced the ice cream ready.

David hopped down. The towel was removed. Jack watched with interest as the salty ice was scraped away from the metal canister and it was lifted out. Anna took the lid off and pulled out the dasher, the louvered gizmo that stirred the cream mixture while it was freezing. Then, using a long spoon, she served up the first bowl and passed it to Jack.

Taken aback, he accepted it with a murmured "Thanks." He waited until everyone else had been served before spooning his first bite. It was rich, cold, sweet, and redolent with vanilla. Delicious.

"Anna uses Mary's recipe, which came down through her family," Delray told him. "I bet it's the best homemade ice cream you ever ate."

"It's the only homemade ice cream I ever ate." He said it before he thought about it. He was hoping the admission would pass without notice, but Delray raised his head and looked at him. Jack shrugged. "My, uh, my folks weren't into things like making ice cream. How'd your meeting with Lomax go?"

Thankfully the diversion worked to change the subject. Delray pulled a frown. "I sent him packing and told him not to bother me again with any offers to buy my ranch. Then he went to work on Anna."

Jack looked across at her. They'd been avoiding making direct eye contact, although he had been aware of every movement she made, and he got a sense that she was just as conscious of him. Their nervousness was silly. They were grown-ups, not kids. They hadn't done anything in the barn except touch hands.

Of course, now that he knew the nature of Delray's feelings, he would never look at her without remembering that.

But now he looked at her inquisitively and Delray said, "Tell him, Anna. He'll get a kick out of it."

With Delray acting as interpreter, she recounted her conversation with Emory Lomax. When she was finished, Jack said, "I thought he was just a jerk. Turns out he's a total creep."

From the hallway, Jack had overheard enough to form a low opinion of the banker. If Lomax were an honest businessman, a person with integrity, he wouldn't have resorted to blackmailing Delray with his connection to Carl Herbold. The way he had come on to Anna proved the guy had no ethics, and that he was an egotistical asshole to boot. It was a dangerous combination.

"Tell Jack what you said to him," Delray said, chuckling. She turned to Jack, but Delray translated her signs into words. "I pretended to be flattered. When he suggested that we get together, I called him an . . . an ugly name," Delray said, amending it because of David. "I told him to take his slimy hands off me or I was going to kick him in the you-know-whats."

David licked out the bowl of his spoon. "Kick him where, Grandpa?"

"I get the picture," Jack said, grimacing. "You should have gone ahead and done it, Anna." She smiled at him. Extending his empty bowl, he said, "Are seconds allowed? Please?"

He watched her as she spooned the ice cream from the canister. Light coming from inside the house through the front windows lit only one side of her face. The other was softened by shadow. Hot as the evening air was, her skin looked cool. She made no wasted motions. When melting ice cream got on her fingers, she unself-consciously licked it off.

Then Jack became aware of Delray watching him watch Anna. He ate the second helping of ice cream in record time, said good night, and left the Corbetts on the porch.

For a long time, he stood beneath the spray in the minuscule shower in the trailer, repeating countless times, "Don't do something stupid and blow it, Jack. Don't blow it."

Chapter Eighteen

*I*t was a wide-spot-in-the-road kind of town. At this time of night, the
sleepy streets showed no signs of life. A single traffic light was per-
ilously suspended above the main intersection, but either it had burned
out or had been turned off at a designated time, because it wasn't even
blinking yellow. Windows were dark. Not even an alley cat stalked the
deserted streets.

But Carl Herbold was on the prowl.

For several days the Bailey farm in northwestern Louisiana had made
a perfect rest stop. Carl couldn't have asked for more comfortable
accommodations. The pantry and food freezer had been well stocked.
There were more channels on the television than he and Myron could
watch. The house had central airconditioning that maintained a cool
seventy degrees.

Carl had got downright nostalgic when it came time to say good-bye
to the place. The widowed Mrs. Bailey and her old-maid sister had lived
there alone ever since G.R. died. Reasoning that relatives and neighbors
were bound to check on the two old ladies periodically, Carl had
decided this morning that he and Myron should move on. It was dangerous to stay too long in any one place when law enforcement agencies—local, state, and federal—were after your ass.

They had left the sisters resting in peace at the bottom of their water
well with bullets in their heads.

Carl had never been good at waiting. He was a man of action. He
and Cecil had nixed the idea of reuniting immediately after the prison
escape. The heat would be on full blast. Cecil would be closely
watched until the authorities became convinced that the Herbold brothers were too smart to do something so predictable and risk Carl's being

recaptured. So they had agreed on this cooling-off period. But with the rendezvous still days away, the idle time was making Carl antsy.

And money had become a concern. While the late Mr. Bailey had provided his heirs a home with all the amenities, the sisters had to have been the most frugal bitches ever to draw breath. They kept no cash in the house. Even when Carl had turned Mrs. Bailey over to Myron to play with, the spinster had sobbingly sworn she had no cash to give them beyond the small amount she carried in her purse. Twenty-seven lousy bucks.

But the joke had been on Carl. After killing both of them, he had spent days searching the house from attic to cellar. None of the typical hiding places had turned up a dime. Who would've guessed the old bitches were telling the truth when pleading for their lives?

Most of the forty dollars Cecil had left them in the car had gone for liquor, food, and gas. They would need money soon. So the plan now was to acquire some cash without creating too much of a ruckus. An in-and-out operation would be ideal.

"That looks like an easy place, Myron," Carl said as they cruised beneath the town's single, nonfunctioning, traffic light. "What do you think?"

"Sure, Carl."

"We'll get us some money and pick you up a few PayDays. How's that?"

He was glad Myron was so agreeable, but he wished his partner in crime wouldn't grin so big. When Myron peeled his lips away from his teeth like that, revealing puffy pink gums, he was one ugly son of a bitch.

The gas station was constructed of corrugated tin and appeared to have been there for at least half a century. The gas pumps in front were the only nod toward modernity, and they looked to be only a couple decades old. Branches of a large chinaberry tree spread across the roof, casting a deep shadow over the entire building, which Carl considered a bonus. The deeper the darkness, the better. He drove around to the back of the building, parked the car, and got out.

Securing the back door was a flimsy padlock, which he opened with a bolt cutter that Cecil had had the forethought to place in the trunk for just this sort of emergency. He led the way through a cluttered storage room, which smelled of rubber and motor oil, into the commercial area. Myron trudged along behind him.

"Shit!"

Carl, hands on hips, thoroughly exasperated, glared at the cash register. He had expected a relic, a brass fixture with buttons with numbers on them and a little bell that rang when the cash drawer shot open. Or maybe even something as crude as a cigar box chock-full of money.

Who would have expected a dump like this in a one-horse town to have a sophisticated, computerized cash register like the one he was looking at? He couldn't seem to buy a break. First, the old ladies had had no hidden treasure trove. Now this.

"How am I supposed to get into that?"

It was a rhetorical question, but Myron, who had found the PayDays in the rack of candies and chewing gums, replied, "I dunno, Carl. Break it."

"You can't break it, you dumb shit. It's got a code, numbers you gotta punch . . . Why in hell am I trying to explain fucking technology to a moron? Toss me one of those Hershey's bars."

"You want almonds, Carl?"

"Why not?"

Myron threw the candy bar underhand. Carl reached out to catch it.

"Hold it right there, you sum'bitch!"

Carl turned toward the shout. The twin barrels of a sawed-off shot-gun were lined up even with his eyeballs. The Hershey's bar fell to the floor.

"Don't shoot," he blubbered. "No!" he cried when he saw Myron out of the corner of his eye about to spring. If that shotgun went off, his head would be ground meat before Myron reached the other man. "We're sorry, Mister. We're sorry. We didn't mean you any harm, we just—"

"Shut up. You," he said to Myron, "keep your hands in sight and move over here by your buddy."

"What should I do, Carl?"

Way to go, Myron. Call me by name. However, Carl was chiding himself, too, for being so careless. He had laid his pistol on the countertop. His back was to it, and it was out of reach. *Stupid, stupid!* The only option left him was to play scared for this yokel. "Do what the man says. We're caught."

Myron's big feet shuffled across the linoleum floor. "Are we going back to the prison?"

Carl swore right then and there that if he got out of this alive, he was going to personally cut out Myron's tongue.

"Y'all them boys that escaped the prison up in Arkansas?"

"Don't shoot us," Carl pleaded, faking a catch in his throat. "We're—"

"Jee-zus," the man exclaimed in a whisper. "Good thing I happened by. Saw your car outside."

Carl asked, "Is this your place?"

"Damn straight. I figured you was just some kids. Never thought—"

"Daddy?"

What happened then was a blur, even to Carl, who enacted it.

The gas-station owner whipped around to admonish his offspring for disobeying his orders and leaving the car, where she had obviously been told to stay put. All Carl needed was that split second to shove the butt of the shotgun into the man's gut. The shotgun never discharged, a miracle that Carl never understood. Myron, acting intelligently, a miracle in itself, snatched up the girl and clamped his large hand over her face, preventing her from screaming.

In less than five seconds, the momentum shifted. Carl and Myron were once again in possession of all the weapons and in control of the situation, while the man who hoped to apprehend them was bent double, retching dryly, and begging for his life.

"Whew," Carl said, retrieving his candy bar from the floor and tearing off the wrapper, "I feel a lot better about this situation now. Don't you, Myron?"

"Yeah, Carl."

Carl bit off a few squares of chocolate. "Better uncover her nose, Myron, or you're going to suffocate her. But keep her mouth shut."

"Please don't hurt her," the man gasped.

"Never entered my mind," Carl said, acting affronted. "Did it enter your mind to hurt this girl, Myron?"

"No, Carl."

"See?" Carl taunted. "We don't want to hurt anybody. And we won't." He rammed the butt of the shotgun into the man's face, making pulp of his nose and knocking out his front teeth.

He fell to all fours, moaning and pleading with God to help him. "Now, see, all that weepin' and wailin' and prayin' isn't going to do you any good," Carl told him. "'Cause you're the only one who can help yourself. All you've gotta do is open up this cash register. Then we'll leave you in peace. Don't you think that's fair?"

"Okay, okay. Just don't hurt us."

The man pulled himself up by a sheer act of will and staggered to the counter. The poor bastard's hands were shaking so badly he could hardly get the thing powered up, but he managed it. He keyed in the code and the cash drawer opened.

"See how easy that was?" Carl clapped him on the back in congratulations, then stabbed him in the kidney with the shank he'd honed in prison. Three vicious thrusts. When Carl withdrew the handmade knife the last time, the man collapsed onto the floor.

"Not a shot fired," Carl mused aloud, smiling. "It's about time I caught a break."

The girl whimpered in terror, drawing Carl's attention to her. He hadn't really taken much notice of her before; he'd had other things on his mind. But now as he stuffed his pockets with the money in the cash drawer, he looked her over.

She was wearing shorts and a striped jersey for a sports team of some kind. Tall socks that covered her thin calves. Athletic shoes. She was around fourteen, he would guess. Not a kid, not quite a woman. But woman enough. He started getting hard. If it weren't for the time it would take . . .

"Tell you what, Myron, I'm going to let you drive for a spell. Would you like that?"

"Gee, Carl, that'd be fun. Can I have some more PayDays?"

"All you want. I'll get them for you. You take her out to the car and put her in the backseat. Don't let her make a sound."

Bless his heart, Myron did exactly as he was told. Of course, he cut off the girl's source of oxygen in the process of keeping her quiet, so that by the time Carl joined them in the car she was unconscious, making the roll of duct tape he had found in the storage room unnecessary. He taped her mouth anyway, just as a precaution.

By the time Myron drove past the city limit sign, Carl was already enjoying himself in the backseat. Immensely.

Chapter Nineteen

They say it was Carl Herbold. Him and that guy he escaped with. They say they's the ones that did it."

"They ain't saying any such thing. They're saying they're *suspects*."

"Same as."

"What country you living in? This is America. We've got a constitution that gives us rights. Innocent till proved guilty, remember? Mornin', Ezzy."

The regulars at the Busy Bee coffee shop on the town square were, as usual, discussing the hottest news story of the day. Whatever the story happened to be, they sliced and diced it as efficiently as those kitchen gadgets on the infomercials that cut up raw potatoes in seven different ways.

It was also customary for them to argue points of that news story, no matter if those points were universal principles, abstract themes, or minute factual details. Today the argument seemed to be focused on the details.

Every morning a cluster of old men gathered at the café. The names and faces changed with each generation, same as the topics under discussion. Wars had been waged, won, and lost. Controversies had arisen and been forgotten. Statesmen and celebrities had been lauded, lambasted, and laid to rest. But the ritual gathering endured. It was as though once a man reached a certain age, his attendance at the Busy Bee became mandatory. As soon as one passed away, another moved in to fill the gap. Upholding the tradition was essential to Blewer's social order.

Retirees for the most part, with a surplus of time on their hands, they were sometimes still there at lunchtime, having switched from coffee to iced tea, irascibly asserting their points of view.

Ezzy had always regarded these old men as rather pathetic. They had nothing better to do than spout their unsolicited opinions about issues that didn't concern them to people no better informed than they. They were human relics, trying to convince themselves that they were vital, contributing components of the society that was forced to subsidize and tolerate them until they died.

Greeting them now, he realized that most were younger than he.

"What brings you out this A.M.?" one asked.

"Coffee, please, Lucy," he told the waitress before addressing the question. "Cora's sister out in Abilene is sick. She went to stay with her for a spell."

Even more than he hated old men who loitered in the coffee shop voicing viewpoints that nobody gave a damn about, Ezzy hated liars. No matter what, he was never going to join the group at the Busy Bee. He had, however, become a liar. Even to himself. *Especially* to himself.

He could polish it up any way he liked, but the plain and simple truth was that after fifty years of marriage, Cora had left him. He had watched her pack her suitcase, place it in her car along with a few pictures of their kids and granddaughters, and drive away. She was gone.

But he kept telling himself that the separation was temporary. He couldn't live the rest of his life without her.

"So you're baching it these days?"

"Seems like," he replied.

"Want some breakfast to go with that coffee, Ezzy?"

He had known Lucy since grade school. He'd played high school football with the husband she lost to a log skidder in a horrible accident. He had attended the funeral of their son, who had died for his country in 'Nam.

Through the decades Lucy's hips had gotten broader and her hairdo higher, but underneath the heavy makeup she used to conceal heartache and the ravages of age, she was the same Lucy he had taught to climb a tree in third grade.

He had eaten cornflakes for two mornings in a row. The smell of hot food had made his mouth water. "Got any biscuits and gravy this morning?"

"Don't I always?"

He took a stool at the counter, putting his back to the table of men in the hope of discouraging inclusion in their conversation. It didn't work.

"You hear about that kidnapping and killing, Ezzy?"

"How could he keep from hearing about it? It's all over the TV and radio this morning."

"Was I talking to you?" the first asked cantankerously. "How 'bout it, Ezzy? As a former lawman, what's your read on it?"

"It was a terrible crime, all right." His eyes silently thanked Lucy for the plate of food she served him. He had always suspected she had a crush on him. She had never outright flirted. He was married, and she wasn't the type to go after another woman's husband. For his part, he had certainly never said or done anything to encourage her. It was just a feeling he got because of the way she always seemed to perk up a little when he came into the café. She gave him preferential service, extra helpings, little favors like that. Like now; there were two fat patties of pork sausage on his plate.

"You think it was Herbold that did it?"

Ezzy's focus remained on his breakfast. "I wouldn't venture to guess. Happened over in Louisiana. Way out of my jurisdiction."

"You can almost see why they killed the man," one mused aloud. "They was robbing him."

"It's the little girl that's the real tragedy."

"For once you're right, Clem. Why'd they have to go and do that?"

"They said on TV her privates was all tore up."

"For heaven's sake!" Lucy exclaimed. "Do y'all have to talk about that? It's disrespectful of the dead."

"Don't go getting riled, Lucy. All I'm saying is that whoever did that to her was mean. He did it for mea'ness' sake and that's the only reason." He stabbed the tabletop with his index finger. "Mea'ness."

"Just like that McCorkle girl. Lord o' mercy. How long ago was that? You remember that, Ezzy?"

He had been thinking how superior Cora's sausage gravy was to the Busy Bee's, letting the conversation eddy around him, hearing it but not really listening. Then all of a sudden it seemed that a thousand fishhooks sank into him at once and that he was being dragged from the cool, shady waters of private rumination up to the surface, where survival meant struggling for every breath.

"'Course he remembers," one said scornfully. Then to Ezzy, "You never did get to prove it was the Herbolds that killed her. You never really knew what happened to that girl, did you, Ezzy?"

He cleared his throat, took a sip of coffee. "Nope, never did."

"Only the river knows the secret," said Lucy.

Ezzy looked up at her, surprised. He had been reading a twenty-two-year-old newspaper clipping just last night, the very one from which she had quoted.

She blushed and seemed embarrassed to have remembered his statement word for word. "I remember reading in the paper that you said that."

One of the Busy Bee's regulars relieved her of the awkward moment by remarking, "Bound to have been those boys. Last anybody saw her alive, she was with them."

"Yeah, but she could've dropped them off somewhere and picked up another fellow."

"Like who?" his friend scoffed.

"Like anybody. She was wild, they say."

"Well, *I* say that's a damn slim possibility. Everybody knows they were involved."

"Then how'd they get to Arkansas so fast? Tell me that. You ever figure that out, Ezzy? Wasn't that business in Arkadelphia their alibi?"

"That's right." Leaving the rest of his breakfast unfinished, he stepped off the counter stool. "How much do I owe you, Lucy?"

She tallied up his bill, and it was so ridiculously low that he doubled the amount and tucked it beneath his plate.

"Thanks, Ezzy." She gave him a smile that revealed a gold jaw tooth.

"You know," said one of the men behind him, "I was just thinking—"

"That's a switch."

"Fuck you and the horse you rode in on."

"Hey, boys, watch the language," Lucy remonstrated. "You know the house rules."

"Sorry, Lucy. As I was saying before I was so rudely interrupted . . ."

Ezzy didn't hear any more. He opened the door, causing the little bell above it to jingle, and let himself out. He pulled on his hat to shade his eyes against the morning sun. The concrete sidewalk was hot beneath his boots as he made his way to the Lincoln. The Stars and Stripes on the pole in front of the courthouse was already drooping from the heat and lack of wind. A lawn sprinkler was clackety-clacking on the plot of grass in front of the Confederate cannon, shooting out a feeble spray that evaporated before the water could find the ground.

Ezzy's car felt like a furnace when he got in. He turned on the ignition to get the air conditioner started. The first sound out of the radio was the morning news report. An intensified manhunt was still underway for Carl Herbold and Myron Hutts, recent escapees from the maximum-security prison in Tucker, Arkansas. They were now suspects in the murders of a gas-station owner and his daughter.

". . . leaving a trail of victims in their wake, starting with two prison guards. They're now implicated in a double murder that took place overnight in the small town of Hemp, Louisiana."

Ezzy turned down the sound. He didn't want to hear about the rape and murder of a fourteen-year-old girl again. Earlier he had watched the story on TV. The man had been discovered dead at his place of business by his wife. She'd gone looking for him when he and his daughter failed to return home from an evening softball tournament in a neighboring town.

The missing girl's body wasn't found until daylight. A Frito-Lay truck driver on the first leg of his route had seen her lying in a ditch. Initial reports were that she had been sexually assaulted before being killed by a gunshot to the back of her head.

Ezzy cruised the streets of the town, disinclined to return to his empty house. He wondered if Carl had killed that man and his daughter and, if he had, whether he was as proud of it as he had been when Ezzy interviewed him in that Arkansas jail more than twenty years ago.

"Well, Ezzy, aren't you a Good Samaritan?" Carl had mocked from behind bars. "Did you travel all this way just to pay me a call?"

Wearing a bright orange jumpsuit, he had looked as handsome as ever. If anything, his smile appeared more dashing than before. Maybe committing murder had added that extra panache.

Ezzy had refused to be baited by his false charm. "You're sinking in a tub of shit, Carl, and there's an anchor around your neck."

"Yeah, well, I'll grant you I've had better days, Sheriff. They've got some piss-poor jails up here in Arkansas, let me tell you. Food sucks. Toilet stinks. Mattress is lumpy. No fun at all."

"I'm afraid you'd better get used to it, Carl."

"Naw, I've got me a good lawyer. He's a freebie, but sharp as a tack. From up north someplace. Has himself a ponytail and an earring. Hates the system. Especially down here in good-ol'-boy country. Thinks all the officials are stupid and corrupt, and I think he's right. He says they might get me for the holdup, but he's pleading me out of that killing. It was an accident."

"Is that right?"

"Look, the guy could've killed my big brother. I had to pop him first or watch Cecil die."

"Save it for the jury, Carl."

Carl's face had turned hard and angry. Brown eyes blazed. "I'm not going to prison for murder, Sheriff. You can write that down. I didn't go into that store to kill anybody."

"Well, even if these fellas here in Arkansas don't nail you, you're going away for a long time."

"How do you figure?"

"If you walk out of this, I'm hauling your sorry ass back to Texas to answer for Patsy McCorkle."

"That chunky girl? Ugly gal?"

A horn blasted Ezzy out of his recollection. Realizing that the traffic light had turned green, he waved an apology to the other driver. With nowhere else to go, he headed for the residential neighborhood where he and Cora had lived nearly all their married life.

He hated the hollow feel of the house as he let himself in. Cora was a small woman; strange that her absence could create such a vacuum. He removed his hat and hung it on a peg near the back door. He went into the kitchen and noticed that he had left the coffeemaker on. He turned it off.

Then, moving into the hallway, he considered what to do with the rest of the day. Watch TV? He had his choice of inane soap operas, inane talk shows, or inane infomercials. Work in the yard? Too hot. And he wasn't good at it anyway. Cora claimed that plants saw him coming and committed suicide before he could kill them.

This interior debate was all for show, a balm for his stinging conscience, because he already knew what he was going to do.

Fighting the allure no longer, he went into the den and sat down behind a massive rolltop desk that he'd inherited from his daddy. He'd been a railroad man and had used this desk every day of his career. Considering it an heirloom, Cora protected the oak finish with weekly polishing. Ezzy unlocked the slatted top and pushed it open. Lying front and center on the desk was the Patsy McCorkle file.

He opened it and stared at her senior picture. He remembered how obscene it had seemed to him when Carl Herbold casually referred to her an as "ugly gal."

"Before you and Cecil came up here to rob that convenience store and kill yourselves an off-duty policeman, you left Patsy McCorkle down by the river, dead."

Carl had stared at him through the bars of his cell, looking for all the world like an innocent man. Finally he threw back his head and laughed. "I don't know what you've been smoking, Ezzy, but you're fucking crazy."

"Everybody who was at the Wagon Wheel that night saw y'all leave with her. I've got dozens of witnesses."

"You've got shit," Carl had shot back angrily.

"You and Cecil weren't with her?"

"Yeah, we were with her. Or more like it, *she* was with *us*. She latched on soon as we walked in. She was drunk. We were getting there. We had some laughs. So what?"

"I've heard y'all were having more than laughs, Carl, that you were putting on quite a sex show."

Carl had grinned and winked at him. "You sound sorry you missed it, Sheriff. Wish we'd've known you were interested. Cecil and me would have shared Patsy with you. Isn't Mrs. Hardge giving you any pussy at home?"

If Ezzy could have reached him through the bars, he might have killed Carl then and saved the State of Arkansas the expense of putting him on trial and keeping him in their prison system for years. Thankfully, he had quelled his temper and left Carl laughing at his back.

He had hoped to get more out of Cecil, who wasn't nearly as cock-sure as his younger brother. But Cecil had corroborated Carl's story. "Yeah, we were dancing with Patsy and all, Sheriff Hardge, but we didn't go to the river with her. We drove a good part of the night, held up that store at seven-twenty in the morning."

That much was true. Ezzy had read the arrest report for the crime, which, ironically, provided the Herbolds with an alibi for Patsy McCorkle. But he'd driven the same route the boys had taken that night. It was just over two hundred and fifty miles. Based on when they were seen leaving the bar, they could have taken Patsy to the river where they had sex with her and still made it to Arkadelphia well before seven-twenty. The time of Patsy's death, which Stroud had established, didn't conflict either.

"Cecil, everybody in that bar saw you and Carl with the girl. I heard the three of you created quite a spectacle, even for that dive. Now don't try and tell me that after all that fooling around, all that drinking and dancing and foreplay, you didn't have sex with her."

Cecil's eyes darted about his cell. He glanced past Ezzy at the jail guard. He chewed his inner cheek. "Okay, okay. She, uh, got me off. With her hand. Under a table there at the Wagon Wheel." He ducked his head and smothered an aw-shucks laugh. "Damnedest thing I've ever done. All those people no more than a few feet away, and there's my dick, flapping around under the table. But that was Patsy. She'd do any-thing for laughs."

"And later?"

"Later?"

"What did you and Patsy do for laughs later?"

Cecil got nervous then and started gnawing on his thumbnail. "What did Carl say?"

"Carl said y'all parted ways outside the bar."

"Yeah, that's right," he said quickly. "We drove to Arkansas and realized we were hungry and since we didn't have any money we decided to hit that store."

"And wound up killing a cop."

"We didn't know he was a cop. Stupid asshole pulled a gun on us. What was Carl supposed to do? He had to protect us from getting killed, right, Sheriff? Sheriff?"

But Ezzy had already turned his back on him and was on his way to talk to the county prosecutor handling the case. He was barrel-chested and red-headed. His florid cheeks looked like balloons about to burst. "Sorry, Sheriff, uh . . . what was it?"

"Hardge."

"Sheriff Hardge. I sympathize with your situation. I surely do. I know you'd like to close the books on your case down yonder. But if I submit these boys to that kind of testing to help clear your case, I'm liable to lose mine. At the very least it would give their lawyers a basis for appeal. They could scream violation of rights. You know defense lawyers these days. Bet they're as bad in Texas as they are here. They pull bullshit out their asses all the time, and felons go back on the streets. If I was to grant your favor, these boys might even get their trials dismissed altogether." He lit an unfiltered Camel and waved out the match. "Sorry. We got 'em first. They killed one of our own. We're gonna keep 'em guests of Arkansas for a long time."

"All I need is a semen specimen. From both of them. How's that going to violate their rights?"

His laugh sounded like a band saw biting into a two-by-four. "Jacking off in a jar? Somebody asks me to do that, I'd consider it a violation of *my* rights."

Chapter Twenty

"Okay, but don't back up."

"I promise I won't."

"You'll stay right there?"

"Right here. Just remember to kick your legs real hard like you practiced."

The water was no higher than David's waist. Even so, looking apprehensive about the four feet separating him from Jack, he took a huge breath and plunged forward. Several strong kicks later, his splashing hands made contact with Jack's. Jack pulled him up and helped him regain his footing on the cool silt bottom of the river.

"Way to go!" Jack gave the boy a high five.

"I did it!"

"I knew you could."

"Can I do it again?"

"Anytime you're ready."

David waded back to his starting place. "It was fun last night having ice cream, wasn't it, Jack?"

"Sure was."

"I wish you were with us all the time. You could sleep in my room."

"Don't you think it would be crowded with both of us?"

Skimming his hands across the surface of the water, David gave it some thought. His face brightened with a sudden inspiration. "You could sleep with my mom. She's got a great big bed."

Jack hid his smile. "I don't think so."

"Why not, Jack? She probably wouldn't care."

"I just couldn't do that."

"How come?" the boy persisted.

"Because you're a family. You, your mom, and your grandpa. I'm not a member of the family."

"Yeah, but—"

"What's that?" Jack held up his hand for quiet. "Sounds like a triangle."

"Yeah, that thing." David made a circular motion with his closed fist as though waving a magic wand. "My mom's s'posed to use it in case of an emergency."

"An emergency?"

Jack grabbed David's hand and thrashed through the shallow water to shore. "Quick, put your shoes on. Get your clothes." Jack scrambled into his jeans and picked up his boots. The triangle had stopped clanging, but Anna wouldn't have used the emergency signal just for the hell of it.

Taking David by the hand again, Jack ran through the woods toward the house. Dusk had fallen. They encountered clouds of mosquitoes but were moving too fast for them to light. Jack tripped over a vine and nearly dragged David down with him.

"How're you doing?" he called down when he regained his footing.

"I'm okay, Jack."

The heavy, humid air didn't make for easy running. By the time they reached the clearing, Jack was sucking hard to draw each breath. He paused and looked frantically toward the house. No smoke. A fire in either the house or the barn had been his first fear. The lack of rain had left everything as dry as tinder. One spark could have ignited a dangerous blaze.

He was relieved not to see one, but something urgent had happened and he still didn't know what it was. Releasing David's hand, he sprinted the remaining distance to the house, where he clambered up the front steps and burst through the door. "Anna? Delray? Where are you? What's the matter?"

He glanced into the living room, but it was empty. As he came back around he ran squarely into Anna, nearly sent her sprawling, and only prevented it by catching her by the shoulders. "What's wrong?"

She pointed him upstairs.

Jack doubled back, rounded the balustrade, and took the treads two at a time. He reached the second floor in seconds. Delray was lying in the hall, steps from the door to his bedroom.

Jack knelt down beside him. He was unconscious. Jack dug his fingers into his neck, feeling for his carotid. There was no pulse. "Shit. Don't die. Not now." Straddling Delray's hips, he began administering CPR. He heard Anna and David running down the hallway toward him.

"David?"

"What's wrong with Grandpa?" There were tears and anxiety in the boy's voice.

"Ask your mother if she called nine-one-one."

"She says she did, Jack."

Anna knelt down on the other side of Delray. Jack glanced at her. "You called?" She nodded. "Good. Good," he said.

Because if help didn't arrive soon, Delray wasn't going to make it.

The doctor was typically guarded. He walked a thin line between glossing over the seriousness of Delray's condition and unnecessarily alarming those who cared about him.

"The preliminary tests show several blockages, any one of which would be serious by itself. His blood pressure is at a critical level. Our first order of business is to bring it down and get him stabilized."

His diagnosis was translated to Anna through an interpreter. Her name was Marjorie Baker. Both of her parents had been deaf, so sign had been her first language. She was a certified level-five translator and a deaf educator. That's how she knew Anna. She had worked with her throughout her schooling, then later became her friend.

Beyond her administrative duties in the public schools, Marjorie Baker was an advocate for the deaf in the rural communities of East Texas. Unlike hospitals in larger cities, this one didn't yet have a Teletype system for the hearing-impaired to use. Consequently, Ms. Baker had been called immediately after Delray was admitted. She had arrived calm and concerned. Jack liked her instantly.

"After his blood pressure is under control and he's stabilized, then what?" she asked, translating the question Anna had signed.

To his credit, the doctor spoke directly to Anna. "Then bypass surgery is called for. Alternatives to surgery, like angioplasty or putting in a stint, are no longer options, I'm afraid. The blockages are too severe."

"Can you do it here?" Marjorie asked.

"The operation?" When Anna nodded yes, he replied, "No, ma'am. I'm a cardiologist, not a cardiac surgeon. I can refer you to several excellent surgeons in either Houston or Dallas. Whoever you select, we'll bring him up to speed on Mr. Corbett's condition and see that he gets all his films, et cetera. It's done all the time. We make the transfer as easy on you as possible."

"Don't worry about any inconvenience to me," Marjorie said, speaking as Anna signed. "I want what's best for my father-in-law."

"Of course," the doctor said.

"Is Grandpa gonna get well, Jack?"

"That's what we're working on."

Ashamed of his tears, David turned toward him and pressed his face against Jack's thigh. "Can you give them any idea of what his chances are?" Jack asked the doctor.

"It's too soon to tell. Honestly," the doctor added when he read the skepticism in Anna's eyes. "Right now, his condition is critical. I won't lie to you and say otherwise. He's in cardiac intensive care. We'll monitor him carefully throughout the night. By morning I should be able to give you a more definite prognosis."

"What about flying him by helicopter to Houston or Dallas tonight?" Marjorie asked the question, but received an enthusiastic nod from Anna for thinking of it.

"In his present condition, that would be risky," the doctor replied. "If it were my father I wouldn't chance it. I'd wait until he had more working in his favor before I moved him." He gave Anna a sympathetic smile and laid one hand on her shoulder. "I realize everything I'm telling you is not what you want to hear. For right now it's the best I can do."

Before returning to his duties, he told Anna that a nurse would let her know when she could see Delray. The promised visit came a half hour later. Anna rushed from the waiting room, following the nurse who had summoned her. Marjorie went with her. Jack stayed behind with David.

"Why can't I go see Grandpa?" he whined.

"Because an intensive care unit is for people who are very sick. It's no place for a little boy."

"How come?"

"You might make noise and disturb the patients."

"I wouldn't make noise."

"Want me to read you a story?" Jack hopefully held up a book.

"That's a dumb book. It hasn't even got any pictures."

The boy wouldn't be distracted. Jack was relieved when Anna rejoined them about ten minutes later. She looked pale and shaken, but smiled for David's benefit and told him that his grandpa was taking a good nap.

"I want to see Grandpa." The boy's lower lip began to quiver.

"He has tubes in his nose and arms, David," Marjorie Baker told him.

"Like the doctor shows on TV?"

"Yes, but it's different in real life. You wouldn't like seeing your grandpa like that, and he wouldn't want you to see him that way. Besides, if you woke him up, it wouldn't be good for him."

Jack addressed Anna. "Do you want me to take him home?"

"No!" David wailed. "I want to stay here with Grandpa."

He began to cry and Anna pulled him onto her lap. She pressed his head against her chest and stroked his forehead, pushing back his hair, which was still damp with river water, Jack noticed. She kissed his brow and hugged him tightly, rocking him back and forth. In a moment his sobs subsided but he still clung to his mother.

"I guess he's staying," Marjorie said, smiling up at Jack. "In all the excitement we haven't been officially introduced. I know your name is Jack."

"Sawyer," he told her, shaking hands. "Thanks for coming. I'm sure Anna is glad you're here."

"She was glad you were there this evening when it happened."

"Yeah, well, I'm glad I could help out."

Marjorie gave him a measured look before she sat down beside Anna and commenced a signed conversation. An hour later, Anna was granted another five-minute visit to the CCU. Delray's condition was unchanged.

The hospital staff urged her to go home for the remainder of the night, but she wouldn't even consider it. It was almost a half-hour drive from the hospital to the ranch. They might get there only to be called back. Delray could take a sudden turn for the better—or the worse. Either way, she wanted to be nearby.

Marjorie offered to stay also, but Anna insisted that she leave. "Only if you promise to page me if the situation changes." Anna made the requested promise.

Jack didn't know what was expected of him. Should he go or stay? Did she want him with her or did she wish he would get lost? Feeling awkward and conspicuous, he sat down on a sofa that formed a right angle with the one Anna and David occupied. He chose a bass fishing magazine from the unappealing and outdated selection of reading material on an end table.

At midnight the overhead fluorescent lights were turned out and substituted with dim table lamps, making the room more conducive to sleep. Only one other family, an older couple, was in the waiting room. The man was stretched out in a recliner. An occasional snore wafted from his open mouth. The woman, presumably his wife, had cried herself to sleep on a sofa. Jack wondered what medical crisis was keeping them here tonight.

David eventually fell asleep in Anna's lap. She carried him to another sofa and covered him with a blanket a waiting-room volunteer had provided. Jack noticed Anna chafing her upper arms and touched her elbow to get her attention. "Cold?" She indicated the air-conditioning vent overhead. He asked the Pink Lady for another blanket and when she brought it to him, he unfolded it and placed it around Anna's shoulders.

"Thank you," she signed.

"You're welcome. Would you like something to drink? Coffee? A Coke? Juice?"

She shook her head, leaned back against the cushions, and, looking exhausted, closed her eyes.

Jack worked his butt into a more comfortable position. It didn't take long for him to determine that bass fishing just wasn't very interesting to him. The second magazine didn't hold his interest any better.

Fact was, he couldn't read for looking at Anna. With her head resting on the back cushion, her throat was arched and exposed, reminding him of the black-and-white photo she'd taken of herself at the fence.

Pretty ingenious of her, setting up what must have been a tricky camera angle. Pretty talented to have thought of the pose and the clever usage of stark light and deep shadow. Pretty pretty.

Was she pretty? Not like a fashion model or a movie star. Unlike classic prettiness, hers wasn't . . . predictable. Her features were more interesting, constantly changing with her mood. Hers was the kind of face that you could gaze at forever, or at least until you figured out why in hell you just couldn't take your eyes off it.

He wondered what she had thought of the incident in the barn. As she crossed the yard that night, skedaddling it back to the house like the hounds of hell were on her heels, what had she been thinking?

Maybe nothing. Maybe she'd been wondering why it didn't rain, or what she was going to cook for breakfast the following day, or if she should buy that new pair of shoes she'd seen in town. Maybe she hadn't given it any thought at all. Maybe it hadn't been an *incident* to her the way it had been to him. It had rocked his world, but maybe it hadn't created a single tremor in hers.

For his part, he'd been on the verge of pulling her close and kissing her mouth. She had run as though afraid that was what he was about to do. But had she been skittish because she wanted him to kiss her, or because she couldn't stand the thought?

He had flattered himself into believing the former. But he could be wrong. She might have been running because he had bad breath. Or BO. Or because she didn't like his looks or find him attractive.

No one would call him handsome. His face didn't look like it had been molded from clay by a master's deft hand, but rather like an amateur had taken a chain saw to a block of wood and hacked it into shape. No, he wasn't going to win any prizes for outstanding good looks.

But he'd never had to buy or beg female companionship. He would know by now, wouldn't he, if his looks were a major turn-off? He'd had women tell him they found his rugged features sexy. Maybe that was it—he was too sexy.

Anna had hightailed it from the barn out of fear. Women had an instinct that went into overdrive when their femininity was threatened. Maybe she'd been afraid that he would act on an animalistic impulse, drag her down into the hay, and ravish her.

Hell, he didn't know what she thought.

All he knew was that he'd had trouble falling asleep that night. When he finally did, he woke up a few hours later drenched in sweat despite the noisy air conditioner blowing frigid air across his naked body, and sporting an erection that *could* have won prizes.

Anna jerked awake. It took a couple of seconds for her to get her bearings. Then she remembered where she was and why, and the grim reality of it compressed her chest.

The last few weeks of Dean's life, she had spent hours in a hospital waiting room. Her vigilance hadn't affected the outcome then, and it wouldn't now, but she couldn't desert Delray any more than she could have deserted Dean.

She turned her head toward the sofa on which David slept and reassured herself that he was still there and all right. She yawned and stretched and rolled her head across her shoulders to work the stiffness out of her neck. She checked her wristwatch; the next scheduled visitation period was still hours away.

She glanced over at Jack Sawyer. He was asleep, his chest rising and falling evenly. His legs were splayed, one knee slightly bent, the other straight. His hands were loosely clasped between his thighs.

She looked at his hands, remembering how it had felt to touch them. She had taught David the sign language alphabet by actually moving his fingers into place. She had used the same method with Jack Sawyer. But his hand hadn't felt like her son's.

Jack's fingers were long and strong. The tips were callused. The backs of them were sprinkled with sun-bleached hair. His nails were clipped, but some of the cuticles were ragged.

David had a child's soft hand. Jack's belonged to a man who often smelled of sunshine, sweat, and hay, whose pulse had been visibly beating in the base of his throat when they stood close, whose breath she had felt against her face, whose gaze had made her feel very warm on the inside.

His eyes came open suddenly and caught her looking at him.

He drew in his legs and sat up quickly. "Everything okay?"

"Yes."

"No word from the doctor?"

"No."

He glanced over at David. She followed his gaze and then, when their eyes reconnected, they smiled at each other. David was sleeping on his back, one arm flung over his head, the other extending beyond the edge of the sofa.

"Wouldn't it be nice to be able to sleep like that?" Jack said. "I guess he was worn out from swimming."

Swimming? Her expression conveyed the question.

"Damn! I let the cat out of the bag."

She followed his lips, but the words she saw on them only puzzled her more.

He realized it and tried to clarify it for her. "That means giving away a secret. I've been teaching David to swim. We've been getting in a little practice every day. Act surprised when he shows you."

She nodded that she now understood.

"We were in the river when you rang the bell."

Jack had been shirtless and shoeless when he'd run into the house. David had been in his underwear, carrying his clothes. She hadn't thought of it until now. Jack must have gotten himself and David dressed while the paramedics were carrying Delray down the stairs and loading him into the ambulance. She had been scrambling around, making certain she had insurance cards and such. It had been a frantic time, but it would have been much worse if Jack hadn't been there seeing to David.

Taking a small spiral notepad from her purse, she wrote him a note to that effect, thanking him for his help.

"I did what anybody would have done," he said after reading her note.

Stubbornly she shook her head. She wrote, "You not only helped me, you saved Delray's life."

He rolled his shoulder in an awkward shrug. "Well, I'm glad I could help out." He sat forward and propped his forearms on his thighs. He seemed to be contemplating near space, but he looked up and asked her, "How'd it happen?"

She filled her notebook with several pages of writing, and by the time she finished Jack had the whole story. Delray had been watching the local five o'clock newscast. After the story about the kidnapping and double murder in Louisiana, he had excused himself and gone upstairs. A few minutes later, feeling uneasy, Anna had gone to check on him and had found him on the floor.

"Thank God you sensed that something was wrong."

She wrote, "I could tell that he was very upset over that news story."

"Because Carl Herbold is a suspect in that crime," Jack said, filling in the rest of the sentence before she could write again.

It surprised her that Jack knew the source of Delray's distress, and her curiosity must have been evident.

"I know there's a connection there." He went on to explain. "Delray and I ran into Ezzy Hardge at the Dairy Queen the other day. He mentioned something about Arkansas, and the boy being too smart to come this way. He said Delray shouldn't worry about it. Since that prison break is the big story out of Arkansas, I put two and two together. But Delray and I had other things to talk about, so I didn't press him for information. Then yesterday I overheard that Lomax character talking about it. From what I gathered, he was saying that folks blame Delray for Carl Herbold's sins."

Anna wrote, "Carl is the stepson I told you about."

"I see."

He seemed to receive this as news, but Anna got the feeling that it wasn't news to him at all. Her communication with other people relied largely on gauging their faces and interpreting their body language. She depended on the facial expressions of others because she couldn't hear the inflections in their speech.

Jack was lying. Not by what he said, but by what he left unsaid. If he already knew the relationship between the escaped convict and Delray, why would he pretend not to? And if he was a drifter, calling no place home, how did he know about it? Carl and Cecil were sent to prison over twenty years ago. Dean had been just a boy. Not even he had known his stepbrothers, except by name. Yet a stranger out of nowhere knew about the stepsons whom Delray no longer claimed.

Jack Sawyer had arrived the day following Carl's escape. Coincidence?

It was certainly something to think about.

Chapter Twenty-One

C ecil Herbold felt he had every reason to be paranoid.

It was his day off. Instead of taking advantage of it and sleeping late, he had awakened early, feeling jumpy even before he got out of bed. He didn't want to leave his apartment, though it seemed to be closing in on him. He couldn't sit still, but he could think of nothing constructive to do that would use up his surfeit of energy. He was hungry but too nervous to eat.

Thinking. That was his problem. He had too much time on his hands in which to think, and when he thought, he got paranoid.

He moved from room to room, peeping through the window blinds, looking for surveillance on the street, all the while realizing that if the heat was out there, he wouldn't see them.

He watched from the window for several minutes but saw nothing out of the ordinary. Traffic was flowing as usual. There were no suspicious-looking vans parked at the curb, no loiterers, no conspicuous persons or vehicles anywhere. But those guys were trained to blend in. Even while in plain sight, they knew how to make themselves invisible.

All right, so maybe he couldn't see them, but he knew they were out there. Sure as God made little green apples, he was under surveillance. He would bet his left nut on it, and he was fairly fond of his left nut.

If they hadn't been watching him before, they certainly were now.

Yesterday morning he had heard on the news about the brutal slayings of the gas-station owner and his daughter in some podunk Louisiana town. Even before it was officially announced that his little brother was being sought as a suspect, Cecil had nursed his own suspicions. It sounded exactly like something Carl would do.

The son of a bitch was supposed to be lying low, staying out of sight, doing nothing that would put the authorities on his scent. That had been the plan. They had discussed it.

But Carl never had taken the logical or safe route. Not in his entire life. He had come out of the womb as crazy as a shithouse rat and did what he damn well pleased, when he damn well pleased.

Had he really gone and raped a fourteen-year-old? He'd always liked them young, but *Jesus*! That was sick. Yesterday at work, old man Reynolds had practically sneered at him each time he looked at him. Coworkers treated him like a leper. They were all assholes. He didn't want their friendship, but, hell, he didn't want them thinking that he approved of Carl's raping a kid.

The telephone rang. Cecil's heart jumped. Letting the slat in the window blind drop back into place, he caught the phone on the second ring and juggled the receiver to his ear. "Hello?"

"Hi, honey."

"Hey," he said on an expulsion of breath. It was his girlfriend. "Where are you calling from?"

"A pay phone."

Unlike his brother, she followed directions. "Good girl."

"Whatcha doin'?"

"Oh, watching some TV, trying to relax."

"Doesn't sound like much fun."

"Believe me, it's not."

"Want me to come over after work?"

He was tempted to say yes. They hadn't known each other for very long, but he was smitten. It was said that when you fell in love for real, you knew it. Now he knew that to be true. He had never felt this way about a woman before.

She was great looking. Blond. His preference. Her figure got the notice of every man around. He loved walking into a public place with her and having every other man there scowling at him with envy.

But it wasn't just her looks that he liked. She was smart. Smarter than him, probably. Nor was she a pushover. She took no shit from anybody. Best of all, she had a real spirit of adventure when it came to sex. She didn't hold it against him that he was a con, either. In fact his criminal past seemed to enhance her sexual appetite and excitability. Just thinking about her now made him hard, but prudence was called for.

"I'd love to see you, honey, but this business with my brother . . . Damn fool is gonna get himself killed." For the benefit of anyone listening in, he added, "Until he's recaptured, I'm just not up to having company."

"You poor baby."

"We still have a date the end of next week, don't we?"

"Sure thing, darlin'. Until then I guess my vibrator will have to do." Cecil groaned.

Laughing, she said, "But it's not as good as you, honey. Miss you."

"Miss you, too. Bye-bye."

He hung up and hurried across the room to the window. One of those skinny-assed cyclists in tight shorts and a doofus helmet was whizzing past. A postman was moving along the sidewalk, pushing his cart and stuffing mail into boxes. Cecil saw nothing to cause alarm.

If the police traced her call to the pay phone, she would be long gone by the time they got there. Cecil had taught her the drill. He had told her that taking these precautions might seem silly and melodramatic, but when you were on parole, you couldn't be too careful.

He had been scrupulously careful. He'd done everything he could to be careful, while Carl seemed to be doing everything possible to mess them up. They had agreed on no deviation from the plan. When he saw that little brother of his, he was going to give him hell.

In the meantime, what he needed to do was send the authorities a false signal. He couldn't just stay here hopping from window to window and let paranoia have its way with him. He needed to do something that would confuse them, throw them off track, make them question their suspicions of him and hopefully relax their surveillance.

But in order for the ruse to work, it had to be something daring and unexpected, something so staggering as to convince them that he was not in cahoots with his destructive little brother.

But what? What could that confounding action be?

Ezzy wasn't yet accustomed to driving the Lincoln.

He had bought it new twelve years ago because Cora said they needed a family car. What for, he couldn't imagine. Until a few weeks ago, his main means of transportation had been a patrol car. The Lincoln had all the bells and whistles available at the time it was manufactured, but he found himself missing the static hiss of the police scanner.

He had the air conditioner cranked up as high as it would go, a luxury because it could be ninety-five outside and Cora would be cold. Their body thermostats had always been irreconcilable. Not even she could be chilled today, though. The pavement looked hot enough to melt the tires as he sped north on the divided highway.

Yesterday, while going through the McCorkle file for the umpteenth time, he came across the name of the man who had been tending bar at the Wagon Wheel that night. According to both his notes and his memory, Parker Gee had been recalcitrant and uncooperative with the investigating officers. Ezzy wondered if twenty-two years had improved his disposition. Thing was, he didn't know where to begin looking for him.

He decided to start at the tavern. It had gone through several incarnations since that summer. As he pulled into the deserted parking lot, he saw it was now called, simply, Blowhard. Ezzy wouldn't hazard to guess why.

The interior was as dark at noon as it was at midnight, but it was much quieter. The present bartender was watching a soap opera on a portable TV while he polished glasses, getting ready for the happy-hour crowd that would descend at four o'clock.

"Parker Gee?" he said after serving Ezzy a complimentary glass of iced tea. "That goes way back. Last I heard he had left Blewer. But I believe he still has family in town."

Ezzy returned home and got out the latest edition of the local telephone directory. He realized he could have started there, but what the hell? Actually driving out to the bar had made it seem more like an official investigation and had given him something to do besides fret over Cora's African violets in the kitchen window, which weren't looking too good.

After a few unsuccessful attempts, he connected with a second cousin. "Parker's in the chest hospital up at Big Sandy."

So today Ezzy was making the trip. He arrived shortly after eleven. The patient he sought had only a portion of his lungs left. Cancer and a desperate operation had taken the rest. If he hadn't been looking for him, he wouldn't have recognized the man in the hospital bed as the formerly robust owner of the Wagon Wheel.

Ezzy reintroduced himself. Unfortunately, pending mortality hadn't made Gee any friendlier. "Yeah, I remember you. Thought you'd be dead by now."

Ezzy was kind enough not to point out that although he had twenty years on the man, it was Gee who had one foot in the grave. "No, just retired."

"Then what brings you all the way up here? This goddamn hospital is hardly a tourist attraction."

Fearing Gee would croak before he could answer his questions, Ezzy got to the point. "I wanted to talk to you about Patsy McCorkle."

"Ain't you given up on that yet?"

"Not yet."

Gee coughed into a handkerchief. "What do you want to know?"

"Anything."

"I ain't got much time. Why should I waste what little breath I've got left on ancient history?"

Ezzy just stared at him, calmly threading the brim of his straw hat through his fingers. Finally Gee cursed beneath his breath and took a sip of water. "She was a slut."

"That much I know."

"There ain't nothing else to tell. I had me a piece of her a few times. Want to hear about what a good fuck she was?" He laughed until a fit of coughing overtook the laughter.

Ezzy would have felt badly about causing this much distress to a dying man, and probably would have desisted if it were anyone else. But Gee was such an unlikable individual that it was difficult to work up any compassion for him. When his coughs subsided, Ezzy continued. "What do you recall of the Herbolds?"

"Just that they were wild. Good-looking boys, but meaner than sin. Every time they came into my place they left drunk, but then so did most of my clientele. Roughnecks. Loggers. Truckers. The real blue-collar crowd was who I catered to."

He exchanged the handkerchief for a heavier towel and held it to his mouth as he hawked up some awful-looking gunk. Ezzy gave him a modicum of privacy by gazing out the window at the heat waves shimmering off the parking lot.

His next words came out as a gasp. "What're you thinking? That Carl's gonna come looking for you, get revenge for a crime you tried to pin on him?"

"So you heard about his escape?"

"Hell, yeah."

Gee barely had enough breath to speak. He was in bad shape and seemed to be getting worse by the minute. If he were about to die, Ezzy needed to get as much information as he could from him.

"Strange that you should say I tried to pin a crime on them. Don't you think the Herbolds had anything to do with Patsy's demise?"

"They could've. But maybe they didn't. How the hell should I know?"

"I'm only asking for an opinion," Ezzy replied, refusing to be goaded by the man's querulousness.

"Look, I already said that Patsy was a flirt."

"You said she was a slut."

"Same damn thing, ain't it?"

"Not exactly."

Staring hard at Ezzy, he took several labored breaths. "She liked men, okay? The more men, the better. She got passed around and she liked it. But some guys might not cotton to sharing. You see what I'm getting at?"

"Jealousy."

Gee staved off a coughing fit by taking another sip of water. "If a man was the jealous sort, he wouldn't have liked what he saw that night."

"Did you?"

"What?"

"Dislike what you saw?"

Gee's laugh was a horrible sound. It prompted another cough, which turned into retching, which required him to reach for the small plastic basin on the bed table. After spitting into it several times, he cackled. "You coming to arrest me, Hardge?"

"No, I know you never left the bar that night."

"You asked?"

"Sure did. But if you put your mind to it, you might remember one of Patsy's jealous lovers who was there that night."

"She'd had just about every man in the place at one time or another. Any one of them might've been upset by the way she was carrying on with Carl and Cecil."

"Nobody in particular stands out in your mind?"

"Nope."

"Nobody she had spurned in favor of the Herbolds?"

Holding the towel to his mouth again, he shook his head no.

"Nobody she had a conversation or argument with?"

He thought about that for a moment, then shook his head impatiently. "No. Look, like everybody told you before, she was with the Herbolds. She left with them. They must've did her. Now, will you leave and let me die in peace?"

Ezzy came to his feet. "Thanks for your time. I didn't count on anything from you, but it was worth a try. The slightest little thing might've helped."

"Helped with what?"

"My peace of mind."

"What's the matter, Hardge? 'Fraid you've been barking up the wrong tree for the last twenty years?" He started coughing hard enough to bring tears to his eyes, and, although it was awfully uncharitable of him, Ezzy thought his discomfort served him right.

He backed toward the door. "If you think of anything, I'm in the Blewer phone book. Good luck to you."

He left the hospital and pulled the Lincoln back onto the highway for the drive home. It had been a long, depressing, and fruitless trip. He hadn't expected a miracle. But just once he would like to experience a breakthrough in this case.

Doors had been shut on it from the morning the body was discovered.

Blewer police had given the case over entirely to him because it had taken place outside city limits. He had received only temporary and lackluster cooperation from the FBI because Patsy's death wasn't officially classified as a murder and there was no evidence of a kidnapping. Other law enforcement agencies from which he had asked assistance really went soft on him when the Herbolds were indicted in Arkansas for armed robbery and murder.

The prime suspects were behind bars and on their way to long prison terms. So what did it matter? Where was the urgency? Other girls were being assaulted, raped, and killed every day, and their assailants were still at large. His perps were in custody. Society was safe from them. Forget about it.

In fact, that was the last thing the Arkansas prosecutor had said to him as he ushered him from his office. "We caught your boys for you and we'll take care of them. Consider yourself lucky and forget about it."

That barrel-bellied, beet-faced prosecutor had probably succumbed to a heart attack years ago, but Ezzy's case was still unclosed and he hadn't forgotten about it. The file on it was residing in the rolltop desk once belonging to his daddy. Because of it his wife had left him, predicting that it would kill him.

Nevertheless he returned to it with the resignation of a hopeless addict. Some men had a weakness for liquor. Others couldn't resist gambling. Even more liked women too well.

This was what Ezzy couldn't resist. This was what seduced him. This was his passion.

Chapter Twenty-Two

"*S*crambled okay?"

"Sure, Jack. I didn't know you could cook." David was setting the breakfast table.

"I wanted to eat so I had to learn."

"Didn't you have a mom to cook for you?"

"She died a long time ago. While I was still a boy." Jack cracked several eggs into a mixing bowl and opened a drawer in search of a whisk.

"Do you have a dad?"

"No."

"Did he die like my dad?"

"Hmm."

"Is Grandpa gonna die, Jack?"

He turned, giving the boy the attention his question deserved. "I don't know, David. I hope not. But he's very sick."

David furrowed his brow and mulled it over. "I wish people didn't have to die."

"Yeah, so do I."

"Guess what, Mom?" The boy's face brightened as he looked beyond Jack toward the doorway. "Jack can cook. He's making me eggs."

Anna was fresh from a shower. Her hair was still damp, but she was dressed in a casual blouse and skirt. She had napped on and off throughout the night, but the rest hadn't been adequate. There were faint circles beneath her eyes.

When the day shift of nurses came on at seven that morning, they ran a check of Delray's vital signs and reported to them in the waiting room that his condition was unchanged.

After his rounds, the doctor updated them. "He didn't get any worse during the night. That's good. This morning we'll be putting him through several tests, and for some of them he'll be slightly sedated. Now would be a good time for you to go home and catch some Z's, because the earliest you'll be able to see him is after lunch."

Even then, Anna was reluctant to leave the hospital. She agreed to go home only after getting the CCU nurse's pledge that she would be called if Delray's condition changed. She looked refreshed by her shower, but her face still showed signs of emotional and physical strain. She also seemed not a little put out that her kitchen had been invaded.

"David was hungry," Jack said by way of explanation. "He was ready for his breakfast, so we started without you. The coffee is ready."

The promise of hot, fresh coffee disarmed her. She poured herself a cup while Jack added a couple more eggs to the bowl and then poured them into a hot skillet. A few minutes later he served them to Anna and David. David shoved a forkful into his mouth and sputtered through the food, "These are the best eggs I've ever ate."

Anna tried to look insulted, but David knew she was pretending and they all laughed.

"Can I join the party?"

Startled, Jack wheeled about. Standing in the utility room doorway was a man in his midforties. Medium height. Nice looking. Hesitant, apologetic smile. "No one answered the front doorbell, so I came on around and let myself in through the back door."

Jack knew he was lying. Even if they hadn't heard the bell, they would have seen Anna's light flashing. Ungraciously, he asked, "Can I help you?"

"Is Delray Corbett here? Does he still live here? His name's on the gate."

"He lives here. He's not at home."

"He's in the hospital." That from David, who had left his chair to stare curiously at the visitor, who in turn was looking curiously at him.

Jack wished he could think of a way to shush David without its being obvious.

"Hospital?" The man made a pained expression. "Jeez. I hope it's not serious."

"He might die—"

"Not too serious."

Jack and David spoke at the same time, contradicting one another.

The man looked at Jack with a mix of reproach and inquisitiveness. Jack looked back.

Jack won. The man relented first and said, "My name's Cecil Herbold. I'm Mr. Corbett's stepson."

Anna had moved into place behind David, settling her hands on his shoulders with instinctual maternal protectiveness. Jack felt similarly protective toward her and the boy. He stepped partially in front of her, separating her and David from the elder Herbold.

"What do you want?"

"To see my stepdaddy."

"He's not allowed visitors. In any case, I'm not sure he would want to see you."

Jack could practically see the chip rising on Herbold's shoulder. "If you don't mind me asking, who are you to say?"

"It's not for me to say. Why don't you ask Anna?"

"Anna?" Herbold looked her over.

"Dean Corbett's widow."

Jack thought Herbold's shock was genuine. "Widow? You're telling me Dean is dead?"

"For six years."

"You don't say? What happened to him?"

Jack gave him a brief explanation.

"Bet that nearly killed Delray. He set such store by that boy. More than he did Carl and me, that's for sure. 'Course we gave him hell." Looking at Anna, he said, "Sure am sorry to hear about Dean, ma'am. That's a damn shame."

Anna acknowledged the condolence with a curt nod.

"So who's this?" Herbold asked, smiling down at David. "This Dean's kid?" He squatted down in front of the boy. "How are you, son? I'm your . . . Hell, what am I?" he chuckled. "Step-uncle I guess."

No longer garrulous, David must have sensed that Cecil Herbold was nobody he wanted to know. Saying nothing, he shrank back against Anna's legs. Herbold rose and addressed Anna with a wide smile. "He's a cute kid. I can see Dean in him."

She hesitated, then signed a thank-you.

Cecil went slack-jawed. He looked at Jack. "She's . . ."

"Deaf."

Herbold's eyes moved back to her. "Huh. Imagine that. But she knew what I was saying."

"She read your lips."

"Well, I'll swan. Isn't that something? She reads lips. I admire a person like you, Anna. Truly I do."

Jack wasn't buying one word of this polite bullshit Cecil was trying to sell them. He wanted the ex-con out of the house and away from Anna and David. "We'll tell Delray you stopped by."

Smiling at Jack easily, he said, "I thought you said I should ask Anna if Delray wanted to see me."

Jack angled his head back toward her. "Be my guest."

Cecil raised his eyebrows in query. "What do you think, ma'am?"

She shook her head no.

Easy smile still in place, he said, "Well, I haven't got anything else to do, so I think I'll take my chances and go to the hospital, try and see him."

"He won't welcome you," Jack told him.

Herbold looked him up and down. "Thanks for the word of warning, uh . . . What was your name?"

"Jack Sawyer."

"Do I know you?"

"No."

"Huh. You married to her, to, uh, Anna now?"

"I'm the hired hand."

"Oh, the hired hand," he repeated, dragging the words out and letting his inflection imply that Jack didn't have a vote regarding who went where when. He took a stroll around the kitchen, taking in every aspect of it, from the bordered wallpaper to the dishes neatly stacked in the glass-paneled cabinets. "Looks different than when I lived here. Did you know I used to live here, David?"

The boy shook his head.

"Didn't your grandpa ever tell you about me and my brother Carl?"

Again David shook his head no.

"No? Oh, yeah, Carl and me ran wild as Indians all over this place." Coming back around to the huddled trio, he said, "It just breaks my heart the way that old man turned his back on us and shut us out of his life."

He gave a sad sigh, then clapped his hands together. "But that's what I hope to fix while I'm here. I came to mend fences. So, I'll be getting on my way and let y'all go back to your breakfast."

He backed up toward the open door connecting to the laundry room. "Pleased to meet you, Anna." He spoke louder than normal, as though volume would penetrate her deafness. "Catch you later, David," he said, winking at the boy. Jack he ignored.

As soon as he passed through the back door, Jack followed. Through the window in the door, he saw Herbold climbing into a ten-year-old Mustang. He was alone. Jack watched him make a careful turn and head for the front of the property. He locked and bolted the door, then jogged through the kitchen, down the center hall, and watched through the front window until Herbold had cleared the gate and was no longer in sight. He bolted the front door, too.

When he turned, Anna was standing there looking as anxious as he felt. It seemed Herbold's visit had robbed them all of appetite. Breakfast had been forgotten. He forced himself to smile for David's benefit. "Hey, Rocket Ranger, have you made your bed this morning?"

"I didn't sleep in my bed last night, Jack."

"Oh, yeah, right."

He looked helplessly toward Anna, who signed something to her son. "It's not time for my programs, Mom," he whined. She signed more. "But *Sesame Street* is for babies." She made a shooing motion with her hands. David, rolling his eyes, went into the living room and turned on the television set.

Jack pulled Anna down beside him on the bottom step of the staircase. He looked earnestly into her eyes. "You should take David and leave."

She stared at him, aghast.

"Go . . . somewhere. Galveston. San Antonio. Somewhere David would enjoy."

She started to get up, but he pulled her back down. "Listen, Anna, listen." He clasped her hands between his before she could indicate to him that she couldn't listen. "You know what I mean," he said impatiently. "Why do you think Cecil Herbold showed up here this morning?"

She shrugged and shook her head, at a loss for an answer.

"I don't know either, but I don't like it. I've been reading about these guys in the newspaper. They're trouble. Delray wouldn't want him lurking around. He wouldn't like it at all, especially with Carl on the loose. I'm going to call the hospital and tell them that under no circumstances are they to let Cecil in to see Delray. You agree?"

"*Yes.*"

"Go get packed and take your luggage with you. You can stop at the hospital for a brief visit with Delray and then leave from there."

She signed what he knew to be an objection to his plan.

"It isn't safe here, Anna," he argued. "Delray was afraid Carl would come here. I think that's one reason he hired me. To have some extra protection around the place. He would want you and David out of danger. I'm acting on his behalf, telling you to do what I think Delray would tell you."

She got up and moved quickly into the office beneath the stairs. Jack followed her. She was writing on a pad. "I will not leave Delray. I will not!"

"These guys are killers, Anna."

She wrote, "I wasn't born yesterday."

"No. Just deaf."

She flung the notepad aside and tried to move past him, but he caught her by the shoulders. "I'm sorry, I'm sorry. That was a stupid, thoughtless thing to say." Her face remained angry and closed. He pressed his fingers tighter around her shoulders. "Delray would never forgive himself if you and David got hurt. I wouldn't forgive myself if you got hurt. Let me help you."

Wriggling free, she backed away from him and picked up the notepad again. When she had finished writing, she turned the spiral booklet toward him. "Delray didn't trust you. Why should I?"

Chapter Twenty-Three

C arl's piss factor was at an all-time high.

The vacant fishing cabin where he and Myron had taken shelter stank of stagnant creek water and mildew. He supposed they were lucky to have found it at all, but its only attributes were its isolation and a roof that provided shade from the brutal sun.

The three small windows and one door didn't allow for much ventilation, so the heat was enough to make a saint yearn for Hell. The mattress on the narrow cot felt like it was stuffed with bowling balls. Myron's farts were so noxious they could be bottled and used for chemical warfare.

Was it any wonder he was in a bad mood?

His misery was such that he was beginning to doubt his decision to include Cecil in his plan. Maybe he should have gone this one alone. After all, this was the big granddaddy of his career, his—what did they call it?—opus? Yeah, this was his opus. His grand finale.

If they hadn't had to hang around waiting to rendezvous with Cecil, he and Myron could have been across the Rio Grande by now, languishing in a tropical paradise, a bottle of tequila in one hand and a señorita who didn't know the meaning of no in the other. Yet here he was, holed up in the backwoods, home to bugs as long as his thumb and snakes as long as his leg, steeping in his own sweat, sweltering in a steam bath of a climate.

But Cecil and his contribution were essential to the quality of life they would have once they reached Mexico. In the long run, Carl supposed this delay and all the hardships it imposed would be worth it.

It was the idle time that was eating on him and making him fractious. With nothing to do except fight off biting insects and count the endless minutes of each day, he was thinking too much. Self-doubt nibbled at him as rapaciously as the rats that came at night to scavenge in his and Myron's trash.

One of the things he was thinking was that he probably shouldn't have killed that guy at the gas station. He hadn't wanted a witness to the burglary. But, hell, the police had lifted prints off the candy counter— Thank you, Myron—in no time flat. The gas-station owner would have identified them a few hours earlier, that's all. They still would have had a good head start. Maybe he should have just tied the guy up and left him.

If he had it to do over again, he might not take the girl, either.

But he got a boner just thinking about that adventure, and knew that whatever other circumstance might have prevailed, he would have taken the girl. And who could blame him? She had been his first woman in twenty years. Twenty years, for Christ's sake! He couldn't work up a hard-on for Mrs. Bailey or the spinster sister. Their saggy bodies had been a turn-off for him, although Myron hadn't seemed to mind the lack of youth and muscle tone.

But that tender young thing in the shorts and tall socks . . . Hmm, hmm, hmm, had she been sweet.

Might not have been the smartest decision to kill her afterward, though. That kind of thing pissed off everybody. The cops, the courts, the public, even other criminals. Every law enforcement agency in three states, along with the feds, was frothing at the mouth over that girl. They were leaving no stone unturned looking for her violator. He was beginning to feel the pressure. Hell, he wouldn't be human if he didn't.

His worst fear was of being recaptured. Because if you go raping and sodomizing kids, and killing them afterward, not only did you get the book thrown at you at trial, if you got slammed back into the joint your ass became the property of every other con, and the guards pretended not to see how rigorously it got reamed. He would live the rest of his natural life either in solitary for his own protection or getting raped every day. What a choice.

But he wouldn't go back to the joint. He would die first. He would rather take a bullet in the head from some redneck peace officer out to bag himself an escaped convict than go back to prison. At least getting shot would be quick and painless. Not like getting raped every day till he died of injury or disease.

Of course he would rather not be recaptured or killed. First choice would be to come out of this alive in sunny Mexico. But between him and Mexico sprawled Texas, eleven hundred miles of a fucking state that had brought him nothing except bad luck since his first arrest as a juvenile.

It would help to have someone to discuss these anxieties with. He might just as well be talking to a stump as to Myron. So even though this goddamn waiting was a necessary evil, all things considered, he would be glad to reunite with his brother. Cecil would share and understand some of what he was feeling.

"Tomorrow's our big day, Myron."

"Uh-huh." He was picking at a scab at his elbow.

"You ready to see some action?"

"Yeah, Carl."

"We'd better get up early in the morning, give ourselves plenty of time. We don't want to get there too early and draw attention to ourselves. But we can't be late."

"Can't be late."

"I hope Cecil knows what the hell he's doing. If he's screwed this up, I'll kill him, and I don't care if he is my big brother." He nudged Myron to draw his attention away from the freshly bleeding elbow. The colorless, unblinking eyes focused on him but registered little. "Just remember one thing, Myron."

"What, Carl?"

"If there's any discussion, any argument, about how things are supposed to go down, you do what *I* say. You got that?"

"Yeah, Carl. Do what *I* say."

"*Me*, Myron."

"Me."

"Goddamn . . ." Carl threw himself onto the uncomfortable cot and stared up at the spider-infested ceiling. His accomplices were a hopeless retard and a brother who periodically came down with a bad case of cowardice. He hoped to God Cecil had been cured of that. For Cecil's sake he hoped that. Because if the shit came down on them, Cecil was on his own this time. Carl was not taking another rap for him. No way.

Cecil had better not do anything stupid, or . . .

Well, he had just better not.

Chapter Twenty-Four

*J*t amazed Anna that a critically ill patient would be assigned to CCU. How could anyone hope to recover in such a busy place? If the noise were comparable to the bright lighting and the level of activity, it must be a very loud environment indeed.

Nurses and other medical personnel bustled about. Several were speaking into the telephones at the central desk. A janitor was mopping the floor while another was emptying wastebaskets. All were dodging an excessively large woman delivering food trays from off a metal cart, which she maneuvered like a tank.

When Anna entered Delray's private enclosure, a nurse was checking the IV drip. He was awake. The nurse made a notation on his chart, then withdrew, leaving them alone.

Anna moved to his bedside and signed, *"I'm so glad you're better."*

"Not so you'd notice." His eyes roved over the paraphernalia that was feeding him, monitoring his heartbeat and respiration, emptying his bladder, pumping oxygen into his nostrils, doing for him what he couldn't do for himself.

"The doctor says you're much better. You look better than you did this morning when I was here." He registered surprise. *"You were asleep, so I didn't disturb you. Were the tests too bad?"*

"Bad enough."

That's all he said and Anna didn't pressure him to elaborate, knowing that he didn't mind the discomfort as much as he resented the helplessness. The worst part of his heart condition was that it was humiliating, making him self-conscious and weak.

Besides, the doctor had already briefed her. "Mr. Corbett is doing as well as can be expected after such a severe heart attack," he told her. The angiogram and sonogram had borne out the original diagnosis. Furthermore, Delray's heart had been damaged by this and previous attacks that had gone unnoticed, probably mistaken for indigestion or heartburn. "A good portion of his heart is infarcted. It can't be healed."

On the upside, he was encouraged by Delray's response to the blood pressure medication. He was in good health otherwise and exceptionally strong for a man his age. The doctor had concluded by saying that he was guardedly optimistic.

"How's David?" Delray asked her now.

She told him that his grandson was being tended by Marjorie Baker in the waiting room, and that he was coloring a picture for his grandpa, which she would bring him on her next visit.

"I'll look forward to seeing that. Everything all right at the ranch?"

She assured him that all was well. She did not tell him about Cecil Herbold's visit to the house. Any mention of his stepsons caused him distress. In his present condition, that kind of upset could be deadly.

Besides, Cecil had already left town. His reason for coming was still unknown, but local police had assured her that he had been followed until he was well out of the county.

"Sawyer seeing to everything properly?"

"Yes."

Delray idly scratched his jaw. "You know I didn't trust him at first." He paused as though waiting for her to disagree or comment. When she didn't, he continued. "I mean, when you think about it, how can you trust a guy who shows up out of nowhere? He seemed harmless. Likable enough. But something was out of kilter. For a while, I thought he might have had something to do with killing those cows."

"But not now?"

"No, not now. Why would he kill my cows but save my life? And he did, you know. He saved my life, Anna."

Jack had worked tirelessly to restore and then to maintain Delray's heartbeat and respiration until the paramedics arrived. With total focus, he had continued pumping on Delray's chest until sweat had dripped off his nose and trickled over his bare chest and streamed down his arms. Even when Anna offered to relieve him, he wouldn't stop. He had done it with an intent and purpose beyond saving Delray's life. It had been as though Jack's life depended on keeping Delray alive.

"If harming me was what he was after, he could have let me die. But still," Delray said, his brows drawing together, "I feel like there's something about him that I'm overlooking. Something I'm missing. But what could it be?"

It could be that Jack had a connection to Cecil Herbold just as Delray did. Different, certainly. But just as solid.

Jack had recognized Herbold immediately. That she knew. He might have known him through the media attention he and Carl had been receiving, but he had known him. He had been alert, wary and cautious, the way an animal is when it senses danger. And this attitude had been instantaneous, before Herbold introduced himself, not after.

"What do you think of him, Anna?"

Because her opinions of Jack Sawyer were conflicted, she lied. *"I don't think anything of him."* Then she compounded the lie. *"I haven't been around him that much."*

She had spent all night not more than an arm's length from Jack Sawyer. She had known when he was truly asleep, and when he had been faking it, as she had sometimes feigned sleep. Why had she played that silly game of 'possum?

Because it was easier to pretend that he wasn't there than it was to pretend that she didn't get a little quivery when he was. It was a self-defense tactic. She didn't want to get hurt or to make a fool of herself.

Striking first had always been her policy with people, especially men. She had developed it to protect herself against randy young men who had wanted to experience the novelty of sleeping with a deaf girl.

The pattern had been set during adolescence. A boy would flirt with her, ask her out, then expect sexual favors in return for his charitable attention. Unable to handle the rejection, the boys boasted of conquests that never took place. As they topped one another's stories, the myths about her grew. So, although there was no basis for it, her bad reputation had thrived. Who was going to believe the silent protestations of a deaf girl? Not the boys hopeful to cash in on the sexual bonanza they'd heard so much locker-room talk about. Not the girls who scorned her as a slut but were secretly jealous of her desirability among their male classmates.

Her parents had urged her to date the boys who called. They desperately wished for her life to be as normal as possible. It seemed reasonable to them that she would have boys calling, and they looked upon that as a positive sign that she was just like any other teenage girl. They didn't know the real reason for the calls, and Anna hadn't had the heart to disillusion them about her popularity.

It hadn't taken long for her heartache to turn to hate. She assumed a bitchy attitude that staved off friendships with men and women alike. It had almost frightened away Dean Corbett. Believing him to be no different from the rest, she had initially declined his invitations. But he persisted until she accepted a date. He seemed to expect nothing in return except the promise of another.

They saw each other nearly every night for months before he worked up enough courage to caress her breast, and then he had stammered a request for permission. Perhaps that was when she knew she loved him.

He proposed marriage immediately after the first time they made love. She teasingly told him that he need not go that far, that she had every intention of sleeping with him again whether he married her or not. He had assured her that it wasn't just sex he was after. He wanted Anna to be his partner for life.

Unfortunately, his life had been all too short. After he died, her chances to meet men had been greatly reduced. She was a hearing-impaired widow, with a young child, who lived with her father-in-law, on a ranch miles from town. Singly, any of those circumstances would have sent eligible bachelors scuttling for cover. The combination of them was a death knell for any social life or romance.

The nasty gossip about her and Delray was another repellent. She caught the speculative glances of people whenever they were out in public together. On those rare occasions, she kept her head high and her expression cool and remote, as she had learned to do early in her life to ward off pity and cruel curiosity.

The gossip regarding her relationship with her father-in-law generated the interest of some men, but they were throwbacks to the presumptive high school boys. The most current being Emory Lomax.

For all her negative experiences, she still had a positive outlook on love, romance, and sex. Dean had been dead a long time now, but she could remember what it had felt like to be in love. The anticipation. The shortness of breath and accelerated heartbeat. The tightness in her throat. The quickening in her belly and itchy achiness in her breasts.

The recollections were quite vivid, actually.

She'd been experiencing them recently. Every time she was near Jack Sawyer.

She had doubted that she would ever be attracted to a man again, but she certainly hadn't expected to feel giddy and flushed in the presence of a drifter with mud on his boots and too much hard living in his face, a man riddled with contradictions.

Jack was very good with David. She could find no fault with his manners. He worked hard. But something about him didn't mesh, and, as with Delray, it frightened her. Especially if it involved the Herbolds.

She wasn't ready to panic and flee, as Jack had suggested. But she would breathe easier when Carl Herbold was once again in custody, and she knew the reason—if indeed there was one—behind Jack's timely arrival.

As for Cecil . . . why *had* he come to the ranch today?

Delray tapped her hand to get her attention, and she shook off her discomfiting thoughts. "What's wrong, Anna?"

Forming the sign for *s* beneath her chin, she then flicked it outward into the *5* sign.

"Don't tell me nothing. You were a million miles away. I know—"

"I'm worried. I want you to get well."

"I'll try, Anna," he said. "But if I don't—" She began signing, but he reached up and forestalled her. "In case this kills me, there are some things we need to talk about."

Anna hoped he wasn't going to make any professions that both of them would later regret. She was relieved when he began talking about business matters. "Don't use David's college fund for anything else. No matter how difficult things get or how much pressure that Lomax character puts on you, keep that savings account for David intact."

She promised she would and urged him not to be troubled about any of that. *"Please rest now."*

He frowned. "There'll be plenty of time for me to rest after I've said what I need to say." Looking into her face, he said, "Anna . . . Anna."

She read her name on his lips, and knew that he was speaking it from his heart. It made her nervous, but she couldn't stop him from saying what he felt he must.

"I was wrong to make such a fuss when Dean first told me he wanted to marry you. I apologize for that."

She wanted to laugh with relief. *"Delray, that's long past. We moved past that years ago."*

"I know, but I still want to apologize. It was wrong of me to protest your marriage. You were good for Dean. And good for me. Especially after he died."

She smiled her understanding.

"I hate leaving you to fend for yourself. I'm leaving you and David with a mess on your hands."

"You're not leaving. And nothing matters except that you get well and come home."

"It matters, Anna. It matters a hell of a lot if I don't get well."

Tears came to her eyes. *"You must get well, Delray. Otherwise I will have disappointed Dean. Because when he died, I promised him that I would look after you. I don't want to break that promise."*

He reached for her hand again and, this time, pressed it against his chest. He rarely touched her. He even went out of his way to avoid touching her. So a gesture as personal as this was unprecedented and proved how important this was to him. He didn't even use sign, because it would have meant releasing her hand. She read the words coming from his lips.

"You haven't failed, Anna. You've kept your promise, at great cost to yourself. No, I know that for fact," he said when she tried to withdraw her hand and sign an argument. "Living with me all these years hasn't been easy for you. Or . . . Or much fun, I guess. I've been selfish."

She shook her head no.

"Yeah, yeah, I have. It's been a much better life for me than it has been for you and the boy."

Anna had never seen Delray cry, not even when he buried his son. The tears in his eyes added yet another degree to the emotion with which he was struggling.

"When Dean died, I was afraid that you would move away from the ranch, take David, and make another life for him and yourself. You could have done that. Maybe you should have. But, anyway, I appreciate that you stayed with me."

Again she tried to pull her hand away and sign, but he wouldn't let her.

"Please let me finish. Now that I've started. I'm not very good at . . . Fact is, I'm lousy at putting into words what I feel. But I hope you know. . . . You've got to know that I . . ."

She hoped he wouldn't profess the love that she had been seeing in his eyes for years. It was impossible to pinpoint exactly when she'd realized that Delray loved her. There hadn't been a brilliant burst of clarity, no precise moment when she was convinced beyond a doubt. Over the course of months and years, it had come to her gradually, quietly and without fanfare, until one day she simply knew, as a woman does.

Neither of them had acknowledged it. She had never given him any indication that she knew his feelings had evolved into something deeper. To do so would have been cruel. Because nothing could come of it.

Moral implications aside, gossip notwithstanding, she didn't return Delray's love. She loved him for accepting her in spite of his initial misgivings. He had taken the time and trouble necessary to learn sign language, and that was an effort for which she loved him. They were bound together by their common love for Dean, and then for David. She was an affectionate and devoted daughter-in-law. But that was the extent of it.

His love for her was different and much deeper.

Had he ever expressed himself, she would have had to leave. She had ardently hoped that wouldn't happen. The ranch had become her home. More importantly, it was David's home. Delray was his only father figure, and the only family they had. Uprooting her son, removing him from everything familiar and loved, would have been traumatic. Apparently Delray had guessed the position she would take. He must have realized the irony of his dilemma—declaring himself would have meant losing her and his grandson.

So they had lived under a tacit understanding: His feelings would remain unspoken, and Anna would pretend not to know of them.

She maintained that pretense now. Bending down, she tenderly and chastely kissed his forehead. When she straightened up and looked down at him, they exchanged a gaze of understanding that was far more puissant than language. Her eyes thanked him for not driving her away by professing his love. His thanked her for not ridiculing him for loving her. Both had their dignity intact.

Chapter Twenty-Five

$\mathcal{S}$ome brainstorms really should be recorded. There should be an encyclopedia devoted exclusively to outstanding ideas so that future generations could use and study them and admire their originators.

However, if there were such a reference book, the element of surprise would be sacrificed. And basic to every brainstorm worth spit was the element of surprise. That's why this one had been so freaking fantastic. No one had expected Cecil Herbold to pay a visit to his wicked old stepdaddy.

He thumped the steering wheel of his Mustang in time to the Boss's voice growling at him through the speakers. Springsteen was a genius at what he did. But Cecil Herbold was no slouch in his field, either. No sirree. He had a real creative flair that had gone largely unappreciated.

Oh, Carl might be gutsier. Carl had more derring-do and dash. But Cecil was the wiser. He was the strategist. The thinker. The planner.

His foot itched to stamp the accelerator. He wanted to give the sweet ride all she would take, really see if she could go balls-out down the highway. That's what his reckless younger brother would do. Drunk on success, Carl might be stupid enough to get a speeding ticket. He might give the laws what they wanted, which was an excuse to pull him over and harass him.

But Cecil was smarter than Carl. He drove within the speed limit. No tickets for him, thank you very much.

Besides, if he sped up, he might lose his tail. "That joker," he muttered with disdain as he raised a can of Pepsi to his lips. Who did the laws think they were dealing with here? Didn't they know he was borderline genius?

Keeping the speedometer just under sixty, he reviewed the day yet again.

He couldn't have asked for it to go any better. It had been fucking *perfect*. That the old man was sick was a bonus he hadn't expected. Someone else might have taken that startling news as a setback. Someone with less imagination might have called it a day right then and there, given up and gone home.

Him, he'd seen it as a golden opportunity and had taken full advantage of it.

He'd gone to Blewer thinking he would drop in on the old bastard at the ranch, make sure his visit was reported by the guys tailing him, then head on back home. When questioned later, Delray would tell them the truth—because Delray Corbett did not lie. (How many times had he and Carl heard that when they begged him to provide them with an alibi? "I won't lie for you sorry boys.")

"Cecil came home to ask my forgiveness," Delray would tell them. Whether he granted it or not was beside the point. It would be told that Cecil had *asked* Delray to forgive him.

That would have been a successful day.

The day had expanded from successful to stupendous when his grief and suffering and remorse and contrition were witnessed by everybody on the third floor of Memorial Hospital.

When he was barred admittance into the CCU, he had caused a scene. Not the screaming, cursing kind of spectacle that Carl would have created. That would have been the wrong strategy. Tears and anguish worked far more effectively in this situation. Everybody in the CCU waiting room had sympathized with him when the frosty nurse in charge had said, "I'm sorry, Mr. Herbold. At the request of the family, no one is being allowed to see Mr. Corbett."

"But I'm family," he sobbed, dryly at first. Then he'd managed to eke out a few tears. "I'm family." His voice had cracked a little, which had made him sound even more pathetic. "I'm not leaving until I see my stepdaddy. There's something I've got to tell him before he dies. Does he know I'm here? Have you asked *him* if he wants to see me?"

Actually if the son of a bitch had known a Herbold was within a hundred miles of his sickbed, he probably would have croaked.

Cecil didn't give a rat's ass about the old man, if he lived or died. In fact, he was rather glad that he had avoided a face-to-face with him. He had been prepared to eat crow and go down on bended knee in front of Delray if that was what had been required to make this act convincing. But he was glad he hadn't needed to go to that extreme. Besides, Delray wasn't an easy man to fool. He wouldn't have been as gullible as the hospital security guard who was summoned.

He was a rent-a-cop who waddled over to Cecil with crumbs of his midmorning snack muffin stuck in his mustache. He asked Cecil what the problem was and Cecil told him. "Well now, I can understand why you're upset. But you're disturbing other people, and we just can't have this sort of commotion here in the hospital." He suggested that Cecil come back at a more convenient time.

When Cecil refused, the security guard looked helplessly at the nurse, who then called the local police.

The officer was old and tired and really didn't give a damn whether Cecil got to see his stepdaddy or not. But he was up to speed on the Herbold brothers. "You're in violation of parole, aren't you, buddy?"

"No, sir. I got permission to come see my stepdaddy. On the condition that I go back tonight and report in. My parole officer has got caller ID on her phone so I can't fake it. Here's her number. Call and check me out."

He had taken the business card Cecil extended to him and dialed the number. He was told that Cecil had permission to leave the State of Arkansas for a visit to his family if he were back by seven that evening. And, unless Cecil was mistaken, he was also told that Cecil was under surveillance, so he couldn't get into too much trouble along the way—such as rendezvousing with, and aiding and abetting, his brother. He was also probably being told that they were hoping this visit was all for show and that Cecil would lead them straight to Carl and Myron.

The Blewer police veteran looked hard at Cecil as he listened to the information coming to him from Arkansas. Finally he said, "Okay. Thanks." He hung up and handed the business card back to Cecil. "You've gone to a lot of trouble for nothing, Mr. Herbold. You're not welcome here. Your stepdaddy's family thinks that seeing you will upset him. They say y'all didn't part on the best of terms."

"That's why I want to see him. My brother Carl and me did some awful things when we lived with him. We about ruined his life. Carl made some mighty strong statements against Delray when Delray refused to help on his appeal. Threats and all.

"I want to tell Delray that I wasn't any part of that business. I did the crime so I did the time. I'm sorry for all the bad things I did. Carl has gone 'round the bend, escaping from prison and all. Raping that girl. He's bound straight for hell. I want Delray to know that one of us turned out all right."

He choked out a dry little sob. "That's all. I just wanted to let him know that I found the Lord in prison. I've been to Calgary. I'm not like I was when Delray knew me. I'm not like my brother."

"I'm sure you'd make Delray right proud of you, Cecil," the disinterested cop said. "But you're gonna have to do it in another time and place. Come on, now. I'll escort you out."

"Okay, Officer," he said, wiping his eyes. "I don't want any trouble."

So he had left. Mission accomplished. It would be channeled through all the agencies searching for Carl that Cecil was a contrite, law-abiding citizen. He had made a pilgrimage to Texas to appeal to his dying stepdaddy to forgive him. He wanted to make restitution—that was a word frequently used by the prison shrinks—for all his past transgressions. He didn't want to be linked to his little brother. Cecil's criminal days were over. They could focus their attention elsewhere.

And he was right about the attention.

He spotted his tail about a hundred miles from Blewer when he stopped to refuel the Mustang and buy a Pepsi and a basket of chicken tenders. Bold as brass and not caring if he was marked or not, he had pulled into the truck stop behind Cecil and parked.

He didn't get out of his vehicle, but waited while Cecil pumped his gas, went in and paid, and returned to his car with his chicken tenders. Cecil had glared at him, he'd stared back, practically begging Cecil to confront him, something Cecil was too smart to do. He had followed him another fifty miles or so before peeling off.

"Hired hand, my ass," Cecil muttered as he crossed the state line between Arkansas and Texas. It was a good cover, but anybody could see that this guy who dressed like a cowpoke and called himself Jack Sawyer was heat. The pickup truck he drove was a nice touch. No question the guy was tough and smart.

Even so, he'd have to get up pretty early to outfox Cecil Herbold.

Chapter Twenty-Six

*J*ack was asleep on his stomach, his head buried in his pillow, the sheets twisted around his legs. A solid knocking on the trailer door brought him instantly awake. He tripped over the sheet as he stumbled from the bed and staggered down the narrow hallway. He pushed open the door.

Anna was wearing a long white cotton nightgown. Her hair was tousled, her cheeks rosy from sleep. She was breathless, apparently from running. She motioned for him to come and come quickly, then made the sign for the telephone.

"Be right there."

Pressing down the painful wake-up call his cock was giving him, he rushed back into the rear end of the trailer only long enough to pee and step into the cutoffs he'd been wearing the night before. He ran from the trailer, catching up with Anna before they reached the house. Once inside, she motioned him down the hallway into the study.

David, still in his pajamas, was speaking into the telephone receiver. "'Cause if you swing too high before you're ready, you could fall and bust your head open and have to get stitches and stuff. Jack says I'm nearly ready to go real, real high, but my mom's still scared for me to. She's back now. She brought Jack to talk to you. Bye."

Handing the phone to Jack, he said, "I heard it ringing and answered it all by myself and then went to wake up my mom like the lady said."

"You did good." Jack scrubbed the top of the boy's head with his knuckles. Taking the phone, he said hello and introduced himself. "Sorry it took so long."

The caller introduced herself as a CCU nurse. "I tried to go through the relay system so I could speak with Mrs. Corbett. Unfortunately," she said, "I couldn't make the connection. The eight hundred number written down here must be wrong. I then tried Mrs. Baker, but she didn't respond to the page."

"I'll translate best I can," Jack told her.

Anna was anxiously watching his face and ignoring David, who was tugging on her nightgown and demanding his breakfast.

"I assume this is about Delray?" Expecting the worst, Jack held his breath. "Is he . . . How is he?"

"His condition is much improved this morning. At least it *was*. The nurse's aide who was bathing Mr. Corbett mentioned his stepson's visit to the hospital yesterday. He became extremely agitated. If we hadn't restrained him, he would have got out of bed and left the hospital. He's still threatening to. We thought his daughter-in-law should know. Maybe she could help calm him."

"Yeah, thanks for calling. She'll be right there."

Jack hung up and faced Anna. David was still pestering her, whining that he was hungry and asking for her to go into the kitchen and fix his breakfast.

"Hey, Captain Rocket Ranger, sir," Jack said, saluting him. "Are you brave enough for a mission? Think you can get your own cereal this morning?"

"Can I have Cap'n Crunch?"

"Why not?"

"Okay!" After clumsily saluting, he raced from the room.

Anna was staring gravely at Jack. He didn't keep her in suspense any longer. "Delray's all right, but very upset. Somebody slipped and told him about Cecil's visit to the hospital."

Raising her fists to her temples, she mouthed a curse. "You took the words right out of my mouth," Jack said, although she wasn't looking at him and didn't realize he'd spoken.

He hadn't known a peaceful moment yesterday until she and David had returned from the hospital around midnight. Without her knowing it, he had followed them when they went into town after Cecil Herbold's visit. He wanted to see if the convict would make good his promise to go see Delray for himself. He hadn't been surprised to find Herbold's Mustang in the hospital parking lot.

Parking a few rows away, he had waited in his pickup until he saw a Blewer policeman escorting Cecil to his car. When he left, a sheriff's car had pulled out behind him and followed him as far as the county line. Jack had taken over from there, tailing him another two hundred miles.

With every mile, he grew more nervous over being away so long.

When he decided to turn around, he broke every speed limit getting back to Blewer and was glad that he arrived at the ranch ahead of Anna. As long as she remained at the hospital she was reasonably safe. With his face now a regular feature of every news broadcast, Carl was too smart to show up in a public place.

It was close to sunset and none of the daily chores had been done. He'd rushed around doing what was absolutely necessary but kept a close watch on the house and on his wristwatch, growing anxious again when the hours stretched out and Anna didn't come home.

Even after dark, the night had been still and hot. The parched earth emanated absorbed solar heat like a radiator. He took periodic strolls around the property, listening for unusual noises, scanning the area for any strange movements in the shadows. Every so often he had to go back inside the trailer and stand in front of the noisy air conditioner to dry the sweat off his skin. Worry had made him irritable, and the heat only made it worse.

With every passing hour, he had imagined a new, unspeakable peril he was sure had befallen Anna and David. Her car could have gone on the blink again and she was stranded in the dark. He was no goddamn mechanic. She should have had that fuel line checked out by an expert.

She and David could have been in an accident. They would be admitted to the hospital ER and someone would ask the name of her next of kin. And she would say that her only next of kin was in CCU upstairs. No one would think to notify the hired hand who was out at the homestead going out of his fucking mind with worry.

And the Herbolds were a constant, gnawing worry. So he had followed Cecil almost all the way back to Arkansas. So what? These were not petty crooks. They'd been born bad and they'd had years in prison to become well-seasoned criminals. Cecil's stunt could have been a smoke screen for brother Carl. Cecil could have staged it as a diversion while Carl had his sights set on Anna and David, the only two people Delray Corbett held near and dear. That was it! They had been abducted by the Herbolds.

He had snatched up the keys to his pickup, ready to speed to the hospital and reassure himself that Anna and David were safe, when he saw her headlights coming through the gate.

By the time the car reached the house, Jack was standing in the shadow of a wisteria vine at the corner of the porch. He should have made his presence known and offered to carry David inside for her. He should have stepped forward and asked for an update on Delray's condition.

But, recalling her harsh final words that morning, and still a little peeved with her even though he'd been frantic to know that she was all right, he had kept to the shadows and watched her lift her sleeping son from the backseat and carry him indoors.

He hadn't returned to the trailer until he knew they were safely inside the house and all the upstairs lights were out. Exhausted from tension and the hours of hard driving, he had collapsed in his bed and fallen into a deep sleep.

He touched her arm to get her attention. "What happened at the hospital? Did Herbold threaten you or Delray?"

She reached for a pad and wrote, "I had taken David downstairs for lunch so I wasn't there, but Marjorie was. Herbold went to the CCU waiting room and demanded to see Delray. He was told he couldn't. He made a scene. Police were called. He was escorted out. That's all."

"That was enough to upset Delray when he heard about it." Jack rubbed the back of his neck. "What the hell was he doing? What was all that about?"

But Anna had no answer for him. In a hurry to dress and leave for the hospital, she had already turned away. She got only as far as the door of the study, where she was met by David, who was sobbing his heart out.

"I spilled the milk," he blubbered. "I didn't mean to, Mom. It was an accident."

Anna looked frazzled, rushed, and at her wits' end as she went through the door and headed for the kitchen. Jack went after her, reached out and grabbed a handful of nightgown, jerking her to a halt.

"Go get dressed," he said calmly when she turned to confront him. "I'll take care of the emergency here. You take care of the emergency at the hospital. David can stay here with me today. Okay?"

"Can I, Mom? Can I?" Tears drying on his cheeks, David excitedly hopped from foot to foot. "I hate the hospital. It smells like when you get shots. Can I stay with Jack, please?"

"I want you to leave. Today. You and David."

Jack had said Delray would wish for them to go away. Jack had been right. Jack always seemed to be right, which was both reassuring and perturbing.

Anna had accepted his offer to baby-sit David, all day if necessary. She would have felt guilty about leaving her son for an unspecified amount of time, and for the inconvenience she was imposing on Jack, except that they seemed to be enjoying themselves even as they mopped up spilled milk. Down on all fours, butts in the air, Jack's covered with faded denim, David's with Star Wars pajamas, they had waved her off with a distracted good-bye.

As soon as Anna arrived at Delray's intensive care cubicle, he began making his argument for her to leave town and take David with her. He looked better with some color in his cheeks, but the cause of that color was concern. It was up to her to calm him.

"We're perfectly safe, Delray."

"You'd be safer somewhere else."

"I will not leave town while you're in the hospital. How can you think I would go away at a time like this?"

"Under ordinary circumstances, you wouldn't. But Cecil Herbold was here yesterday. That makes these circumstances anything but ordinary."

He didn't know that Herbold had come first to the house. Had he known that, he might have gone into cardiac arrest.

"I'm not going anywhere. I'm staying right here with you."

"Please, Anna. Do this for me. You and David are all I care about. I sheltered Dean from those boys, best I could. Never would let them get near him. Cecil and Carl are my responsibility, my mess. You sure as hell don't deserve to inherit them. Please, Anna, I don't want to die fearing—"

"Well, how's the patient?" The doctor breezed in, cutting short Delray's plea.

Anna wrote him a quick note. "He raised quite a ruckus this morning."

"So I heard."

"Did his distress do any damage to his heart?"

The doctor glanced through the records in a metal notebook. "I see a blip here on his EKG. That was probably when he was threatening to sue us." He frowned at Delray, who scowled at him. Laughing, the doctor decisively snapped the notebook closed. "I take it as a good sign that he has that much energy and feels that strong." Looking at Delray, he asked, "How would you feel about a helicopter ride?"

Chapter Twenty-Seven

$\mathcal{M}$ ind if I go across the street and cash my paycheck?"

Russell, seated at his desk with his feet propped on the corner of it, tipped his newspaper down and glowered at Cecil. Of course it was hard to tell that he was glowering because he frowned habitually. "It'll count as your break. Fifteen minutes."

"There might be a line."

"Fifteen minutes." He went back to his newspaper.

The son of a bitch, Cecil thought as he slipped on his sunglasses and stepped out into the syrupy heat. It wasn't like he had asked for any special favor. He used his coffee break every Friday morning to go to the bank and cash his paycheck. That had been his routine since working at the garage. Russell just got his rocks off by being an asshole.

Behind the tinted lenses of the sunglasses, Cecil scanned the street but saw nothing out of the ordinary. The cops were probably still scratching their heads about his trip to Blewer yesterday. Thinking about the confusion that must have created caused him to chuckle. He wondered if Delray ever learned that his stepson had paid him a visit. If so, he hoped the old man died from the shock of it.

He went into the drugstore and ordered a lemon Coke at the soda fountain, asking the waitress to put it in a cup he could take out. He paid for his drink, a roll of root beer–flavored candy, and a hot-rod magazine. Back on the sidewalk, he strolled to the corner. Sipping his drink through a straw, he waited for the light to change.

He crossed the street, then doubled back on the opposite side. He paused in the shade in front of the bank to finish his lemon Coke, then, like any model citizen, placed the empty cup in the trash can conveniently provided by the local Rotarians.

Compared to the blistering heat outside, the air-conditioned bank lobby felt like the Klondike. He removed his sunglasses and slid them along with the roll of candy into the pocket of his uniform shirt, on which his name was embroidered in red.

The magazine slid from beneath his arm and fell to the floor. As he bent to pick it up, he glanced toward the door and spotted the bank guard. No more than nineteen, he had hair the color of carrot juice and plump cheeks made ruddy by acne. He was opening the door for a lady pushing an infant in a stroller.

Cecil walked to the island in the center of the lobby. He had brought a deposit slip from his checkbook with him. Using the ballpoint pen tethered to the counter with a little gold chain, he filled out the deposit slip and endorsed his check. He tried not to think about the cameras mounted high at intervals along the wall.

He compared the lines at the two tellers' windows. In one stood a fat man with an astoundingly full key ring dangling heavily from his belt and sweat rings staining the armholes of his shirt. The woman with the baby stroller was now behind him. She was cooing to the kid, trying to keep him entertained while she waited her turn.

The teller in the second window was helping an elderly couple. Behind them was a mustachioed biker in a bandanna-print do-rag and leather vest. His bare arms sported an array of lavish tattoos.

While Cecil was still debating which line would move the fastest, a man in a business suit and horn-rimmed glasses stepped around him and got in line behind the mother, effectively cutting in line in front of Cecil.

"Asshole."

The man turned. "Pardon me?"

"Never mind," Cecil muttered. He got in line behind the biker.

The elderly couple was having trouble understanding the mechanics of travelers' checks. The biker shifted impatiently in his thick-soled boots and crossed his decorated arms over his stomach.

In the next line, the fat man concluded his business and lumbered out, the keys jangling like sleigh bells. The mother stepped up to the window. The yuppie in the gray suit was tallying the ledger in his checkbook.

Finally the teller in Cecil's line suggested that the elderly couple have a bank officer explain how travelers' checks worked. She summoned one over, who escorted the old folks to his desk. The biker took their place at the window. Cecil inched forward. Sensing someone behind him, he turned.

"Hey, Ceezeel."

"Hey, Pepe."

He was another mechanic that worked over at Russell's. Pepe was Mexican and, as far as Cecil could tell, associated only with other Mexicans. They'd never exchanged more than a few words, but the guy seemed okay. "Russell give you grief about coming over here?"

"Same as always, man," Pepe replied.

The biker pocketed the cash the teller had counted out for him, told her to have a good one, and left. Cecil stepped up to the window and slid his paycheck and deposit slip across the cold marble shelf.

"Good morning, how are you today?" the teller said, glancing down at the deposit slip. "Fifty back in cash, right?"

"Please."

"Any particular way you want that? Tens, twenties?"

The mother in the next line thanked the teller and wheeled the stroller around. As she moved away, the yuppie stepped to the window. The teller greeted him with a good morning.

The handgun materialized out of nowhere.

It appeared in Carl's hand as though by magic.

"Don't even think about pushing any alarm button," he said in the same polite voice with which he'd said "Pardon me?" to his brother only moments before. If the situation hadn't been so tense, Cecil would have cracked up over his brother's disguise and yuppie affectations. "Just empty your cash drawer, quietly and calmly, and no one will get hurt."

To the teller at his window, Cecil said, "I'll have what he's having," quoting a well-known movie quip and producing the pistol he'd had tucked into his pants beneath his shirt since dressing that morning.

Behind him he heard his co-worker say, "Fuck," which, with his Spanish accent, sounded more like *fawk*.

"What I really want is all that money you keep on hand on Fridays," Cecil told the teller. Every Friday was payday at the tire plant miles outside of town. Employees stopped by this bank to deposit their checks and take out cash for spending money. The bank always had plenty of cash on hand on Fridays.

Carl's teller whimpered, "Oh my God."

"Shut up or die, bitch," Carl growled at her.

Cecil's teller was more cooperative. She produced a canvas bag stuffed with banded legal tender. "Thank you," Cecil said politely when she pushed it across the counter.

"Connie, are you crazy?" the other teller hissed.

"Well I don't want to give my life for this stupid bank job, do you?"

"You're gonna fawk up your parole, man," Pepe was saying.

" 'Xcuse me, pal, I'll just be a sec." The biker had returned. He shouldered in between Cecil and the counter. "Say, ma'am, I was recounting my money outside, and you . . . What the fu—"

Cecil slammed the barrel of his pistol into the biker's mouth, cracking several teeth and busting his hairy lip. The blood that spurted onto Cecil's shirt was the same color as the monogram on the breast pocket.

Several things happened at once.

Pepe said, "You fawking crazy, man," and Cecil told him to shut up.

Carl's teller screamed and ducked beneath the counter.

Carl swore, "Shit!"

The biker staggered backward from the blow. Then, realizing what he'd interrupted, bravely made a lunge for Cecil's gun.

But it was Carl who shot him in the throat.

Pandemonium erupted. Up till now, nobody who wasn't directly involved had realized that a robbery was taking place. Men and women alike began screaming and ducking for cover. The woman with the stroller shrieked and threw herself over her baby, protecting him with her own body. The baby started wailing.

"Myron!" Carl shouted.

"Yeah, Carl?"

"Give us the bag."

Myron was wearing a stringy black wig beneath a baseball cap to conceal his distinctive hair. Sunglasses shielded his strange eyes. Had the guard not been distracted by the earlier commotion at the teller's window, Myron might not have made it past him carrying the duffel bag from which he removed a sawed-off shotgun before tossing the bag to Cecil.

Brandishing his pistol, Carl jumped onto the counter and shouted for everybody to stay down while Cecil went around with the duffel bag and began dumping the contents of the cash drawers into it. No exploding bags with blue ink for the Herbold brothers, thank you very much.

Myron was covering the bank guard, who looked ready to heave onto his polished shoes.

"Hey, you," Carl shouted down at him. "Do you have a gun?"

"Yes, sir," the guard replied between chattering teeth.

"Get his gun, Myron."

Myron did as he was told. "If he moves, kill him," Carl instructed.

"Okay, Carl."

But Myron got confused and a little trigger happy when two local policemen rushed in. Later, a special edition of the town newspaper devoted entirely to the robbery explained that the two patrolmen had been alerted by a passerby that something was amiss inside the bank.

Courageously but imprudently, they didn't wait for backup and instead went in alone. Immediately assessing the situation, one of them fumbled for his pistol. But before it had cleared his holster, Myron shot him with the shotgun. Upon seeing his partner practically cut in two, the second cop wet his pants and sank to his knees, covering his head with his arms. With a burst of ill-timed bravery—or maybe simply adrenaline—the bank guard sprang up. Myron shot him with the second barrel.

"Goddammit," Carl spat, sounding thoroughly disgusted with the tide of blood spreading across the marble floor. "Reload, Myron."

"Okay, Carl."

Cecil zipped the duffel bag. "Ready. Let's get the hell out of here."

"I don't think so."

Connie the teller was now cupping a pistol between her hands. But she didn't address the warning to Cecil, Carl, or Myron. She directed it to the second cop, who had regained his courage and was reaching for his gun.

Connie the teller shot him straight through the heart.

Chapter Twenty-Eight

*E*zzy watered the leafy plant in the living room window. He had given up on the African violets. They were goners. As for the living room plant, he didn't have the faintest idea what it was called or whether or not it needed watering. Maybe he had already overwatered it. But when Cora came back, she might take the African violet decimation better if at least one of her plants had survived.

Ezzy always thought in terms of "when she came back." Not "if she came back." He hadn't allowed himself to think that she wouldn't.

He hadn't allowed himself to get too depressed over yesterday's wasted trip to see Parker Gee, either. His visit to the dying man had used up a day; that had been the extent of its value to him.

Well, that and the decision it had forced him to make: He was dropping the McCorkle case.

It was over for him. He was calling it quits. For the last twenty-two years he had been chasing his tail. He was tired. Through. Finished. He wanted his life back. He wanted his wife back. It was over. Forget about it.

This morning he had awakened with renewed resolve to expunge it from his consciousness. Of course, he didn't delude himself that this was going to be an easy withdrawal. Breaking a twenty-two-year-old habit was no small feat. Keeping busy at something else would be key. So he had moved from room to room trying to remember the million and one projects on Cora's "honey do" list that he had never gotten around to doing.

Thus far he had repaired the cord on the floor lamp in the den. He had oiled the hinges on the back door. He had replaced the casters beneath the legs of the sofa and had determined that no way in hell did he know

how to stop the ceiling fan in the bedroom from wobbling. He scheduled an electrician to fix that.

Problem was, Cora ran a tight ship, so Ezzy quickly ran out of
projects.

After watering the unidentified plant, boredom set in with a
vengeance. Was he hungry? Maybe. Should he go to the Busy Bee for
lunch? The same crowd would be there. Same nosy questions. He
wasn't in the mood.

So he heated up a can of Wolf brand chili and carried a bowl of it and
some crackers into the den. He turned on the TV set just for the background noise, finding comfort in any human voice. Way behind on his
reading, he picked up a three-month-old edition of *Reader's Digest* and
scanned the index looking for something to spark his interest.

He was well into the account of a man being swallowed by a whale
like the Sunday school story of Jonah when the local noon news came
on. The lead story was of a bank holdup that had left two policemen, a
bank guard, and a customer dead. The thieves had escaped with an
undisclosed amount of money. Although the community was small, it
was a rich bank because of the nearby industry—a tire factory.

Security cameras helped identify the robbers as prison escapees
Myron Hutts and Carl Herbold, along with Herbold's brother Cecil, a
parolee who lived and worked in the town.

Astonishingly, bank employee Connie Skaggs had also participated
in the robbery. The thirty-two-year-old childless divorcee, described by
a co-worker as "just a regular person," was captured on videotape fatally
shooting one of the policemen.

"We're confident of catching these killers and bringing them to justice," said the emotional chief of police, who had lost half his force
when two of his four officers tried to thwart the robbers. "You don't go
shootin' cops in this town and get away with it."

The Herbolds and their accomplices were to be considered armed
and extremely dangerous. Ezzy's chili cooled as he listened to the report
about the net that law enforcement agencies had thrown over Arkansas,
the northwestern corner of Louisiana, and northeast Texas.

The reporter on the scene then returned control of the broadcast to
the anchorman, who introduced a psychologist. Dr. Something-or-
Other launched into a monotonal lecture on the traumatic toll such a
violent event takes on witnesses and the families of victims.

Ezzy muted the sound. Mechanically spooning the tepid chili into his
mouth, he stared at the silent television screen. The psychologist's seg-
ment was followed by a diaper commercial. That preceded one featur-
ing a woman showing off her daisy-fresh toilet to an envious neighbor.

Like an old firewagon horse, Ezzy was charged and ready to run. His earlier resolve was as dim a memory as the necktie he got last Father's Day. Minutes ago, his spirit had had the wherewithal of a couch potato. Now it felt energized, eager, pumped.

He had been the first lawman to tussle with the Herbold brothers. He had been the first peace officer to jail them. Now they had committed a violent crime in a neighboring state and were on the lam.

Carl and Cecil had been mean boys. Psychologists would probably attribute their meanness to being without a father during their formative years, to their weak and passive mother, to their harsh stepfather who had tried to discipline them but hadn't loved them. Was it any wonder they'd been ornery youngsters?

But they were men now. Accountable. Now they were being mean because they liked it. After this morning's holdup and murder, they had nothing to lose. Men who were going for broke were the most dangerous. The Herbolds needed to be caught before they hurt someone else.

Suddenly Ezzy was on his feet. He carried his chili bowl into the kitchen and splashed cold water over it. The water instantly congealed the chili grease into an orange wax, but Ezzy left it in the sink that way.

Grabbing his hat, he was out the door and into his car in seconds, moving with more vigor and sense of purpose than he had since it was suggested that he retire.

The central room at the sheriff's department was empty save for one officer manning the telephone. He broke a smile when he saw Ezzy. "Hey, Ezzy. What brings you 'round?"

"Hey, Souder. How's it going?"

"You liking retirement?"

"It's okay."

"Take some gettin' used to, I guess."

"I guess. Is your new boss in?"

"Yeah, yeah," the officer replied. "Just came back from lunch over to the café. Brought back a piece of Lucy's coconut cream pie."

"Think he'll mind if I pop my head in?"

"You know where the door's at."

Ezzy knocked politely. Sheriff Ronald Foster looked up from his slice of pie, licked meringue from the corner of his mouth, and motioned Ezzy in. He was a spit-and-polish graduate of Texas A&M. He had won the election for sheriff by a wide margin because he was built like a wrestler and had a strong, confidence-inspiring demeanor. He was a solid family man with a pretty wife and three children; he was a deacon in the Baptist church. Sharp blue eyes telegraphed both "I love

Jesus" and "Don't fuck with me." He had a Marine haircut and, if Ezzy was right, he fancied himself to be a lot tougher than he was.

If he was irritated by Ezzy's unannounced visit, he was too polite to show it. His handshake was firm, dry, and hearty. "Sit down, Ezzy. Sit down. Want some of this pie?"

"No thanks. Looks good, though."

"I've never known Lucy to make a bad one."

Taking the offered seat, Ezzy asked how he was liking the job, and Foster replied, "Can't complain." And when he asked Ezzy about retirement, Ezzy lied and said the same.

"I'm sure you heard about the bank robbery up in Claredon, Arkansas, this morning," Ezzy began.

"The wires have been humming. Big manhunt is underway, even down this far."

"That's why I'm here, Ron. I thought maybe you could use an extra deputy."

The young man, who was occupying the chair Ezzy still considered his, fixed an unblinking stare on him. "What for?"

This was the tricky part: pleading his case without suggesting that Sheriff Foster wasn't up to the job. "Just in case those boys come down this way again."

"So you heard about yesterday?"

Yesterday? Yesterday? What about yesterday? "Yeah," Ezzy said, faking it. "Over at the Busy Bee. The boys over there were talking about it this morning."

The new sheriff shook his crew-cut head. "Still can't figure why Cecil would show up here. My guess is that he just wanted to throw everybody off track. He and Carl must have been planning this robbery for months, if not years. It was too well organized. I reckon Cecil thought a good diversion would be to come down here to see his stepdaddy."

"Nobody ever accused those boys of being stupid." *Cecil was here yesterday to see Delray?* As soon as he left here, he was going to call on Delray, see if he could get any more information out of him. The sheriff's next statement dashed that plan.

"Cecil went to the house first, then created quite a scene at the hospital. Got everybody all bent out of shape."

Ezzy nodded, although he had no idea what he was agreeing with. "That's what I heard."

"With Delray in critical condition, that's all that deaf lady needed."

"Damn shame, all right." Although Ezzy was tucking away the shocking information Foster was inadvertently giving him, in the back of his mind he was thinking, *Since when have I become such an adroit liar?*

"Well, anyway, he's Arkansas' problem now. Cecil's got more on his mind than Blewer and the people in it. I've certainly had no indication that he and Carl are headed this way."

"You had no advance warning that Cecil was coming yesterday, either."

"The FBI is in constant contact with this office, Ezzy. First sign of trouble, we'll be up to our armpits in federal agents."

"All the more reason to swear in as many local boys as possible."

"But there's been no sign—"

"There's no telling what those crazy sons of bitches might do." Seeing that Foster was becoming impatient and hearing the desperation in his own voice, he forced a little laugh and shrugged with faked nonchalance. "It wouldn't hurt, would it, to have an extra pair of eyes watching out for them?"

"No, it wouldn't *hurt*. I just don't think it's necessary." Foster smiled, and it was as phony as Ezzy's laugh had been. "You know better than anyone how strained this office's budget is."

"You wouldn't have to pay me." *Jesus, please don't force me to beg to this pup.* Although he figured that since he'd taken to lying so well, Jesus might turn a deaf ear to his prayer.

To appear less eager, he leaned back in his chair, propped his foot on his knee, and hung his hat on the toe of his boot. "It was just an idea, you understand. Wanted you to know I was available if the need for an extra man arises."

The young sheriff stood and rounded the desk, indicating to Ezzy that the visit was concluded. He was being dismissed, just as he had been by the prosecutor in Arkadelphia all those years ago. The world belonged to younger, stronger men.

"I can't tell you how much I appreciate your offer, Ezzy. But I wouldn't dream of calling you back into public service. You've earned your retirement. Every hour of rest and relaxation you can get, you should take and enjoy.

"Besides," he said with a chuckle, "Miss Cora would never speak to me again if I drafted you into active duty." He slapped Ezzy on the shoulder as a means of propelling him through the door he pulled open. "Good to see you. Thanks for stopping by."

The door was soundly closed behind Ezzy's back. He glanced at the dispatcher, who quickly averted his eyes to the paperwork on his desk. He was embarrassed for the old man who just didn't know when to hang it up.

With what dignity he could muster, Ezzy put on his hat. "See ya, Souder."

"Yeah, see ya, Ezzy. Take care now."

Ezzy trudged down the sidewalk, wishing he could wind back the clock and rethink his decision to come here and ask for a job.

Sure, sure, it would have been rejuvenating to be in on a tri-state manhunt. Being back with the guys on a stakeout, bullshitting about nothing to stave off boredom and the jitters, drinking bad coffee—it had been an appealing pipe dream.

But it wasn't just the return to that camaraderie that had jump-started him. It went much deeper than that. In the back of his mind, he had thought that maybe if he helped to apprehend the Herbolds now, even if his contribution was small and inconsequential, it might assuage his conscience for not getting them the first time.

He should have known better. Life didn't work like that. If you failed to catch a pop fly that lost your team the World Series, no matter what else you did in your career, that screwup was what you were best known for.

By going to Foster all he had succeeded in doing was humiliating himself. He didn't blame Foster for not embracing the idea. It wasn't a very practical one. The acting sheriff had been courteous. He had phrased it in the politest terms possible, but in essence what he said was "Nobody needs you, Ezzy."

Sadly, he was right.

Chapter Twenty-Nine

*S*ix Flags has this roller coaster that makes you go upside down.
Twice! Mom thinks I might be too little to ride it, but I'm not, am
I, Jack?"

"There'll probably be a sign that tells how tall you have to be."

"I think I'm tall enough."

"You'll have a great time."

"Can you come, too, Jack?"

"No, I won't be there. Want to take along your dinosaur book for the
time you're not at Six Flags?"

"Yeah, cool."

Jack placed the book in the suitcase on top of the folded shorts and
T-shirts. He ran down the list of essentials that Marjorie Baker had given
him over the telephone. "That's everything. We won't latch it, though,
until your mom gets here. She might want to add something at the last
minute."

The interpreter had called on Anna's behalf with the good news that
Delray was being transported to Dallas by helicopter that night. Anna
and David would go by car in the morning. By the time they arrived,
Delray would be awaiting bypass surgery. Marjorie had graciously
offered to accompany Anna to facilitate her communication with medical personnel and baby-sit David when necessary.

For David, it would be a grand adventure. In exchange for minding
well and not whining when he was at the hospital, he had been promised
a trip to the theme park in neighboring Arlington. Well acquainted with
its attractions through television and print advertising, he hadn't stopped
talking about it. Throughout the afternoon, during dinner and bath time,
he had chattered nonstop.

Jack's opinion of mothers had gone up several notches. The good, loving, patient ones who did this day after day deserved sainthood. He was tired, and not a little concerned because Anna was driving home alone after dark. He suggested to David that he go to bed early. "That way, you'll be rested up for your trip."

"But I'm not tired, Jack," the boy protested. "And I don't have to go to bed till the little hand's on the eight."

Jack was beat. He longed to lie down and stretch out. The hours he'd spent following Cecil Herbold yesterday had taken their toll on him. Today he'd stayed busy catching up on the chores he had let slide yesterday, while also tending to David, which he had discovered was a full-time job.

But the little hand wasn't on the eight yet. "Okay then, how about a game of Old Maid?"

They played at the kitchen table while eating chocolate sundaes. David won three games straight. Jack couldn't keep his mind on the game for worrying about Anna. The Herbold brothers had outdone themselves today in a small town in Arkansas. Cecil's long round-trip to Blewer the day before hadn't left him too tired to participate in a bank robbery that had left four innocent people dead.

Despite the extensive and well-organized manhunt, he and his brother remained at large. Cecil knew that Delray was in the hospital and that his daughter-in-law and grandson were at the ranch alone except for the hired hand. Jack couldn't think of a good reason why they would risk recapture by coming here. But it hadn't made sense for Cecil to appear yesterday, either. He didn't like it.

"How come they didn't use metal?"

"Who?"

"Are you listening, Jack?"

"Sure I'm listening. I was just trying to figure how I can get you to draw the Old Maid."

"I play good."

"You sure do."

"When the Indians made knives like yours, how come they didn't use metal?"

"Because they didn't have it. They used materials they had, like stone and obsidian."

"What's obsindium?"

"Obsidian. Volcanic glass."

"Glass from a volcano? Cool!"

"Hmm."

"How does a volcano make glass, Jack?"

And if Cecil or Carl came here, what would he do? What could he do without creating a shitstorm for himself?

"Jack?"

"Uh, I don't know, David."

"I thought you knew everything."

"No. Not near everything."

David won that game and they shuffled the deck. David dealt. "You know the other day when I had to pee and you said it was okay if I peed outside, only not to make a habit of it?"

"Hmm."

"And we both peed?"

"Hmm."

"My mom said—"

"You told your mom?"

"Sure."

"Great," Jack said under his breath.

"Mom said the same as you. It was okay in a 'mergency, but not if there was a lady around."

"Good advice. Listen to your mother." He had the Old Maid again.

"And I asked her if my penis would ever get as big as yours."

Jack's head came up. "What?"

"She said it would but I had to grow up first."

"What's that?"

"You know, Jack." David rolled his eyes. "Your *penis.*"

"No," Jack said, holding his hand for silence. "I heard something."

"That's Mom's car."

Man and boy scrambled through the utility room and out the back door. David was in a rush because he thought it was his mother. Jack hurried because he feared it wasn't.

But it was Anna's car. David bounded down the steps, talking and signing at the same time. "Mom, Mom, guess what? My suitcase is all packed and I'm ready to go to Dallas. What time are we leaving tomorrow? As soon as I wake up, or do we have to eat breakfast first? Jack let me ride one of the horses today. He held the reins and led it around the corral, but I got to sit in the saddle all by myself, and don't worry 'cause I held on real tight to the saddle horn and didn't fall off. My dinosaur book is in my suitcase, too. I already took my bath and we're playing Old Maid."

How much of that Anna understood, Jack couldn't guess. She got out of her car and knelt down to hug her son close. Then she lifted him off the ground and hugged him even tighter. David wrapped his legs around her waist and returned her hug, his small hands patting her back.

Jack's eyes connected with Anna's over the boy's shoulder.

And he knew.

Eventually David wiggled free and she released him, letting him slide to the ground. "We had sundaes and Jack let me pour the Hershey's on it. I didn't spill any. I can make you a sundae if you want one, Mom, 'cause I know how."

She signed to him. David told Jack, "She says some other time, but not tonight. She's tired."

"Then I think we'd better get her inside." As they went in, Jack tried to catch Anna's eye again but she avoided looking directly at him.

In the kitchen, she took a carafe of orange juice from the refrigerator and poured herself a glass.

David was still chattering. "Guess what we had for dinner, Mom? Hot dogs. Jack makes good hot dogs. He's going to teach me how to play checkers so I can surprise Grandpa when he comes home."

Anna's smile slipped. Quickly she turned to place her empty juice glass in the sink.

"Know what, David?" Jack said. "I think she's tuckered out. I know I am. What say we all go to bed? Why don't you walk your mom upstairs? I'll lock up before I leave."

"The sooner I go to bed, the sooner I can get up, right, Jack?"

"You bet."

David slipped his hand into Anna's. "Come on, Mom. I'll take care of you."

Anna stroked his cheek, but David seemed not to notice the tears shining in her eyes.

"Good night, Jack."

"Sleep tight, David. See you in the morning."

Jack cleaned up the sticky sundae dishes and placed them in the dishwasher. He left the kitchen to take some damp dish towels into the utility room. When he returned, he was surprised to see Anna there.

She looked weary and fatigued, her spirit as whipped as her body. She had removed her sandals and pulled her shirttail from the waistband of her skirt. Her makeup had worn off, and her eyes looked watery, red, and weak.

"Delray . . . ?"

She gave a slight nod, then moved soundlessly toward one of the cabinets. Jack intercepted her. "Whatever you want, sit down and let me get it."

That she consented so readily indicated just how exhausted she was. She took a seat at the kitchen table, reaching for her notepad and pen. "What would you like?" When she pointed to a tea canister, Jack filled the electric kettle and plugged it in.

He brought a cup and saucer to the table and sat down across from her. "Did you tell David?"

Sighing, she shook her head and made the sign for sleep.

"I think you made the right decision. Tomorrow's soon enough."

She wrote that David would be disappointed that the trip to Six Flags was canceled.

Jack gave her a rueful smile. "Well, he's a kid."

"Thank you for staying with him today."

"No problem."

"I had no idea I'd be away so long. I—"

Jack reached across the table and took the pen from listless fingers. "I enjoy David. I didn't mind staying with him. I'm glad I could help."

She signed "Thank you."

Jack signed "You're welcome."

The telephone rang. He pointed toward it and asked if she wanted him to get it. "Please."

"Hello?"

"Is this Mr. Sawyer?"

"Yes."

"It's Marjorie Baker. I'm calling to see if Anna made it home safely."

"Just a few minutes ago."

"How is she?"

"About like you'd expect. Very tired."

"Would you give her a message for me? Tell her I placed a call to a funeral director. She and I have an appointment at nine in the morning."

"That was awfully nice of you, Ms. Baker."

"It's the least I could do. Got a pencil and paper?"

He wrote down the pertinent information, then said, "If I could just trouble you . . . ? I don't want to tire Anna any more than she is by making her write it out, but I'd like to know what happened. Last I heard, Delray was on his way to Dallas for surgery."

"He suffered another heart attack. All efforts to resuscitate him failed."

Jack listened as she gave him a brief account. "I see," he murmured when she finished. "Well, thanks. I'll give Anna your message."

"Tell her not to hesitate to call if I'm needed."

"Thanks again."

He hung up just as the kettle started whistling. He carried it to the table and poured boiling water over the tea bag Anna had selected, then returned to his seat across from her.

"Want something to eat?" Declining any food, she stirred a teaspoon of sugar into the berry-flavored tea and took a few sips before again raising her eyes to his. He passed her the slip of paper with the time and place of the appointment for the following morning. She read it, acknowledging it with an absent nod. "Ms. Baker told me they worked on Delray for almost half an hour."

She wrote, "They did everything they could. They just couldn't bring him back."

"Christ, Anna, I'm sorry."

The features of her face began to work with emotion. The tears he had seen shimmering in her eyes earlier began to slide down her cheeks. Jack scraped back his chair, ready to go to her, but she waved both hands in front of her to stave him off.

He lowered himself back into his chair. "What caused it? Hearing about Cecil's visit?"

Wiping the tears off her cheeks, she wrote, "Possibly."

"Did news of the bank robbery this morning reach the hospital?" When she nodded wearily, Jack asked, "Do you think Delray heard it?"

She raised her shoulders, then wrote, "I don't think so, but he was already worried. He didn't die peacefully."

Jack just looked at her, giving her an opportunity to elaborate.

To what she'd already written, she added, "I don't think he knew about the robbery, but he was afraid of what Carl and Cecil might do. He died worrying about them, the ranch, and his bank loan. About David's future."

When she glanced up, Jack said, "About you, too, I'm sure."

"What about me? Did Delray talk to you about me?"

She was becoming agitated. He could tell that by the two emphatic slashes she'd drawn beneath the last word. "Not at any length, Anna. He just hinted to me that maybe he'd been unfair to you."

Brows drawing together, she wrote, "Unfair how?"

"Uh . . ." Having painted himself into a corner, he now didn't know what to say. Delray hadn't actually admitted to him that his possessiveness had been unfair to Anna. He had implied it, but Jack couldn't put words in a dead man's mouth.

Anna scribbled across the pad then turned it toward him. "You don't know anything about it."

"I know he loved you."

In a flash, she was out of her chair and leaving the kitchen. Jack almost upset his chair going after her. She went out the front door and closed it behind her. Ignoring the hint, Jack followed her onto the porch. She was leaning into one of the support posts, her cheek resting against it.

Jack took her by the shoulders and turned her around. She resisted, but he didn't let go. "Of course he loved you, Anna, and he didn't have to tell me for me to know it. Any fool could have figured it out."

She signed something, a quick, brusque sign.

Jack shrugged helplessly. Switching from the word sign to the alphabet, she spelled out *How*? "How did I know he loved you? Because he could have taken advantage of your unique circumstances. He didn't."

Then it was Anna's turn to shrug with misapprehension.

"Okay, I'll spell it out, too. He didn't make sex a condition of providing you a home. That could be chalked up to shyness or morality or a dozen other things, I suppose. But I think Delray loved you too much to dishonor you by even suggesting that you sleep with him. And don't shake your head and look bewildered like you don't understand what I'm saying, because I know you're getting at least the gist of it."

She averted her head and squeezed her eyes shut. Taking her chin in his hand, Jack turned her face back toward him. She opened her eyes, but gave him a cold, remote stare.

"You're right, this isn't any of my business. But I see what you're doing."

Her angry look said "Okay, what?"

"You're laying a big fat guilt trip on yourself because you didn't love Delray the way he loved you." He pressed her shoulders. "Don't do it, Anna. You've got nothing to feel guilty about. You sacrificed so much for him. Your education. Your photography. A social life. Even speech. You couldn't love Delray back. He knew that. Which made him love you all the more for staying with him."

At first she looked ready to tackle that argument, but then he felt the tension ebb out of her. Her shoulders slumped. The muscles of her face relaxed, and her haughty expression became one of profound sadness. She lowered her eyes.

Although unintentional, that downward sweep of eyelashes was sexy as hell. Mentally Jack crooked his finger and summoned forward the mental image that he had kept on standby all day. Since morning, he had kept it in the wings of his mind for later recall. Now was a good time to summon it to center stage.

She had rushed straight from her bed to fetch him in the trailer. The nightgown she'd been wearing had thin straps, but it hadn't been designed with seduction in mind. It wasn't a fancy negligee, not by a long shot.

But it had looked soft and airy, not very substantial. Like it would melt in your hand like cotton candy does in your mouth. She hadn't been wearing much, if anything, underneath it.

He hadn't been able to think about that then, not with the CCU nurse on the telephone talking about a life-threatening situation. Then David had spilled his milk and Anna had rushed off, and, what with chores and baby-sitting David, Jack had been denied time to luxuriate in the recollection of Anna in her nightgown.

But now he let his imagination curl around the thought of her shape—the way it had looked in the black-and-white selfportrait—beneath that sheer cloth. The dew of the grass had left it damp and clinging to her calves. Something about that and her bare feet had made her seem fragile and in need of protection. Her skin had looked soft and smooth, a striking contrast to his hairy chest and legs. He had felt like a gorilla hulking over a butterfly.

And he felt much the same now. Standing this close, he sensed the gentle rise and fall of her chest with each breath. One small move from either of them and they would be flush up against each other. Actually, it wouldn't even require much motion; just a slight inclination and they would be belly to belly.

With any other woman, he wouldn't have to think about it. Instinct would guide him. He would know when the time was right to reach for her. He would know where to place his hands, how to touch her, what to caress, when to kiss, when to start removing clothes. With consensual strangers, he knew the protocol. He took them to bed at night and left them in the morning, physically refreshed but emotionally disconnected.

But with Anna, standard practices didn't apply. Anna he knew. He knew her circumstances, her family, knew how vulnerable she was tonight, and knew how she would hate him later if he exploited that.

This wasn't something that had just come up—no pun intended. It wasn't a spur-of-the-moment lech. He hadn't been seized by a sudden raging lust. Desire had set in when he first laid eyes on her, and it had been building ever since. For days he refused to acknowledge it, even when he noticed her watching him from the back door while he worked in the corral, even when he realized that the episode in the barn had held some meaning for her. Flattering, yeah, but he hadn't pursued it because . . . well, because he wasn't going to be here long.

And because he wasn't his father.

The biggest deterrent, however, had been Delray. Knowing how he felt about Anna . . . Well, it just wouldn't have happened. Not in a million years. He wouldn't have let it happen even if Anna had initiated something with him.

But Delray was no longer here, and Jack wanted badly to touch her. But he didn't. Because it could go one of two ways. She would either respond to him and they would engage in mind-blowing sex. Or she would tell him to keep his grubby paws off her and send him packing.

Either way, he'd be screwed.

So he dropped his hands from her shoulders. Actually they sort of slid down her arms all the way to her wrists before he broke contact and stepped back. She raised her head. His tongue felt thick, but he managed to say, "You'd better go inside, Anna."

She must have sensed from his expression that it was in her best interest to do so, that staying a second longer could upset some delicate balance, that within heartbeats everything could change, and that unless she were willing to let that happen she should immediately remove herself.

Hesitating only briefly, she quickly sidestepped him and slipped inside the front door.

Jack watched her go, whispering his eulogy to the dead man. "Delray, you were a hell of a lot better man than I would have been."

Chapter Thirty

"What's with him anyway?" Connie Skaggs was keeping well to her side of the getaway car's backseat.

Myron was folded into the opposite corner. The space between the front and back seats barely accommodated his long legs. His knees poked up almost on a level with his chin.

"Is there something wrong with him, or is he just spooky as hell?"

Addressing her in the rearview mirror, Cecil said, "He's a little different, honey, is all. But Carl says once you get used to him you hardly notice his strangeness. Isn't that right, Carl?"

"Yeah, that's what I said." Carl sat hunched down in the front passenger seat, his shoulders pulled up so close to his ears that his shirt collar bracketed his mouth and made his mumble even more inarticulate.

"Well he gives me the creeps," Connie stated candidly, as though Myron weren't within earshot. "He'd better keep those pasty white hands off me."

"He's not going to bother you," Cecil assured her.

"I'm just saying . . ." She let the implied threat dangle for a moment. Then, protectively folding her arms across her middle, she turned her head away from Myron to stare out the window, although it was dark and there wasn't much to see.

With his head lolling forward, Myron had snoozed through the conversation. A bead of saliva clung precariously to his lower lip.

Cecil wished that Connie felt more kindly toward Myron. Or, short of that, that she had kept her low opinions of him to herself. This situation needed no additional drawbacks. Having the four of them compacted into such close quarters for an extended period of time would create a fertile breeding ground for dissension. If they didn't tolerate each other's idiosyncracies, the tension could get fierce. Already Carl was in one of his dark moods.

He had removed the necktie and jacket of the pinstripe suit he'd worn into the bank. But he still had on the suit trousers and polished wingtips. Cecil wondered where he'd stolen the outfit. It sure as hell didn't belong to him.

When they had spoken in the bank, Cecil barely recognized his brother with his sideburns shaved off and his hair slicked down. The plan had been for them to meet there at the designated time. Carl's disguise had taken Cecil aback for an instant, but it had been effective. A casual observer never would have connected the buttoned-down executive with the escaped convict. That's what made Carl so damn special. He was clever as all get out.

But for somebody who had pulled off a daring bank robbery worth several hundred grand, his baby brother didn't seem very happy. Carl should be experiencing a heady rush, a high. He should be celebrating their success. Instead, he was about as merry as a gravedigger. This was of paramount concern to Cecil, who knew from experience that nothing good ever came from one of Carl's black depressions.

Hoping to divert a disaster, he tried to lighten the mood by engaging Carl in conversation. "You two pull that job the other night at the gas station?"

"What do you think?" Carl muttered.

"Figured it was you." Cecil nudged him playfully with his elbow. "Sounded like the kind of mischief that would appeal to my little brother." Less jovially Cecil added, "I guess you had no choice but to get rough with that kid, right?"

Carl turned his head, his eyes seeming to lock into place when they connected with Cecil's.

Cecil smiled nervously. "You gotta admit that was pretty raunchy, what y'all did to that girl. Not that I don't understand. Because I do. I mean, what they say now is that rape isn't about sex. It's about control."

Carl stretched his arm across the back of the seat. "Is that what they say?"

"I heard it on *America Undercover.* You know, on HBO."

"No. I don't know. Where I was at we didn't get HBO."

Cecil wished like hell he'd never brought this up. "They did this documentary on rape, and that's what they said."

"Well, they were wrong. I shot a wad into any hole I could find and never once thought about controlling myself."

"That's disgusting!"

That from Connie. Carl looked into the backseat. "Is anybody talking to you? No. I didn't hear anybody say a goddamn thing to you."

"Connie, please," Cecil said in an attempt to stave off trouble between Connie and his brother. "Be quiet. Me and Carl are talking."

"What am I," she asked testily, "invisible?"

"No, it's just that—"

She interrupted. "Long as I'm here, I'm entitled to my opinion."

"What the fuck were you thinking, Cecil?"

Although the verbal eruption awakened Myron, annoyed Connie, and startled Cecil so much that he nearly swerved the car off the road, he was relieved that Carl had finally exploded. He didn't have to dread it any longer. Now the air could begin to clear. Even so, he didn't partic-ularly like the tone Carl had taken with him.

"What'd I do?"

"What'd I do?" Carl mimicked. "I want to know when you got it into your thick skull to bring her along."

"Why aren't you asking me?" Connie said.

"Because I'm asking my brother."

"I can speak for myself!"

"Shut up!" the two brothers barked in unison.

Awake now, Myron went rooting for a booger in his right nostril.

"I met Connie at the bank," Cecil began. "You know, on Fridays when I went to cash my check? We started talking. Every Friday I'd look forward to seeing her. Then she shows up at the garage, asking for me to fix her car. One thing led to another. We hit it off and began going out."

"I don't give a shit about your love life," Carl said scornfully. "I want to know why you brought her into this. A goddamn broad? Are you crazy? I don't like it. Not a bit. Not a fucking little bit."

Whenever Carl got that evil glint in his eyes, whenever he could say an entire paragraph with practically no movement of his lips, it was time to talk fast. Nervously, Cecil said, "Connie talked about how much she hated the bank and her co-workers. How they were always sucking up to the bosses. How they were all snobs. How she wished she could pay them back for snubbing her and treating her like dirt. And so it just came to me one night."

"Like a vision or something?" Carl asked sarcastically.

"Well, yeah, sort of." Ignoring Carl's snort of derision, Cecil contin-ued. "I started teasing her, saying things like, 'We ought to rob that bank. That'd show 'em.' Stuff like that. Then I wasn't teasing anymore, and she knew it, and she said yeah, we ought to do just that."

"Satisfied?"

Once again Carl threw a glare in Connie's direction. Then to Cecil: "You damn blind fool. She pussy-whipped you. That's what happened. She fucked you into bringing her along."

"Give me some credit, Carl," Cecil said angrily. "It's not like that. She's been a huge help. Do you think we could've pulled it off so smooth if it wasn't for her? She was working it from the inside, and we needed that. You yourself saw her kill that cop."

"Which turned up the heat on us."

"Which saved your hide!" Connie shouted from the backseat. "He was aiming at you, jerk face. Besides, don't blame me for the heat. You drew first blood when you killed that biker. And this booger-eating freak did his share of killing, too."

Carl looked across at Cecil. "Seems, big brother, that the only one who didn't kill somebody is you. But that's the way it usually goes down, isn't it?"

Cecil slammed on the brakes and brought the car to a screeching halt in the middle of the road. Not that it mattered. There was no other traffic on this ribbon of macadam that wound through dense piney woods. If the road had a name or number Cecil wasn't aware of it. It was unlikely that it appeared on any map. He had boasted to Carl that the hideout he had prepared was so well hidden in the thicket that daylight had to be piped in.

But he wasn't being cute or funny now when he turned to Carl and demanded to know what he had meant by his snide remark.

"What I mean is that every time something gets fucked up, it's me has to shoot us out of it," Carl said nastily before turning to Connie again. "Did Don Juan here ever tell you about his wussing out in Arkadelphia?"

"My gun jammed!" Cecil exclaimed in a high, thin voice.

"That's what you told me at the time, but what you testified to in court was that when push came to shove you couldn't pull the trigger, that you couldn't bring yourself to shoot that guy."

"That's what my lawyer told me to say. He made me say that, Carl. You had that fire-breathing liberal Yankee lawyer with the ponytail. Fat lot of good his high ideals did you, huh? My lawyer said to show remorse, and so I did."

"Yeah, well, I'm inclined to believe what you testified to on the witness stand. Meaning, little brother, that you're a chickenshit coward."

Cecil lunged across the seat and seized Carl by the throat.

Carl jammed the barrel of his pistol into Cecil's stomach.

Connie screamed. "What in the hell are y'all doing?"

Cecil fell back, gasping for breath and clutching his midriff.

Carl started laughing, replacing the weapon in his waistband, then reached across and clasped Cecil's red face between his hands. "I was just testing you, big brother. Wanted to see if you'd finally got some starch in your drawers, and, by God, I think you have. Whooee! The way you came at me. You see that, Myron?"

"Yeah, Carl."

"We could have used him back in Tucker to help us with those mean niggers, couldn't we, Myron?"

"Sure could've, Carl."

"You're all crazy, is what," Connie huffed. But she was laughing, too, now that the pressure had eased up and everybody had let off a little steam. "Crazy as bedbugs."

Carl lightly slapped Cecil's cheek. "You okay, Cec?"

Cecil was still trying to catch his breath, but at the risk of disappointing Carl, he signaled that he was fine.

"Then get this chariot cranked up again and drive, big brother, drive. Let's get to this cabin of yours, so I can get out of these goddamn clothes. Me and the late G. R. Bailey didn't share the same taste when it came to fashion."

"Who's G. R. Bailey?"

"History. Him, his old lady, and her pudgy sister," Carl said. "In fact, everything's history. I'm looking only to the future. We've got lots of plans to make, Cec. Sooner the better. Je-*sus*, it's good to be back in business!"

"Sure is, Carl," Cecil wheezed. "Feels damn good to have the Herbold brothers reunited."

Carl turned to Connie. "I'm hungry. Can you cook?"

"Eat shit and die."

Again, he laughed and clapped Cecil on the shoulder. "Smart and sassy. No wonder you like her."

Nothing called forth tradition more readily than death. Even if the deceased had fallen out of favor with God and man, customs were steadfastly upheld. Delray Corbett's passing did not go unnoticed and unobserved by the community in which he had lived.

The morning following his death, the newspaper ran an obituary written from the factual information supplied by Marjorie Baker on Anna's behalf. The Benevolent Committee of the church was in charge of food, the delivery of which fell to ladies who Anna figured had drawn the short straws. Feeling awkward talking to someone who couldn't talk back, they arrived at the house bringing casseroles, cakes, platters of fried chicken and baked ham, and, as soon as it was even moderately polite, departed.

Delray was buried between his wife and his son with a minimum of fanfare. Old-timers were the ones who clung to funeral rituals, but it was also the old-timers who remembered the Patsy McCorkle incident and the connection that Delray had to it through his incorrigible stepsons. That guilt by association followed him even into his grave.

During his lifetime, he had cultivated only a small number of true friends. He had shunned them in favor of his self-imposed exile for the past several years. So only the few who felt the most obligated attended the service in the chapel of the funeral home. Still fewer followed the hearse to the cemetery for the interment.

Anna, seated with David in the shade of a canopy, gazed out over the handful of people in attendance. A few of Delray's former domino-playing buddies were there. She was surprised to see one of Dean's friends who had been a groomsman in their wedding but whom she hadn't seen since Dean's funeral.

When Dean died, she had thought it wrong of Delray to sever contact with these young men, who also were grieving their loss. It wasn't until later that she realized that Delray had felt threatened by them. In addition to not wanting them around to remind him of Dean, he hadn't wanted them around her. He had considered any man a possible suitor and therefore his competition.

Marjorie Baker was the only friend she could claim at the gravesite. Not even Jack Sawyer had come. He excused himself by saying that he would be of more use working at the ranch than sitting at the funeral, and that he didn't have the proper clothes to wear. But Anna wondered if those excuses were the real reason for his not attending.

She didn't see that it made much difference.

Upon concluding his remarks, the minister closed his Bible and came over to where Anna sat. "My prayers are with you and David, Anna." Speaking through Marjorie, she thanked him, and it was over.

David had been solemn and abnormally still throughout the two services, his exuberance for once stifled. He was probably overwhelmed by the foreignness of the hushed voices and soft organ music, the flowers and muted lighting, and the casket with its spray of yellow chrysanthemums.

Kneeling on his level now, Anna told him that it was time for them to leave and asked if he wanted to tell his grandpa good-bye. He looked at the casket and, for the first time, seemed to make the connection between the strange ceremony he had just observed and his grandfather. Assailed by the permanence of death, he pressed his face into Anna's shoulder and began to cry. She held him close. She didn't rush him, but let him cry wetly and noisily.

Eventually, he raised his head and swiped the back of his hand beneath his nose. *"Ready to go now?"* she asked.

"Can we go to McDonald's for lunch?"

Smiling tearfully, Anna agreed that that was a good idea. Hand in hand, they moved toward the limousine provided for the family. Unfortunately, just before reaching it, Emory Lomax stepped forward and blocked her path.

He had been born under a lucky star. What other explanation could there be for this incredible stroke of luck? He was a favorite son of the angels, of the good fairies, of elves and nymphs. Whoever the hell it was that doled out the good fortune loved Emory Lomax. He'd been lavished with it.

When the minister began the final prayer over Delray Corbett, Emory bowed his head, but he kept his eyes open and smiled down at the green cemetery turf. Corbett was dead. It just didn't get any better than this. Just when Connaught and the suits at EastPark were getting antsy and demanding results, Emory had had the pleasure of phoning them to report that the biggest obstacle to their acquisition of the prized property was being buried that morning.

A meeting had been scheduled as early as day after tomorrow. He was on a roll.

"Amen," he said, in chorus with the minister.

The kid was crying. Anna Corbett was holding him. Respectfully, Emory joined the dispersing congregation, giving the family some private moments at the grave. The epitome of decorum, he walked back toward the row of parked cars with his head slightly bowed, his gait slow and respectful, when actually he could barely keep himself from dancing a little jig and hurdling the headstones.

He would be EastPark's hero. The rewards would be so tremendous that just thinking about them made his head spin. His ranking in the company would skyrocket. He would bypass the grunt work and all the wannabes in lowly positions who couldn't hold a candle to Emory Lomax.

The bank and its stuffy president and his tight-assed heir, his unattractive secretary Mrs. Presley, all could kiss his ass. He was gone, baby. There was nothing now to stand in his way.

Well, there was *one* small matter to clean up. One tiny snag that could cause a major unraveling if not tied off.

Emory frowned behind his RayBans. He wasn't sure how to go about handling it. It could be real tricky. It would require . . .

He was thinking so hard about it, he almost missed Anna as she walked toward him flanked by a tall, gray-haired broad and the kid. He stepped in front of them.

"Mrs. Corbett." He sandwiched Anna's hand between his, stroking and patting it. "I'm so sorry. So very sorry."

Enunciating carefully so she wouldn't miss one heartfelt word, he expressed his shock and grief over her father-in-law's untimely passing. "At a time like this, words are so inadequate."

She nodded coolly and tried to reclaim her hand. He continued to hold it and pressed a business card into her palm, then closed her fingers around it. "It's vital that you call me at your earliest convenience. You'll be facing some difficult financial decisions which should not be put off. You'll need some guidance."

She yanked her hand away and signed something, which the tall broad interpreted. "Anna says thank you. She also says that she appreciates your offer, but that Delray left all their financial matters in good order."

Emory's smile faltered. "Your father-in-law was a meticulous man. That's why I admired him so much."

She treated him to another of those snooty, condescending nods.

The kid tugged on her hand. "I'm hungry, Mom. Can we go now?"

Emory could have throttled the little bastard, although he smiled down at him. "Hold your horses, sonny. Your mother and I are talking."

Well, no they weren't, because Anna mouthed good-bye and turned toward the limousine where a chauffeur was holding the door for her.

An image of Connaught's scowling face wavered in front of Emory, as real to him as the heat waves that shimmied up from the pavement. He began to sweat inside his dark suit.

"Uh, Mrs. Corbett," he said to forestall her. Then, realizing that he was addressing the back of a deaf person, he reached out and grabbed her arm, which she immediately pulled free.

"Forgive me for detaining you any longer. It's hot out here, and your boy is hungry, and I know this is already a stressful day for you, but, well, some matters take precedence even over . . . uh . . ." He nodded back toward the grave.

Anna had impatience stamped all over her.

Emory blurted out, "I know who poisoned your cattle."

Chapter Thirty-One

$\mathcal{J}$ack was heating a can of tamales on the small butane-powered range in the trailer when David knocked on his door. "Mom says we have enough food to feed an army and it'll ruin if we don't eat it and do you want to eat with us. You do, don't you, Jack?"

Jack removed the pan of tamales from the burner. "Sure, thanks. Tell your mom I'll be there."

"Aren't you coming right now?"

"Five minutes."

Jack used the time to run a brush through his hair and change his shirt. He even splashed on some aftershave. The primping was silly, but, well, he couldn't remember the last time anybody had invited him to supper.

When Anna and David returned from the funeral, Jack had been on a ladder knocking down the dirt dauber nests beneath the eaves of the house. With enviable resilience, David exploded from the passenger door of the car as soon as it came to a stop. "Jack, Jack, wha'cha doin'? Can I help? We went to McDonald's."

Jack came down the ladder. "Good, huh?"

"Yeah. Can I climb up?"

"A few rungs. Not too high. Be careful."

Anna hadn't been as sprightly as her son. She had alighted slowly and moved as though the black mourning dress were made of chain mail. It had looked too heavy and hot for the season and too large for her small frame. Dark sunglasses had concealed her eyes, but beneath them her face was drawn and pale.

"How are you?" he asked.

She signed that she was okay.

"You haven't had any real rest since leaving for the hospital two days ago. Why don't you go inside and lie down? Take the whole afternoon for yourself. I'll watch David."

She signed something that Jack asked David to translate. Hanging on to the ladder with one hand, the boy had shaded his eyes against the glaring sun with the other. "She says that's nice of you, but before anything else I gotta go inside and change my clothes."

"Good idea." Catching the boy around the waist, Jack swung him down. "You do that, then meet me back out here, ready to go to work. Okay?"

"Okay, Jack!"

"Don't leave your clothes scattered all over your room. Put them away for your mom."

"I will." He dashed inside, letting the door bang shut behind him.

"It would be nice to have that much energy," Jack had remarked as he came back around to Anna.

Smiling after her son, she nodded.

He removed his hat and wiped his forehead with a handkerchief. "This heat is something else, isn't it? Sure could use some rain."

Banalities. But he hadn't known what else to say. He had wanted to console her about Delray, but, as he had learned, those were treacherous waters. He had wanted to ask how the funeral had gone, but she could have come back by saying that if he had wanted to know, he should have attended. Best not to wade into that, either. That narrowed it down to lame comments about the weather.

All morning as he went about his chores, he had mulled over what he should do. The conclusion he reached was that he should be gone by the time they returned from the funeral. He could make a clean break. No good-byes. No explanations for why he was leaving or why he had come in the first place. Maybe a brief note wishing them well and *adios.*

That would have been the smart thing to do. But, dammit, he just couldn't disappear on the day they buried Delray. The Herbolds held a grudge against their stepfather, but Delray's dying didn't necessarily mean that Anna and David were out of danger. Jack couldn't leave. Not until Cecil and Carl were safely behind bars again.

But you've still got no business slathering on the Old Spice and going to supper at her invitation, he told himself as he let himself in through the back door, damn near breaking his neck by tripping over the threshold.

In the kitchen, David was setting the table. Anna, looking a little flustered herself, was scurrying around setting bowls and platters of food on the antique sideboard. She indicated to Jack that he should serve himself buffet-style and handed him a dinner plate.

He was amazed at the outpouring of generosity by the people to whom Delray hadn't even been friendly. Jack had never experienced anything like this abundance of neighborly sympathy. As he spooned up potato salad and marinated cucumbers, baked beans, and honey-glazed ham spiked with cloves, he thought back to his mother's death.

He had grown up in Baytown, across the bay from Galveston. His mother had supported them by working in a dry cleaner's ten or more hours a day. When she got home from work, she ate a quick meal and went to bed, sometimes crying herself to sleep. One of Jack's earliest memories was of feeling helpless to relieve his mother's apparent misery.

On Sundays, her only day off, she had slept late, then did limited housekeeping and grocery shopping and retired early to get a head start on the coming week. The grueling routine didn't leave much time for anything else. They rarely did anything frivolous or fun. Surviving consumed the majority of their time.

Jack woke up one morning and found her dead in her bed. He'd called the police, who'd called the coroner, who'd made arrangements to take away the body. A routine autopsy revealed that a brain aneurysm had burst, killing her instantly. Without fuss or muss, she was laid to rest.

His old man had shown up about a week later.

Jack hadn't known where to reach him to notify him of his wife's death. He hadn't been at the last address Jack's mother had for him, so he was there by chance for one of his periodic visits.

His father was only fifteen years older than Jack, younger than his wife by ten years, and much more handsome than she was pretty. He had derived cruel delight in pointing that out to her often. Jack was told that he had been the harvest of a wild oat. "Sown one Saturday night when I was shit-faced and looking at her through whiskey goggles," his father had told him. When informed of her pregnancy, his father had married his mother, but that was where he felt his obligation ended.

Whenever he did grace them with a visit, Jack hoped with a child's innocent optimism that he would stay. He took Jack places. He laughed. He made his mother smile. Jack could hear her giggling in the night and knew that she was happy his daddy was in bed with her.

But the happiness was always short-lived. A few days into the visit, the inevitable fighting would start. His dad bragged about the women he slept with when he was away. It was no empty boast. He had girlfriends among the local women, too. They called the house asking for him after he left.

Sometimes he got drunk and yelled a lot. A few times irritated neighbors called the police, who came to settle him down. Jack wished for a father like other kids. He missed his dad when he was gone. But life was more peaceful and predictable when he was away.

Although his mother died young and unhappy, the only tears cried over her passing were Jack's. If his father ever visited her grave, Jack never knew about it. After coming home and finding Jack an orphan, he left again, telling his son, who was trying his damnedest to be brave and not to cry, that he had some business matters to finalize. "Then I'll be back for good. I promise."

He didn't return for six months. By that time the state had placed Jack with foster parents.

When his mother died, nobody had come around with home-baked cookies and coconut cakes like the ones on the Corbetts' sideboard. No one had lent a helping hand to Jack. The only hand extended to him was the open palm of the landlord demanding the rent, which he couldn't pay because his old man had taken all the money in the house with him when he left.

"I like this fluffy stuff with the baby oranges and the pineapples in it. Try some, Jack."

Following David's recommendation, Jack tried the gelatin salad, and it was good.

All of it was good—the home-cooked food, the homey ambience, the whole damn scene. There was only one thing wrong with this picture: him. No amount of grooming was going to change the fact that he didn't belong here. He didn't fit, and he was a damn fool for pretending even for one evening that he did.

This wasn't his house. This wasn't his boy. He wouldn't tuck him in and listen to his prayers, then go off to bed with the woman. Because she wasn't his either and never would be. He believed that.

And yet he just couldn't stop looking at her. His stare drew hers like a magnet so that it became a source of irritation to David, who several times thumped on the table to get her attention, whining, "Mom, I'm talking to you."

Her nap had done her a world of good. Her tired, teary eyes had their blue sparkle back. The sleep had restored some color in her cheeks. She had exchanged the unflattering mourning dress for a pair of blue jeans and a ribbed tank top. The top was tight, but her hair was loose, brushing her shoulders every time she moved her head. Some glossy pink stuff was making her lips shine.

Bad idea to look at her mouth, though.

"May I be excused, Jack?"

"Hmm?" Distracted, he turned to David, who repeated his question. "Shouldn't you be asking your mom's permission?"

"I always asked Grandpa."

Jack looked toward Anna, who told David he could leave the table. He went into the living room to watch television. Over Anna's protests Jack helped her put away the leftovers and load the dishwasher. When the chores were done, he edged toward the back door, ready to thank her and leave.

But she motioned for him to follow her into the study, where she booted up the computer. Jack sat as he had before, straddling the chair seat backward and positioning it so he could see the computer screen and Anna could see his face.

She typed, "I need your advice."

"Okay. Shoot." The last word seemed to confuse her. He smiled, then said, "That means 'go ahead.' "

Delray had explained to him how the deaf must distinguish the appropriate usage when a word has several applications. In this case "shoot" could be used as a noun meaning the sprout of a plant. Or it could be the exclamation "Oh, shoot!" Or the verb to shoot. Or the idiom, as he'd used it. Anna had an excellent command of English. She was rarely stumped.

"Please read this and give me your opinion," Jack read off the computer screen. Having typed that, Anna pulled a letter from a file and handed it to him.

The letterhead belonged to a regional timber company. According to the letter, the outfit wanted to partially clear some of the Corbetts' wooded acreage. The company was offering to pay a competitive market price for the timber, which they estimated would amount to somewhere in the vicinity of fifteen thousand dollars. Jack whistled softly when he read that part.

While he'd been reading the letter, Anna had been typing, "Delray wouldn't even consider it. He didn't want to change anything. He didn't want the forest thinned out, especially by someone else. What do you think?"

Jack massaged the back of his neck. "Well, it says here they'll plant seedlings to replace the trees they cut down, which is good for the ecology. They're going to pay you for the timber, *and* they do all the work. You should have a lawyer look at the contract before you sign, but what have you got to lose except the trees?"

She wrote, "I can live without the trees. I can't live without money. Lomax was at the funeral."

"The vulture."

"Exactly," she typed. "I'm afraid he'll call the note if I don't agree to sell to EastPark. I must start repaying the principal. With the beef market as it is . . ." She looked to see if Jack was following her thought.

"It supports you, but doesn't make any extra."

"This timber deal would give me some needed cash," she typed. "Delray turned down similar offers. But if I don't sell some of the timber, I might lose the whole property. To me it makes good business sense."

Jack smiled at her. "Lady, you don't need my advice. In fact, I should be asking for yours on how to handle my own financial affairs."

She laughed and it was a beautiful sound. "I'll call them tomorrow," she typed. Then her expression grew troubled, and she wrote, "Is it wrong of me to go against Delray's wishes the same day as his funeral? This letter is already weeks old. If I don't give them an answer they might withdraw the offer."

"You're the boss now, Anna. The last thing you should do is defend the way you manage the ranch. Especially to me. I'm no judge on how folks should manage their lives."

She looked into his eyes for a long time, then turned back to her keyboard. "What is your story, Jack?"

He smiled wryly. "I don't have a story."

"Everybody has a story."

"Not me. And, anyhow, it's not very interesting."

Her expression told him that she didn't believe that. It told him something else, too—that even though they had met less than two weeks ago, she knew him pretty well. She had been compensated for her deafness with the perception of anyone who has lost one of his or her five senses. Whereas the blind usually have sharper hearing and sensitivity, Anna possessed incredible insight into an individual's thoughts.

Jack read the words as they appeared on the blue computer screen. "You're going to leave, aren't you?"

He signed his answer. *"Yes."*

Her eyes moved from his hand up to his lips, then to his eyes.

It might be less than an hour, or a day or two, maybe a week at the outside, before the Herbolds were either captured or killed. Whenever it was, Jack would leave. Leaving was a foregone conclusion. He couldn't stay.

He didn't look forward to it. When he came here, he hadn't counted on getting so personally involved. He wouldn't trade the experience of knowing Delray, Anna, and David. Collectively and individually they had made an impact on him, no denying that. They had given him some good memories to take with him. To most folks that wouldn't seem like much, but to Jack Sawyer it was a lot, a hell of a lot. It was the best he could hope for.

Anna signed a single-word question. He didn't recognize the sign, but it was safe to guess. "When? Soon, Anna."

She cast her eyes down, but only briefly. One corner of her lips twitched slightly with what he took for regret. Then, turning back to the keyboard, she wrote, "Will you do something for me before you go?"

"Of course. I won't leave you high and dry. You make up a list of projects, and I'll see that they're all finished before—"

She stopped him with a wave of her hand. "No, a favor," she typed. "A personal favor."

Chapter Thirty-Two

"*H*ere's what I think." Cecil speared a dill pickle with his pocketknife and pulled it from the jar. "I think we ought to lay low for as long as we can."

"How long do you figure is long?"

"Several days. Maybe even a week."

"A week? Jesus! Are you stupid or just plain crazy?"

"Hear me out, Carl. We ought to let things cool down before we venture out. You want one?"

Cecil offered the harpooned pickle to Carl, who actually recoiled. "Fuck, no. It smells like dirty feet. Who planned our menu, anyway?"

"Connie and me have been stocking up on groceries when they came on sale. Anything nonperishable. Because we didn't know how long we'd be here, and there's no refrigeration."

"No shit," Carl muttered as he drank from a can of lukewarm Budweiser.

Throughout the day his mood had gone from foul to fouler. The hideout cabin belonged to somebody Connie knew, a cousin's brother-in-law or some such nonsense. Carl had tuned her out as she explained the lineage.

Her description hadn't sounded very promising. He'd held out little hope that he was going to be charmed by the accommodations, but he had clung to a sliver of a chance that he would be pleasantly surprised.

Unfortunately, the structure lived up to his low expectations and then some. They had arrived late last evening, but even darkness couldn't conceal the cabin's defects. It wasn't much more habitable than the hut he'd shared with Myron for the last few days leading up to the bank robbery.

That was the only thing he felt good about—the robbery. At least that much of Cecil's planning had panned out. Not every bill had been counted, but they had left the bank with more cash than Carl had anticipated.

What a damn shame that it had to be split four ways.

Sitting on that much cash was making him antsy to spend some. He was rich now. Money bought power, respect, and fear. People were going to know who Carl Herbold was. From here on, folks would sit up and take notice of him. Enemies old and new would shiver in their shoes whenever they heard his name. Cash in hand was as good as a sword. Carl planned to wield it mercilessly, hacking down anyone who opposed him. All his life he'd had to answer to other people, assholes for the most part. Not anymore.

But it was hard to accept that he was a rich man who left fear and trembling in his wake. Look at him. He was eating unheated pork'n'beans from the can in a hot, dirty one-room cabin in which a varmint had died not too long ago and left an indelible odor. He was cut out for a better life than this, and he wanted it sooner rather than later.

He crumpled the empty beer can in his hand. "Why wait so long, Cec?"

"Because every cop within a five-hundred-mile radius is on the lookout for us."

"The car's clean," Carl argued. They had switched cars fifteen miles from the bank. Connie had left the second car parked at a twenty-four-hour truck stop, where vehicles came and went at all hours, the theory being that it would go unnoticed. "They won't be looking for this car, Cec. Unless you lied to me."

"Why don't you just lay off him?" Connie piped in.

"Why don't you just kiss my ass?" Carl shot back.

"The car's clean," Cecil quickly interjected. "So are the plates. But if we're on the road, we're exposed. Somebody is going to recognize us. The smart thing to do is reduce the risk factor."

"Pretty fancy words there, big brother. Nonperishables. Radius. Risk factor. You've been watching a lot of HBO." Carl hitched a thumb toward Connie. "Or did she teach you all those big words?"

"All I'm saying is that we should stay here until our pictures aren't showing up on TVs all over the state," Cecil replied. "You want one of these peaches, honey?"

He offered a can of spiced peaches to Connie. She fished one out with a plastic spoon, then picked it up with her fingers. Smiling suggestively at Carl, she took a bite, virtually sucking the flesh of the fruit off the pit. Juice dribbled down her chin. The symbolism didn't escape him, and he realized that was her intention.

Laughing, she wiped away the sticky syrup with the back of her hand, and playfully poked Cecil in the gut with a fingernail painted the color of an eggplant. "Since I've been seeing you, my table manners have gone to pot. My mama would have a conniption fit."

Carl scowled into the can of pork'n'beans. He had pretended to turn the ass-chewing he'd given Cecil into a joke, but he'd meant every word he'd said. This bitch had made herself useful during the actual holdup. Having an insider had helped, no doubt. She had also proved her mettle by blasting that cop to kingdom come; no argument there, either.

But the last thing a group of men needed when they were on the run was a Connie Skaggs throwing in her two cents' worth every step along the way. This one had a fatter mouth than most, and she wasn't afraid to speak her mind. Even more bothersome was that she wasn't afraid of him.

Cursing, Carl jammed the plastic spoon into the can of Van Camp's and set it on the table with a hard thump.

"You through with those, Carl?"

He motioned for Myron to help himself. He had scraped clean a can of ravioli and was swabbing the bowl of his spoon with his tongue. Before that, he'd polished off a tin of sardines. Now he started on the beans.

This is fuckin' great, Carl mentally grumbled. He should have a señorita with tits that would knock your eyes out straddling his lap while he swilled hard liquor and smoked an expensive cigar. Instead he was stuck in this stinking godforsaken shack in the middle of nowhere. His companions were his cowardly brother, a piece of tail that was nothing to brag about, and an idiot with the eating habits of a goat.

He didn't like the way Cecil had taken charge, either. Who had anointed him lord and master? Connie. Yeah, she was the culprit who had filled Cecil's head with a lot of crap about who should be boss.

Carl knew how easily Cecil could be swayed. Connie had played him like a fiddle. He had been easily flattered into thinking he was braver and smarter than he was.

When the time came, Carl would set him straight.

In the meantime, he would play along. He opened a package of salted peanuts with his teeth, spit out the chunk of cellophane, and poured the nuts into his palm. "Another thing I don't get about this plan of yours, Cecil, is why we're taking this route. We're traveling due south. If my geography is right, if you start in far northeast Texas, shouldn't you head southwest if you want to bump into Mexico?"

"Not enough places to hide out there," Cecil mumbled. Connie had stuffed one of the slippery peaches into his mouth and he was talking around it.

"Can I have one?" Myron asked.

Connie hesitated, then slid the can across the table toward him. He plunged his skinny fingers into the can and fished out a peach. "Oh, Jesus," she screeched. "You whitewashed freak! You ruined them! Do you think I'd eat one of those now?"

"Shut up," Carl thundered. "Can't hear myself think when you start that goddamn caterwauling. What were you saying about places to hide?"

"If we strike out across west Texas, they can spot us by plane, helicopter."

"There're fewer towns, fewer cops."

"But nowhere to take cover. Too many wide-open spaces with nothing but tumbleweeds and jackrabbits. Besides, that's the route they'd expect us to take."

Carl fell back in his chair as though flabbergasted. "Using fancy words, *and* an expert on what the laws think. Whew, I'm impressed, Cec. Aren't you, Myron? Aren't you impressed with how my big brother has thought this all out?"

"Sure, Carl."

"Cut it out, Carl. I just think—"

"Why don't you let him talk?" Connie was glaring at Carl, her expression cantankerous, her lips tightly pursed. "He could explain it to you if you would shut up for just one minute."

Rage bubbled inside Carl, instantly reaching a boiling point. Each blood vessel became a lava flow of fury. He could easily have wrung her neck, but he quelled the murderous impulse and deliberately kept his voice low and even. "Nobody tells me to shut up. Especially a cunt. And especially when I'm talking to my own brother."

Unfazed by his insult, Connie crossed her arms and harrumphed. "This is supposed to be fun. An adventure. I don't see why you have to be so pissed off all the time."

"I'm not pissed off," Carl argued quietly. "Myron has seen me pissed off plenty of times before, and this isn't pissed off. Myron, do I look pissed off?"

Myron spat a peach pit onto the table. Taking Carl's question seriously, he gazed at him thoughtfully. "Sort of, Carl."

Cecil jumped in. "For Christ's sake, knock it off. Both of you. Connie, cool it. Carl, just listen to my plan. Then if you don't agree, we can discuss it. Fair?"

"Oh, yeah, fair. Just like the United fuckin' Nations." Carl held his hands out to his sides, indicating that his older brother had the floor.

"I say we go straight south till we reach the coast. Hug the coast all the way to Corpus Christi, then hook a hard right, go in somewhere in the neighborhood of Laredo."

"Drive through East Texas?"

"We might slip across the Louisiana state line some."

"I don't like East Texas, big brother. You ought to know why."

"On account of our stepdaddy and that McCorkle bullshit?" Laughing, he looked at Connie and winked. "Should we let him in on our secret?"

Carl braced himself, knowing in his gut he wasn't going to like what was coming. "Secret?"

"Delray is in the hospital, bad off. Could die any minute now if he hasn't already." Cecil hadn't grinned this big since he busted the cherry of his first virgin.

"How do you know?"

"I went to see him."

"What? When?"

"The day before the robbery."

"Why?"

"Just to throw everybody off," he chortled. "It worked, too. Like a charm."

He proceeded to tell Carl about his escapade, re-creating the scene he had made in the hospital. "They fell for it, too. Every frigging word. Even had me a female parole officer." Again he winked at Connie. "This cop called the number on the card I gave him and got Connie on the phone. She filled his ear with what a good boy I am. Guess he knows better now, huh, sweetheart? Guess he—"

"You dumb fuck."

"Huh?" Cecil whipped his head around to look at Carl, who was glowering at him.

"I told you he'd be pissed," Connie remarked as she studied a chipped fingernail.

"It worked out great, Carl."

"It put every lawman between here and Brownsville on the alert!" he shouted. "I wanted them to think we'd forgotten all about Blewer and Delray and all that shit. Now you . . . Ah, Jesus, you're stupid!"

"Don't call him stupid."

"Shut up, Connie," Cecil shouted. Rounding on Carl, he said, "I'm your older brother, and I'm goddamn sick and tired of you talking down to me. It was a brilliant plan and it worked."

"It worked to rally everybody around Delray and Dean—"

"Dean's dead."

"Dead?"

"Long time now. His widow and son live with Delray."

"She can't hear." Carl looked sharply at Connie. "That's right," she said with a know-it-all inflection that made him want to slap her. "She's a deaf mute."

Carl mentally gnawed on the information. "What about Hardge? Hear anything about him?"

"Nothing. He's probably dead by now. So, see? No harm done."

"You forgot about the undercover guy." Cecil looked at Connie as though he now shared Carl's desire to slap her. In her own defense she said, "He might just as well know everything, Cecil."

"What about an undercover guy?" Carl demanded.

"He was at the ranch, trying to pass himself off as a cowhand."

"How do you know he wasn't?"

"Just a feeling," Carl replied. "He had that edge, you know? They might've been afraid you would show up there after your breakout, stationed somebody there to keep an eye out."

"FBI?"

"Don't know. Maybe a federal marshal. He followed me out of town, but I gave him no reason to be suspicious, so he turned around and slunk back to Blewer. I swear to God, Carl, we've got nothing to worry about."

Carl forced himself to relax. "Seems like you're right, Cec. Sorry I blew a gasket."

Cecil relaxed with a soft chuckle. "We're all a little nervous and uptight, but you've got to get a better grip on that temper of yours, baby brother."

Carl grinned disarmingly. "Never have mastered that. Not to this day."

"So, okay, can I continue outlining our route?"

"I'm all ears."

Cecil went over his plan again. "Once we leave here, we'll have two days of hard driving. Max."

"Two days max."

Confidence again in place, Cecil reached across the table and playfully socked Carl's shoulder. "Mexico ain't going anywhere, I promise."

More than anything, Carl hated to be talked down to. It was doubly insulting coming from a dyed-in-the-wool chickenshit like Cecil. But he forced a smile.

Believing he had a concession, Cecil stretched expansively. "Until then, relax and enjoy being out of prison. We've got all the comforts of home right here."

He placed his arm around Connie and drew her close to his side. Giving Carl another sly look, she snuggled against Cecil and slid her hand down the front of his shirt to his belt. The purple fingernails flirtatiously tapped his belt buckle before slipping beneath it.

Cecil blushed, then excused them and they went outside.

Watching them go, Carl muttered, "You've got all the comforts of home, big brother."

Chapter Thirty-Three

*J*ack reread what Anna had typed onto the computer screen. "A favor?"

She had designated a *personal* favor. She wasn't asking him to perform a chore that just any hired hand could do. The adjective placed her request in another category. It conjured up all sorts of activities of an intimate nature. He cleared his throat. "Well, sure, I'll help you out any way I can."

She clacked the keyboard keys. Jack read, "I'd like to photograph you."

He released a small laugh of relief. Or disappointment. He wasn't sure which. "You want to take my picture? Why? What for?"

She left her chair and brought an album down from the bookcase, but not the same one she had shown him before. Placing it in front of him, she waited expectantly as he opened the leather cover.

Mounted on black paper, the first photo was of a group of children playing with total abandon in a lawn sprinkler. Sunlight shone through the jetting streams of water and was reflected in the puddles in which the children splashed. As in her other photographs, the arresting quality was the contrast between light and dark. The technique captured the unfettered joy that can only be found in the very young, while the troubles awaiting them in adulthood loomed.

The background of the next photo was a rough clapboard wall. In front of it sat two old men facing each other across an upturned barrel, on which they were playing dominoes. The white dots stood out sharply against the black dominoes. One of the players was a black man, the other was white.

Next, a worker's hands. Only his hands. In close-up. Covered with dirt. Dark soil packed beneath the jagged fingernails and collected in the creases of his callused knuckles. Those hands cradling one perfect white rose.

A woman seated in a wooden rocking chair silhouetted in front of an open window. Sheer curtains billowing into the room. At her breast a nursing infant. Head bent. Dark hair concealing her face and falling over her pale breast. Anna's hair. Anna's baby. Anna's breast.

"Lord, Anna. Why do you . . . Why have you . . ." Jack shook his head, at a loss for words. "Why don't you do this professionally? I don't know a damn thing about pictures, but these are *good*. Aren't they? Have you ever shown them to someone who could do something with them?"

He turned the pages of the album, studying each photograph a second time. "They're editorials. Each one says something. Something important, and . . . and identifiable. They're too good to hide in albums. They should be seen and enjoyed."

Obviously pleased by his comments, she returned to the computer. "I thought about selling them for posters. Greeting cards. Things like that."

"Yes. Why haven't you? What happened?"

She smiled ruefully and gave a small shrug as she typed. "Circumstances. Dean's illness. Then David. Then——"

Jack laid his hands on top of hers, stilling them on the keys. "Delray didn't encourage you, so you stored your camera in the attic and tried to forget about it."

"Yes," she signed. Typing, she told him, "I tried to forget about it, but I couldn't. It's still in here." She pressed a closed fist against her heart. "Maybe if I weren't deaf and could express myself some other way, I wouldn't love it so much. But I have much to say, and this is the best way I know how. I want to start again. This time I'd like to try and sell my work. At least share it."

"Go for it."

"First I need a larger collection. It may take me months, perhaps a year, to put together a collection that will interest a buyer. That picture of David and me was the last one I took. That was five years ago. I need lots of practice. It won't be easy, but if I'm ever going to do it I must start now. Will you let me start with you?"

"I agree with everything you're saying. There's no time like today to start over. And you've got talent. That's obvious. It'll be wasted if you don't jump in with both feet. But since this collection is so important, why in hell would you want pictures of me in it?"

"You have an interesting face," she typed.

"So does the bearded lady at the circus. You don't want pictures of her, too, do you?"

"I'm _serious!_" she typed. "Your face says so much."

He laughed. "It says you need to have your eyes checked."

But she continued staring at him, peering closely into his face. Soon he stopped laughing. He even stopped smiling. Because she turned in her chair and scooted forward to the very edge of the seat. Then, raising her hands, she placed them on either side of his face. Her touch was so light that her skin was barely even making contact with his, but she might just as well have pressed sizzling branding irons against his cheeks.

He followed the movement of her eyes as they surveyed the individual features of his face. As she angled her head to one side or the other, her hair whisked across the back of his hands. His fingers were gripping the back of his chair so tightly that they were numb; his knuckles must surely be white, but he didn't look down to see. He didn't move for fear of breaking some magic spell that had caused her to want to touch him. He could see himself reflected in her pupils and wondered what in hell she saw in his mug that was so damn captivating.

But he let her look her fill. He didn't say anything. He didn't pull away. He remained motionless. He wouldn't have moved if Elvis had materialized out of the wall behind her.

Inching closer still, until her hips were barely balanced on the edge of the chair seat, she extended her fingers up to his eyes. Beginning with the spidery lines that radiated from the corners of them, she explored with her fingertips. When they finished with his eyebrows and the vertical cleft between them, they tiptoed across his prominent cheekbones. Her index finger traced the length of his nose from bridge to tip.

Her hands cupped his jaw as before, but now they applied pressure to the rigid bone. Her thumbs met at the center of his chin just below his lower lip. One stroked outward, then the other, then they met in the center again, and remained only briefly before she withdrew her hands, which she closed into fists and tucked beneath her chin like a child who'd been caught doing something naughty.

Jack's heart was beating double-time. Not because unique erotic experiences were new to him. They weren't. He'd lost his virginity in junior high with the class slut up against a locker bank during the one and only school dance he had ever attended. During a slow dance she had dragged him from a gymnasium festooned with crepe-paper carnations and streamers. They'd found a deserted, darkened hallway and, by the time the Bee Gees had finished singing about nobody getting too much heaven no more, Jack had been there and back.

Once while tending bar at a debutante ball in Fort Worth, he'd been sucked off by a multimillionaire's daughter who could have taken a gold medal if fellatio were an Olympic event.

In Kansas City during a Pink Floyd laser show, a girl he'd never seen before or since had unbuttoned his jeans and fondled him to climax with one hand, while smoking a potent joint with the other.

In Billings he'd fulfilled a barrel racer's fantasy of doing it on horseback during a snowfall.

These events stood out in his memory because they were slightly bizarre, at least in comparison to his other encounters. Mostly he took his sex straight and simple, with ordinary women with whom he had two things in common: loneliness and physical need.

But none of his experiences—consummated sex or mild flirtations—were as erotic as Anna's touching his face. Because she had done it with intense curiosity, and genuine interest, and maybe just a tad of caring.

Jack Sawyer hadn't known much caring in his lifetime. Oh, he'd had people extend him courtesies, but those rare kindnesses usually came from people who were nice to everybody. No one had ever really *cared* for him.

Not his mother, who had kept him only to use as leverage against the man who had spurned her for many others. Not his daddy, who talked a good line but had never really given two shits about anybody except himself.

But Anna . . . She had cared enough to share with him her dreams, which she'd been unable to share with Delray, and possibly even her husband. She had trusted his judgment or she wouldn't have asked his advice about the timber contract. She had cared enough to make herself pretty before inviting him to supper. She had cared enough to invite him.

Several seconds had passed since she took her hands away, but her eyes were still on his mouth, not like she was looking to read his lips, but like she wanted to kiss him. She lowered her hands from beneath her chin and placed them over his, where they still gripped the back of the chair like it was the only handhold keeping him on the planet. She raised her eyes to his in a silent but stirring invitation, then dropped them to his mouth again.

Whispering her name, he moved his head a fraction of an inch closer, half afraid that she would bolt, more afraid that she wouldn't.

She tilted her head. Her lips parted receptively.

Lord help me, he thought as he leaned down, in his mind already feeling her lips and tongue, tasting her kiss.

Ezzy felt like a damn fool. He almost hoped she wasn't home so he could leave without being forced into conversation, but with his conscience clear.

Since no one responded immediately to the doorbell, he took two steps to his right and peeped through the window of the living room. The TV was tuned to a sitcom. Only Delray's grandson was watching it, although upon closer inspection Ezzy saw that the boy was actually sleeping. The doorbell hadn't roused him.

Hearing footfalls approaching, he moved back into place directly beneath the porch light so she could easily see and identify him. The door opened a crack and Anna Corbett's face appeared in the narrow space.

Ezzy couldn't remember the last time he'd seen her, but it must've been a spell. He'd forgotten how pretty she was, especially now with her cheeks flushed. He recalled Anna as a schoolgirl, with long skinny legs and big blue eyes. Her eyes were still big and blue, but her legs were no longer skinny.

"Evenin', Mrs. Corbett," he said, tipping his hat.

Recognizing him, she opened the door all the way, inviting him in by stepping aside.

"Thanks." Ezzy stepped into the entryway and removed his hat while balancing a casserole dish on the palm of his other hand. "Mrs. Hardge and me were sure sorry to hear about Delray. We wanted you to know."

She nodded and mouthed "Thank you" as she also signed it.

"I'm sorry I couldn't attend the service this morning. I had business to attend to."

Devastated by Foster's rejection, depressed by the emptiness of his house, which so closely mirrored his life, he had punished himself further by returning to the place where Patsy McCorkle had died.

Same heat, same biting bugs, same sluggish river, same frustration. He'd sat on the hollowed trunk of the fallen tree for a long time, swatting at ants and mosquitoes, sipping Dr Peppers that grew tepid in his hand, and wishing he could roll back the clock twenty-two years.

He wanted to know what happened to the girl. Just that. That's all.

He didn't wish to exact punishment on whoever had killed her. Maybe punishment wasn't even called for. Maybe her death had been accidental. He wasn't motivated by revenge. The toll the incident had taken on him and his family was grounds for vengeance, he supposed, but he would gladly sacrifice retribution just to know the circumstances under which she had died and who was ultimately responsible.

He wanted only to *know,* so he could die in peace.

"Anyhow," he said now to Anna Corbett, "I brought you this lasagna." Awkwardly, he handed her the dish. "My wife would have come herself, only she's at her sister's out in Abilene. She sends you and the boy her condolences."

He had no idea how much of what he was saying she understood. Her parents had opted not to place her in classes for deaf children, but to enroll her in the Blewer school district, where she had attended regular classes with an interpreter. Ezzy had heard that she was as smart as a whip and that her only handicap was that she couldn't hear.

He had no experience with the hearing-impaired beyond watching the man in the First Baptist Church sign the Sunday morning services for the group of deaf people who came from several Protestant congregations in the county. Ezzy especially liked to watch them sign the songs. They looked prettier signed than they sounded coming from the choir. And sometimes watching the sign language made the preaching seem to go faster.

Best he could tell, deaf people were just like everybody else, so he couldn't really account for feeling so awkward as he stood in the entry hall of Anna Corbett's house. He didn't know if his discomfiture had to do with the situation or her handicap.

Maybe the former, because duties such as this usually fell to Cora. He had helped scrape up countless blood smears on the highway and zipped what remained of a Henry, or Joe, or Suzy—somebody's loved one—into a body bag. He had notified their next of kin. There his responsibility ended—when the official duty was performed. That was when Cora took over. She upheld their social obligations and attended the funerals.

When told of Delray's passing earlier today, she had asked, "Was there a good turnout at his funeral?"

"I didn't go."

"Why not? Did you at least take something?"

"Take something?" he repeated stupidly.

He'd only mentioned Delray Corbett's death to fill the chilly silence between their two telephones. He had used it as an excuse to call her, when all he had really wanted was to hear her voice and, if the mood was right, to ask her please to come home. She had seized on the opportunity to talk about something other than their separation.

"For goodness' sake, Ezzy, you've got to take something."

"It's not like Delray was a bosom buddy, Cora. Not even a close acquaintance."

"But we've known that man practically our whole lives. And now that poor girl has to raise her son all by herself. I doubt if anybody has offered to help her because the gossip about her and Delray has been so vile. Some women, even in my circle who profess to be Christians, can be downright vicious."

"What gossip?"

"Good Lord, Ezzy! Didn't you ever bring your head up out of that McCorkle case long enough to take a look at what was going on around you?"

"Maybe I heard and just forgot. I don't usually pay attention to gossip," he said, trying to sound just a shade self-righteous and superior.

"I swear," Cora said with a long-suffering sigh. "There's been talk for years."

"That they . . . ?"

"Yes. That after Dean died their relationship changed and became closer than it should have been. But I don't see that it's any of my business. Whether they slept together or not, she's lost him. You've got to take something."

Ezzy was dumbfounded by the rumor. Delray Corbett and his daughter-in-law? Not just living under the same roof, but sleeping under the same covers? Had Delray been capable of passion? Was romance possible with someone so cold and standoffish, so rigid and stern?

"Hell, I can't imagine Delray taking off his clothes to shower, much less getting naked and nasty with a woman."

"Are you trying to provoke me, Ezra?"

"No." *Yes.*

Another vexed sigh. "I store the funeral food on the right side of the freezer chest."

"The *what*?"

He'd had no idea that Cora was so well prepared for any catastrophe that might befall their friends and neighbors. After they hung up—without his having mentioned a reconciliation—he'd gone to the freezer chest in the utility room and on the right side found several sealed casserole dishes labeled as to contents, the number of people they would serve, and heating instructions.

Anna Corbett was holding one now. "Once it thaws completely," he said, "just heat it up for about thirty minutes at three fifty. You understand?" he asked dubiously.

Nodding, she turned away to set the cold, wet dish on the hall table, then wiped the condensation on the seat of her blue jeans. As she did,

Ezzy noticed what a nice shape she had. He tried to keep his eyes above her neckline, because he suspected she wasn't wearing a brassiere. Maybe that accounted for her apparent nervousness. She kept tugging on the bottom of her T-shirt, rubbing her palms together, and rolling her lips inward like she was embarrassed, like she had been caught unprepared to receive company.

Yeah, she was a pretty little thing. But when he thought about her and Delray going at it in bed, he just flat couldn't picture it. Even on a lonely, cold, winter night, he couldn't see Delray snuggling against anybody. The gossips were wrong about this one. Or he was no judge of character.

"Well, I best get on my way, Mrs. Corbett. You need anything?"

She shook her head.

"If you think of something, just call." Wondering if he'd made a horrible gaffe, he asked, "*Can* you call somebody?"

She nodded vigorously.

"Okay, then. Good. You tell whoever you contact that I'm available if there's anything I can do."

Nodding again, she opened the door for him. He stepped out onto the porch, but was reluctant to leave. He didn't want to frighten her, but he felt compelled nevertheless to mention the Herbolds. He turned. "Mrs. Corbett, I heard about Cecil Herbold's visit the other day. Did he threaten you or your boy?"

She shook her head and mouthed no.

"I don't know how much news you've heard—what with the funeral and all—but he and Carl linked up and robbed a bank. They're still at large. Did you know about that?"

She nodded yes.

"I'm surprised nobody's out here guarding your place."

She held up her finger indicating for him to wait and ducked back inside. When she returned she was writing on a small tablet. She turned it to him. He read, "The authorities offered to guard the house, but Delray turned them down."

"Maybe you ought to think twice."

She wrote, "I'm not afraid. This is the last place they would come."

"You're probably right," Ezzy told her, although he didn't necessarily believe it. It had been his experience that criminals often gravitated to friends and family. The hotter their trail, the more likely you'd find them making their way back to a familiar place, one they called home.

If she were his kin, he wouldn't let her stay out here all alone even if she had her hearing. But he had no authority, either professional or personally, to insist. So he said, "You see anything, you call somebody. Pronto. You understand? You've got your boy to worry about."

She smiled at him, writing, "We'll be fine. Jack's here."

"Jack?"

She nodded toward the barn. Ezzy turned and saw a man sliding the barn door closed. He appeared to lock it, then struck off toward a trailer parked about a hundred yards from the house, his long stride eating up the distance between the two buildings.

"Oh, yeah, your ranch hand," he said more to himself than to Anna. He remembered Delray introducing him at the Dairy Queen, a man wearing a cowboy hat and slouched in the corner of the booth. Polite fellow. Much leaner, younger, and stronger than Delray. The type that made women go all aflutter.

Ezzy cleared his throat as he came back around to Anna. "Pardon me for asking, Mrs. Corbett, but do you feel, uh, comfortable being out here alone with a man who's worked for you such a short time? Do you trust him?"

She bobbed her head, leaving no room for doubt.

Ezzy wondered if the guy was that trustworthy, or if she were just naive, or if the gossips were right. For all he knew, the young widow was a hot number who'd worn ol' Delray plumb out until he finally succumbed, and now had plans for the hired hand to take his place.

To Ezzy, she didn't look the type, but, God knew, he'd been wrong before.

Chapter Thirty-Four

They came early, shortly after daybreak, two of them.

Their tight-fitting uniforms were brown. Their boots were spit-polished. Wide-brimmed cowboy hats and mirrored sunglasses obscured their faces except for the grim, unsmiling lips.

"Mr. Sawyer?"

Jack had heard their car and had stopped his work to watch them approach. "Yeah?" He leaned on the handle of the shovel he'd been using to dig a hole for a new support post for the feed trough in the corral.

Already the day was stifling hot and he was dripping perspiration. But when he reached toward his back pocket for a handkerchief to blot up sweat, the two lawmen tensed. One even dropped his hand to the six-shooter strapped to his hip. Jack pretended not to see the precaution. He shook out the handkerchief and used it to wipe his face. "What can I do for you gentlemen?"

"We're from the Blewer County sheriff's office."

"Uh-huh."

"Came to ask you a few questions."

"About what?"

"Heard that Mr. Corbett—the late Mr. Corbett—had some cattle poisoned last week."

"I was with him when he found them," Jack said. "Three of them. Two more died the next day."

"Common enough poison, Dr. Andersen said." The deputy shifted his wad of tobacco from one cheek to the other. "Over-the-counter stuff. Nothing fancy. Easily obtainable. But in the right hands strong enough to do some damage."

"The sheriff's office is investigating?"

"That bother you, Mr. Sawyer?"

"No. I advised Delray to report it. He thought otherwise."

"Anybody hear you advise him?"

"We were alone."

"Hmm."

"How come, do you suppose, that out of all the cattle ranches around here, Corbett's was the only one hit?"

"I don't know."

"Give it a shot."

Jack propped the shovel against the trough he'd been repairing. "My guess would be that someone had a grudge against Delray."

"Like who, for instance?"

"I'm not from around here, and haven't been here long."

"So you wouldn't have any idea?"

Jack said nothing.

Eyeing him suspiciously, the younger of the two hiked up his holster. "Well, we weren't investigating until yesterday. Corbett didn't bring us in. We wouldn't have even known about it, except that somebody brought it to our attention. A concerned party. So we called the vet and he gave us the skinny."

Jack divided a puzzled look between them, although he wasn't puzzled at all. He knew why they were here. Sheriff's deputies didn't pay courtesy calls this early in the morning. "And?"

"And"—the tobacco-chewer paused to spit—"we'd like for you to come on back to town with us so we can talk about it some more."

"Am I a suspect?"

"You and everybody else."

"But I'm the one you're arresting."

"We're not calling it an arrest."

"Then what are you calling it?"

"We'd just appreciate your cooperation, is all."

"But I'd feel better if you'd unstrap that knife and hand it over," his partner added.

Moving carefully, Jack unsnapped the scabbard and detached it from his belt. One of the deputies stepped forward and took it from him. Jack said, "You're making a mistake."

"Maybe, but all the same you're coming with us, Mr. Sawyer."

"Can I drive my own truck?"

"We've got plenty of room for you to ride with us."

"Please. One of you can ride with me. I'd just like to have my own truck, so that after this is cleared up, I won't have to trouble you to bring me all the way back."

They exchanged glances. The older, larger one with the chaw nodded. "Okay. I'll ride with you."

The most humiliating part wasn't being escorted off the property with two all-business sheriff's deputies flanking him. It was having Anna witness it from the front porch. "Did you speak with Mrs. Corbett?" Jack asked as they approached the front of the house and he saw her watching solemnly.

"We told her why we were here, yeah. I'm not sure she got it."

"She got it," Jack said testily. Looking up at her, he said, "I didn't do it, Anna. Swear to God, I didn't."

But she looked wounded, disillusioned, her eyes bleak and vulnerable. They'd haunt his dreams for years, those eyes.

"Jack?"

David came through the front door. Jack had been thankful that at least David wasn't seeing this. It was bad enough having to face Anna. But Fate was a hateful bastard. David was there now, barefoot, his belly button poking out from beneath the top of his Spider-Man pajamas, looking sleepy and sweet and apprehensive as his eyes moved from the patrol car to the unsmiling men standing on either side of Jack.

A few weeks ago, Jack probably would have pretended not to see or hear him. He would have turned away without acknowledging him. After all, what was David to him? Nothing.

But he couldn't do it. Not now. He remembered how it felt to have his trust betrayed by a person he wanted badly to love. He remembered how it had wrenched his young heart to watch his father turn his back and walk away, not knowing when he would return. Or if he would. Even as he smiled up at David, Jack cursed the Corbetts for resurrecting those painful memories, for making him *feel* them again.

"Hey!" he said with false cheerfulness. "You're up mighty early."

"What are the policemen doing, Jack?"

Jack pushed back his hat brim with his thumb and glanced first at one of the deputies, then the other, as though noticing them for the first time. "They just came to talk to me."

"Are you going with them?"

"Hmm."

"Where?"

"Downtown."

"For how long?"

"I don't know."

David began to look worried. "Are you coming back?"

"I hope so."

"Today?"

"I might be away longer than that."

"Do you want to go?"

"Sure," Jack said. "I've been looking forward to it." He had hoped to reassure David that he was all right, but he might have overshot his mark.

The boy's chin drew up and tightened. His lower lip began to tremble. "Are you mad at me?"

"Of course not."

"Didn't I do my jobs good yesterday?"

"You did everything fine. I couldn't have asked for a better helper. It's just . . ." Jesus this was hard. "It's just that I've got to go now."

"Can I come?"

" 'Fraid not."

A tear rolled down the boy's cheek. "When will you be back?"

The damaging effect of a false promise would be worse than the truth. *"Come on, son, don't be a crybaby. Like I told you, I'm only leaving to finish up some business, but I'll be back. And this time I'll stay. We'll be together all the time. I promise."*

With his father's lying words echoing in his head, Jack said, "I might not be back, David."

The boy began to cry harder. His shoulders shook. "Go ahead then and leave!" he shouted. "I hate you." Kneeling, Anna drew her son to her. He threw his arms around her neck and buried his face in her shoulder.

Jack took a step forward, but the deputies shouldered in, halting his progress. "Let's go," one said in an undertone. They walked him to the pickup, then one veered off in the direction of the patrol car.

The pickup's keys were in the ignition. As Jack started the motor, his companion said, "I'm trusting you, Sawyer. Don't do anything stupid."

"I want this cleared up worse than you do. Don't worry."

"I'm not worried." He hitched his chin forward. "Take off."

Jack took one last glance at the front porch, where Anna was still comforting David. Dejectedly he engaged the truck's gears and drove out the gate, the patrol car practically in his tailpipe.

Chapter Thirty-Five

I'm sorry, Mrs. Corbett. You can't see him right now. He's behind closed doors with Sheriff Foster."

"Did you tell Jack I was here?"

"No, son, I didn't," the clerk replied, smiling kindly at David. "He's awful busy right now."

"Not too busy to see me."

"Sorry, son, the answer's no."

David turned to Anna. "I want to see Jack and tell him I'm sorry."

Usually well behaved, David had been acting bratty since his crying jag on the front porch. Feeling sorry for telling Jack that he hated him, he wanted to apologize. He had nagged her with a million questions for which she had no answers.

When was Jack coming back?

Was Jack coming back?

Did Jack know he didn't mean it when he said he hated him?

Had she been mean to Jack? Is that why he looked forward to leaving?

Why was he going with the policemen?

Were they putting Jack in jail?

And so it went until Anna thought she would go mad. What was she to tell him? That Jack had left of his own accord and was happy about it? Or that he was being arrested and had no choice except to leave?

Either way, her son would be devastated. She tried to console him, but nothing worked. He wouldn't let the matter drop and he wouldn't be distracted from it. When he became so misbehaved, she reprimanded him for crying more over Jack's leaving than he had over his grandfather's death, although that scold stung her conscience. She had lived in the same house with Delray for years, but the regret she had experienced upon watching Jack being escorted away under suspicion of a crime had been sharper and more intense than what she had felt when she walked away from Delray's grave the day before.

Unwilling simply to wait for whatever happened next, she decided to pay a visit to the sheriff's office and see if there were any concrete answers to be had. However, to salve her conscience, she had stopped at the cemetery first. Delray's grave was disturbingly fresh, but the flowers were beginning to wilt in the unbearable heat. She suggested to David that they divide them among Grandpa, Grandma Mary, and Daddy's graves. *"Don't you think Grandpa would like to share his flowers with them?"* she asked. Sullenly, David nodded.

The task took the boy's mind off Jack temporarily, but Anna's was spinning around the question of whether or not Jack could have done what the authorities obviously suspected him of doing.

They wouldn't have come for him unless they believed he was responsible. Did they have evidence linking him to the poisoning? How could he have done something like that? And for what reason?

She searched for a possible motive, but came up empty.

Jack had looked her in the eye and denied the accusation, but was he lying? Ordinarily she could read people very well. Had her attraction to Jack blinded her? Had she missed something in his face, his eyes, his mannerisms, that would have signaled an unsavory inner character?

If he were completely innocent, why had he acted so skittish when Ezzy Hardge came to the house last evening? As soon as she identified the caller at the door, Jack had told her he had things to do and had left through a back door.

She had hoped he would return after Ezzy left. She had hoped they would resume what had been started before the former sheriff's inopportune visit. She had hoped Jack would kiss her.

Last night when she finally gave up hope of Jack's returning, she had resented Ezzy's bad timing. Perhaps it had been a blessing. It might have prevented her from becoming involved with a man who was cruel, heartless, and devious enough to poison a rancher's herd.

But she couldn't believe it of Jack Sawyer. She wouldn't believe it until he confessed it to her. She wanted to ask him point blank if he had done this horrible thing, and if so, why. She wanted to ask him herself while looking into his eyes. She wanted to know. She had to know.

But the clerk at the reception desk in the sheriff's office was being uninformative and inflexible. He was polite but firm in refusing her and David's request to speak to Jack, telling them only that Jack Sawyer was unavailable, and that he didn't know for how long he would be held.

She also got the distinct impression that he was talking down to her because of her handicap. She had written everything out on a notepad, not wanting to rely strictly on David's interpretation for something this important. The man spoke to her as he would to a child—a child who wasn't very bright.

On her pad she wrote, "I don't wish to press charges against Mr. Sawyer. Not until I've spoken to him and am convinced that he's guilty."

"It's not for you to say, Mrs. Corbett."

"But it was _my_ cattle," she wrote. "My father-in-law chose to handle the incident himself."

"Don't matter. If Sawyer broke the law, it don't matter none what you want to do about it. The state'll prosecute him."

Her usage of English was far superior to his; that made his condescension even more infuriating. He used an incoming telephone call as an excuse to tell her that she would be notified of any progress on the case. He suggested that she "go on home now"—"like a good little girl" being implied. Then he started speaking into the phone and ignored her as though she weren't there.

Anna left, practically having to drag a protesting David along with her. Outside, the heat was intense, but she stood on the sidewalk and considered what to do next. There seemed to be nothing she could do for or about Jack Sawyer. David was cranky and whiny. A long afternoon spent trying to entertain him in his current frame of mind held no appeal. A movie? She checked her wristwatch. Too early even for the matinee showings. Lunch? Still too early.

As Anna glanced up and down the street indecisively, something caught her eye. She had seen it before, of course. But now it leaped out at her like a gaudy neon sign, luring her inside. Giving David's hand a firm tug, she marched smartly down the sidewalk.

The shop was cool, quiet, and well maintained. Keeping a close eye on David to see that he didn't meddle with the expensive merchandise, Anna shopped the new generation of cameras and lenses.

The store had opened several years ago. Anna had been curious about it, although until now she had never ventured inside. She had barely allowed herself to glance at the display windows, fearing the temptation would be too strong to resist.

Because it was the only store in Blewer that specialized in photographic equipment, the inventory was extensive and pricey. The array of gadgets and accessories was mind-boggling. She longed to test the cameras locked inside the glass display cases, but knew they were priced well beyond her budget. Until she was earning some money with her photographs, she must be content with her outdated equipment.

Her only purchase was a few rolls of black-and-white film and a recently published book on technique.

"... have to send that film off to be developed," said the man attending the cash register. She hadn't caught his first words. "Can't get black-and-white film developed anywhere in Blewer any longer."

She nodded.

"I don't believe I've seen you in here before. I know most of my customers."

She motioned David over and signed for him to explain to the man that she was deaf. When he did, the man wasn't embarrassed or put off as people frequently were. He didn't look askance and stammer an apology. Instead his face lit up around a broad smile.

"What's your name? You aren't by any chance Anna Corbett?"

Flabbergasted, she smiled and reached across the counter to shake his hand.

"Pete Nolen," he said, grinning from jug ear to jug ear while he pumped her hand. "I'll be switched, if this doesn't beat all. Wait'll the wife hears. Always wanted to meet you and thought I'd never get the chance. Come over here."

Rounding the counter, he guided her toward a wall where dozens of framed photographs were on display.

"Here you go! Right there!" He tapped a black-and-white enlargement of a photo Anna immediately recognized as one of her early works.

Making certain she could see his lips, he explained. "A year or so ago I was trying to sell some new equipment to the photography department up at the junior college. Spotted this hanging on the wall and thought it was excellent. I asked the professor if he knew the photographer, and he told me about you. About you being deaf and all? He said it was a shame you quit school, 'cause you had more talent in your little finger than most of his students could ever hope to have. It took some persuading, but I came away with this picture."

He gazed at the photo with obvious appreciation. The subject of it was an old house. It stood in silhouette against the overexposed western sky at sunset. It could have looked foreboding, except that light shone through every window and projected soft pools of it onto the front porch.

"It just says 'home' to me, 'cause I grew up in a farmhouse that looked about like that one. It's been on this wall ever since I got it. People respond to it. Relate, you know? It gets a lot of comment. I could've sold it a hundred times over, but it's my only Anna Corbett, so I wouldn't part with it. You ought to do more work."

She lifted the sack containing her purchases and shook it slightly.

He caught her meaning and grinned even wider. "Good! I'd like to see 'em when you shoot 'em." He plucked a business card from his wallet. "Number's right there. Here and home. You need anything in the way of supplies, call me. Or if you just want to talk photography, I never tire of the subject. Can't tell you how pleased I am to finally meet you, Mrs. Corbett."

Emory Lomax belched into his white paper napkin, wadded it up, and tossed it down onto the bone pile that had formerly been a slab of baby back ribs. "Was I lying about the food? This boy knows ribs, doesn't he?"

There were three of them, Connaught and two vice-presidents, sharing the booth with Emory. Connaught and one of the flunkies sat facing Lomax, while the third shared his bench.

So uptight they squeaked when they walked, they murmured agreement that it was indeed superb barbecue. Playing his role of host to the hilt, he signaled the waitress and ordered another round of longnecks. Usually he didn't drink anything stronger than iced tea at lunch, but this was a special occasion. Beer wasn't a very sophisticated beverage. Not like the martinis and single malts they were probably accustomed to. But beer went with barbecue, and he had brought the suits to the best barbecue shack in East Texas.

They had flown up from Houston in a sleek company jet that looked like something the villain of a James Bond movie would use to flit around Europe. Emory picked them up at the Blewer County Municipal Airport, which was a clearing in the middle of what was, essentially, a cow pasture without the cows. It was nothing more than a buckled runway, a rusty tin hangar, and a cramped office with a couple of fuel pumps out front.

"This is one of the first things we'll need to revamp," Emory remarked as he escorted them to his car, his pride-and-joy Jag. "As soon as Phase One gets underway, I see us modernizing this airport for the weekenders flying in. What do you say?"

Taking their cue from Connaught, the other two nodded in sync like a duo of puppets, which was the manner in which they acknowledged almost everything. They were tight-lipped and noncommittal, but Emory wasn't put off. He understood. It was SOP. It was the way moguls conducted their business affairs. There was a lesson to be learned from them.

Now that they'd finished eating, Emory sensed their impatience. Connaught occasionally would glimpse disdainfully at the jukebox, which had blared forth throughout their meal. He also gave the extravagant, diamond-studded gold timepiece on his left wrist a frequent glance. As soon as the waitress transferred the four frosty longneck beer bottles from her tray to their table, Emory got down to business.

"It's sewn up. The Corbett place is as good as ours. As long as Delray was dying, he couldn't have picked a better time." He shot them smiles all around. "Meaning no disrespect, of course."

"What about Mrs. Corbett?" one of the puppets asked. "Did she inherit?"

"Everything."

"Isn't that a problem?" Connaught asked. "You told me she was as set against selling as her father-in-law."

Emory leaned back and stretched his arm along the back of the booth. "That might have been the case of the matter as long as he was alive. Honor thy father-in-law. She didn't want to cross him."

"But you believe she'll come around now?"

"I'm sure of it," he replied with a casual confidence. "How's she going to run that ranch alone? She can't. She's a deaf mute. Won't take long for her to see the light. Give her a week, two at the outside, and she'll realize there's no way she can handle it. And of course"—he paused to insert a chuckle—"I'm going to be right there reminding her of all the hardships she'll face if she tries to go it alone. I'll be encouraging her to sell before y'all change your minds and start looking for another property."

The suit across the table from him pushed his untouched beer aside. "What makes you think you wield any influence over her?"

"Well, there's the note the bank's holding. I can use that as leverage. Then she's already had that one scare with the herd." Snickering, he added, "There could always be another unfortunate mishap."

"Is this Mexican of yours trustworthy?" asked the man sitting beside him.

"Long as you pay him, Jesse Garcia would screw his own mother with twelve people watching."

"You're sure the poisoning can't come back to you?"

"Absolutely. In fact, even as we speak, somebody else is being booked for the crime."

He saw no point in telling them about the worrisome hired hand, who was too cagey- and competent-looking for Emory's comfort. His first impression of the cowboy was that he was an arrogant son of a bitch who might go poking his nose into other people's business. Emory couldn't risk having anybody around Anna Corbett undermining the sound advice he was going to be giving her. He needed to be rid of the hired hand.

And then there was Garcia. Despite what he had told them about the Mexican, he made Emory nervous, too. What if somebody offered him more than fifty dollars to finger the person who had hired him to poison the salt lick in Corbett's pasture? It wasn't the Mexican's standard practice to rat out his clients, but who knew? He might be having a bad year and need the money.

So what had Emory done? He had conveniently taken care of the two niggling problems at once. As the banker whose collateral was in jeopardy, he had called the sheriff's office and shared with them his concerns about the senseless killing of valuable stock and the coincidental hiring of a new hand. They had assured him they would check into it.

As easily as that, he had removed himself from the poisoning by casting suspicion on someone else. The sheriff's office would be occupying the cowboy while they conducted an investigation. It could take a long time. Time in which Emory would work on Anna without interference.

It was goddamn brilliant if he did say so himself.

"Trust me," he said, "I've got all the bases covered. Garcia is a genius. I've even thought about using him again. Anna Corbett dotes on her kid. Which opens up several avenues of possibility. For the right price, I'm sure Garcia could get real creative."

The three men from EastPark exchanged an uneasy glance. Noticing it, Emory quickly added, "Of course I'd rather not apply that kind of pressure. That would be a last-resort tactic, to be used only if absolutely necessary, and only after discussing it with you beforehand."

"We hope you understand, Mr. Lomax," one of the veeps said, "that if your name is ever connected to a crime, EastPark will disavow all knowledge of it. We never sanction criminal activity."

Bullshit. Connaught probably conducted a handful of criminal activities before breakfast. Emory knew it, and Connaught knew that he knew it, but Emory agreed. "Of course. I'm just talking off the top of my head. Most of these options won't be exercised. What I'm counting on most, what will be most effective, is our personal relationship."

As hoped, that piqued interest. You could practically see Connaught's ears pricking. "Your personal relationship with whom?"

"Mrs. Corbett."

"I wasn't aware you had one."

Emory lowered his arm from the back of the booth and shrugged self-consciously. "I didn't want to let on about it. In case y'all misinterpreted my interest in the project. I pride myself on keeping my business affairs separate from my personal life. But from both points of view, I think Mrs. Corbett—Anna—will be making a mistake she'll regret forever if she declines your offer. I'll hammer that point home. If she won't listen to me as a financial adviser," he said, winking, "I'll simply have to use some other form of persuasion."

Again the men exchanged concerned looks. "Mr. Lomax, the laws on this type of land acquisition are very strict. Furthermore, they're carefully monitored by the federal government."

"I'm well aware of that, yes," Emory said, pulling a somber face.

The suit sitting next to Connaught said, "It's imperative that you keep your involvement with us separate from your responsibilities at the banking institution with which you are affiliated."

Who did these assholes think they were talking to? Emory Lomax knew the rules of this game; he'd been playing it for years. Although miffed by the implied insult to his intelligence, he maintained his solemn, obsequious expression. "Of course. That's been understood from the beginning."

"It's even more important that nothing unethical or, God forbid, immoral—"

"Hey, y'all!" Emory interrupted, holding up both hands. "You've got nothing to worry about."

Reducing his voice to an undertone, he leaned across the red plastic basket in which his order of ribs had been served. "It's not like I need to seduce the woman. Anna is . . . Let's see, how can I phrase this delicately? Since she's been deprived of normal language skills, she's found another way to communicate. Get it?"

"You're saying that the two of you already have a relationship of an intimate nature?"

Emory was fed up with the high-flown language. "No, what I'm saying is that I've been fucking her for a couple of years now. Almost to the day I started handling their accounts. At first I thought the old man was slipping it to her. That's what the gossips said and, as far as I know or care, they were right. But she came on to me something fierce, so I thought, hell, why not? I'm single. She's a knockout. And . . ." He inched forward as far as the booth allowed. "Know the best part? She can't talk. Now, I ask you, is that a dream fuck or what?"

That drew a smile even from iron-ass Connaught.

Emory said, "Stand by for further developments, gentlemen. Should be in the bag any day now."

That brought the meeting to a close. Emory left enough cash on the table to cover four rib dinners, eight beers, and a miserly tip. Back-slapping and glad-handing his guests to the door, he repeatedly assured them that he had the situation under control, all the while springing gushers of sweat from his armpits and wondering how in hell he was going to make good these boasts.

He was so preoccupied with his dilemma he didn't notice the diner seated back-to-back with him in the next booth.

Chapter Thirty-Six

*W*hen family and friends paid compliments to her photography, Anna had dismissed them as biased. But Pete Nolen's opinion of her work was valid. He was a professional who could differentiate good work from bad. He had understood exactly what she was trying to say with that photograph of the farmhouse. Of course Jack—

She didn't let the thought form completely, because thinking about Jack made her sad, and she was going to let nothing dampen this moment. Unlikely as it seemed, she had a fan! She wanted to bask in the glow of the shopkeeper's praise. Unfortunately, there was no one to tell of this news, no one with whom to share this momentous occasion.

When they arrived home, she was so pumped she immediately loaded her camera with film, gathered her equipment, took David outside, and started posing him on the swing Jack had rigged for him.

But the heat was oppressive, the atmosphere so sticky it seemed that the air clung to their skin. David got cranky and wouldn't cooperate. Before long she surrendered to the climate and her son's recalcitrance. As they trudged back inside, she noticed white, puffy thunderheads on the northwestern horizon, and thought how delicious a cleansing rain would feel.

She fixed David a grilled cheese sandwich for lunch and let him picnic on the living room floor and watch a video about dinosaurs while he ate. She went upstairs to her bedroom for a few moments alone.

After Dean died, she had redecorated the bedroom so that every time she entered it she wouldn't be reminded of the days and nights her husband had lain in the bed, struggling for each breath and fearing his own mortality.

Decorated in shades of apricot and ivory, it was a soothing room, with baby portraits of David scattered about in silver frames. A few of her and Dean. One with Delray and Mary. Her favorite books lined the shelves of the open cabinet in the corner. An area rug broke up the space between the bed and the window, in front of which was a rocking chair. The room was personal but uncluttered. It wasn't fussy, but uncompromisingly feminine.

Too feminine. Very chaste.

Some nights she was assailed by a loneliness so dense it was palpable. She hated sleeping alone. She longed to have someone lying beside her to touch in the night, to feel his breath against her skin, share his body heat, and know that she wasn't alone in her dark silence.

Other nights her desires took a decidedly more carnal turn. Following her periods, when she had always been easily aroused, she would have erotic dreams in which she and a faceless man were engaged in incredible sex. Sometimes she awoke in the throes of orgasm. Other times she awoke just prior to climaxing, and for the remainder of the night she was feverish and restless. On those nights, she hugged her pillow tightly and pressed it between her thighs.

Yes, she missed sex.

Jack Sawyer had made her realize how much.

Pushing the thought aside, she moved to the dressing table, sat down on the tufted stool, and looked at herself in the mirror. What she saw terrified her. Because what she saw was a woman who had remained voluntarily mute for six years.

Following Dean's death, she simply hadn't had the heart to continue practicing her speech. She'd been wrong to give it up. Everything she had learned to that point was probably lost to her now and might be impossible to regain. But she had to try.

The encounter in the sheriff's office earlier today had been unpleasant and humiliating, but beneficial. It had made her realize that if she were going to oversee the ranch, and negotiate contracts with timber companies, and stave off land-grabbing opportunists like Emory Lomax, and sell her photographs, and combat the ignorance and prejudice of people who spoke down to her because of her handicap, then she must relearn how to speak.

She did not underestimate the task ahead. She accepted the limitations. Never would she be able to conduct conversations relying entirely on speech. Having been born profoundly deaf limited her capabilities, but it did not restrict her to absolute silence.

Too long she had relied on others, even her young son, to speak for her. No more. She must learn to speak for herself. She *must*.

Opening her mouth slightly, she exercised her vocal cords for the first time in years. She felt the vibration as the air moved across them and knew she had made a sound. It was probably just as well that she couldn't hear the noise that had come out, or she might never try again.

She hesitated, reminding herself that thousands of hearing-impaired people relied solely on sign language and chose never to learn to speak. They led rewarding, productive, fulfilled lives.

But she and her parents had decided when she was a child that she would combine sign language with lip reading and speech. Deaf educators and private tutors had dedicated themselves to teaching her. Hours had been spent in front of a mirror as she was now, following the instructions of patient, caring therapists.

She had been good at it and had become very proficient. Then Dean had died. Intimidation and self-pity had caused her to give up the skills she had worked so hard to acquire. Delray's selfish wish for her to remain locked in silence had been a good excuse for her to become indifferent to it. She realized that now. She'd taken the coward's way out.

It took a lot of courage to admit that. It took even more to face the mirror and confront not only the seemingly insurmountable task ahead of her, but also her fear of it, her fear of trying and failing.

Taking a deep breath, she forced herself to sit up straighter. *Start with the basics,* she told herself. Bilabial stops. *P* and *b.* The first sound was nonvoiced, the second voiced.

P. How to utter a *p*? Lower the jaw and open the chamber of the mouth, but keep the lips closed. Separate them with a puff of air. She did it. It looked right in the mirror. She did it a second time, holding her fingers an inch in front of her lips so she could feel the air as she expelled it. Yes, that felt right. Did it sound right?

Now a *b.* That sound required the same action of the lips, but the vocal cords had to be activated at the same time.

Concentrate, Anna. You can do this. You have done this.

Placing her hand against her throat, she tried only the vibration, then made an adjustment and tried it again. The third time, she combined it with the movement of her lips. Too much air? She repeated the action, holding her fingertips near her lips and cutting back on the expulsion of air. Yes, that time it felt right. But was it?

Her hand seemed to weigh a thousand pounds. She let it fall into her lap and remain there. Her shoulders sagged. Suddenly she felt exhausted, due in no small part to emotional distress and not physical fatigue. Nevertheless, she felt too tired to move.

As she stared at her reflection, she watched her eyes fill with tears. Would she ever be able to make herself understood? Would she make a fool of herself? Would she make the people to whom she tried to speak feel uncomfortable, make them look away with embarrassment and pity for her?

Worse, would she embarrass her son?

David was unself-conscious of her impairment because he didn't know any better. But what would happen when he enrolled in kindergarten next fall? Because of her, the other children would make fun of him. They would call his mother a dummy.

At first he probably would rush to her defense. But the time would come when he would be ashamed of her, and resent her for being different, and wish that his mom was like all the others.

One way or another, her deafness would influence his development. In order to cope, he might grow a real chip on his shoulder and become a belligerent bully. Or he might become introverted and shy, keeping his anxiety bottled up inside. Whatever the effect, it could be profound and might radically change her son's personality. How sad it would be if her outgoing, engaging little boy was reduced to less than that because of her cowardice.

She couldn't let that happen. If not for herself, she must relearn speech for David's sake.

With renewed determination, she impatiently wiped away her tears and faced the mirror again. Placing her fingertips against her lips, she tried another consonant. One more difficult. A *j*.

As in Jack.

Chapter Thirty-Seven

$\mathcal{M}$r. Lomax, I'm glad you're back, there's—"

"Later, Mrs. Presley. These my messages?" He swept up the pink slips as he passed her desk on the way into his office.

"Yes, sir, but there's—"

"I said later. Get me an Alka-Seltzer, will you?"

The barbecue had given him a bellyache. The beer had left him with a dull headache. And the land developers had been a pain in the ass.

After lunch they had asked him to drive them out to the Corbett ranch. A half hour out, a half hour spent looking around, a half hour back. Not until he had waved them off toward Houston in their space-age private jet did he feel like he could draw an easy breath. For the moment they were pacified, believing that the deal was in the bag.

Emory's nuts were in a vise.

Returning from lunch over an hour late and getting a sour glance from the bank president because of it, Emory had his heart set on the cool, quiet serenity of his office. He needed some downtime to plot what his next move would be.

Leaving his secretary with the request for the Alka-Seltzer, he slipped into his office, removed his damp suit jacket, and hung it on the hook behind the door to dry out. Flipping through his message slips, he moved around the corner of his desk. His tall wingback leather chair was facing the window. He spun it around.

"Hey, Emory."

The cowboy sprang from the chair like a striking rattler, grabbed Emory by his necktie, reversed their positions with a brain-joggling spin, and shoved Emory into the chair that was still warm from his body heat.

Before Emory could even register what had happened, the Corbetts' ranch hand had him pinned to the chair with a wicked-looking knife. The sharp tip of it was at his throat. Emory gripped the padded armrests of his desk chair in stark terror.

"Enjoy your lunch?" the cowboy asked pleasantly. "I thought the barbecue sauce was a tad too tame and the pickles too salty, but otherwise it was pretty good. I had a chopped-beef sandwich. I noticed you and your fancy friends had ribs."

The door opened. "Mr. Lomax—"

"Call security!"

"Yes, sir."

"Wait a minute!"

To Emory's consternation, Mrs. Presley, mouth slack with astonishment, holding a foil packet of Alka-Seltzer in one hand and a glass of water in the other, stopped dead in her tracks when the cowboy barked the order.

Then in a gentle voice he said, "While you're at it, Mrs. Presley . . . is that your name, ma'am? Along with the guard, bring in the bank officers. I'm sure they'll be interested to hear what Mr. Lomax has to say about one of their best customers. You might want to stick around, too. In fact, round up everybody. I think everyone who works with Emory would find what I have to tell very interesting."

Emory laughed nervously. "Why, you ol' son of a gun! When did you hit town?" Working up every ounce of courage he had, he moved aside the knife and clapped the cowboy on the shoulder. "Mrs. Presley, this cut-up, who nearly scared the wits out of you, is a fraternity brother of mine. Uh . . ."

"Jack."

Emory cackled, releasing pent-up fear. "Jack here was always pulling jokes like this when we were at Stephen F."

Except for faltering on the name, it sounded convincing. His diploma from Stephen F. Austin University was hanging on his office wall. He had regaled Mrs. Presley with elaborate stories about his Greek fraternity life, which were grossly untrue because he had never been invited to join one.

To his vast relief, the cowboy sheathed his knife. "Hope I didn't scare you too bad, ma'am. I couldn't resist pulling a good one on my old buddy here." His hand landed on Emory's shoulder like an anvil. Emory nearly buckled beneath the grip of strong fingers.

The secretary smiled tentatively. "What about the—" She held up the packet of Alka-Seltzer.

"Never mind. But thanks."

Still looking uncertain, she backed out through the door and pulled it closed.

Unfortunately, the Jack person didn't go anywhere.

He took his knife out of the scabbard again and sat down on the edge of the desk just above the lap drawer and facing Emory, whose mouth was so dry he could hardly make the moving parts work. However, he did manage to hiss, "Are you *insane*?"

"If I was insane, I'd've already slit you open from gullet to gonads. Only a thread of sanity has kept me from it. You should be grateful for that, Emory. Can I call you Emory? Of course I can, seeing as how we're fraternity brothers."

"I want you out of my office, or I'll—"

"No, now, see, Emory, you're not in a position to be threatening me. Frankly, I'd love nothing better than for you to call in the guard and make a scene, because then I could recount for anybody listening the conversation I overheard at lunch today. I was sitting right behind you in the next booth and heard every lying, treacherous word."

Looking into the steely eyes, Emory didn't doubt for a minute that Jack would do what he said.

"Think about it, Emory. How well do you think the lurid account of your fictitious love affair with Mrs. Corbett would go over with the bank president? The other officers? Particularly the women officers. Hmm? You see where this is leading, Emory?"

Emory did see where this was leading, and it was straight toward disaster. Especially if he wanted a career in banking. He couldn't give up his job here until his sideline with EastPark paid off. He owed a huge amount on the Jag. Repossession was out of the question.

"It would be my word against yours." He forced a laugh that sounded like a sheet of sandpaper scraping across a concrete sidewalk. "Who's going to believe you?"

"Oh, I'm sure most of the ladies would. Anna Corbett can't be the only woman you've repulsed with your sexism and slimy come-ons."

"You're bluffing, cowboy. If you were serious, you wouldn't have ambushed me in my office. You'd have denounced me in the bank lobby where everybody could hear."

"The only reason I didn't was to spare Mrs. Corbett the embarrassment of having her name linked to yours."

"Ahh, so you're sweet on the deaf widow. Touching. Go ahead and make a fool of yourself." He snorted with derision. "Didn't you overhear the part about her and old Delray? That row you're hoping to plow? That old man has been tilling it for years."

The cowboy's eyes narrowed and Emory feared that he'd gone too far. Who was this guy, anyhow? Where had he come from? Emory knew nothing about him. He was stupid to be provoking a man who was still tapping the blade of a knife against his palm, a knife that might have ended other lives. He wouldn't be surprised if Jack what's-his-name carried out his threat of disembowelment right then and there.

Thank God he hadn't connected Emory to his being arrested this morning. If he had, Emory knew he would already be dead. He was here only to defend Anna Corbett's honor. Was Emory Lomax one lucky bastard, or what?

Jack stared hard at him for several moments, then he relaxed. "I'm going to let that remark pass, Emory, because you're not worth killing over such a ridiculous statement. A word of advice, though. You'd better catch up with the rest of society. Men don't talk like that about women unless it's in the strictest confidence."

"I was among friends. You were the one eavesdropping."

"Hmm, true. And of course you never would have guessed that I was anywhere near that barbecue café. You thought I was safe behind bars, didn't you?"

Oh, shit. He stretched his neck out of his tightening shirt collar. "I have no idea what you're talking about."

"Emory, Emory," Jack said, tsking and shaking his head. "Your nasty little scheme didn't work. The sheriff's office had absolutely no evidence against me, and after questioning me, they realized that I wasn't motivated to do that to Corbett. I demanded that either they book me for a crime or let me go." He spread his hands away from his body. "Needless to say . . . And the real funny thing is," he continued, "Jesse Garcia and me hit it off right away."

Shit, shit, double shit.

"I paid him a call after lunch. Introduced myself. Halfway through the bottle of tequila, he happened to admire my boots. Said his favorite uncle in Mexico had been a bootmaker of some renown. By any chance had my boots been made in Chihuahua by a cobbler named Julio?" Jack grinned. "Lo and behold."

Emory snickered. "Do you expect me to believe that?"

"Oh, I was lying," he confessed. "But your problem is that Garcia believed me. Of course he was a little drunk. He got misty reminiscing about Uncle Julio, who died last winter. He told story after story while I listened. It was a little early in the day for tequila, but all the same, we got to the worm, and I made a friend for life."

And Emory was screwed.

As though reading his mind, the cowboy smiled down at him. Not pleasantly. Dangerously. "If Garcia fingered you—"

"He wouldn't."

"If it meant either giving you up or going to jail? What do you think? Or if it came down to you or me, who do you think he would give over to the police?" He tapped him on the chest with the point of the blade. "You, Emory. He'd finger you. Faster than a chili pepper moves through a gringo. Then how long do you think your business partners would stick around? They would abandon you in a snap. They said as much over their rib baskets."

Of all Jack's threats, that was the one that frightened Emory most. Connaught played high-stakes poker every day, and he dealt from the bottom of the deck. But he would disown a dealer who got caught at it. Emory nursed no illusions about Connaught's loyalty; he had none except to himself.

"Okay, okay," Emory said, as though he were a little bored by now, "you've made your point, John Wayne."

The ranch hand squinted at him, taking his measure, as he had the first time he saw him in the Corbetts' living room. "What really concerns me, Emory, is that you think I'm bullshitting you."

He stood and leaned over the chair again, putting his face on a level with Emory's. The tip of the knife nicked the skin over his Adam's apple.

"If you mess with Anna Corbett again, I'll kill you. Do you remember what I said earlier about your gullet and your gonads? I meant it. I'll hurt you bad. Do we have an understanding?"

Oh, yeah, they did. They for damn sure did. Emory was convinced as he'd never been convinced of anything else in his entire life that this man was capable of killing him.

Because he couldn't nod for the risk of having his throat cut, he croaked, "Yeah."

"Good, good." Jack pulled back his knife and wiped a droplet of blood onto the leg of his blue jeans before sliding it into the leather scabbard. "Be seein' ya."

Chapter Thirty-Eight

"*I*'d give just about anything for a lemon Coke."

Connie Skaggs was balanced in the open window, one bare foot propped near her hip on the sill, the other barely skimming the floor as she indolently swung her leg back and forth. Her toenails were painted the same obnoxious color as her fingernails.

The top two buttons of her blouse were undone. Occasionally she dabbed at her deep cleavage with a wet paper towel. Her skirt was bunched up around her plump thighs, high enough to be inflaming but not so high as to reveal the prize.

She had the attention of all three men. Carl figured she was lapping it up.

"You know the kind I'm talking about, Cecil," she said wistfully. "Like they make at the drugstore soda fountain."

"I drank one right before the robbery."

"Lots of shaved ice. Two wedges of fresh lemon." She took a deep breath, expanding her chest and mashing against the damp cloth of her blouse large nipples as dark as her toenails.

Oh yeah, she knew exactly what she was doing, thought Carl. Myron was masturbating. He hadn't unzipped, but he was sitting on the floor in the corner, his legs splayed, his lips slack, his eyelids at half-mast as he stared at Connie while massaging himself.

Cecil must have noticed Myron's self-absorbed activity, because he joined her at the window, stepped in front of her, and discreetly pulled her skirt to a more modest level. Placing his arms around her, he bent down and nuzzled her neck. "I'd fix you a lemon Coke if I could, honey. Once we get to Mexico, you can have all the lemon Cokes you can drink."

She tried to wiggle free, saying crossly, "Stop that. It's too hot for mugging."

"It's never too hot for mugging." He chuckled, going for her neck again.

"I mean it. Get away." She swatted at him and he released her, looking wounded.

"Okay, okay."

Carl's lip curled with contempt. Any bitch slapped at him, he'd knock the shit out of her. But his big brother was a pussy. Always had been. Apparently always would be. He had hoped that prison and parole had toughened Cecil up. But if it had, the toughness hadn't weathered Connie Skaggs' influence. The bitch had deballed Cecil. He was more of a wuss now than before, when he hadn't been able to bring himself to blow away that guy in Arkadelphia who'd tried to stop the convenience-store robbery.

"I don't mean to be so grumpy, Cecil." Connie lowered her leg from the window ledge. She stood and leaned into the open window, bracing her hands on the sill, looking out at the dusty landscape and affording them a good view of her ass. "It's just so damn hot, it's making me cranky. There's not a leaf moving outside."

Carl agreed with her on that point. The heat had set him on edge too. The air was so dense it felt like an extra garment. Each breath required a conscious effort. He was leaking sweat from every pore. It trickled over his ribs, down his spine, and into his butt crack. The hairs on his arms and chest clung wetly to his skin.

It was too damn hot to move. Even the flies had stopped buzzing. Earlier in the day they had driven him crazy, zooming around the cabin like miniature F-16s, crashing into the walls, biting viciously when they landed on exposed skin. Now, too enervated to fly, they lethargically crawled around wherever they had last lighted—on empty cans and food wrappers and sticky spots on the table where Myron had dribbled anything he lifted toward his mouth.

Connie turned back into the room and flounced over to the table, where she took a drink from a can of orange soda that had recently been visited by one of the very houseflies Carl had been watching. "My mama used to say that when it got this hot and still, it was bound to rain."

"Did it?"

That was the first time in an hour Carl had uttered a word. The sound of his voice seemed to surprise them. They looked across at him where he was sprawled in a chair tilted against the wall. Cecil had returned from the window and was once again sitting backward in a wooden chair at the table, his chin propped on the top slat. Myron still sat spraddle-legged in the corner, a faint smile on his lips, his eyes more vacant than usual, a wet spot staining the front of his pants.

Connie turned to Carl. "Did it what?"

"Rain."

"Sometimes," she retorted. "Sometimes not. My mama wasn't always right." Going up on tiptoes, she worked her rump onto the table. Carl wondered if the broad knew what chairs were for. She seemed to prefer sitting on the surface of just about anything other than a chair seat.

"Take me, for instance." She dug into a bag of fried pork skins, put one into her mouth, and talked around it as she crunched. "Mama punished me hard for not minding her. I got whippings you wouldn't believe with my daddy's leather belt. She forced me to wear dumb, ugly clothes that I hated. While I was in school, anytime I did something wrong, I had to kiss up to the teacher and say I was sorry.

"She marched me to that holy roller church of hers twice every Sunday, Wednesday nights too, and made me wave my hands in the air and yell 'Praise Jesus!' like the other ignorant fools. She thought if she did all that, I'd turn out to be a good girl." Leaning forward from the waist, she shimmied her breasts and gave the room at large a wink. "Mama was *wrong*."

Cecil laughed, but his eyes were uneasily monitoring her chest and the flimsy modesty her blouse provided.

Carl grinned at her and motioned toward a six-pack of beer. "Bring me one of those."

"They're hot."

"So'm I."

He figured that a savvy bad girl like Connie would catch his double meaning, and she didn't disappoint. Without breaking eye contact, she tore one of the beer cans from the plastic webbing, hopped down off the table, and sauntered toward him wagging her rear end and swishing her skirt against her legs.

When she reached his chair, he didn't retract his legs and feet, which were stretched straight out in front of him. Peering up at her from beneath his eyebrows, he challenged her to do what he knew she was just itching to do.

Her predictability almost took the fun out of it.

She straddled his outstretched legs, planting her bare feet wide on either side of his thighs. "Want me to open it for you?"

"Yeah. Why don't you do that?"

"I think I'll have one too," Cecil said from across the room.

Connie ignored him. So did Carl. She shook the can of warm beer before popping the top. As expected, it spewed. Suds showered her chest, ran over her hands, dripped onto Carl's lap. Squealing and laughing, she slurped up the foam oozing from the open can.

Carl grabbed her wrist. "That's supposed to be my beer."

She extended the can toward him, placing it close to his mouth. He sipped beer from the top of it, then she tilted it forward and poured it directly into his mouth. He swallowed, but she didn't stop pouring.

"Come on, take it all," she cajoled in a singsong voice. "How much can you take? Need help?"

She placed her mouth next to his and alternated the spout between them, pouring first into his, then hers, playfully vying over who got the most beer. She spilled more than they drank, but the sloppiness made it even funnier.

"You two are wasting a perfectly good beer," Cecil remarked.

About the time the beer ran out, Carl dug his hand into the waistband of Connie's skirt and gave it a swift tug, causing her to land hard on his lap. She dropped the empty beer can and pushed her fingers through his hair, gripping his head. Her mouth was open and wet and slick when it covered his.

"What the—"

Cecil shot from his chair and came across the floor in angry strides.

Connie's mouth had gone after Carl's tongue with the strength of a Hoover, but Carl managed to pull away long enough to shout, "Myron!"

He came to his feet with the alacrity of a crane, but after two giant steps, he intercepted Cecil while he was still a few yards from where his girlfriend was sucking the lungs out of his brother. Myron clotheslined him. Carl heard his brother's teeth breaking like old crockery, and felt the thud when he hit the floor.

"What the hell are you doing?" Cecil shrieked. "What *is* this? Carl? Connie?"

But she seemed to have forgotten that Cecil existed. Carl also dismissed him. As long as Myron was standing over him, he was out of commission. Poor Cecil didn't know it yet, but he was as helpless as a newborn mouse trapped by a veteran alley cat. Myron could entertain himself for days with a weakened victim.

Connie was grinding her crotch against his. Roughly he opened her blouse. Her heavy breasts tumbled out, nearly smothering him. She crammed a nipple into his mouth. "Hard. He never sucks them hard enough."

Carl not only did as she asked, he bit her. "Hey!" She slapped him.

He slapped her back, busting her lip. She gaped at him, stunned. She touched the wounded spot with the tip of her tongue and dabbed up blood. "You son of a bitch."

Then she attacked his zipper with the greed of a miner who had just spotted gold in a rock pile. He grunted half in gratification, half in pain when she freed his stiff cock and squeezed it tightly with her sweaty hands.

Reaching beneath her skirt, he yanked on the narrow thong until her panties gave way. She went up on tiptoes, balanced for a second, then came down on him.

Carl, leaving her to do all the work, peered around her at his brother, who was groveling on the floor like a blind man who'd lost his cane. A froth of blood, mucus, and saliva dripped from his mouth. His cheeks were wet with tears and he was making the most godawful mewling sounds. The sight of him sickened Carl, and made him ashamed they shared a last name.

Cecil looked up and caught Carl watching him. "How can you do this to me?"

"Don't blame me that she's a fucking whore. You're the one who brought her along, big brother." He gathered up Connie's skirt and held it above her hips so his brother could see her ass in action.

With a feral cry, Cecil made a foolhardy lunge toward them that cost him a blow to the head by Myron's fist. He staggered backward, then went down on his knees. Hanging his head and drooling bloody gunk onto his chest, he sobbed.

"Say, who're you calling a fucking whore?" Connie panted.

"You like me better than him?"

"You're better at this, that's for sure."

"Aw, come on now," he said with feigned bashfulness.

Throwing her head back, she closed her eyes and rode him harder. "Oh, Jesus, don't stop, don't stop."

"I wasn't thinking of stopping. I was thinking of giving Cecil there a real show."

She was so lost in the act, it came as a cruel shock when he lifted her off him, turned her around, and shoved her down to the floor, where she landed on all fours. "What are you doing?"

"Shut up." Just as he entered her, he placed his hand on the back of her head and gave it a hard push. Her face smacked the wooden floor, painfully rearranging bones and cartilage. She screamed.

Cecil crawled toward her in a futile rescue attempt. Myron kicked him in the ribs. They splintered and he yowled.

Carl grinned up at Myron. "When I'm done with her, you can have a turn, Myron."

Myron, grinning and guffawing, ground his heel into Cecil's kidney.

Chapter Thirty-Nine

*K*eeping one eye on his rearview mirror, Jack pulled out of the bank parking lot into traffic. He doubted Emory Lomax would have him arrested for assault with a deadly weapon. With the duel threats of Garcia's betrayal and EastPark's disfranchisement, the last thing Lomax wanted was interaction with any branch of law enforcement. Much as he would like to see Jack Sawyer neutralized, Lomax couldn't risk baiting another legal snare in which he himself might become trapped.

Even so, Jack didn't trust him.

Who could tell what a conniving weasel like Lomax might do? Men like him were inordinately buoyant and had a way of resurfacing even after sinking for the third time. Having no scruples, loyalty, or love for anyone, they did what they wanted, when they wanted, with no regard for anything except their own desires. They paid allegiance only to their own greed. Nothing served as a conscience.

With the possible exception of self-preservation. That's what Jack was betting on. Lomax wasn't to be underestimated, and that included his survival instinct. He was gambling that Lomax valued his own skin more than he did vengeance. He was reasonably confident that his threats had derailed Lomax's scheme to secure the Corbett property. At the very least he had put a crimp in Lomax's schedule.

He pulled into a full-service gas station. "The oil might be a quart low," he told the attendant after asking him to fill up the tank.

"Sweet truck, mister."

"Thanks."

The young man looked to be in his late teens. He continued to admire the pickup as he washed the front windshield. After pumping the gas, he opened the hood, checked the dipstick, and told Jack he was right about being low on oil, and disappeared into the garage to get a can. That's when Jack spotted a police cruiser in his side mirror. His gut clenched. Had he been wrong about Lomax?

But the squad car drove past without the lone officer giving him a glance.

His showdown with Lomax had accomplished what he had hoped it would, but, in hindsight, it had been a rash and foolhardy thing to do, motivated in part by his own ego. Now it seemed like a silly adolescent game of one-upmanship.

He certainly could have staged a less dramatic confrontation. His theatrics had daunted Lomax, but for how long? The effect might be short term. When Lomax had time to recover and think about it, his pride might prompt him to double his efforts. Jack's grandstanding might have made matters worse for Anna, not better.

It was presumptuous to think she wanted his help anyway. Delray had suspected him of sabotaging the herd. Her father-in-law's suspicions, coupled with those of the deputies who had escorted him away this morning, might have convinced Anna that he was guilty. The hours of questioning he had undergone hadn't bothered him nearly as much as the reproach he'd seen in her eyes as he'd tried to explain to David why he was in custody of the deputies.

All the way around, for a variety of reasons, she and her son would be much better off if Jack Sawyer were out of the picture. With this full tank of gas, he ought to drive away from Blewer and everyone in it. He could leave with a clear conscience, knowing he had benched Lomax long enough for Anna to consult another financial adviser.

Arrogant and smug is how he had felt when he left the bank. Now he cursed himself for being so reckless. He'd walked out of the sheriff's office today, but the next time law officers came after him it might not be so benign an experience. He'd been a damn fool to threaten Lomax. With his knife, no less. That was as good as waving a red flag. Yeah, the sooner he was away from Blewer, the better.

The service-station attendant returned with a can of oil. "This brand okay?"

"Sure. Fine."

While the oil was draining into the engine, the boy strolled back to the driver's side, propped one foot on the gas pump, and leaned against it. "Gum?" He offered Jack a stick of Big Red.

"Thanks."

When they were both chomping, he remarked, "I'd've remembered this truck. You ain't a regular."

"No."

"Headed in or out of town?"

"Haven't decided yet."

The young man glanced up and down the street. "I's you, I'd head out."

"Why?"

"Nothin' excitin's gonna happen 'round here. That's for damn sure."

"It's a pretty quiet town, all right."

"Unless them Herbolds show up. Then there might be some fireworks." He smacked his gum as though he welcomed the possibility. "My old man knowed 'em when they lived here."

"No kidding?"

"Says they's bad news. Says they might be headed back here, but I say who'n hell would want to come to Blewer, especially straight from prison? If it was me just broke out, I'd hit the big cities and find me some recreation." He winked and popped the gum between his molars. "Know what I mean?"

"Yeah, I know what you mean." Jack raised his hips off the seat and dug into his front pants pocket. "How much do I owe you?"

Taking the hint, the young man moved around to the front of the truck, tossed the empty oil can into a trash barrel, and lowered the hood. "Cash or credit card? If you pay by cash, you get a five percent discount and a free beer Koozie."

Jack handed him two twenty-dollar bills through the open window. "I'll take the discount. Skip the Koozie."

"You sure? My girlfriend and me collect 'em."

"Be my guest."

"Cool. Be right back with your change."

During their conversation, Jack had reached a decision: He wasn't going anywhere. Not until the Herbolds were either recaptured or killed in the attempt. Anna might order him out of the trailer and off her land, and he couldn't blame her if she weren't entirely certain of his trustworthiness. But he couldn't leave Blewer as long as Carl and Cecil were still at large and posing even a hint of threat to her and David.

"Here you go."

The young man gave him his change. "Thanks for the good service," Jack told him.

"You bet. Thanks for the Koozie." Nodding past Jack's shoulder, he added, "Wherever you're headed, Mister, if I's you, I'd try and outrun that."

Jack looked through the truck's rear window, and for the first time noticed the dark storm clouds gathering on the horizon.

"Dumb sons o' bitches."

Lucy approached the counter with a carafe of fresh coffee. "Who is, Ezzy?"

"Excuse my language, Lucy. I was just watching your TV there."

He was taking a coffee break from boredom. For working folks it was near quitting time—beyond the afternoon coffee break, verging on cocktail hour, too early for supper. Ezzy was the only customer in the diner.

He and Lucy had been discussing the upcoming Blewer Bucks football season, but he had kept one eye on the small TV she kept on the work counter between the malt mixer and the microwave. He had noticed when *Oprah* signed off and the first edition of the local evening news came on.

The lead story was about the manhunt mounted for the convicts, who were still being sought more than a week following their escape. But there was a new chapter to the story. In northwestern Louisiana the bodies of two elderly women had been discovered on their farm at the bottom of the water well. Carl Herbold and Myron Hutts were shoo-in suspects; their fingerprints were found all over the house. Now law enforcement agencies in three states were coordinating efforts to capture them, along with Cecil Herbold and Connie Skaggs.

The TV station was broadcasting live shots of a roadblock, where uniformed officers were barricaded, armed to the teeth, behind their patrol cars. The camera caught one yawning. That was what had caused Ezzy to curse.

After refilling his coffee cup, Lucy propped her fist on her hip and watched the broadcast with him until another story was introduced. "Who're you calling dumb, Ezzy?"

"Well not the Herbolds."

"You think the cops are going about this manhunt all wrong?"

He looked at her wryly. "If you'd escaped from prison, killed four people, then robbed a bank and killed some more, would you be traveling down a major highway?"

"Lord, Ezzy, I don't know. You're the crime expert."

He harrumphed. She was the only one who thought so. "Those roadblocks are a waste of time and taxpayers' money."

"So what's your opinion?"

He sipped his coffee thoughtfully. "If I was them—the Herbolds—I'd hole up somewhere till things calmed down. Sooner or later those police forces aren't going to pay men to sit on their thumbs and yawn on TV. They'll cut back on the manpower. Something else will distract them. They'll look the other way." He tapped the counter with his blunt index finger. "That's when I'd make my move and not before."

Even though he didn't order it, she served him a slice of apple pie. "Want ice cream on that? Or whipped cream? Some cheddar?"

"No, this is fine." He didn't want the pie, but to keep from hurting her feelings, he picked up a fork and dug in. It was delicious, though the crust wasn't as flaky as Cora's. "I knew those boys, Lucy. They weren't book smart, but they were cagey little bastards. I'd bet my next retirement check that they've got the law figured out. Instead of setting up traps the Herbolds are too smart to walk into, those officers ought to be out beating the bushes for them."

"That's lots of acreage to cover on foot, Ezzy."

"I know. It's impractical. No, it's impossible. I'm just saying that's how they'll be found. If ever."

"You think they could get away?"

"Wouldn't be all that surprised if they did. Especially if Carl's running the show, and he usually did."

"Be a shame if they escaped. Can you imagine him killing those helpless old ladies in cold blood? And that teenage girl?" She shook her head in a manner that said the world was going to hell in a handbasket. "Maybe you ought to share your theory with somebody, Ezzy."

"They wouldn't listen to me," he grumbled.

"Bet they would."

He knew better. He had offered his services to Sheriff Ron Foster and had been turned down flat. He wasn't going to humiliate himself again. "Nobody wants my services, Lucy. They think my brain is kaput just 'cause I look old and decrepit."

"Now you're fishing for compliments." Reaching across the counter, she playfully slapped his arm. "You're a far sight from old, Ezzy Hardge. And a long shot from decrepit, too."

"You haven't seen me getting out of bed."

Only after speaking the words did he realize that she might read something into them. Sure enough, when he looked up at her, he was met with a soft and misty gaze.

His hand was unsteady as he reached for his cup of coffee. "Take my word for it, it ain't pretty. Cora teases me about being creaky."

He was no longer looking at Lucy, but he sensed her deflation. She said nothing for a while, then quietly said, "She's sure staying away a long time."

"Um-huh."

"When is she coming back?"

"Any day now," he lied.

"Hmm." There was another silence long enough to stretch out in. Then she cleared her throat. "Well, till she gets back, I'm happy to cook for you. Anytime."

Relieved that the boundaries had been reestablished, he looked at her across the blue Formica and smiled. "That's right decent of you, Lucy. Thanks." He forked up the last bite of pie, took a final sip of coffee, and stepped off the counter stool.

Treating him more like a visitor than a customer, Lucy walked him to the door. Since he had come in, there had been a distinct change in the weather. The sky had grown dark. The wind was whipping at the canopy above the door, making it pop like a mainsail.

"Looks like we might get some rain finally," Lucy said.

"Looks like."

"You be careful out there, Ezzy."

"Thanks again for the pie."

"Ezzy?" He paused, turned. Lucy was twisting a dish towel between her hands. "The other day, after you left, those old geezers . . ." She pointed toward the table where the spit-and-whittle group collected each morning. "They said that Carl Herbold had vowed to kill Delray Corbett."

"Not a threat any longer. Delray's heart attack beat him to it."

"What happened to make him say such a thing?"

"After his conviction for killing that bank guard in Arkadelphia, Carl filed for an appeal. It was granted, but he fired his lawyer and asked Delray to foot the bill for a new one. Delray told him he was on his own. Said he had done the crime so he could pay the consequences. Said Carl should be glad he wasn't having to face murder charges here in Blewer County for Patsy McCorkle.

"Carl swore up and down he had nothing to do with her death. Delray called him a liar and publicly denounced him. The boy went berserk and spouted all sorts of dire threats. He lost on appeal and blamed his stepdaddy for not coming through with a better lawyer. In fact, he blamed Delray for everything. Said if Delray had loved them, he and Cecil might have turned out different."

"Was their meanness Delray's fault?"

"Maybe. Some. But not altogether. Those boys were already bad when he married their mother."

She glanced toward the empty table before bringing her worried eyes back to him. "They also said that . . . that Carl had vowed to kill you."

"Just talk from a bunch of old men who've got nothing better to do than jabber about other people's misfortunes."

"Did he?" she persisted.

"Something to that effect," he said reluctantly. "He said he was a repeat offender only because I jailed him so many times on pissant charges when he was a kid. On account of me, he said, he had a long record and that's why the courts in Arkansas came down on him so hard."

"It still bothers you, doesn't it?"

"Naw. Con talk, Lucy, is all it was. Can't take it seriously."

"No, I mean that McCorkle girl's death. It still bothers you."

Her insight surprised him. Or was his preoccupation visible? Did it show up like a tattoo? It bothered him to think it might be that obvious to folks, but he answered her honestly. "It comes to mind now and then."

Her overmascaraed lashes didn't even blink. His pat answer hadn't satisfied her. Why was it that the women in his life were the most intuitive females on the face of the earth? "Yeah, Lucy, it still bothers me. And, actually, I think about it a lot."

"Those boys never had to answer for it." Her lined face formed a grimace of compassion for his torment. "And it haunts you 'cause you believe they did it."

"Not quite, Lucy. I'm coming to believe they didn't."

The wind was even stronger than it had looked through the window of the Busy Bee. Moving down the sidewalk toward his car, Ezzy squinted against the grit the gale churned up from the gutters. He held his hat on his head with one hand while using the other to fish his car keys from his pocket.

Earlier in the day, middle-school band students had gone from car to car parked in the downtown area and put flyers under windshield wipers. Freed by the wind, the announcements of the fund-raising pancake supper were swirling around like a swarm of bright pink butterflies.

Across the street from the café a kiddie pool featured in the sidewalk sale at the Perry Bros. store was tumbling along the sidewalk. It blew out into the street, forcing a van to swerve in order to miss it.

Ezzy got into his car and turned on the headlights. Even though it was hours before sundown, low scuttling clouds had made the sky as dark as twilight. Motorists were driving recklessly and fast, trying to reach their destinations before the approaching storm broke. On his way home, he witnessed several near collisions.

He drove with more caution than he wished. Eager to get home and ponder the words he'd unexpectedly heard himself say to Lucy, he regarded the storm as a gross inconvenience.

But, inevitably, his adrenaline kicked in. He began thinking like an official faced with an emergency that jeopardized public safety. There would be a potential for flash flooding. Pylons should be rounded up and made ready to place at low crossings before some fool tried to drive through high, swift water and got his car swept into the river. The fire department should be on the alert to sound the civil defense alarm if a funnel cloud was sighted. Every deputy in the department should be mobilized.

He caught himself speeding toward the sheriff's office before he remembered that he didn't belong there. He would be sitting out this storm, and all the storms to follow.

Arriving at home, he heard the first rumblings of distant thunder, which underscored his dejection. The house was unnaturally dark. Switching on lights as he moved through the gloomy rooms, he went outside to the back deck and pulled the lawn furniture and Cora's prized hibiscus plants beneath the overhang for protection.

He thought about calling her to ask if they'd had any rough weather in West Texas, maybe make her feel a little guilty that she wasn't here to share a lonely, stormy evening with him.

But he didn't want to expose himself to rejection again. Not yet. Eventually he would beg if he had to, make promises he probably wouldn't keep, do anything to get her to come home. But he wasn't up to it tonight.

The last time he'd called, she had rebuffed his tentative approaches toward the topic of their reconciliation. Worse, she had ignored them, stopping him cold whenever he ventured in the direction of anything personal. Instead, she had squandered his time and long-distance budget by talking about Delray Corbett's funeral and the food he should take out to Anna.

He went back indoors but stared out the patio door, past his deck and beyond. Ugly storm clouds stretched across the horizon as far as he could see, bringing to mind Anna and her boy. He wondered if they would be okay out there all by themselves. Probably. Besides, if there was any trouble, her hired hand was nearby.

He went into the living room and switched on the TV. Using the latest technology, the weatherman was standing slap-dab in the middle of the state map, moving his hands over the multicolored radar pattern of storms. They spread over the entire eastern third of Texas, stretching from the Red River all the way down the Sabine, nearly to the coast.

Weatherwise, it was going to be an eventful night.

Ezzy climbed aboard his Barcalounger, prepared to ride out the night in front of his television set. But for all the warnings and watches issued by the National Weather Service, the threatening storms seemed of minor importance. Free now to square off with the hypothesis he'd shared with Lucy, he focused on it, viewing it from every angle, like a gladiator sizing up his opponent. And that's how he thought of it—as a silent, invisible enemy that had stalked him for years while he remained blissfully, stupidly unaware.

Not until this afternoon when this reversed possibility pounced on him with the impetus of a mountain lion and sank its claws into him had he realized why this case had haunted him. Not because he was convinced that the Herbolds were involved. But because he *wasn't* convinced.

Maybe he'd been too close to it from the start. The discovery of the dead girl's naked body in his county had caused him to leap to a quick but logical conclusion. Maybe he had wanted the Herbold brothers to be guilty because they were a tragedy waiting to happen. It was only a matter of time before somebody tangled with them and wound up dead. Ezzy had skipped ahead a few chapters, that's all.

They'd had a fairly good alibi in that they'd been driving to Arkadelphia. They'd been photographed robbing a convenience store there early the following morning. But, presuming them to be guilty, Ezzy had massaged the facts to make them fit. Not perfectly, but pretty good. Say as good as a size eight shoe fit a woman who really wore an eight and a half. He had made it work.

But Carl's avowal of innocence had always bothered him. His vehement denial was the real grain of sand in the oyster shell of Ezzy's case. Why would Carl own up to every other wicked deed he'd ever done but adamantly deny that he had even left the Wagon Wheel with Patsy that night? Ezzy had figured he was just being ornery. But maybe not. For once in his miserable life, maybe Carl had been telling the truth.

What was most troublesome was that if Carl and Cecil hadn't left the tavern with that girl, someone else had. Someone else had taken her to the river, used her sexually, then left her dead in the weeds. Someone else held the answers to the questions that had plagued Ezzy for almost a quarter of a century.

Had he spent his career, and a good part of his life, trying to prove that Carl and Cecil were there, when actually another man had heard Patsy McCorkle take her final breath? Had he allowed a guilty man to go scot free?

Damn him for a fool if he had.

Chapter Forty

*I*t's really better this way. Right, Myron?"

"Right, Carl."

"We did what we had to do."

"Yeah."

Myron was eating Vienna sausages from the can. The packing gelatin oozed between his fingers faster than he could lick it off.

"Did I ever tell you about our stepdaddy, Myron?"

"You said he was a bastard."

"To put it mildly, Myron. To put it mildly. Our mama came home one night wagging this loser with her and announcing that he was going to be our new daddy. Fat chance of that. Right off, me and Cecil hated him and made no secret of it. From the day they got married, it was them against us. All we needed was each other. My brother and me made a good team."

He sighed heavily. "But Delray ruined Cecil, is what I think. My brother must have taken some of his lectures to heart, because the older Cecil got, the more of a pussy he became. Wasn't too long before he completely lost his sense of humor and spirit of adventure. It came to a head that morning in Arkadelphia. He got spooked and left it to me to kill that off-duty policeman. Now, how's that for a brother?" he asked in disgust.

"I just couldn't trust him after that, Myron. Not even on this job. He argued with me about every single detail, didn't he? You were here. You heard." He looked across at Myron, adding earnestly, "If I had done things Cecil's way, we'd've been fucked."

"Yeah. Fucked." Myron picked at a pimple on his chin and drank from a can of beer, seemingly indifferent to the conversation and to sharing the cabin with two corpses.

In many ways Carl envied Myron. He wouldn't mind temporarily slipping into Myron's vacuous universe where nothing mattered except the appeasement of whatever appetite happened to be gnawing. Just for a little while. Just long enough to get over this hump. Myron didn't seem to care, or even remember, that he had tortured Cecil into such a sad state that he was begging for death by the time Carl put the pistol to the back of his head.

When you looked at it from that standpoint, he'd done his brother a huge favor. Killing him had been act of mercy, not murder.

Nevertheless, the incident had left a bad taste in his mouth. Sharing the cabin with the bodies wasn't helping his nerves any, either. He wished he and Myron had carted them outside, or that they would rot faster than they were so he wouldn't be forced to continue looking at them. They hadn't started stinking yet, but when they did, what then?

With no more concern than he would give two tow sacks of potatoes, Myron had dragged the bodies into a corner so they wouldn't clutter up the center of the floor. They lay exactly as he had left them, in a jumble of bloody clothing and lifeless limbs.

Apparently it didn't bother Myron to look at Cecil's death mask, or Connie's blood-streaked legs, or the necklace of dark bruises around her throat. Myron was an ardent, if artless, lover. Connie hadn't taken to his rowdy style of romance and had fought him to her last breath. But she was a whore. No great loss to anybody.

Carl tried real hard to work up some sadness over his brother's death, but all he could muster was regret that Cecil had died as he had lived— a gutless coward. If he had shown some spine, he might still be alive. Instead he had died blubbering like a baby, and that was cause for disdain, not grief.

"He never could go the distance," Carl said, speaking his private thoughts aloud. "I could give you a hundred examples of how he chickened out at the last minute. He always backed down when things got rough, and left me to do the dirty work for him. But he was my brother. I'm gonna miss him something terrible."

Although Carl doubted Myron knew shit about sibling relationships, the retard nodded agreement.

On a happier note, he said, "Your share of the money just doubled, Myron ol' boy!"

Myron peeled his lips back in a wide grin.

Carl shuddered. "Jesus, Myron. Don't you know what a toothbrush—"

The gunfire cracked through the cabin like a whip. He and Myron dove for cover.

* * *

David aimed his fingers toward the ceiling and pretended to be firing laser weapons at descending aliens. They were slimy, icky, ugly creatures with snot coming out their noses and hairy warts on their heads. They had webbed hands and a long tongue that could kill people if it touched 'em 'cause there was poison on it. Not even Rocket Rangers were safe. That's what he was. Rocket Ranger XT3. He was the leader, the bravest of all the rangers. The aliens were scared of him.

"*Pskoowou! Pskoowou!*" He fired his laser weapon, and it blew up the warty head of the leader of the aliens. He had killed them all.

Rocket Ranger XT3, this is base zero, zero niner. What's your position? Rocket Ranger XT3, do you read?

David adjusted his make-believe headset. "Zero, zero niner, this is Rocket Ranger XT3. Mission accomplished."

He glanced over at his mother, who lay on her side facing away from him. She had come downstairs to get him, saying he had to take a nap. He'd put up his best arguments. He wasn't tired. Naps were for babies. Kids on TV didn't have to take naps. Rocket Rangers didn't for sure. But a Rocket Ranger didn't have a mom, either, who gave him mean looks that said he would soon be in serious trouble if he didn't obey.

So David had trudged upstairs behind her, saying words like *damn* and *hell* and *butt*, ugly words she couldn't hear.

That was one good thing about having a mother who was deaf. You could talk back without her knowing. And you could pretend to be asleep until she fell asleep, and then you could fire rockets and stuff and the sounds didn't wake her up 'cause she couldn't hear them.

But he had killed all the attacking aliens and so now he was bored.

He counted out loud to one hundred, a new skill his mom had recently taught him. Then he tried counting backward, but he lost interest somewhere in the midseventies.

He practiced clicking his tongue against the roof of his mouth, seeing how loud he could do it. Whenever he'd done this around Grandpa, he would frown and tell him to cut it out, that it was rude and annoying. Jack hadn't minded, though. Jack and him had had a contest to see who could do it the loudest. Jack could do it real loud. Louder than anybody.

Thinking about Jack made him feel sad again and he sorta wanted to cry, but he didn't because that would be babyish. He rolled to his side and stared beyond the edge of the pillow into near space. Mom had said that Jack might not come back and he was afraid she was right 'cause when the police on TV took away people, they hardly ever came back. They got killed or put in jail or something.

If Jack didn't come back, nothing was going to be fun anymore.

Things would go back to being the way they had been before Jack came, only Grandpa wouldn't be here either. It would be just him and Mom.

Mom was okay. She cooked good stuff to eat. She played games with him and didn't get mad if he won. When he was sick she pulled him onto her lap and rocked him even though she said he was getting almost as big as her. Or if he was scared—or just 'cause and for no special reason—it felt good to let Mom hold him and lean his head against the fat part of her chest.

But Mom was a girl. She was always scared he was gonna drown or poke his eye out or break his neck or something. When she was around he couldn't pee outside. She didn't like farts, either. Girls thought farts were about the worst thing ever. At least Mom did.

Today when he was crying because Jack left, she had told him he probably wouldn't miss Jack at all when he started going to school. She said it would be exciting to go every day.

Smiling so that her teeth showed, she had said. *"You'll learn to read."*

He had reminded her that he already knew how to read.

"You'll learn to read better. And you'll make lots of friends with boys and girls your age."

He had nursed a secret longing to have a friend. One time Mom and Grandpa had an argument about him going to preschool. He hadn't been able to follow all the signs, but most of them. He had sorta hoped his mom would win and that he could go to preschool and play with other kids. But his grandpa had said that Mom could teach him everything he needed to know at home, and that he would be in school soon enough, so he hadn't got to go.

Maybe when he got to kindergarten he could get on a T-ball team. Or soccer. He might be good. He was pretty good at running and stuff. Maybe he could go to birthday parties like the kids on TV. But he wasn't sure he would know what to do at a birthday party. The other kids might not like him. They might not want him on their T-ball team, either. They might think he was stupid or something.

He would sure feel better if Jack was around. He could talk to Jack about stuff. When he talked to Mom, she just said dumb Mom things. She said that everybody was going to like him and that he would be the teacher's favorite. But how did Mom know that?

Jack would understand. But Jack wasn't here. He had got in his truck and driven off with one of the policemen. What if he never came back? Not ever.

Wait a minute!

Jack hadn't taken his stuff! He wouldn't leave forever without his stuff! He would come back for it, wouldn't he?

And then he got the best idea.

Cautiously, he looked over at his mom. She was still sleeping. Moving slowly, he inched to the edge of the bed. Watching her for signs of waking up, he eased himself off the bed until his toes touched the floor. One of the planks creaked beneath his weight and he froze, until he remembered that his mother couldn't hear it. She would only sense a vibration, so he was very careful to walk on his tippy-toes across the room. At the door, he glanced back toward the bed one last time. She hadn't moved. He pulled the door closed.

As he went down the upstairs hallway, he noticed how dark it was. His mom sure was sleeping a long time. It must be suppertime already. Maybe even past supper.

On the way downstairs, he halfway expected to hear her coming after him. If he asked her permission to do this, she would probably say no, so now was a good time. He could get there and back before she missed him.

When he came back, he would go upstairs and hide the stuff under his bed, then he would wake up his mom and tease her about being a sleepyhead and tell her he was hungry for supper. She would never know that he had left the house, something he was forbidden to do unless he had checked with her first. Never, ever, was he to go beyond the yard without her or Grandpa. The "yard" was the grassy part with the white fence around it.

It was a dumb rule. He was old enough to go to school, wasn't he?

He unlocked the front door and stepped out onto the porch, being careful to pull the door closed behind him. On the porch, he paused. Everything sure looked funny. Sort of green and weird. The sky looked scary, too. He saw jagged forks of lightning and heard the thunder that followed.

Maybe he should wait and go another time.

But he might not have a chance as good as this.

Before he could talk himself out of it, he ran down the front steps and across the yard. He crawled beneath the fence and angled off toward the barn. As he ran past the corral, he noticed that the horses were acting strange. They were running along the fence, first one way, then the other, like they were trying to get out. They snorted and stamped, tossed their heads, and rolled their eyes. He wouldn't like riding them today, not even with Jack holding the reins and leading.

He paused again, wondering if maybe he had fallen asleep after all.

Was he having a dream? But when the lightning flashed again, he knew he was awake.

He ran faster. If he didn't hurry, he might get rained on and then Mom would know that he'd gone outside without asking permission.

Despite his seat belt, Jack went airborne when his truck ran over a pothole. He banged his head on the ceiling of the cab. "Son of a bitch!" He swore not because of the pothole or the pain to his head, but because even though he was pushing the truck toward eighty miles an hour, it seemed to be mired in quicksand.

He had hit the pothole because his eyes were on the sky, not the road. He knew the warning signs because he had experienced them before. Once in Altus, Oklahoma; once in a small town in Missouri, the name of which escaped him now. When the sky looked like this, and the atmosphere took on this greenish cast, the conditions were right for a tornado.

He glanced at a familiar landmark as he sped past and knew that he had only a couple more miles to go. "Come on, come on," he said, urging the truck to perform at maximum capacity. Thank God he'd had that oil level checked.

Raindrops as heavy as sinkers began spattering the windshield. A gust of wind disturbed the preternatural stillness. Then another gust, stronger than the first. In under a minute the branches of the trees lining the highway were in a frenzy. Falling twigs and leaves got caught in his windshield wipers. It began to rain harder. He glanced at the turbulent sky and cursed again.

The sudden rainfall after months of drought made the surface of the road dangerously slick. When he finally reached the gate and applied the brakes, the truck went into a skid. Managing to stop it about thirty yards beyond the gate, he pushed it into Reverse and fishtailed backward, then dropped it into Drive and shot through the iron arch.

His first thought upon seeing the house was that all the rooms were dark. Why weren't the lights on? Were they here? Or had Anna, frightened by the threat of dangerous thunderstorms, gone into town to wait them out? Possibly with Marjorie Baker?

Jack didn't even take time to shut the door of his truck. As soon as he cut the engine, he clambered out and ran up the front steps to the porch. Not bothering to ring the bell, he pushed open the door. The wind caught it, ripped it from his hand, and slammed it against the interior wall.

Although that made a racket loud enough to raise the dead, he shouted, "Anna! David!" He raced into the living room. It was empty and the television was dark. Running from room to room, he shouted for David. He opened the cellar door in the kitchen and hollered down, but he couldn't even see the bottom of the narrow stairs for the darkness below. Besides, David would have replied if they had taken shelter there.

"Where the hell are you?"

Jack went back to the entry and ran up the staircase, taking the treads two or three at a time. David's room was empty. He ran toward Anna's and burst through the door. She was lying on the bed. "Anna!" In three strides he was across the room, shaking her awake.

She sat bolt upright, obviously terrified from having been awakened so abruptly from a deep slumber, shocked to see him in her bedroom standing over her and breathing heavily.

Knowing he must look like a wild man, he held up both hands palms out. "Where's David?"

She glanced at the rumpled empty space beside her and registered alarm. Jack said, "There's a storm coming. We've got to find David. Hurry!"

Sensing his urgency if not catching every rushed word, she scrambled off the bed and followed him from the room. They checked Delray's bedroom, the attic, the closet in David's room, underneath his bed. There was no trace of the boy.

Jack gripped her shoulders. "Where could he be?"

Frantically, Anna shook her head.

Nearly stumbling over each other, they ran downstairs. "I've already checked down here, but let's do it again." He took the time to look directly at her so she wouldn't miss any words. "I'll search this side of the house. Meet me back here."

In less than sixty seconds they were back in the foyer. Anna's hands were in her hair. She was seconds away from hysteria. Jack bolted through the open front door, ran to the end of the porch, and looked toward the northwest.

And saw it.

An angry finger of destruction dipping down from a curtain of cloud. "Shit!"

He grabbed Anna's hand and leaped off the porch, dragging her with him. She managed to land on her feet. He raced for the storm cellar, which he knew to be on the far side of the corral. Delray had pointed it out to him shortly after he began working for him.

Jack saw that the horses were terrified, and he regretted being unable to do anything for them, but they were safer in the corral than inside the barn, which could collapse on them. Even if they weren't safer outside, his priority was seeing to Anna and David's safety.

But Anna wasn't cooperating. She dug her heels in as they approached the storm cellar. He stopped and turned to her. "Get in the cellar." Even though it didn't matter how loudly he spoke, he was yelling above the roar of the wind. "I'll find David."

She wrested her hand free and began running in the opposite direction of the cellar.

"Goddamn it!" Jack started after her.

She reached the barn seconds ahead of him and struggled to pull open the heavy metal door. The wind tore at her hair and clothes. Raindrops struck like needles, but she seemed unaware of anything except finding her son.

Jack pushed her aside and grabbed the handle of the barn door. "David!" He cupped his hands around his mouth. "David!" He jogged down the center aisle, checking each stall and the tack room, shouting as he went, but when he reached the opposite end, the boy was still not to be found. He slid open the rear door.

"Oh, Jesus."

That he didn't shout. He spoke it as a prayer.

Chapter Forty-One

$\mathcal{T}$he funnel cloud had spun itself into a full-fledged tornado, but it was still trying to decide whether to remain airborne or skim the ground. With every second it gained velocity and strength. The ranch lay directly in its present path. They had maybe two minutes. Probably less.

While Jack was still trying to assimilate their peril, Anna shoved him out of her way and dodged his attempt to grab her and hold her back. She ran across the open field toward the trailer.

Jack ran after her, overtook her, and kept running. As soon as he reached the trailer, he banged on the aluminum side of it, then nearly yanked the door off its hinges in his haste to open it. "David! David!"

The boy was cowering in a corner of the built-in sofa.

Terror-struck, teeth chattering, he said, "Am I in trouble?"

Jack scooped him into his arms. "Just glad to see you, buddy."

Anna had just reached the door of the trailer when Jack leaped through the opening with the boy in his arms. "The cellar!"

This time she didn't hesitate or argue, but instantly reversed her direction. They sprinted back across the field and past the barn. The distance had never seemed so far. Hard as they were running, it seemed to Jack they were making no progress, until suddenly they were there.

David was clinging to his neck so tightly that it was left to Anna to open the cellar door. She had difficulty lifting it, then the wind caught it and slammed it against the ground. Jack glanced over his shoulder. The twister had dipped lower and was cutting a furrow through the field they had just crossed. Faster than his eyes could register the bizarre sight, fence posts were being plucked from the ground and sucked up into the whirling funnel. The sound was horrific.

Anna scrambled down the steps ahead of him and David. Jack passed the boy to her, then fought with all his strength to lift the door up so he could close it. For what seemed like an eternity, he played tug-of-war with Mother Nature at her most ferocious. The tin roof of the barn was being ripped off sheet by sheet. One sailed past him. Ten yards closer and it could have sliced him in half.

Putting all his strength into it, gritting his teeth, he managed to get the door up, then ducked beneath it as it slammed shut almost on top of him. He bolted it from the inside.

Plunged into total stillness and stygian darkness, and reeling from the battering he'd taken from the gale-force winds, he lost his balance on the concrete steps and stumbled down them.

"Jack?"

He followed the direction of David's quavering voice. But it was Anna's hand he found reaching out for him through the impenetrable blackness. When their hands touched, they clasped tightly. He moved forward carefully, feeling his way, until he was crouched in front of them, touching them. David's leg, Anna's shoulder, her hair, the boy's cheek.

His arms closed around them. While the storm raged outside, he held them protectively. Anna buried her face in one side of his neck, David in the other. His hands cupped the backs of their heads, pressing them closer. Things were hurled against the cellar door with such impetus that David whimpered in fear. Anna felt the vibrations; she shuddered.

Jack whispered reassurances, knowing the boy could hear them, hoping that even though Anna couldn't, she would be comforted by the movement of his breath in her hair. Her hand lay trustingly on his thigh. David's small fist gripped a handful of his shirt.

And he knew that this was what mattered. They mattered. He mattered to them. All the rest of it—*all* the rest of it—evaporated into insignificance.

His throat became painfully tight with emotion. He squeezed his eyes shut to block out the loneliness of his past. He hugged Anna and David closer, cherishing their nearness. Their warmth seeped into him far deeper than his skin. This moment would be locked in his memory forever. Nobody could take it from him. This one time, this moment, he experienced love.

Jack could have held the embrace forever, but eventually David became restless. He wiggled free. "Was it a twister, Jack?"

Reluctantly Jack released them and sat back on his heels. "That's what it was, all right."

"Wow, just like the movie." Now that the danger had passed, David was excited. "Do you think it blew our house down? Or picked up our cows and carried 'em off?"

Jack chuckled. "I hope not."

Anna's hand found his in the darkness. She bent his fingers back so his palm was flat, then she traced letters against it. "L . . . i . . . g . . . ? Light? Light." He patted her knee, indicating that he understood. "David, is there a light in here?"

"It hangs down from the ceiling."

Jack stood up and waved his arms around until he connected with a single lightbulb. When he pulled the short chain, he blinked against the sudden glare.

"Wow! Look at that spider!" David exclaimed.

But Jack was looking at Anna, and Anna was looking at him, and although she was as wet and bedraggled as a lost kitten, he thought she had never been more beautiful. He noticed how snugly her wet shirt was clinging to her. It fit like a second skin, hid nothing. With admirable chivalry, his eyes moved back to her face, but staring at it posed no hardship. It was so goddamn beautiful, why would he need to look farther? Ragged as he must look, something in her eyes told him he looked pretty good to her, too.

"Hey, Jack? Jack?"

"Leave the spider alone, David," he replied absently. "This is her house, not ours."

"I know, but she's crawling toward Mom."

His daze interrupted, Jack brushed the harmless spider off the wall behind Anna, then took a look around. The ceiling of the cellar was only about four inches above his head. He estimated the enclosure to be twelve feet long and eight feet wide, with two cots along each wall. It was on one of the cots that Anna was still sitting. David had gotten up to explore.

On the back wall were several shelves stocked with candles and matches, lightbulbs, canned food and a can opener, a jar of peanut butter, a sealed glass canister containing a box of saltine crackers, bottled water, and a heavy-duty flashlight with extra batteries.

At the front end were the steps leading up to the door, which set at a forty-five-degree angle. Jack went up the steps and put his ear to the door. Turning to Anna, he said, "The worst is past, I think. But it's raining hard and I hear thunder. I think we should stay a while longer."

David interpreted her signs. "Mom says whatever you think, Jack."

"Okay. We'll stay awhile."

"It's neat in here," David said, bouncing on the balls of his feet. "Can we spend the night in here?"

"That probably won't be necessary."

"Darn." Then, immediately recovering from his disappointment, he asked, "Are you back for good? Why'd you leave with the policemen? Did you miss us?"

Anna clapped her hands and motioned David forward. His exuberance was instantly doused by her stern expression. Suddenly downcast, he shuffled toward the cot until he was standing in front of his mother.

Anna placed her fingers beneath his chin, brought his head up, and began to sign. As she did, her eyes filled with tears.

Jack watched as David's lower lip began to quiver. "I didn't mean to scare you half to death, Mom. I just wasn't sleepy and didn't want to take a nap and I was thinking about Jack and how I wished he'd come back and that if I went out to the trailer and got some of his stuff and kept it in my room, he'd be sure to come and get it and I'd see him again and ask him to stay with us."

Anna waited until he finished, then signed another reprimand.

By now David was crying too. "I know I went past the fence, but I had to, Mom, to get to the trailer. I didn't know a tornado was gonna come. I didn't know you'd be waked up and think I was disappeared and maybe kidnapped. Am I gonna get a spanking? I'm sorry." Covering his eyes with his forearm, he began to sob.

Anna pulled him against her, rocking him slightly and crying silently herself until both their tears subsided. Finally she eased him away and began signing. "Three days!" the boy wailed.

Jack asked him what was going on.

"I can't watch TV for three whole days."

"If you ask me, you got off light." Surprised that Jack wasn't siding with him, David tilted his head up to look at him. "You broke several rules, David. The worst thing you did was scare your mom. Moms have to know where their kids are. That's the number one rule."

"I know," he mumbled contritely. "She freaks out if she can't see me."

"Then you knew not to sneak off, right?"

"Yes, sir."

"Don't do it again."

"Okay."

"Promise?"

"Promise."

"Now promise your mom."

David signed a promise to her. Smiling forgiveness, she wiped the salty tear tracks off his cheeks. He said, "Can we have supper now?"

Jack and Anna laughed.

While they were snacking on peanut-butter-cracker sandwiches, the single light went out.

Ezzy groped his way through the house, moving from room to room, wishing to heaven he could remember where Cora kept a flashlight for emergencies such as this. For a former law enforcement officer, he was shamefully unprepared. He ought to know better.

The only thing that surprised him about the electricity blowing was that it hadn't blown earlier. As the frontal system moved southeasterly across East Texas, it clashed with warmer, moister Gulf air, creating vicious thunderstorms that spawned funnel clouds and tornadoes. Warnings of large hail, high winds, and torrential rain were issued so fast the weathermen couldn't keep up with them.

He cursed when he banged his thigh on the corner of the kitchen table. A bolt of lightning illuminated the room long enough for him to see his way clear to the pantry, and he'd just discovered a flashlight on one of the shelves when the telephone rang. The battery in the flashlight was dead. "Dammit!" he swore as he reached for the phone. "Yeah?"

A woman's voice said, "I'm trying to locate a Sheriff Hardge."

"I'm Hardge." He was no longer sheriff but that was a technicality he didn't correct.

"My daddy was Parker Gee. He died this morning."

Standing in pitch-black darkness relieved only by blinding lightning flashes that made his kitchen seem surreal, Ezzy needed a moment to sort through his mind's roster of names to find Parker Gee.

He then recalled the patient in the chest hospital. The former bartender with the nasty disposition and the nicotine-stained fingers, the thready voice, and the wracking cough that produced blood. He was surprised Gee had lasted this long.

"Hate to hear that, ma'am."

"He brought it on himself. Craved a cigarette right up till the last. Can you believe it?" Apparently there'd been no love lost between father and daughter. She sounded more bitter than bereaved.

Rubbing his bruised thigh, Ezzy asked, "How can I help you?"

"He gave me a message to pass along to you, but I have to tell you it makes no sense."

"I'm listening."

"Do you know somebody named Flint?"

Ezzy stuck his finger in his ear so he could hear her above the thunder that rattled the windows of the house. "Flint, you say? That the first or last name?"

"I don't know. Daddy said, 'Tell Hardge find Flint.' That's what I'm doing. The last few days they were giving him high doses of pain medication. He was loony as a goon. Didn't know me or my kids. So I wouldn't lose sleep trying to figure out what it means. Probably doesn't mean anything. The funeral's day after tomorrow, in case you're interested."

She gave Ezzy the time and place of the burial then said good-bye and hung up. Ezzy wouldn't attend the funeral. He didn't like the man. The only thing he had in common with him was the McCorkle case. The strange message must relate to it. But how? Was there ever any mention of someone named Flint in his notes? Not that he recalled. Just before dying had Gee remembered another customer in the bar that night? A man named Flint?

At least Ezzy assumed it was a man. Could have been a woman.

The phone rang a second time. "Hello?"

"Ezzy?"

He could barely hear through the crackling static, but it wasn't Parker's daughter calling back. "Yeah, who's this?"

"Ron Foster. Your offer still good to help out? We could sure as hell use you down here tonight. Could you—"

The line went dead, cutting off the new sheriff in midsentence, but that was okay. They didn't have to ask him twice.

As though suddenly endowed with excellent night vision, Ezzy facilely navigated his way into the den and unlocked the gun cabinet, from which he took a rifle and his pistol and holster, and boxes of ammunition for each.

In the garage he located his slicker where it had been hanging since the last time he'd used it. He tossed it into the front seat of the Lincoln along with the guns. He disengaged the automatic garage door opener and raised the door manually. Lashing winds and rain nearly knocked him down.

By the time he had backed his car into the street and pointed it toward town, it had begun to hail. The stones pounding the car were the size of lemons and made a horrible racket as they beat the Lincoln all to hell. He didn't bother to turn on his windshield wipers. They would have been totally useless against such meteorological fury.

When he turned on his headlights, they reflected off the falling hail and rain, making a glaring curtain out of the barrage. Lights off, barely able to see beyond the hood ornament, he drove at a snail's pace, straddling the center stripe because the gutters were flooded.

He was still several blocks away from the sheriff's office when he heard the sirens. At first he couldn't distinguish them from the howling wind, but once he realized what that keening sound signified, he stopped his car in the middle of the street. The fire department didn't sound the warning sirens unless a funnel had been sighted.

"Lord, Cora, you ought to see your old boy now."

He pulled on his slicker, which, considering the severity of the storm, would be about as effectual as a rubber with a hole in it. Then, taking a deep breath, he opened his car door and stepped out into nature's temper tantrum.

He raised his arm to provide some protection for his eyes. Hail stones hammered him. One struck him in the temple and he yowled in pain. Half staggering, half running, he headed for the ditch that ran parallel to the street. The bottom of it was already flowing like a river, but it wasn't out of bounds yet. He needed only a slight depression . . .

He had no longer to think about it. In all his seventy-two years, he had never experienced a tornado, but he'd seen the documentaries about them. He recognized the sound.

He threw himself into the ditch and, barely keeping his head above the churning water, covered it with his hands.

The next several minutes seemed to last for a hundred years.

At first Ezzy kept his head down, but curiosity got the best of him. Just as he looked up, the steeple of the church at the end of the block splintered into a million flying fragments of wood and steel. Its bell was sucked into the vortex of the funnel and clanged like it was heralding the end of the world.

The county tax office was demolished before his eyes.

A car was picked up and spun around several times before being hurled back down to earth. It crumpled like a tin can.

Trees were pulled out of the ground as though a giant were weeding his garden.

Windows shattered with explosive force, and Ezzy hoped to God that if any people were inside those structures they had protection from flying glass.

Then he saw the Dumpster, the kind contractors kept at construction sites. It was tumbling down the street. Ezzy's first thought was *What a ridiculous way to die.* Big as a boxcar, it rolled end-over-end directly toward him with the velocity of a speeding freight train.

He uttered an unmanly scream and plunged his head into the water.

The damn thing rolled right over him. Only the slight depression in which he lay had saved him.

He didn't know this for several minutes, however. Not until the tornado had cut a destructive swath through his town did he crawl out of the ditch like a primitive life-form. Sitting on the sloping ground, he gazed at the devastation around him.

The Dumpster had crashed into a live oak about twenty yards from him. It was wrapped around the trunk like a tight sleeve. Nothing but piles of debris remained where buildings had stood. Graceful old trees lay toppled with their roots obscenely exposed. The church bell had landed in the parking lot of a florist shop, crushing the neon sign.

Slowly Ezzy came to his feet. His knees were wobbly. Bracing his hands on them, he bent at the waist and took several deep breaths. Tentatively, he touched the sore spot on his temple and pulled away bloody fingers. The hail stone had broken the skin and raised a knot as big as an egg. Otherwise, he seemed not too much the worse for wear.

Assessing the damage on this street alone, he realized that the people of his county were going to need him. The sooner he got on the job the better. He hobbled back to his car, which, in the quirky way of tornadoes, had escaped with only the rear windshield being busted out. As he slid behind the wheel and shut the door, he glanced back at the Dumpster and shook his head with dismay.

He ought to be dead.

He thanked God that he wasn't and wondered why he had been spared.

He wasn't a particularly religious man. In fact, he harbored a lot of theological doubts that gave Cora fits and kept her constantly praying for his doubtful afterlife.

But he thought he had this one figured. Whoever or whatever God was, he was merciful. He had spared Ezzy's life tonight. And Ezzy knew why—he hadn't fulfilled his purpose for being here in the first place. His time wasn't up. His job on earth wasn't finished.

Tonight, he'd been given another chance.

And another clue.

Chapter Forty-Two

$\mathcal{J}$ack worked his feet out of his wet, mud- and manure-caked boots and left them on the floor of the utility room along with his socks.

When the lights went out in the cellar, he had groped along the shelf where he'd earlier seen a flashlight. Using it, he'd lighted candles. They'd huddled in the cellar for another half hour, until he determined that the winds had subsided noticeably and all he could hear against the door was heavy rain.

When he had opened the door, rain had showered down on him, but what he noticed most was the change in temperature. It had dropped by twenty degrees. In spite of the rain, the air felt and smelled fresh. The storm had migrated toward Louisiana. Frequent lightning flashed in the eastern sky.

As they came out of the cellar, he and Anna were relieved to see that the house was still standing. "It looks intact. Let's go check." He carried David as they ran through the downpour, dodging the deepest puddles. On the way, they all caught a case of the giggles, an outlet for other emotions that were more difficult to deal with. By the time they reached the house, they staggered up the front porch steps, wet through to the skin and weak with laughter.

Inside they did a quick inspection of rooms. A tree limb had broken out a living room window, exposing the furniture to rain. Shingles had been ripped off the roof above the second-story hallway, creating several leaks. The electricity was still off and the telephone was dead, but there appeared to be no substantial damage to the structure.

The leaks were easily handled by placing kitchen pans beneath them. Jack picked up the largest pieces of broken window glass, then tacked a Hefty bag over the open casement to prevent more rain from coming into the living room. Leaving Anna and David with plenty of candles burning, he'd gone back outside to the corral to see if the horses had been injured. One had a gash on his flank, but it didn't look too deep. Miraculously, the others seemed to have escaped being struck by flying debris. He couldn't check on the fate of the cattle or the remainder of the property until daylight.

Now, leaving his footwear behind, he went into the kitchen and relit the candle he'd left on the table when he went out. Upstairs, he saw flickering candlelight coming through the partially opened bathroom door and heard David's voice. He knocked on the doorjamb and poked his head around.

"It's okay, Jack, you can come in."

The boy had just gotten out of the tub. The floor was strewn with wet towels. He was putting on his pajamas. "I got to take my bath with candles." Two were burning on the dressing table, one on the tank of the commode. They cast dancing shadows on the walls and ceiling. "It was cool. The candles make the bathroom look like a cave, don't they?"

David would think back on this entire evening as one big adventure. It had probably been as much fun for him as the postponed trip to Six Flags would have been. He was naive to the danger he'd been in while inside the trailer. Jack shuddered to think about what might have happened to David if he had been only one minute later arriving.

"Where's your mom?"

"Waiting for me to say my prayers."

"Then you best get to them."

"Will you come?"

"If you want me to."

He and David entered the boy's bedroom together. Anna was turning down the bed and looked at Jack inquisitively as he followed David into the room. She also looked fresh from a bath. She was dressed, but her hair was wet. Not from rain. A shampoo. She smelled like flowers, which only made it more noticeable that he smelled like the corral.

He shrugged self-consciously and pointed at David. "He, uh, wanted me to hear his prayers."

David climbed into bed, adjusted his pillow, arranged the stuffed animals he had chosen to sleep with, checked to make sure his dinosaur book was within reach on his nightstand, then folded his hands beneath his chin, closed his eyes, and began reciting his prayers.

Jack bowed his head and closed his eyes. He wished Anna could hear the sweet purity of her child's voice as he asked God's blessing on those he loved. Of all the things she missed hearing—music and crashing waves and the wind through cottonwood trees—this was perhaps the thing she would most love to hear, and Jack's heart broke for her that she couldn't.

"God bless Jack and make him not leave."

Jack raised his head. He looked quickly at David, then at Anna. She must have been reading David's lips because she looked at Jack at the same moment, and when their eyes met she quickly looked away. Bending over David, she kissed him good night and signed that she loved him.

"I love you too, Mom."

"'Night, David."

"Jack, are you going to be here in the morning when I wake up?"

"Sure. I'm counting on you to help me see what kind of damage that storm left us."

"Cool!"

Anna blew out the candle on the nightstand. David snuggled down into his pillow and closed his eyes. He was almost asleep before Anna and Jack reached the door.

Out in the hallway, they faced each other across their lighted candles. "This is going to seem very presumptuous. Presumptuous," he repeated when she signaled that she hadn't understood. "Rude." She nodded. "Would you mind if I use your shower?"

She motioned him toward the bathroom.

"Because the trailer . . . The trailer . . ."

She tilted her head to one side, a listening posture for hearing people. But her eyes were on his lips and that distracted him. "Uh, best I could tell, you lost most of the barn's roof. Insurance should cover it. Some fencing was ripped up. Goddamn if the thing didn't pull sod right out of the ground. I've never seen a tornado do that before. The toolshed is a total loss. Tomorrow I'll do a more thorough check. Sort of hard to tell how extensive the damage is in the dark and with this rain. I might have missed some things."

He followed her fingers as she spelled out the word *trailer*.

He looked away from her for a moment, then, knowing she would see it for herself in the morning, told her, "Smashed flat like a tin can that has been stamped on."

She stared at his mouth as he said the words, and even for a moment longer. Then she lowered her eyes and stared at nothing. The water dripping from the leaky ceiling into the pots and pans produced a funny, discordant percussion she couldn't hear.

Jack almost touched her, but pulled back his hand just shy of making contact with her forearm. She saw the motion, however, and looked up at him again. "We got lucky, Anna."

She glanced into David's room. Jack watched her throat as it worked hard to swallow. On the verge of tears, her head came back around to him.

"Going back to what we were talking about before," he said, "I'd like to shower if that's all right. Unless you'd rather . . ." He was so taken with the play of candlelight and shadow across her face, that his request dwindled to nothing.

When his lips stopped moving, she raised her eyes to his.

"Unless you'd rather I didn't."

"Help yourself," she signed, spelling out the words.

"Okay, then. And I'll, uh, I'll rack in my truck. It won't be the first time, and it's not that bad."

Before he even stopped speaking, she was waving her hand for him to stop.

"What?"

She made the sign for sleep and pointed downstairs.

"On the sofa? You sure?"

She nodded.

He shifted from one bare foot to the other. "Come to think of it, that might not be a bad idea. With the power off and all, maybe I should stay—"

She nodded more emphatically and a little impatiently.

Jack quit while he was ahead.

"Okay, then, well . . ." He stood there a moment longer, at a loss for what to say or do next, only knowing that he didn't want to say good night and separate just yet. "Well, I'll, uh, take that shower now and let you, you know, get to bed. You must be exhausted. Good night."

She signed *"Good night,"* then turned and went down the hallway toward her room, using her candle to light the way, stepping around the pans that had collected a good amount of rainwater already.

Jack stood beneath the shower for a long time, letting the hot spray beat against his skull, then between his shoulder blades, massaging out the tension. He soaped and rinsed and soaped again, then continued to stand under the water until it turned cool.

After drying, he slipped on a pair of clean jeans and a T-shirt, spares he kept in the toolbox of his truck for just this sort of emergency. He wiped out the tub, and gathered up his and David's wet towels, intending to take them downstairs to the utility room along with his wet clothes.

But when he stepped out into the hallway, he heard quiet sobs coming from Anna's room.

He debated it. For about half a second.

Dropping his wet bundle on the floor, he moved down the hall and peeked into her bedroom. She had placed the candle on the nightstand and turned down the bed, but she was sitting in a rocking chair near the window, staring out at the rain, crying.

She was unaware of his approach until she saw his reflection in the windowpane. Startled, she quickly wiped the tears from her cheeks, stood, and turned to face him. "I don't want to disturb you, Anna. I just wanted to see if you were all right."

For a long moment she did nothing except look back at him. Finally she formed the sign for the letter *b* with her right hand, raised it to her lips, moved it forward and down, as though blowing him a kiss. *"Thank you."*

"For what?"

She gave him a retiring look, then signed David's name.

Huskily Jack replied, "For Godsake, Anna, you don't have to thank me for that."

She shook her head stubbornly and formed the sign again. Except this time, her fingers remained against her lips, which began to tremble, and as Jack watched, tears overflowed her eyes again.

"Hey. Hey." He took the steps necessary to reach her and placed his hands on her shoulders. "Everything's okay now. You were scared. Hell, *I* was scared, but nothing really bad happened. David is safe. That's all that matters."

From there it seemed only natural to draw her against him. Placing his hand on the back of her head, he tucked it beneath his chin. Her tears were absorbed into his T-shirt. Awkwardly, he patted her back. "Everything's okay. This is a delayed reaction to anxiety, that's all. If it makes you feel better to cry it out, you go right ahead. Bawl your eyes out. You've earned a good cry. I'll stay as long as you want me to."

As before in the cellar, she wasn't reading his lips, but the literal translation of the words was unimportant. Their meaning was understood. She laid her fingertips against his larynx, listening to him through her sense of touch. He kept talking, whispering actually, conveying his reassurances through vibrations.

"David scared the living daylights out of you, disappearing like that. And to make matters worse you had a tornado bearing down on you. But it turned out all right, didn't it?"

She kept her head down, but her fingers moved up to his lips and rested there lightly, barely touching. "I can't say as I blame you for crying. I've felt like crying several times this evening. I got real choked up listening to his prayers. So I know how you feel." He rubbed her back in a circular motion. "Let it out. I'll be right here."

He stopped speaking but her fingertips remained against his lips. He kissed them softly. Then again. She turned her hand horizontally across his lips and he kissed her palm. When her hand moved to brace his jaw, he dropped a light kiss on her temple, then her cheekbone.

Where his lips remained.

Forever.

While his heart raced like a son of a bitch.

He tilted his head down and across as she tilted hers up and across, and their lips grazed each other. They reversed angles and glanced off each other a second time, only not as rapidly. His arms tensed, tightening the embrace. Then, pressing her lips with his, he kissed her.

He thought *Oh, Lord, oh, Lord,* because her mouth was very soft and so sweet and temptingly receptive.

Moments later, it was he who initiated the exchange of tongues, but she responded favorably.

Everything else in Jack's world receded. Worries and regrets fell away like unlocked leg irons. A curtain was drawn across his history. He existed only in the here and now, immersed in Anna. His senses were saturated with her. The flowery smell clinging to her skin and hair. The feel of her small body curving into his. The incredible taste of her mouth. Nothing in his lifetime compared to this.

When it was snatched away, he reeled from the abrupt loss.

He opened his eyes to see her backing away from him, her lips rolled inward, her chest rising and falling rapidly. And he cursed himself for a goddamn fool. Yeah, he was caught up in it. He was crazy with lust. That didn't mean she was. Why should she be? Look at them. She was gorgeous and he was . . . well, sure as hell not gorgeous. She had been married, but there was a quality about her that was almost innocent, and he wasn't even close to that. Women's intuition being what it was, Anna would know he was the last thing she needed in her already complicated life.

He raised one hand imploringly. "Anna, I apologize. I—"

He ceased talking when she tugged her shirttail from the waistband of her jeans and rapidly undid the buttons. He was immobilized first by shock, then by the sight of that smooth strip of exposed skin. Her breasts were covered, but they held the fabric away from her body, and that was sexier than if she'd been naked. Maybe. He still wanted to see her naked.

She stood taut as a wire. Holding her breath. Expectant.

He moved toward her and slid his hands inside her blouse. They bracketed her rib cage for a few seconds while his eyes probed hers, then he pulled her against him and resumed the kiss.

Her skin was as soft as he'd imagined it, her body as responsive as he'd hoped, her appetite for him as strong as his for her. Her arms went around his neck, and in that locked embrace he walked forward until she came up against the wall. Lowering his head, he kissed her neck, her chest, her breasts. She made a sound low and deep in her throat and he kissed that arched column before returning to her mouth.

She angled her middle up and forward to rub against his. He dropped his hands to the rear pockets of her jeans and raised her higher against him, pressed her tighter. With her hands on his shoulders, she pushed against him aggressively, rotating their positions until his shoulder blades were against the wall. She raised his T-shirt and pressed open-mouthed kisses on his chest and belly. He felt her tongue against his skin and when it flicked one of his nipples, it nearly took the top of his head off.

He fumbled with the buttons of his fly, but when they were undone, it was Anna who reached inside. He hoarsely called her name on a sound that could have been a laugh, or a sigh, but was definitely caused by pleasurable surprise. Her caress was a gentle squeeze that milked a drop of semen from him.

"Ah, God," he groaned.

His wits seemed to flutter away from him on a million rising wings. Knowing he couldn't take much more before he embarrassed himself, he reached for her hand and pulled it away, managing to pant, "I don't want to spoil it. I want to touch you, too."

She must have understood him, at least the essence of it, because she led him to the bed, where she removed her blue jeans. As she stepped out of them she also took off her blouse. He could find no flaw in her, and that seeming perfection intimidated him.

He stood there feeling gauche and awkward, but she showed no such timidity. She slipped her hands inside the seat of his jeans and eased them down, smoothing her hands over his buttocks. His penis jutted between them; she studied it with frank interest. Between her small hands, his sex felt full and heavy and hard. This rampant evidence of his virility restored his self-confidence. In fact, he was suddenly drunk with vanity.

She had lovely breasts. Perfect, in fact. The nipples tightened against his caressing fingertips and tongue. He sucked them delicately as he skimmed her tummy with the backs of his fingers. His knuckles brushed past her navel.

Her underpants were silky. Inside them the hair was soft. Her center was very wet.

*   *   *

She lay still beneath him for what seemed like a long time, yet it wasn't long enough. It could never be long enough. She wouldn't have minded if he'd fallen asleep and not moved until morning. She liked the feel of his weight on her, the pressure of him inside her.

But he wasn't asleep. Occasionally she felt his fingers moving in her hair, gently caressing her scalp. His rough cheek rubbed against her earlobe. His teeth nipped her neck. She hoped he was doing what she was—basking in the intimacy.

But eventually he disengaged himself and eased onto his side. She rolled to her side to face him. They nuzzled. She felt his lips moving against her cheek and pulled back to see what he was saying. "Did I hurt you?"

She shook her head.

"I thought you . . . you know, sort of tensed up when . . ."

She smiled and laid her fingertips against his lips. His penetration had hurt a little. It had been a long time since she'd been with a man, and she had had a baby since then. How like Jack to notice her subtle reflex.

The mild discomfort had lasted only an instant, however. Then she had hugged his hips with her legs and immodestly urged him to penetrate deeper. She blushed now thinking about how lusty her participation had been. She had made it practically impossible for him not to make love to her. So afraid that he would stop after that first kiss, she had seized the initiative.

She had wanted him. If tonight hadn't ended with them like this, she would have regretted it forever. Whatever happened tomorrow would happen. But she was with him now, and he was gazing at her in the same dreamy fashion with which she knew she was gazing back.

He stroked her cheek with his index finger. "You're so beautiful, Anna."

She spelled out the words *"So are you."*

He guffawed. "Me? Beautiful? That's funny."

"You are." Her fingers formed the letters insistently.

"I thought my face just said a lot."

She could tell he was teasing her. *"That, too."*

His smile gradually relaxed as his eyes searched hers. "What's it saying to you right now?"

Painstakingly her fingers spelled out the words. *"That you are very happy to be here, like this."*

He said, "Well, it ain't lying."

"What did you say?"

"I said it ain't—"

She waved that off. *"I got that. What did you say when . . ."*

"When . . . ?" He left the question dangling and raised his eyebrows quizzically.

She gave him a long, puissant look.

"Oh, you mean when I, when you, when we . . . came?"

She nodded.

"Hell, Anna, I don't know. Does it matter?"

"Only if you called another woman's name."

"I promise it wasn't that."

"Good."

He placed his thumb against her lips and stroked it across them. His smile was sweet and a little sad. "I honestly don't remember what I said, Anna, but whatever it was, it couldn't come close to describing what I was feeling."

She buried her face in his chest hair, but she held her hand up so he could easily read the words she spelled out. *"I wish I could have heard it."*

He tilted her head back. "I wish you could have, too."

She was tempted to tell him that she had started practicing speech again, but she hesitated. What if she couldn't relearn what she had forgotten? The skills she had painstakingly developed might be hopelessly lost from disuse. She might build up his hopes and later disappoint him. Disappointing herself would be bad enough. Disappointing him would break her heart.

So better not to tell him yet. When she spoke his name for the first time, she wanted to do it well. Until she was certain she could, she would remain silent and practice in secret.

Instead, she told him, *"I know what your voice sounds like."*

"Oh, yeah?"

She nodded and placed her hands on his cheeks, then rubbed them up and down over the stubble. "Whiskers?" He thought about it for a moment, then said, "That's not a bad description. My voice isn't very refined. It's sort of scratchy."

His sappy grin made her laugh because she knew her grin was just as sappy. They kissed, briefly and lightly. Then deeply and intimately. And they couldn't stop touching each other. Her fingers combed through his chest hair, which was a novelty for her because Dean's chest had been smooth. From there she explored the ridge of his collarbone and his shoulder, before her hand covered his biceps. Curiously she squeezed it, and he flexed the muscle.

She spelled out, *"I have two questions."*

"Yes, I know I'm a hunk. And, no, I don't let it go to my head."

She slapped his arm.

"Sorry, I couldn't resist." He kissed her quickly and readjusted his head on the pillow. "Shoot."

She held up one finger, indicating the first question, *"What happened this morning?"*

"At the sheriff's office? They let me go. Lack of evidence. I didn't do it, Anna."

"I know. I didn't believe you could have poisoned our herd, but—"

He took her hands. "You had every right to be suspicious. Just for the record, it was Emory Lomax."

She wasn't surprised but she asked him how he knew.

He told her about a fix-it man named Jesse Garcia and about his confrontation with Lomax in the bank. By the time he finished, she was laughing at the word picture he had painted.

"You threatened his manhood with your knife?"

"I don't think anything short of that would have got his attention."

Holding his face between her hands, she kissed it randomly before her mouth settled on his. She tried to deepen the kiss, but he angled his head back and looked at her seriously.

"Anna, I don't want you getting hurt by me being here."

The statement puzzled her, but the seriousness of his expression alarmed her. She shook her head.

"Yeah, you could," he argued. "When it comes right down to it, you don't know anything about me. Did Delray happen to tell you what I told him? That I move from job to job? That I'm a—"

"Drifter," she spelled out.

"Right. Well . . ." His eyes probed hers. "You haven't asked why I live the way I do."

No, she hadn't. Furthermore, she realized that it wasn't important to her. She knew what she needed to know about him—that he was kindhearted and gentle, proud, protective, strong, smart. Important to her was the man he was now, not his past, which obviously troubled him. Whatever the circumstances that had brought him into her life, she was glad for them, not regretful. But that was too much to say by spelling out each word, so she told him simply, *"I know what is important to know, Jack."*

"I could argue that," he said, frowning as though debating it. Then he said, "There's something else you should think about. People are nasty. It's human nature to be spiteful. You're a prime target for gossip of the worst kind. It's nobody's goddamn business who you sleep with, but somehow, because you're a widow, and you're deaf, the gossip is juicier."

She hated what he was saying, but she knew it to be the truth. *"Did you hear any gossip about Delray and me?"*

"Yes." He must have read her distress because he rushed to say, "I never believed it. I knew it was lie. But when they talk about you sleeping with your hired hand it's going to be the truth."

"Yes, and I'm glad."

"Me, too." He laid his palm against her cheek. The intensity of his facial expression said more than the words she read on his lips. "God damn me for a selfish bastard if you get hurt because of me, but I wanted to be with you, Anna. I've wanted this since the first time I saw you."

She remembered him as she had first seen him in his battered straw hat, scuffed boots, and sunglasses, offering to help her with her car. That memory would be with her the day she died. Maybe she had started loving him right then.

She knew she loved him now.

Snuggling her body closer to his, she kissed him without restraint, hoping that her kiss conveyed a small measure of the emotion he had awakened in her. She placed her hand low and started to caress him, loving the musky smell, the heat and firmness of his sex. He indulged her. More than that, he seemed to revel in her curiosity.

But curiosity gave way to carnality and her touch became more erotic. His eyes turned dark with heightened arousal. His face grew tense with pleasure. When she took him into her mouth, she felt the vibration of his moan. Again and again she read her name on his lips, knowing when he whispered it softly with intense feeling, knowing when he mindlessly cried it out in passion.

They loved completely.

She thrilled to feeling him gloved snugly inside her, of watching his eyes move over her, appreciating the curves and contours of her body. She watched his lips fasten to her breast, but her eyes closed while experiencing the sweet tugging of his mouth. His tongue traced the grooves at the tops of her thighs. He pressed his face into the softness of her belly and kissed her navel. Turning her over onto her stomach, he kissed his way down her spine, then catnapped with his cheek resting in the small of her back.

Her own level of sensuality surprised her. She and Dean had enjoyed a healthy sex life, but she had never felt this free and uninhibited. Maybe because Delray was always sleeping in the room down the hall. Maybe because Dean hadn't been as imaginative a lover. For whatever reason, with Jack she was shameless.

Never more so than when he parted her thighs and applied his mouth and tongue to her until she experienced a melting orgasm. Just when she would think it over, another sensation would ripple through her and she would ride it like a wave until it crested. Finally, she reopened her eyes to see Jack bending over her, smoothing the damp hair off her forehead and smiling tenderly. "You've never been loved like that before?"

She could tell it pleased him when she tiredly shook her head no.

"Ah, well, that's good. I mean I'm glad I could do that for you."

Angling her head up, she kissed him, tasting both of them on his lips, then smiled as she closed her eyes and drifted off to sleep.

After another brief nap, they made love again, this time face to face, more slowly and with less passion, but with heightened emotion and meaning. Then Jack wrapped them both in the sheet and carried her to the rocking chair, where he held her on his lap. They communed through their skin, with each breath, every heartbeat. Dialogue was unnecessary. They needed no conversation. They had their silence.

As dawn was breaking, without even raising her head from his chest, Anna told him what was in her heart. Although she signed, Jack understood. Because he lifted her hand to his lips and, after kissing her palm, spoke against it. She felt the words.

"I love you, too."

Chapter Forty-Three

*C*arl had laughed himself sick. When he realized that he'd mistaken a crack of thunder for a gunshot, he'd rolled over onto his side on the grimy floor of the cabin and laughed until he cried.

"Shit, Myron, I thought we were goners for sure," he said, wiping tears from his eyes. "Thought some backwoods peace officer had got lucky and stumbled across our hideout."

The joke had been lost on Myron, but he laughed anyway.

However, the thunder was a forerunner to a storm that was no laughing matter. There were times during the turbulent night when Carl had cursed fate for playing this last rotten trick on him. He had escaped prison without getting a scratch on him. He had executed a brilliant bank robbery and getaway. He was well on his way to a life of leisure.

A man with all that going for him was not supposed to die at the whim of a tornado.

Throughout the evening, he and Myron had stood at the windows and watched the dark, glowering clouds. The hushed, green atmosphere gave Carl the heebie-jeebies. With darkness came an even greater foreboding, punctuated by ferocious lightning the likes of which Carl had never seen in his life. Rain, hail, and high winds hammered the cabin for hours. The roof leaked like a sieve. It was a challenge to find a dry spot in which to try to sleep.

Carl harbored a secret fear that God was sorely pissed at him and that the storm was punishment for all his misdeeds. Between that worry, the spine-chilling sounds that accompanied the storm, the rain pouring in through the roof, and the stiffening corpses in the corner, he'd passed a miserable night.

This morning was a different story.

He had awakened to the happy chirping of birds, cooler temperatures, and sunny skies. After relieving himself against the exterior wall of the cabin, he got into the car and started the motor. "Come on, come on," he said impatiently as he turned the dial on the radio, trying to find a local station.

Myron appeared in the open doorway of the cabin, his pink eyes even pinker from sleep, his white hair forming a frizzy halo around his head. "Wha'cha doin', Carl?" He idly scratched his balls as he peed into a rain puddle.

"Bring me a Coke, will ya?"

He'd give one of the hundred-dollar bills out of the bank bag for a cup of strong, black coffee, but the tepid soft drink was the only source of caffeine available. For almost half an hour he remained in the car, sipping the drink and listening to the radio. When he went back inside, he felt refreshed and energized, and it wasn't just a caffeine rush.

He tossed aside the empty cola can and rubbed his hands together vigorously. "Myron?"

"Huh?" He was stuffing packaged doughnuts into his mouth. His lips were dusted with powdered sugar, making him appear even more ghostly pale than usual.

"We're getting out of here."

"Okay, Carl."

"I mean right now." As though Myron had disagreed, Carl argued his case. "I've been listening to the radio. Know what all the news is about?"

"What?"

"The storm. Roads and bridges washed out. Damage estimated in the millions. Dozens of people killed. A lot more than that missing and feared dead. You know how those newsmen talk, all somber and serious like? Well, all they're yapping about this morning is the storm. It hit East Texas hard. The weathermen couldn't even count the number of tornadoes. Flash floods galore. Roofs blown to hell and back. Houses and businesses destroyed. Cars swept into flooded creeks. Power out just about everywhere. Phones, too. The governor asked the president to declare it a disaster area. This morning everybody's busy trying to set things right again. Know what that means?"

Myron swallowed a doughnut whole. "What?"

"It means that nobody's looking for us." He pointed outside toward the car and its radio. "Not one word about us on the news. Not *one*. Do you think they're gonna be chasing us down when there's a granny lady and her kitty cat stuck in her floating house trailer? Hell, no! Search and rescue. That's what they're gonna be doing today. And probably tomorrow, and the day after that, too. Now's the time for us to move." He laughed. "This is what you call providence, Myron. Hell, we couldn't have planned it better!"

"Cecil said we gotta stay here a week."

"Yeah, Cecil said," Carl repeated with a scornful snort. "Cecil didn't know shit. He would probably quarrel with this decision, but I know an opportunity when I see one, and this one all but bit me in the ass. So let's hump it. We're leaving."

They gathered up all the unused food so they could eat on the road. They also took a package of toilet paper, canned drinks and bottled water, and anything else Carl deemed useful. While Myron was placing his supplies in the backseat of the car, Carl went around to the trunk to make certain the duffel bag full of money was still there. He doubted Cecil would have double-crossed him, but he wouldn't have put it past that Connie.

The bag was still there, and from what he could tell it hadn't been tampered with. While he was at it, he slipped several hundred-dollar bills from the bag into his pocket. Spending money, he told himself. To cover travel expenses. Myron would never miss it from his share.

Carl watched his partner trudge from the cabin to the car with a case of soft drinks under each arm. Myron was always the same. He never got upset or afraid. He never lost his temper or got rattled. His idiocy protected him from normal human reactions and emotions.

It was a crying shame that such a sizable sum of money was going to be squandered on an idiot who would never fully appreciate its value and the possibilities it afforded. Maybe he should spare Myron the headache of appropriating his share of the cash. The responsibility would be too much for him. It would only confuse him.

Besides, how much cleaner could it be than to discard him here along with Cecil and Connie? He could check all his baggage here, so to speak. He would be responsible only for himself and accountable to no one.

Ah, the prospect of total freedom was sweet!

Myron placed the drinks in the seat of the car, then turned back toward the cabin. Carl pulled the pistol from his waistband, eased back the hammer, and took a bead on the back of Myron's haloed head.

But before he could pull the trigger, he reconsidered. There were miles to go before he reached the Mexican border. Myron was dumber than dirt, but he was also an extra pair of hands and a strong back. He did what he was told without argument. He came in handy when it came to grunt work. He was a mule. You didn't shoot a good mule just because it was ugly and stupid. You kept it around because it was useful.

Deciding to keep Myron for the time being, he tucked the pistol back into his waistband and closed the trunk of the car.

In under fifteen minutes they were ready to leave. Myron took his place in the passenger seat. Carl returned to the cabin for a final look around to see if they'd left behind anything that might later be needed.

His eyes came to rest on the two bodies. In the morning light, they looked grotesque. They were beginning to bloat. Their open wounds were fly-blown. Shortly they would begin to stink.

He felt a stab of remorse, but dismissed it as quickly as he had dismissed his fear of God's wrathful punishment as soon as the storm had passed.

He didn't let himself think anything other than that Cecil and Connie had got no better than they deserved. She had been a low-class cunt who had weaseled and fucked herself into a situation where she didn't belong. She had been trouble waiting to happen. He'd known it the minute he met her.

It wasn't so easy to gloss over his brother's murder. But it too was justified. Cecil had been a hopeless coward. And a stubborn one. He just wouldn't admit to his little brother's superiority.

Survival of the fittest was the fundamental law of nature. Carl had rid humankind of two weak links, that was all.

He gave them a mock salute. "*Adios,* y'all."

"From what I picked up on the radio in my truck, the power is out nearly everywhere," Jack told Anna over their breakfast of bread and jam. Food in the refrigerator had already begun to spoil. "They're saying it might be days before the utility company can restore it. Everything is in chaos. For the time being, we're on our own."

Following breakfast, he climbed onto the roof of the house and assessed the damage. He would need shingles to make permanent repairs, but in the meantime he patched the leaks with tarpaper. He figured he could rebuild the toolshed as soon as he collected the necessary materials. The barn roof was a total loss and would require professionals to replace it. When telephone service was restored, he would call the vet about the horse's injury, but he'd looked at it again, and it didn't appear to be serious.

Those chores completed, he expressed to Anna his concern about the welfare of the cattle and suggested that she and David go with him to check it out. He was nervous about leaving them alone without a telephone.

Anna packed a picnic lunch of nonperishables, although David insisted on carrying his separately in his *101 Dalmatians* backpack. Anna took along her camera and assorted gear, thinking that pictures taken directly after the storm might come in handy with insurance adjusters.

Evidence of the storm stretched beyond the iron arch demarcating the Corbett ranch. Jack maneuvered the pickup around debris and tree branches littering the road. Power lines had been ripped from toppled poles. They saw a signpost that had been folded double. A sheet of corrugated metal from the roof of the Corbett barn was spotted half a mile away, looking like a piece of crumpled tin foil. An old windmill lay on its side in the middle of the pasture, its blades scattered around it.

As Jack rounded a bend he nearly collided with a cow. He slammed on the brakes just in time to avoid running over the animal. Several head had wandered across the road and were grazing placidly in the ditch on the opposite side.

"Leave it to those smart Corbett cows to find the section of fence that's down."

Saying that, he got out of the truck. Waving his arms, flapping his hat, and whooping, he herded the cattle back across the road to their pasture. Luckily he'd brought along a tool kit and a few spare boards and was able to make temporary repairs to the fence. To his mental shopping list he added barbed wire.

He parked the pickup outside the cattle guard. "We'd better go the rest of the way on foot. I'd hate to get the pickup stuck in the mud."

Anna had put on a pair of Delray's boots. They were huge on her, but they protected her feet from the mud and standing water. David wore an old pair of boots, but Jack carried the boy most of the time as they walked the circumference of the pasture. The herd had weathered the storm well. From what Jack could see, they hadn't lost a single head.

He thought that just short of a miracle, although he'd heard of these storms doing some peculiar things, like annihilating one side of a street while leaving the other side untouched. Sometimes they traveled along the ground for miles, leveling everything in their path. Other times they skipped along like a stone over water, leaving only patches of devastation. This twister must've veered sharply to the east, missing the pasture where the cattle were grazing and sparing the herd.

As they made their way back to the truck, Jack wondered what David thought about his holding Anna's hand. If David noticed, he didn't comment on it. In fact, he seemed unaware that the nature of their relationship had changed, but then they hadn't blatantly advertised it. Jack had sneaked downstairs to the living room couch before the boy woke up.

It wouldn't have done for David to surprise them where they shared the rocking chair by the window, Anna sprawled on his chest, her legs draping over the arms of the chair, both of them drowsy after making slow, sleepy sex, letting the motion of the chair do most of the work.

So he had kissed her one last time and carried her to the bed and left her there, although it had been damned hard to do. It was hard to keep his hands off her now. Every time he looked at her, he wanted to touch her. And he looked at her a lot.

It was the staring that David finally noticed.

Jack had spread out a quilt in the bed of the pickup because the ground was too wet for a bona fide picnic. They were eating a lunch of peanut butter sandwiches, fresh fruit, and bottled juice drinks. His gaze connected with Anna's, and held, and she smiled at him in that special way a woman smiles at a man after good sex.

It was a small and subtle smile that spoke volumes. It said that she knew all your secrets and made you wish to hell you knew hers. Every time Anna gave him that you're-thinking-about-fucking-me-aren't-you? smile he wanted to pinch himself to make sure he hadn't dreamed last night.

He hadn't. It had been real. She had even told him she loved him, and she hadn't been stoned or drunk or trying to get at his wallet. Incredible as it was, she had told him she loved him and he believed her.

Their stare lingered longer than either of them realized. That's when David noticed. "How come y'all aren't talking? Is something wrong? Are you mad?"

Jack ruffled David's hair. "Nothing's wrong. I'm just staring at your mother."

"What for?"

Jack looked across at Anna, speaking as much to her as to the boy. "Because she's so pretty."

"You think she's pretty?"

"Hmm."

David looked at Anna as though seeing her through Jack's eyes. "She's okay I guess," he said, biting into his sandwich.

"David?" Jack hesitated, then said, "Would it be all right with you if your mother and I were together?"

He screwed up his face with misapprehension. "We're already together, Jack."

"I mean, you know, if your mother and I were like boyfriend and girl-friend."

David frowned, but it was more from disappointment than displeasure. His idol had just tumbled off the pedestal. Sounding betrayed, he said, "I didn't know you liked girls, Jack."

"I guess I didn't when I was your age. But I sort of grew into liking them as I got older."

"I won't."

"Don't be so sure."

"I won't," David repeated more adamantly. He divided a look of bewilderment between them, but he ended on Jack. "You want my mom to be your girlfriend?"

"Yeah, I do. I want that a lot."

"Kiss her and stuff?"

"Yeah."

David rolled his eyes. "Well, if you want to, okay."

"Thank you," Jack replied solemnly.

"But you still like me, too, right?"

"Absolutely. You're my main man." Jack high-fived him.

Reassured, David dug into a package of potato chips and stuffed the whole handful into his mouth. "After lunch can we go swimming?"

Jack laughed at the boy's casual regard for their romance, but he was also relieved. He could tell by Anna's expression that she had been following the conversation and felt the same relief he did. Neither could have been happy if their relationship troubled David.

He convinced David that swimming wouldn't be a good idea until the river waters receded to a normal level. But to keep the boy's disappointment at bay, and to extend for himself what was his first day of family life, he drove them to the forested part of the Corbetts' property.

"David, did you know your mother is very smart? She's decided to sell some of the timber off the land and let the loggers replant seedlings."

"Cool!" David exclaimed. "Like on the Discovery Channel? Can I watch when they cut down the trees?"

"We'll see. But for right now you can mark a few."

"Wow!"

The carpet of undergrowth and pine straw had acted as a filter, trapping the rainwater underneath and leaving the surface dry enough to walk on. When they saw a tree that Jack thought the timber company would be interested in, he slid his knife from the scabbard, handed it to David, and let the boy carve an X into the bark.

Once when David was distracted by his job, Anna placed her arms around Jack's waist and lifted her face to his for a kiss. Needing no more encouragement than that, he kissed her meaningfully and felt himself grow hard.

When at last they pulled apart, he mouthed, "Sorry." But he wasn't. Tilting his hips forward, he nudged the cleft of her thighs. She nudged him back, her eyes holding a promise for the night to come.

As they continued their hike, she experimented with her camera and various attachments. She prevailed upon him and David to pose until David complained of the purple spots behind his eyes caused by the flash. Jack suspected she got off some candid shots as well using natural light, because once after he and David stood up from their inspection of a hidey-hole in a tree trunk, he caught her lowering the camera from her face and smiling with satisfaction.

With the afternoon sun came a return of the heat. The wet ground began giving off steam, and they decided it was time to return to the house. Jack rolled down the windows in the cab of the truck. Anna sat in the middle, allowing David to get out and open and close the cattle guard gates as they drove through them, a chore the boy enjoyed.

Anna rode with her hand resting on Jack's thigh. It was an unconscious gesture—comfortable, trusting, possessive—that she wasn't even aware of. But Jack was. He covered her hand with his and when he did, she looked up at him and scooted closer until he could feel her breast beneath his triceps, her hip comfortably against his. Familiarity. With a woman. One woman. Something else new to him.

Anna's hair blew against his cheek and neck. The fragrance she wore reminded him of intimacies they had shared last night. David talked incessantly, but rather than being an annoyance, his chatter added to Jack's contentment.

He didn't know whether to cry or to crow.

He had never known life could be this good.

It was so good that he didn't trust it to last.

Nothing this good lasted.

It would end.

How it would end scared him.

Chapter Forty-Four

*T*he pickup rolled to a stop. "What time is it, Jack?"

"Going on three o'clock."

"Good, I haven't missed *Gilligan's Island*." David opened the passenger door and nearly fell out of the cab in his haste to alight. Running up the front steps, he bounded across the porch.

"You forgot the electricity's not on!" Jack hollered after him. But the front door had already closed behind him.

Jack helped Anna out of the truck. "He's a bundle of energy today." Pulling her against him, he added, "Not me. Not after all that exercise you put me through last night."

She tried to look affronted but couldn't keep from smiling. He hugged her tightly and quickly, then set her away and began unloading the bed of the pickup. She carried her camera and related gear. He took the quilt and food hamper. "Soon as we get this stuff inside, maybe we should go into town and see what's going on, ask about the electricity and such. What do you think?"

She made the sign for food.

"Right," Jack said. "If any stores are still standing they've probably already been picked clean, but maybe we can still find some groceries that don't require refrigeration. Good thing the cookstove is fueled by gas."

Reaching around her, he opened the front door and pushed it open. Anna went in ahead of him. He followed.

The blow was struck with staggering force.

He'd been kicked in the head by a horse once. He was working as a wrangler on a dude ranch in southern California, a place where rich people paid huge sums of money to play cowboy for a week. The gelding was known to have a nasty disposition. He'd been rubbing him down after a trail ride when he saw the horse's nostrils flare and realized what was coming. He had dodged, but not quickly enough. The hoof had caught him in the head.

This was much worse.

With the horse, he'd had a millisecond to brace himself. This time nothing had prepared him. It had come out of nowhere, delivered by an entity unseen. The side of his head sustained the full thrust and all the impetus behind it. It literally knocked him off his feet. He went airborne and seemingly hung there forever before crashing into the entry wall. A stabbing pain shot through his side and he knew the collision had left him with at least one broken rib.

He landed in a heap on the floor, swallowing the nausea that filled his throat. He clutched his head and closed his eyes, cursing the pile-driver that had hit him, because nothing short of that could have caused this much blinding, debilitating pain.

He could actually feel his brain bouncing around the inside walls of his cranium like a ball on a roulette wheel. Only when it finally resettled was he able to open his eyes, astonished that he still could get them open and that the blow hadn't killed him or knocked him unconscious.

Acting on instinct, he tried to stand but managed only to come up onto all fours. When he raised his head, the surrounding walls did a hoochie-coochie and the floor undulated. The motion made him sick. He hung his head between his shoulders and retched.

"Aw, Jesus. Will you stop that?"

Jack's arms collapsed beneath him and he fell onto his side, sending another searing pain through his torso. The broken rib was acting like a branding iron on his vital organs. He clenched his teeth to keep from crying out.

"Now look at the mess you made on the floor. How about it, sweetheart? You gonna give him hell about puking on your wax job?"

Jack opened his eyes again. The vertigo had abated a little. At least the rhythm of the dance the walls and floor were performing was slower now than before. Nevertheless, he had to swim through waves of nausea before he was able to pull things into focus.

The man was tall, handsome, deadly.

Jack knew that immediately, and with that knowledge came another gush of vomit, which he was able to keep down only by the sternest act of will.

The guy had one hand clamped over David's mouth, hard enough to hold the boy against him. In the other hand was a pistol aimed at the side of David's head. Anna was flattened against the opposite wall, staring at the man in terror, her eyes wide and white. All the blood had drained from her face.

Their assailant was addressing her. "Didn't your mama teach you that it was impolite to ignore folks when they were talking to you?"

Anna continued to stare at him.

Pushing David ahead of him, he moved closer to her. "What's the matter, honey? Cat got your tongue?"

She stood frozen, petrified.

The man poked her lightly in the belly with the barrel of the pistol. "Come on now. Speak up." He moved the gun barrel down past her waist and rubbed it against her pubic area. "Bet I can make you talk." Lowering his voice to an obscene whisper, he said, "Bet I can make you scream."

"Deaf."

Jack's voice was little more than a croak, but it brought the man's head around. He looked at Jack shrewdly through eyes honed sharp by years of imprisonment.

"She's deaf," he rasped. "She can't talk."

The cold eyes narrowed with even more suspicion, but his disarming smile was in place. "You wouldn't lie to me, would you? I don't advise it."

"She's deaf."

To Jack's surprise, he threw back his head and laughed, showing even rows of straight, white teeth. "I didn't know whether to believe it or not, but, by God, it's true. My brother said—*Ow!*"

Suddenly he yelped and flung David aside. He waved his hand in pain, then inspected the red teeth marks on his palm. "You little fucker, I'll teach you to bite me." He advanced threateningly toward David.

"No!" Jack shouted.

Anna screamed.

"Leave my mom alone," David cried as the man reached down, grabbed him by the front of his T-shirt, and jerked him off his feet. David began flailing his arms and kicking. For several seconds the man had his hands full trying to subdue the boy.

Jack, fearing the pistol would go off in the tussle, forced himself to his feet, then staggered in the general direction of the struggle.

"Stay back!" The gunman thrust the pistol at Jack's chest as he pushed David against Anna, who clutched the sobbing boy to her chest.

As Jack saw it, he had two choices. He could die a brave fool's death, or he could use his head and realize that he would be no good to Anna and David if he got himself shot. His impulse was to attack the son of a bitch. But what purpose would defending them serve if he got killed in the process?

So he did as ordered and stayed back.

The man grinned and rolled his shoulders as though to relax them. "Now that's more like it. No need for everybody to get all excited."

"I'm not excited," Jack said calmly.

"Well then, good. We don't have a problem, do we? We shouldn't. 'Cause we're family. Here I was on my way south, and I say to myself, 'I can't pass up an opportunity to meet my nephew and sister-in-law, now can I? No, sir.'" He gave Anna a wide smile. "No blood relation, I'm glad to say." His eyes moved over her. "Dean did good for himself. I swear, everything that kid touched turned to pure gold, and that includes you, honey."

"What do you want, Herbold?"

He turned to Jack. "None of your goddamn business." Then vanity got the best of him and he cocked his head to one side. "You called me by name. You know me?"

"You serious?"

Carl laughed and bowed slightly. "I'm a regular TV personality, aren't I?" Giving Jack no time to reply, he said, "Let me guess. You're the one says he's the hired hand."

Jack remained stonily silent.

"Yeah, Cecil told me about you."

"Did he tell you about Delray?"

"That he was about to cash it in?"

"He did."

"He's dead?" Carl looked at him skeptically.

Jack said, "I can show you the obituary in the newspaper."

"Won't be necessary." Thoughtfully, he rubbed the barrel of the pistol up and down his cheek as though scratching an itch. "Does my heart good, thinking about that motherfucker roasting in hell." He savored his vision for a moment, then refocused on Jack. "So what's with you?"

"Nothing's with me."

"That's not what Cec said. He said he thought you were law. Federal maybe."

Jack almost laughed, but the pain in his side made him gasp instead. "Cec was wrong."

It was obvious Carl didn't believe him. "You're just the hired hand."

"That's it."

"Now that Delray's dead, you planning to take over?"

"No. I'm just sticking around until Mrs. Corbett gets on her feet."

Carl grinned and gave him a slow once-over, then glanced at Anna before returning to Jack. "Not what it looked like to me. To me y'all sure seemed friendly. Going on picnics together and all," he drawled, indicating the food hamper that Anna had dropped when he grabbed her. He bent down and picked up an apple that had rolled from it, polished it on his sleeve, then took a large bite that crunched loudly as he chewed. "You fucked her yet?"

Jack said nothing, knowing Carl was trying to bait him so he would have a good excuse to kill him. He probably planned to kill him anyway, but as long as he could delay it, they stood a chance of escape or rescue.

Anna was watching him, following his dialogue with Carl as best she could by reading their lips. He hoped she also could see his right hand as it moved against his belt. His fingers formed each letter slowly, so as not to attract the other man's attention.

To use up time and keep Carl distracted, he remarked, "Your brother's not with you." His fingers formed the letter *k*.

"No, Cecil couldn't make it today."

"Where is he?" *N.*

Carl's smile faltered. "You sure you're not law? You ask a lot of questions about stuff that is none of your goddamn business."

Jack hoped he could keep Carl preoccupied until Anna noticed and interpreted what he was signing. *I.* "I figure Cecil is dead."

"Shut the fuck up!"

"Why, Carl," Jack taunted. "You sure are touchy when it comes to talking about your big brother." *F.* "What'd you do? Kill him so you could keep all the bank money for yourself?"

He pointed the pistol at Jack. "Look, I'm warning you. I told you to shut up."

E. Jack had no illusions about how dangerous Carl Herbold was. But even the most hardened criminal had an Achilles' heel. He had found it on the first probe. Fratricide was a heavy load of guilt to bear, even for a seasoned killer.

If Anna had noticed the signal he was sending, she hadn't acted on it. He started over. *K.* "What about the girl? What's her name, the teller who helped in the robbery." *N.* "Where's she, Carl? Or did you dispose—"

Carl backhanded Anna in the face.

The attack was so vicious and unexpected that for an instant it immobilized them all. Then David started screaming at Carl, Carl started laughing, and all Jack could do was let the rage surge through him because Carl still had the pistol aimed at his midsection.

"That's right, big-shot hired hand, or whoever the hell you are. You keep up the smart-ass chatter and she gets the back of my hand. For starters." Anna was holding her hand to her bleeding lip, but her posture and her eyes were full of hauteur as she glared at the convict. "Or maybe I'll fuck her in the ass while you and the boy here watch. Now that I think on it, I'd like that better."

Jack was powerless. If he gave Carl any excuse to kill him, he would do it and still sleep well tonight. Losing his temper was not an option, but it took all his willpower to stand and do nothing when his impulse was to rip out the guy's throat.

Each breath sent a shaft of pain through him. It hurt like hell to talk, but his voice was the only weapon available to him. "You're real tough, Carl. Who'd you pick on while you were in prison? There weren't any women and children around."

Carl released a heavy sigh, shook his head, and made a tsking sound. "So much for trying to be a nice guy." Immediately he grabbed Anna by the hair and shoved her to her knees.

Myron was hot. It had done no good to roll the car windows down because there wasn't any wind. The sun was shining through the windshield and causing him to sweat. He had drunk three Cokes already. Carl had told him to stay inside the car. If he couldn't get out to pee, he had better not drink any more Cokes even though he was real thirsty.

He was also bored. Boredom was making him sleepy. Twice he'd nodded off, only to be brought suddenly awake when his body twitched.

If he fell asleep and didn't guard the money, Carl would get mad and yell at him and call him a retard. He didn't want Carl to get mad. Carl was his friend. He couldn't let Carl down.

But he was hot and bored. And a little scared.

It had been a long time since Carl left. He had said he had something to take care of. "Remember what I told you, Myron? Two things I was gonna do when I got out?"

"Kill the motherfuckers who got you put in prison."

"Right. Well, one's down. Cecil. There are a couple to go." He had checked his revolver, spinning the cylinder. Myron liked when Carl did that 'cause he looked like a cowboy in the movies. He liked cowboy movies.

"Shouldn't take long, Myron."

But it was taking long. Carl should be back by now. What if something bad had happened to him? What if he'd been caught? What if he didn't come back at all?

The possibility filled Myron with fear. He didn't know the way to Mexico. What would he do with the money they'd stolen? Where would he sleep tonight?

The pores of his face leaked anxious sweat. He dragged his sleeve across his forehead to keep sweat from running into his eyes. His shirt was sticking to him. His crotch itched with a heat rash. The sweat made it sting. He fidgeted in the seat. His hands were slippery with sweat. He set the pistol on the seat beside him and wiped his palms up and down his pants legs to dry them off.

If Carl didn't come back for him, he would be real scared.

But if he didn't do exactly what Carl had said, Carl would be mad. He remembered what Carl had told him.

"Now here's the plan, Myron. Are you listening? Okay, good. I'm leaving the money here with you. The money we took from the bank, remember?"

"I remember, Carl."

"Good. It's in the trunk, okay?"

"Okay."

"I can't take it with me, because a man toting a duffel bag would attract unwanted attention. So I've got to leave it here. Understand?"

"Sure, Carl."

"Don't doze off."

"I won't."

"You're the guard. You can't let anybody sneak up on you. You've got your guns?"

"Right here, Carl." He raised the pistol in his hand to show Carl that he had his gun ready. A loaded shotgun lay across his knees.

"Good going," Carl had said, and Myron had felt proud. "Now, if anybody comes near the car, shoot them."

"Okay, Carl."

"I mean it, Myron. This is important. Don't talk, don't do anything, just shoot anybody who comes close."

"Okay, Carl. Can I have a Coke?"

"Sure."

Carl had set a whole six-pack of Cokes on the seat beside him.

"Where're you going, Carl?"

"I told you, Myron, I've got something to do."

"Can I come?"

"Jesus."

And he blew out his breath like he did when he was fixing to get mad and Myron heard him say something about him looking like a walking fright show and that he might just as well have an Uzi tucked under his arm as have Myron tagging along.

Myron didn't know what all that meant, but that was what Carl had said, and that was why he had to stay in the car and guard the money in the trunk and shoot people if they came up to him.

But Carl had been gone a long time. He was getting scared. His slippery index finger toyed with the trigger on the shotgun lying across his lap. He whimpered in fear over the possibility of being left alone. He wouldn't know what to do if Carl didn't come back. He wouldn't know how to get across the border and find sweet Mexican pussy all by himself.

He stared at the spot on the horizon where he'd last seen Carl, willing him to reappear. He sucked on his lower lip and gnawed his inner cheek. He wiped the sweat off his forehead again. He glanced over his shoulder through the back window.

What he saw caused him to utter a sound of utmost distress.

It was a car, slowing down, pulling up beside him.

Chapter Forty-Five

What a difference twenty-four hours made, thought Emory Lomax.

Yesterday he had marked the long hours until the end of the workday when he could retreat and lick the wounds inflicted by the man named Jack who'd attacked him in his office. He had tucked tail and slunk home, where he had swallowed several aspirin to kill the headache the beer at lunch had given him. Unfortunately, he had later resurrected it with several glasses of bourbon. He wasn't a good drinker; the bourbon had gotten him shitfaced.

Then the storm struck. Each flash of lightning and every thunderbolt had seemed aimed for the center of his skull, its sole purpose being to add to his misery. But beyond intensifying his headache, the storm had affected him very little.

He hadn't known when the gale-strength winds tore away his window shutters and sent his metal trash cans tumbling down the street. He was unaware of the hard rains that had overflowed his gutters and flooded his garage up to the wheel axles of his Jag. He knew nothing of the tornado until this morning when his radio alarm clock woke him with the news.

As the storm was wreaking havoc on his community, he had been drinking his way into a drunken stupor, at times wallowing in self-pity, occasionally sweating in fear that his duplicitous machinations would bring him to ruin, continually seething over Jack the Cowboy's insults.

Now, as he sped in air-conditioned comfort along the road that led to the Corbett ranch, he asked himself for the umpteenth time just who the hell that guy thought he was to talk to him with such condescension. He had entered his office uninvited. He had threatened him with bodily harm. Holding a knife to his throat, no less! Jesus, what audacity.

On the measuring stick of life, this Jack person didn't even register. With a swaggering hard-body and a face like the Marlboro Man, the guy was a contemporary version of a saddle tramp, a joke, a ne'er-do-well without two nickels to rub together.

Why in hell he had let the guy browbeat him on his own turf, he couldn't fathom. Of course it had been a surprise attack. He had lain in wait and ambushed him. Undoubtedly that was one reason he had surrendered with shameful haste.

Another was that he'd just concluded a disturbing meeting with Connaught and company, hotshots and high rollers to whom he'd made rash promises that would be difficult to keep.

Getting on Jesse Garcia's bad side was also a quelling thought, but this Jack character had admitted to lying during their meeting, so he might have been lying about all of it. How did Emory know any such meeting had taken place? He had never heard of Garcia turning on one of his clients. At the risk of damaging his business reputation, it seemed unlikely he would start double-crossing his customers now. Not even for the sacred memory of Uncle What's-His-Name the bootmaker.

Chalk up his intimidation to any or all of those extenuating circumstances. Or to the unaccustomed drinking at lunch. Or to the oppressive humidity of yesterday afternoon. To a mind fart. To whatever.

The important thing now was that he recognized the cowboy's grandstanding for what it was. Anna Corbett's ranch hand was jealous of him, so he had flexed some muscle. Big deal.

On the other hand, the acquisition of the Corbett property *was* a big deal. Standing between him and achieving that prize goal were a few macho threats issued by a man who wasn't fit to polish his shoes.

This morning Emory had awakened with a bitch of a hangover, but with a clearer head and a firmer understanding of what he must do. The conquest of Anna Corbett could not be postponed. It must begin in earnest today.

She might continue to give him the cold shoulder, but when she got to know him, she would thaw. The only way she would get to know him was to spend time with him. That's what he intended to do. Today would be a courtesy call. He would offer her his services and, over the next several weeks, grant her unlimited favors, professional and personal.

When she became dependent on his generosity and kindness, he would really turn on the charm and let her think she was being courted—but only until the deal was closed. He wouldn't mind sampling the goods, but he'd be damned before he saddled himself with a deaf broad and her bratty kid.

Cowboy Jack had warned him to stay away from her. "Ooooh, I'm scared," Emory said to the luxurious dashboard of his Jag. What was the guy gonna do? Slit his throat? Beat him up? Emory scoffed. Scare tactics. That's all it amounted to, and Emory wasn't falling for it.

"Give a cowboy a freaky-looking knife and he thinks he's Jim fuckin' Bowie," he muttered as he applied his brakes.

Up ahead a car was parked on the shoulder of the road. From what Emory could tell, there was only one person inside, in the passenger seat.

He didn't have an altruistic bone in his body, but he was politic. He prided himself on being very good at covering his ass. If the car was broken down and the individual was a bank customer who later said that Emory Lomax had breezed past without stopping to render aid, that would be bad public relations. Bad all the way around, because his relationship with the bank president was already tenuous.

But if it were said that Emory Lomax was a regular Good Samaritan, that he had inconvenienced himself for a person in need, that would earn him some much-needed brownie points.

Genial smile in place, he pulled up alongside the car.

"You could have called."

Cora's voice was as icy as Ezzy had ever heard it. She was upset, which, in Ezzy's present state of mind, was just too damn bad. He felt like telling her to "deal with it" and hanging up.

"You knew I'd be worried," she said in remonstration.

"Did I?"

That crack really ticked her off. She sighed in a huff. "I didn't call to quarrel with you, Ezzy. Even out here I've been hearing news reports about the storms in East Texas last night. The TV said a tornado practically leveled Blewer. I've been calling for hours and just now got through. Then when you didn't answer the house phone . . . well, put yourself in my place. Wouldn't it upset you not to hear from me? I was imagining all sorts of horrible things."

"The sheriff called yesterday evening and asked did I want to help during the emergency."

"So you dropped everything and rushed right over."

Her sarcastic tone made him sound like a pathetic individual who had lost all pride and self-esteem, and who would jump at a chance to prove his self-worth. "Yeah, I did," he said. "It felt good to be needed and wanted by somebody. Anybody."

It wasn't like him to try to score major points in a quarrel with Cora, but dammit, he'd barely escaped being killed by a tornado. Moreover, he'd been up all night drinking bad coffee and eating vending-machine snacks, monitoring the police radios, and dispatching younger, able deputies to go out and do the job he was too old to do.

Dispatch. When he reported in, that's the assignment they'd given him. Not search and rescue. Not flood control. Not any sort of man's job. He was good enough only for what an old lady could do. All they needed was somebody to receive and send messages, the only qualification being that his body had to be warm. That's the job they'd assigned a veteran law enforcement officer with fifty years' experience.

The worse thing about it was that he hadn't told them to go screw themselves and walk out. He'd done it. Then when the telephone service was restored earlier today, he'd been further humiliated. They'd taken him off dispatch and placed him at a desk to answer incoming calls from the general public and direct them if necessary.

In his view he was entitled to be a little testy, especially with the wife who'd elected to leave him.

She asked, "When did you eat last?"

"Don't worry about it. Lucy's been seeing to it that I get fed."

"Lucy at the Busy Bee?"

"You know any other Lucys?"

"I was just asking."

"Yeah, Lucy over at the Busy Bee," he repeated snidely. "I've been taking all my meals there."

That capped her. She was silent for a long time, and Ezzy enjoyed her stewing. *Let her wonder,* he thought.

Finally she said, "Even though you're about as pleasant as a boil on the butt, I'm relieved to know you're all right."

He wasn't exactly all right, but he let it pass. The knot on his temple wasn't worth mentioning. He wasn't dead, seriously injured, or trapped beneath an I-beam in a collapsed building, and that's what she meant by all right.

"How did the house fare? Was it damaged?"

"Haven't been home to find out." He tried to sound indifferent. "Electricity's out all over the county. We're on emergency generators here in the office. Crews are working 'round the clock, but downtown is in a helluva mess and that's where the main transformers are. Got to hand it to the phone company for getting our service back on this soon. Which leads me to tell you that the lines are ringing off the wall. I've got to go, Cora."

"Okay then, well . . . You're sure you're okay?"

"Right as rain."

"Call me back when you take a breather."

Ignoring the misery in her voice, he gave her a clipped "Bye now," and ended the call. If she was so all-fired worried about him, she could damn well get into her Buick and come home.

As soon as he disconnected, the telephone immediately rang again. "Sheriff's office."

"Yeah, uh, sir, I got a passel of snakes in my yard. When the creek water went down, there they was, squiggling all over the place. The wife's gone ballistic. One of the dogs done got bit."

In the background Ezzy could hear hunting dogs barking, a woman shrieking, and an unidentifiable pounding noise. He asked the routine questions and jotted down the man's answers on the standard form. When he gave Ezzy his rural address, Ezzy asked, "So y'all've got your phone service back?"

"No, sir, we ain't. It's deader than a hammer. I'm callin' on my cell phone."

Ezzy promised that a deputy would be along as soon as possible, but added that it might be a while. He cautioned the man to be careful until help arrived, but he didn't tell him that they would probably be finding snakes in the house for weeks or months to come. He'd known that kind of infestation to happen after floods.

The next call came from a man who was angry at his neighbor. "If he'd kept that sorry fence of his in better repair, it wouldn't have blown into my swimming pool."

Ezzy advised him to take it up with the neighbor and not to clutter the telephone lines with such a petty, personal complaint. The chastisement didn't sit well with a man already irate. When he started cussing Ezzy out, he hung up on him.

He just wasn't feeling too charitable today. His tolerance level had maxed out hours ago. Anybody who rubbed him the wrong way was liable to get his head bit off. When the telephone rang again, he practically snarled at the caller.

"Sheriff's office."

"Who's this?"

"Ezzy Hardge."

A pause. "Didn't you retire?"

"How can I help you, ma'am?"

"I'm not sure you can. In fact I know y'all are awful busy over there. I probably shouldn't even be calling. It's probably nothing."

"You got a name, ma'am?"

"Sorry. It's Ella Presley. Over at the bank? I'm Emory Lomax's secretary."

Too bad for you, Ezzy thought. "Is the bank open today?"

"No, sir. Our electricity is off and several windows were blown out. We just got our phones back on. Some of us came in to, you know, to help clean up the mess."

"Y'all been robbed or what?" he asked drolly.

"No, no, nothing like that. The reason I'm calling is, well, Mr. Lomax left a while ago, and the president called an emergency meeting of all the bank officers for four o'clock this afternoon, and I haven't been able to reach Mr. Lomax to notify him of the meeting."

To Ezzy this sounded like another personal problem. What was it with people today? Had the tornado sucked all the common sense out of Blewer County? He was slowly losing what little patience Cora's call had left him. "Mrs. Presley, I don't see where—"

"I wouldn't bother you, except that Mr. Lomax is never out of touch. Never. I'm always able to reach him either on his cell phone or his pager. But he doesn't answer his phone and he hasn't responded to my pages."

"Maybe he turned them off."

"He wouldn't. What really bothers me is that he was on his way out to the Corbett place. Mrs. Corbett—you know, the deaf lady?—well she's a bank customer. Mr. Lomax personally handles her account. He was worried about her maybe not having any electricity or phone service, so he told me he was going out there to check."

Ezzy smiled at Mrs. Presley's naiveté. Lomax had turned off his pager because he was with Anna Corbett and didn't want to be disturbed. Recalling how she'd looked the other night, Ezzy couldn't say he blamed the banker, although he couldn't imagine a quality lady like her having any romantic interest in an asshole like Lomax.

"He'll show up before too long," he said with unconcern. "I wouldn't worry too much if I were you."

"I wouldn't, except for what happened yesterday afternoon."

Ezzy stifled a yawn and propped his cheek on his fist. He even closed his eyes. "What happened yesterday afternoon?"

"A man came into the bank and asked to see Mr. Lomax. When I told him he wasn't back from lunch yet, he told me he would wait and sailed right past me into Mr. Lomax's private office."

"What man?"

"He and Mr. Lomax claimed to be old college chums, but one of the tellers told me later—while we were on coffee break—that he was no more a fraternity brother of Mr. Lomax's than he was a Chinaman. She said he was the Corbetts' ranch hand and probably hadn't even gone to college."

Ezzy's eyes opened. He lowered his fist and eased forward until both elbows were resting on the desk and he was massaging his forehead with his free hand. This was getting more interesting. "Why would two grown men try and pass him off as a fraternity brother?"

"It's even weirder than that, Sheriff. I don't think they're friendly at all. I heard raised voices behind the door, like they were arguing. And no matter how they tried to trick me into thinking it was a prank, that business with the knife—"

"Knife?"

"Didn't I tell you that part yet?"

"No, no, you didn't." Ezzy grabbed a notepad and pencil. "But I'd sure like for you to tell me now."

Chapter Forty-Six

$\mathcal{E}$ zzy despised Emory Lomax. It was damned foolish to give that weasel a second thought, much less devote an hour of his time to him. That's how long it would take him to drive out to the Corbett ranch and back again. Fifteen minutes after leaving the sheriff's office, he was still debating whether or not to return to town.

His eyes were grainy from lack of sleep. Despite what he had told Cora, he was so hungry his stomach thought his throat had been cut. Thinking back, the last thing he'd eaten that hadn't come wrapped in cellophane was the piece of apple pie Lucy had sliced for him yesterday afternoon.

He was suffering a burning pain between his shoulder blades caused by hunching over a desk all night charting routes for deputies who called in and reported themselves lost while trying to locate stranded motorists or other citizens in equally perilous circumstances.

He'd sat so long his joints were stiff and his arthritis was killing him. Too much coffee had left him with breath that would have brought a camel to its knees. He was in bad need of a shave and shower.

Overall, he felt like hell.

He must have looked it, too, because Sheriff Foster had ordered him to take a two-hour break. He ought to have his head examined for squandering half of it checking on Emory Lomax. Good thing Cora didn't know that he was off on another wild goose chase based solely on gut instinct. She'd give him grief.

It wasn't Lomax's welfare as much as it was curiosity about the hired hand that had him dodging storm debris and speeding toward the ranch. Delray's hired hand must have some mighty strong feelings of dislike toward Lomax to have pulled a knife on him. Or was it Anna Corbett that had sparked that much emotion from the man? Was he dealing with plain old-fashioned jealousy? If so, the romance sure had progressed quickly. Although love worked that way sometimes. Look at him and Cora.

Yeah, look at me and Cora.

He had intentionally ended their telephone conversation on a sour note. Now he felt bad about that. Pure spite had caused him to dismiss her concerns. He should call her and apologize. He'd call when he got back to town. As soon as he got back.

Returning his thoughts to the business at hand, he recalled that day at the Dairy Queen when Delray had introduced him to his new employee. He hadn't struck Ezzy as an overly friendly, chatty sort. But he hadn't seemed like a short-tempered hothead either.

Of course, Emory Lomax could test the patience of a saint. Like the time he had stormed into the sheriff's office demanding that Ezzy do something about the birds that were "voiding" on his English import while it was parked in the lot reserved for bank employees.

Ezzy had listened to every feverish word of the tirade, and when Lomax finally ran out of breath, Ezzy calmly asked if he truly thought the sheriff's office could do anything about the shitting habits of sparrows. Lomax had stamped out, leaving the deputies and office staff in hysterics.

It was in no way remarkable that the new man in town didn't like Lomax. Few people did. Many who had applied to Lomax for a loan would probably enjoy killing him. The difference was that nobody Ezzy knew of had acted on the impulse to the extent that this man had.

But if Lomax had felt his life genuinely threatened, why hadn't he reported the assault to the police? There'd been no such report. Ezzy had checked. Maybe the incident had been a joke between college buddies after all and the secretary had simply read it wrong.

However, no matter how it came down, you couldn't have folks pulling knives on each other. Even in jest that was a dangerous business. That's why he was on his way out to the Corbett place. If Lomax was paying a call on Anna Corbett and bumped into the hired hand while he was out there, and either or both of them had a heavy crush on her, you had all the makings of a combustible situation.

And dammit, he *did* have a gut instinct that there was more to this situation than met the eye. Call him crazy, old, and delusional, call him a fool, but he had fifty years' experience in these matters, and something here was out of joint. At the very least it bore checking out.

Last night when he'd reported in, Foster, in a rushed and harried manner, had said, "Consider yourself deputized." Legally, Ezzy was acting in an official capacity, although he doubted that Foster would clear him to run down a missing-person report. But what Foster didn't know wouldn't hurt him. Besides, he was still busy with the aftereffects of the storm, so why bother him with something this trivial?

For all his physical miseries, it felt good to be driving an official car again. The Lincoln had been blocked in by someone who had double-parked. When he asked if he could take a squad car on his break, the deputy pulling telephone duty had waved him out by tossing him a set of keys.

The car felt as comfy and familiar as the old flannel robe that—to Cora's consternation—he had rescued from the Goodwill bag about a dozen times. A chance to drive a sheriff's unit again was a valid enough reason to be on this errand. He might just as well be following up Ella Presley's call as catching a short nap that would only make him crankier, or checking his house for storm damage that he wouldn't know how to repair, or puzzling over the nebulous clue to the McCorkle case left to him by a dying man.

Cora would have given him grief about that, too.

Myron was close to tears.

Carl was still gone and he was getting real scared.

He was also afraid he had done something wrong.

Carl had told him to shoot anybody who came near the car.

But he had let the man in the car go past and he hadn't shot him. The car had slowed down when it pulled up alongside the driver's door. The man had leaned forward and looked in at him. Then he had sped up and driven off real fast before Myron got a chance to shoot him.

It panicked him to think of Carl finding out. But it panicked him even more to think that Carl wasn't going to come back for him and that he would be alone and wouldn't know what to do when it got dark. He would rather Carl yell at him and call him a retard than leave him.

He thought about scooting behind the wheel and driving in the direction Carl had gone. He could go find Carl. But he didn't know the way. What if he couldn't find him? What if Carl came back and he was gone? Then Carl would really get mad at him for not doing what he said.

So he continued to sit and sweat and guard the money.

But the next person who came by, he would shoot. Then if Carl found out about the other one, he wouldn't get so mad.

That decision reached, Myron didn't even whimper in fear and anxiety when he noticed the approaching car. He saw it in the exterior side mirror. He didn't turn around and look at it, but kept his head forward. It slowed down and pulled to the shoulder behind his car. He was glad it had stopped, because he wanted to shoot somebody and make Carl proud to be his friend.

It was a police car. It was white with blue letters on the side. It had a shiny light bar across the roof. The lights weren't on, but a car with letters on the side and lights on top represented the enemy. Carl hated cops worse than anything. Carl would be extra happy with him if he killed a cop.

The driver opened his door and got out.

"Hey, bud, you having trouble with your car?"

Myron watched him in the mirror as he started forward down the driver's side of the car.

When he got closer, Myron could hear his footsteps in the gravel.

His finger was sweaty, but it tightened around the trigger.

"Need some help here?"

When the officer bent down and smiled at him through the open window, he raised the shotgun and fired.

Emory Lomax slipped a canister of breath spray from the breast pocket of his jacket and squirted the essence of peppermint into his mouth. He checked his reflection in the rearview mirror and was relieved to see that his recent fright hadn't left him looking shaken.

He had slowed down to offer assistance to the passenger of the broken-down car, but when he pulled up even with it, he'd received the scare of his life. The eyes staring back at him were colorless, yet rimmed in pink. They were set in a bloodless face surrounded by hair that looked like a Halloween wig. He'd never seen anything like it, and it had scared the hell out of him.

Piss on good intentions and public relations. Even if the spook were a bank customer—he didn't think he was; who could forget that face once you'd seen it?—he wasn't about to stop. Gunning his motor, he had gotten the hell out of there and hadn't slowed down until he reached the gate of the Corbett ranch.

Before getting out, he smoothed down his hair and practiced his smile in the mirror. The place seemed unnaturally quiet. There was no one around. As he climbed the front steps, Emory was irritated to note that his collateral had suffered some storm damage, most notably to the barn. The house, however, seemed okay except for a broken front window.

He was about to ring the doorbell when he remembered that the electricity was probably out. He rapped the doorjamb smartly three times. Immediately the door was answered by none other than the man who now topped his shit list.

Rudely, Jack said, "What are you doing here, Lomax?"

"Not that it's any of your business, but I came to see Mrs. Corbett. Would you please summon her to the door?"

"She's unavailable."

"What does that mean, 'unavailable'?"

"It means she's not available. I'll tell her you came by."

The man's gall was infuriating. He didn't even have the courtesy to look him straight in the eye. Instead he was looking beyond him, his eyes darting from one side of the yard to the other. "See ya."

He tried to close the door, but Emory stepped forward and stopped it with his hand. "Look here, Jack," he sneered. "I'm insisting that you call Mrs. Corbett to the door."

"She can't see you right now. In any case, she doesn't even want to."

Emory blustered, "How do you know what she wants and doesn't want? Isn't it for her to say whether or not she wants to see me?"

"I'm saying it for her. Now go away."

The hired hand was shooing him away like a stray dog. Emory wouldn't stand for it. "Who the hell are you to talk down to me?"

"Look, Lomax, sometime we'll get together over a beer and I'll list all the reasons why I think you're an asshole. But that's not why I'm asking you to leave. I'm asking you to leave because it's in your best interest to do so."

"Is that right?"

"Believe me."

"Well, I don't believe you. It's in *your* best interest that I leave."

"Okay. But it's also what Mrs. Corbett wishes."

" 'Mrs. Corbett,' " he scoffed. "How polite. And how phony. Everybody in town knows what you do for her. You took over where the old man left off, right? Did you at least change the sheets after he died, or did you jump right in and take—"

"Shut up."

"Or what?"

"Just go."

"Not before I tell Mrs. Corbett that if she wants me to be nice to her, she'd better start being nice to me." He tried to push the man aside, but he resisted. "I'm coming in."

"I can't let you inside."

"Over, around, or through you, I'm coming in." Emory was tired of being condescended to by Anna Corbett and her ranch hand. He couldn't let them insult him like this and get away with it. If she would stoop to sleep with the likes of this cowpoke, she didn't deserve the kid-glove treatment.

As of now, all bets were off. No more Mr. Nice Guy. He would strike back with a vengeance. He would call her note, repossess the property, hand it over to Connaught, and become a corporate hero.

He would teach the deaf broad to snub him!

But he wanted to tell her this himself, while he was angry and his resolve still fresh. Regardless of her deafness, he would make himself understood.

But first he had to get past this guy. Again Emory tried to shove him out of his way, and when he stood his ground they became engaged in an undignified struggle.

"I will not be turned away by the hired hand," Emory panted scornfully.

He pushed against the man's chest with all his strength and had the pleasure of seeing his face turn white with apparent agony. He stumbled backward into the entry. Seizing the opportunity, Emory barged inside.

Confusion brought him up short.

Anna was kneeling on the floor.

The kid was pinned against the wall with a gun to his head.

The guy with the gun—

Gun?!

Chapter Forty-Seven

$\mathcal{D}$avid was terrified. He had seen a man shot to death only a few feet away from him. He was crying and it must have been loud because Carl grabbed him by the shoulder and shook him hard. "Shut up that bawling, kid. Hear me? Shut up."

Anna reached for her son, and Carl pushed him toward her, saying, "Shut the damn kid up."

She didn't know what Carl had in store for her when he shoved her to her knees, because just as he did, Lomax arrived. Jack's back had been to her, so she hadn't been able to follow what he said, but she could tell by the way he had stood in the partially open doorway that he had tried to protect Lomax, probably by persuading him to leave. The man's arrogance wouldn't allow him to back down. Lomax burst through the door; Carl had killed him instantly.

David clung to her tightly, his small body racked by shudders. Jack raised his index finger vertically against his lips, asking David to please be quiet. David nodded and did his best to be manly, but he continued to hiccup sobs.

How quickly the priorities of a lifetime are rearranged, Anna thought. Since David's birth, she had fretted over the embarrassment her impairment might cause her son. Those worries seemed trivial now. If their lives were spared, if they were allowed to go on living, what difference did it really make that she couldn't hear?

She fervently wished she could turn back the clock. Only minutes ago they'd been naively unconcerned for the future. Now they were in danger of dying soon. Why had this happened now, just when she and Jack had found each other?

Jack. He was in tremendous pain. He must have broken a rib when he fell into the wall. He continued to hold his side, and his face was white with pain. She could tell that each breath was a gasping effort to override the agony. His lips were tense and moved unnaturally, although she could read everything he said and realized that he was attempting to speak distinctly so she could follow his dialogue with Carl.

She had also seen him spelling out the word *knife*, and remembered, as he obviously had, that his knife was still in David's backpack. After marking the trees with it, David had asked if he could keep it for a while, and Jack had consented, but on the condition that he carry it sheathed and in his backpack. There it remained, in a child's backpack covered with spotted dalmatians.

But how to get it without Carl's seeing?

David must have dropped the backpack when Carl grabbed him as he entered the house. It, along with her photography gear and the food hamper, had all been kicked into the corner. Carl stood between it and Jack. She was closer to it, but had no more chance of retrieving it than Jack did. If he even tried, Carl would kill him. Of that she had no doubt.

Seemingly indifferent to having just taken a stranger's life, Carl nudged the bleeding body with the toe of his shoe. "Who's he?" Emory Lomax had landed on the floor in a supine position, his sightless eyes staring at the ceiling, his face still registering puzzlement.

"He's dead," Jack said. "What difference does it make to you who he was?"

"None, I guess." He scowled at Jack. "Remember me warning you not to lie to me?"

"So?"

"So, the stiff here was more honest about the nature of your relationship with my sister-in-law."

Anna signed, *"Don't call me that, you son of a bitch."*

"Whoa, whoa. What was that?" Laughing at her, he moved his fingers to mimic sign language. "What'd she say?"

"I don't read sign," Jack told him.

Carl looked skeptical, but he let it pass with an uncaring shrug. "Doesn't matter. I can guess what she said from her expression."

She hated that he found her so amusing. She hated that he mimicked her like cruel children had done when she was in school. But to tell him off in sign would only give him more ammunition to ridicule her. She had learned early to ignore taunts from people too stupid and insensitive to realize that when they made fun of her they only embarrassed themselves.

He was talking to Jack again. "You lied to protect the woman and kid. Sweet. Real sweet."

"Do whatever you want with me," Jack said to him. "I won't even put up a fight if you'll let them go."

"No!" Anna shot to her feet and took a step toward Jack. Carl grabbed her arm and spun her around abruptly.

"Now where do you think you're going? If you're so eager to be near a man, I'm right here." He drew her up flush against him. She didn't flinch, only glared at him haughtily.

"What's so special about you, hmm? You've got one man beating down your front door, another willing to die for you. You must be in heat is what I'm thinking. You're putting out a scent that's got 'em panting after you."

He peered into her eyes more closely. "Can you understand what I'm saying? You're one of those . . . what do they call them? Lip readers? Aren't you a lip reader, sweetheart?"

She gave him a stony stare.

"I bet you'll understand this good enough."

He moved his hand over her breasts, then reached between her legs and groped her. Reflexively she squeezed her thighs together and slapped at his hands, which only made him laugh. His silent laughter looked obscene.

She felt his breath on her face, but she didn't give him the satisfaction of averting her head in disgust, not even when he raised his fingers beneath his nose and sniffed them. He winked lewdly. "Nice."

She didn't hear Jack's approach, but she felt it a heartbeat before he barreled into Carl, who rapped his temple with the butt of the pistol. Jack collapsed. She crouched down beside him. The blow had opened a two-inch gash on the side of his head. Already it was bleeding profusely. David started crying again.

Despite his own pain, Jack reached for David and tried to quiet him. But even though he was speaking to David and stroking his head, he was looking at her. She'd never seen a smile so sweet or so sad. It was as though Jack's entire life had come down to this moment, as though he were resigned to this being the last few moments before the end of his life, and that it was no better than he had expected it to be. The futility suggested by his smile broke her heart.

She wished that she could tell him everything would be all right. She wished that she believed everything would be all right. Instead she laid her fingertips against his lips and he mouthed *"I love you"* against them as he had this morning—in what seemed another lifetime.

Carl knocked her hand away from Jack and roughly hauled her to her feet. "I hate to break up this touching scene, truly I do. But I came here for one purpose and one purpose only, and that was to get revenge on my old stepdaddy."

"You're too late," Jack said.

"To kill him, yeah. But that doesn't mean I can't get some satisfaction. Since I can't snuff Delray, guess I'll have to settle for those he left behind."

"If you came here to kill us, why haven't you already done it?"

"Are you that anxious to die, hired hand?"

"Just curious."

Carl shrugged. "That's fair, I guess. Fact is, I don't want to spoil my fun. I waited over twenty fucking years in prison for this day. I want to prolong the pleasure, same way I did with Cecil. He deserved a slow, painful death for being such a goddamn coward, and that's what he got. Damn shame I didn't get to kill Delray, too. I would've liked to make him suffer for all the years he cost me. The good news is, he's dead." He leveled the pistol on Jack. "The bad news is that—"

"The bad news is that your partner seems to have run into some trouble."

Following Jack's nod toward the open front door, Anna turned at the same time Carl did.

The pale man smiled through the blood running down his face. "Hi, Carl."

"Jesus Christ, Myron!"

Carl grabbed the front of Myron's bloody shirt and yanked him across the threshold. He looked through the door but saw only a beat-up orange pickup and a shiny Jaguar that must've belonged to the stiff.

"Where's the car, Myron?" he screamed.

"The car?"

Carl slammed the door shut and bore down on Myron. "What happened? Why'd you leave the car? Where's the money?"

Myron's idiotic grin collapsed. "The money?"

"The money from the bank, Myron. *Jesus!* What were you thinking to go off and leave it?"

Agitated, Myron dragged his sleeve across his face, smearing the blood and sweat. "I shot the man like you told me to."

Carl wanted to kill him. The need to kill him pulsed through his veins. He envisioned wrapping his hands around Myron's long, skinny neck and squeezing until his strange eyes bulged out of their sockets.

He saw himself shooting him in the face again and again, until that stupid expression was reduced to pink mush and the ugliness was pulverized.

But until he knew about the money, he had to keep Myron alive. He forced himself to take several deep breaths. Eventually the blood vessels in his head no longer felt ready to burst. More calmly he asked, "Where's the money, Myron? What did you do with it?"

"It's still in the trunk."

"Where's the car?"

"You know where it's at, Carl."

"Same place I left it?"

"Yeah."

"Where're your guns?"

Myron replied only with a blank stare.

"Your guns, your guns!" Carl shrieked.

Myron was near tears. "I must've left 'em."

Again Carl had an almost uncontrollable impulse to kill him with his bare hands. He had left all the weapons save his pistol with Myron, not wishing to be weighted down with hardware should a nosy passerby stop to offer him a ride. Even his shank was beneath the driver's seat of the car. He was down to one lousy pistol and a few extra bullets, and it was all Myron's fault.

Quaking with rage, he stifled it enough to ask what had happened. "Tell me what happened, Myron."

Myron's smile returned. "I shot the—"

"*What* man?"

"A cop. He came up close to the car. You said for me to shoot anybody who came close to the car."

"Good job, Myron."

"I blowed his head off with the shotgun."

The kid had started to whine, and it was an aggravating distraction. Carl wanted to scare him into shutting up, but first he had to find out how Myron had come to have what looked like a bullet wound in his shoulder and another long stripe of open flesh along the side of his scalp above his right ear. But if he pressured Myron for answers, he would become even more confused and, God knew, Myron didn't need to become more confused.

"Who shot you, Myron?"

"The cop."

"The one you shot?"

"The other one."

Carl swallowed. "There were two?"

"Yeah, Carl. One stayed in the car. When I shot the first one, the one in the car got out and started shooting at me." He turned his head to look at his wounded shoulder. "It hurts real bad."

"We'll get some medicine for it later. What happened to the other cop? Is he dead too?"

"I guess so. I shot him."

"You shot him but you don't know if he's dead? You didn't check? You left without making certain that both of them were dead?"

Myron's face worked with indecision. "He was screaming."

"Screaming," Carl said, plowing his fingers through his hair and expelling a long breath. "And you left the money."

"I was scared, Carl. My arm hurts. I came to find you. I'm sorry I forgot the money. Are you mad at me, Carl?"

"Shut up!" Carl shouted. "Just shut the hell up and let me think!"

This was serious. What should he do?

He could forget his revenge, leave now, and return to the car, the money, the key to his future. But what if someone had come along and discovered the slain cops? Or cop, singular. One might still be alive. With only one revolver, in a shoot-out of any magnitude, he could wind up dead or recaptured. Not an option.

Besides, he wasn't sure he could trust Myron to hold down the fort here even long enough for him to make a clean getaway. Myron was a total shitbrain. As soon as Carl left, this guy, this ranch hand, whoever he was, would make hash of Myron. The guy was smart. Cecil had said he had an "edge," and on that point he agreed with his brother. In no time flat he could outfox Myron. Then he would be coming after Carl, calling the cops, or otherwise fucking up his plan.

If they shot everybody here and got it over with, he and Myron could return to the car together, but he would still be faced with whatever uncertainty awaited them there, and only one of them would be armed.

And if they killed everybody here they'd have no hostages to bargain with.

Christ, what to do?

He had to think. Had to keep his head and reason it out. That's what he was good at, thinking it out. Planning. But this was the worst jam he'd ever been in. Maybe Cecil would have an idea. But Cecil was dead. He had killed Cecil.

Best not to think about that because it only gummed up his brain.

But who the hell could think of anything with that kid carrying on?

It was enough to drive a man crazy. With a burst of temper, he spun around and pointed the pistol at the squalling child.

"Officer down!"

Ezzy had been so lost in thought that the frantic words coming through the police radio didn't register at first. When they did, he jerked erect in his seat and turned up the volume.

"Officer down!"

Ezzy reached for the transmitter. "This is BC-Four. Who's this?"

The county had started using UHF radios a few years ago. Although the ten-code system was still used for some transmissions, most were voice communications. Units were identified by letter-and-number sequences.

Ezzy was answered only by a low moan, so he repeated his transmission in a louder, more urgent voice. "Can you hear me?"

"I think Jim's dead."

Ezzy reached several hasty deductions. Jim Clark was the only Jim in the department. His partner was a relatively new man, practically a kid, named Steve Jones. He was in obvious distress, probably wounded, very scared.

Calmly Ezzy asked, "Steve, that you?"

A moan, but an affirmative one.

"Ezzy?" His name crackled through the speaker. "Ezzy Hardge?"

"Get off the goddamn radio so I can talk to this kid," he yelled to the dispatcher who had cut in.

"Where you at?"

"County road Fourteen-Twenty," he replied impatiently. "Headed east. Clear the radio."

Another voice. "Jim called in a few minutes ago, Ezzy. Said there was a forty-six on Road Fourteen-Twenty south of River Road. They were stopping to check it out, see what the trouble was. Late-model gray Honda Civic. Texas plates Harry Gary Roger five five three."

"Ten four," said Ezzy. "I'm practically there."

"Ezzy, you ain't—"

"Steve Jones?" Ezzy said, interrupting. "Listen, son, I'm on my way. Hang in there, you hear?"

There was no answer. Ezzy cursed and floored the accelerator. He sped through the stop sign at the state highway's intersection with River Road. Moments later, he spotted the sheriff's unit parked on the shoulder behind a gray Honda. Both doors of the patrol car were standing open. There was no other sign of trouble except for the body sprawled in the road. Buzzards were already circling.

Ezzy screeched to a halt behind the sheriff's unit. He opened his door, crouched behind it, and drew his pistol. He looked at the body in the road. It was Jim, all right. His own mama couldn't have identified him by what was left of his face, but he was recognizable by his boots. High-dollar Lucchese boots. Which he always wore and always kept polished to a high gloss. The pointed toes, now turned up to the sky, were spattered with blood.

He crept from behind his cover and ran in a crouch to the rear of the other patrol car. He moved to the right side and poked his head around to look up the passenger side. Wedged in the open door he saw the younger deputy.

Ezzy rushed to him. The radio transmitter rested in his outstretched hand. There was a godawful lot of blood beneath him, coming from his knee, which appeared to have been shattered by a shotgun blast. He was barely conscious. Ezzy slapped him lightly on each cheek. "Steve, it's Ezzy. Help's on the way, son. Which way'd he go?"

In all his days of law enforcement, Ezzy had never known someone to shoot a cop or two then leave his car behind and set off on foot. Even assuming the perp's car was somehow disabled, why hadn't he taken the patrol car, at least for a few miles? It was a puzzling set of circumstances.

Young Jones appeared to be in shock. His face was chalk white and beaded with sweat. He kept his teeth clenched to keep them from chattering. "Did he get Jim?"

"'Fraid so, son."

"That freak. Like a . . . a ghost."

Ezzy's heart thumped solidly against his ribs, once, then seemed to stop for several beats before resuming. "Big, gawky guy?"

Jones nodded. "My leg gone?"

"Naw, you'll be all right," Ezzy told him with more confidence than he felt. "Was this guy alone?"

"Yeah. Get him, Ezzy."

Ezzy was hoping that was what the young deputy would say. "Sure you don't want me to wait till—"

"No. Get him. He went . . . yonder." He pointed with his chin.

"On foot?"

"Bleedin'. I think I hit him."

Ezzy patted him on the shoulder. "You did good, son."

Tears came to his eyes. "I let Jim down."

"Nothing you could've done different."

After assuring the officer again that medical help would be there soon, Ezzy jogged back to his car, his arthritis making ice picks of his kneecaps. But at least he still had both knees.

Over the radio, he informed other units of the exact location of the shooting. "Ambulance is on the way," he was told.

"You'll need the coroner, too. Proceed with extreme caution. The suspects must still be in the area, on foot, but armed and dangerous. Could be escaped convicts Myron Hutts and Carl Herbold."

"Ezzy, this is Sheriff Foster," he said in his most formidable paramilitary voice. "Are you still at the scene?"

Ezzy didn't respond, not even when the sheriff repeated his question. He turned off the radio and sped away, steering around Jim Clark's body. He was afraid to drive too fast at the risk of missing a trail. He was afraid to drive too slow and risk their getting away.

He swiveled his head from side to side, hoping to catch sight of Myron Hutts. And hoping just as earnestly that he spotted the convict before the convict spotted him. Killing one more cop would hardly matter to either him or Carl Herbold now.

Wouldn't it be something if Carl Herbold succeeded in carrying out his death threats? What a coup it would be for the whole criminal population if Carl got the lawman that first put him in jail. Carl would become the prisoners' poster child.

Ezzy laughed, but there was no humor in the sound. If he let Carl kill him, Cora would never forgive him.

He topped a rise and sighted the Corbett ranch up ahead to the right. Parked out front were a pickup truck and a Jaguar he recognized as Emory Lomax's. The emergency had taken his mind off that problem. He—

Ezzy braked so hard his car went into a skid and nosed into the ditch on the far side of the driveway. He'd almost missed it—a trail of blood leading out of the tall weeds in the ditch straight up the driveway to the house.

He got out of the car. Cocking his pistol, he crouched beside the post supporting the wrought-iron arch.

Then he heard the unmistakable crack of a gunshot.

Chapter Forty-Eight

"The next one's for the kid if he doesn't stop that infernal bawling."
Carl had fired the pistol into the wall, deliberately missing David
but only by a hair.

That's when Jack realized a truth.

Unequivocal. Unarguable. Absolute.

He would have to kill this man.

Of course he would try for a nonviolent resolution. He would try to
prevent bloodshed. He would exercise all other options first. But from
his position on the floor, as he looked up at Carl Herbold, he knew with
unshakable certainty that he would be forced to make him stop breathing.

The certitude made him feel very old. World weary. Defeated. He
wanted to shake his fist at God and demand to know why.

But he wasn't even allowed the luxury of introspection. There was no
time for it. Carl was ranting over David's crying. Jack tried reasoning.
"He's five years old. He's scared. He just saw you shoot a man in cold
blood. Your friend there isn't exactly the man-on-the-street. In these circumstances, what do you expect a child to do?"

"I expect him to shut up!" Carl shouted.

"You're making more racket than he is."

"Who asked you?"

"Why don't you let his mother take him upstairs, put him to bed?"

"You think I'm stupid? She doesn't leave my sight."

"The phones are out. There's no electricity. What could she do?"

"I said no."

"Something to drink might help. In the kitchen—"

"Everybody stays here where I can see them."

Jack glanced toward the corner. "Maybe if he had something to play with. His backpack has some toys in it."

Out of sheer frustration over Jack's persistence, Carl mulled it over. Finally he motioned toward the corner, saying to Myron, "Give the kid his bag."

Myron bent down and picked up the backpack, then carried it over to Jack. David gazed at Myron with fear and awe. Jack was glad the boy was momentarily distracted because it seemed more natural when he passed the backpack to Anna instead of handing it to David.

Her eyes locked with Jack's for an instant, then she unzipped the bag and slipped her hand inside.

Carl jabbed his finger for emphasis. "Now, I don't want to hear another peep out of him."

Jack said, "Will terrorizing us make your situation any better?"

"You don't know shit about my situation." Then, "What situation?"

From the bag Anna removed a loincloth-clad action figure that held a shield in one hand and brandished a sword in the other. She waggled it in front of David. He smiled and reached for it.

Taking breaths deep enough to form words cost Jack dearly, but he knew that dialogue would buy them precious time. "You're in a world of hurt, Carl. I can tell what's going through your mind."

Carl gazed back at him belligerently, but he was still listening. "Like hell you can. You don't know anything about me."

"I know you'd like to kill your partner there."

Myron was slumped against the wall, clutching his wounded shoulder and gazing blankly at David as he bounced the Roman warrior along the floor. He seemed not to hear or comprehend Jack's hypothesis. Nor had he shown any curiosity over Lomax's body, which he'd had to step over twice in order to deliver the backpack.

Jack said, "Myron let you down, screwed up your plan, made you furious. But you can't eliminate him. Even wounded as he is, you might need him to go back for the money."

When Carl shifted his eyes toward Myron, Jack knew he was on the right track. "You should have killed us sooner."

Carl hefted the pistol. "Of all you've said, that makes the most sense."

"Because now it's too late."

"Okay, smart-ass. I'll play. Why's it too late?"

"Because if that second cop is still alive—"

"He's not."

"You think he might be, though, don't you, Carl? At the very least you know it's a good possibility."

He let Carl ruminate on that for a few seconds. Anna put her hand into the backpack and it came out holding a wad of Silly Putty, which she playfully molded over David's knee.

Jack continued. "By now, that officer has called for help. In a matter of minutes cops're gonna be all over you, in which case you'll need hostages. Without hostages, you don't stand a chance of getting out of here. Dead, we're no good to you. Hope you got your jollies by torturing us, because it really screwed you, Carl.

"Lastly, you'd like to take Lomax's car and go back for the money yourself, then run like hell, leaving poor Myron to fend for himself. That would be your first choice." Jack frowned. "But there's one major drawback. You're afraid to take the risk. You're afraid that if you return to your car, you'll be walking straight into hell. A sticky predicament for a man with only one pistol."

"These hayseed laws?" he scoffed. "I could whip them with one hand tied behind me."

"I don't think so, Carl. And neither do you."

"Don't do my thinking, okay?"

"If you weren't worried about it you would have already been out that door. Something's holding you back."

"If you're so smart, how come I'm the one standing holding the gun and you're the one on the floor with nothing?"

"Know what I think, Carl?"

"I don't give a rat's ass."

"You didn't kill David when he was crying. You didn't kill me, either, and I've been provoking as hell. I think you know your time is running out. You're getting nervous about your future. What's left of it. Or maybe it's the afterlife you're scared of. Bottom line, I think you're a gutless coward."

Carl drew back his foot to kick him, but Jack was poised for an attack. He grabbed the heel of Carl's shoe. When he did, Anna plunged the knife into Carl's thigh, high and on the inside. She withdrew it; blood spurted out in a perfect red arc that sprayed the wall behind them.

Carl screamed.

Jack used the man's raised foot as a lever to topple him backward. "Run, Anna!" he shouted.

She couldn't hear him, but she reacted with incredible speed. Yanking David into her arms, she jumped over Lomax's body and ran toward the door. Jack opened it for them and shoved them through.

"Myron!" Carl shouted.

Galvanized by Carl's frantic cry, Myron pounced. To Jack it felt as though a sack of cement had landed on him. He fell facefirst onto the floor, Myron on top of him.

"Take the gun, Myron!"

Carl, maniacally trying to stanch the geyser of blood spraying from his severed femoral artery, slid the pistol across the oak planks toward Myron. When he reached for the gun, Jack scrambled from beneath him, dove for the corner, grabbed the only weapon available, and rolled onto his back.

Myron pointed the pistol in the general direction of the corner.

Jack depressed the button on the flash attachment of Anna's camera and held it down. It fired shards of brilliant light as fast as a machine gun fires bullets.

Blinded by the strobe, Myron's first shot went wide. His second, fired as he reflexively raised his hand to protect his eyes, shattered the foyer chandelier. Glass rained down.

Jack didn't waste a second, but bounded to his feet. As long as Myron had the pistol, he had to fight him. He ducked his head and rammed it into Myron's stomach. The albino careened backward, his head striking the wall with a sickening noise. Jack encircled his wrist, squeezing it hard, shaking it with all his might to try to loosen the gun from Myron's grip. He used the weakness caused by Myron's shoulder wound and pounded his hand against the wall several times.

Jack's own strength was almost exhausted when the long, pale fingers finally relaxed and the pistol fell to the floor. Jack kicked it out the door, then hit Myron as hard as he could in the face. He gave his throat a hard chop with the side of his hand. Myron crumpled to the floor, unconscious.

Jack spun around in time to see Carl dragging himself along the floor using his free hand. The other was pressed tightly to his thigh wound. Jack was tempted to run from the house now, but then he spied what Carl was after.

Jack's knife. Anna must have dropped it in her haste to flee the house. Now it lay only inches from Carl's grasping fingers. Jack lunged for it, beating Carl to it with barely a second to spare.

He turned Carl over onto his back and pinned him to the floor with one knee on his chest, the other on his right biceps. The blue point of his knife found a soft, vulnerable spot behind the convict's jawbone.

Carl whimpered, "No, please. Please. Don't."

Jack's face dripped bloodstained sweat onto Carl's as he bent over him. His breathing was fast and raspy from his struggle with Myron. But he was unaware of his exertion or his broken rib or the myriad minor injuries he'd sustained in the fight.

He felt supremely alive, oxygen-rich, bloodthirsty.

For all the crimes Carl Herbold had committed against innocent people, even for the crimes he had committed against the not-so-innocent, he should pay with his life.

"You need killing real bad."

Jack pressed the knife deeper into the soft underbelly of the man's chin, opening the skin, causing a thread of blood to trickle down the blade. Carl thrashed his uninjured left leg. His voice cracked around another plea for mercy.

The temptation was overwhelming. The desire blazing and irresistible. The rightness and morality of it compelled Jack to push the rippled blade into Carl's throat.

"I give you to the devil, you son of a bitch."

The distance between the wrought-iron gate and the house was at least seventy-five yards, most of it in the open. The blood trail marked the way. Ezzy dashed from tree to bush to anything else that would provide him cover. With still about twenty yards to go, he paused to catch his breath behind a large pecan tree from which a child's swing was suspended. He could hear raised voices coming from the house, but at this distance he couldn't make out the words.

He checked his pistol to assure that all the chambers were loaded, then stepped around the tree. As he did, a blood-curdling scream issued from the house, followed by the shouted words, "Run, Anna!"

A second later, Anna Corbett darted through the front door with her child in her arms, running like her life depended on it, and Ezzy was certain it did. She crossed the porch, ran down the steps, and started across the yard. Ezzy met her about halfway between the parked vehicles and the house and practically had to tackle her in order to get her behind the old orange pickup. She fought him like hell until she recognized him and realized that he was trying to protect her.

"You're all right, you're all right."

The kid was crying. She was clutching him tightly and patting his back, but she was looking frantically toward the house, and Ezzy wondered who was left inside. The hired hand? Lomax? Hutts and who else? The Herbolds? Had they come home? Would she be able to tell him if he asked?

Two shots were fired in quick succession.

"Jesus Lord," Ezzy muttered. No time for questions.

He took Anna's chin in his hand and turned her face toward him, ordering, "Stay here!" He crept around the rear of the truck, then sprinted to the porch and crouched down at the side of the front steps where he was out of sight of anyone inside.

He leaned against the wooden trellis material that screened the gap between the ground and the underside of the porch. He counted it a miracle that he had made it this far without being shot and conceded that his critics were right: He was too old for this shit. Taking deep breaths, he concentrated on slowing down his heart.

From the open front door he heard sounds of a struggle—flesh meeting flesh, thumping noises that were unmistakably those of bodies hitting walls, grunts of effort and groans of pain. He raised his head just enough to peer over the edge of the porch. As he did, a pistol clattered out the front door and slid across the porch, coming to rest a few feet from his nose.

He stared quizzically at the weapon. "What the hell?"

It was just beyond his reach. He couldn't get it without exposing himself, and he was reluctant to do that. Anna's hired hand might enjoy knowing he had backup, but as long as the criminals were unaware of Ezzy's presence, he held a slight advantage.

He was still debating the next course of action when the man he suddenly remembered was named Jack stumbled out. Bent almost double at the waist, he crossed the porch with lurching footsteps. Momentum more than his own muscle coordination propelled him down the steps. He managed to remain on his feet, however, and, holding his right side with his left hand, staggered across the yard on legs that looked ready to buckle at any second.

Chapter Forty-Nine

$\mathcal{T}$hank God, thank God, thought Anna when Jack cleared the door.
He was in pain from his broken rib, that was apparent. Blood
streamed from the blow Carl Herbold had struck on his head. His face
was bruised and scratched. But he was alive.

She willed him not to stumble and fall. Anxiously she watched as he
made it across the porch and down the steps. *Only a few more yards,
Jack, and you'll be safely with us.*

He had almost drawn even with Lomax's car when Carl appeared in
the doorway of the house.

He braced himself against the doorjamb with a hand that was wet
with his own blood. The right leg of his trousers was soaked with it, and
the knife wound continued to gush crimson. Already his skin was as
pale as a cadaver. Dark circles ringed sunken eyes. His lips looked
bloodless. Life was literally draining from him.

But he wasn't dead yet. He had enough strength to shuffle forward,
bend down, and pick up the pistol lying on the porch. He had enough
life in him to raise his arm.

Anna sprang up from behind the pickup truck. She reached across the
hood of it as though to extend Jack a lifeline.

He smiled at her.

Warn him, Anna, warn him!

As though she had spoken it a million times, his name felt familiar as
it vibrated across her vocal cords. Her tongue found the correct position
against her palate. Her lips cooperated almost unconsciously.

Years of coaching and practice helped, of course. The patience of
teachers counted for something. Unheard sounds, endlessly repeated,

worked their way out of her memory, resurfacing now when she needed them.

But without the loving, life-saving will to speak his name, she would have remained mute.

"Jack!"

Time stopped. Motion was freeze-framed. She watched his face register stunned surprise. His eyes lit up. The lines around them deepened as a smile broke across his lips. Her mind photographed him far better than any camera could. This would be the picture of him that she would carry with her forever.

Then time resumed at a frenzied pace, making up for that which had been lost. His joyous expression was replaced with a grimace of agony as the bullet from Carl's gun struck him in the back. His arms reflexively flew upward. His palms were face out, as though he were raising them in surrender. He pitched forward, landing first on his knees, then falling facedown.

Anna screamed and was about to round the hood of the truck to run to him when she saw Ezzy Hardge crouched at the edge of the porch, frantically waving her back.

Carl raised the pistol again. This time he aimed it at her.

Carl watched the hired hand disappear through the front door. He was ashamed of his groveling, ashamed of the way he'd pleaded that his life be spared. The way he'd blubbered, he'd been no braver than Cecil.

He was in a shitload of trouble. He was bleeding like a stuck pig, and if it wasn't stanched soon he was going to die. He'd once watched a guy bleed out from a shank stuck in his liver. It hadn't been Carl's quarrel, so he had done nothing to stop the fight or to help the loser. He'd just stood there along with everybody else, making bets on how long it was going to take, and watching the guy's blood eddy down the shower drain until it ran out.

He didn't want to die like that. He didn't want to die, period. He sure as hell wasn't going to die without taking this cuss with him.

He forced himself to crawl to the door. Myron, he noticed, was out cold, his mouth gaping and drooling. Carl wished he'd had a convenient opportunity to kill him for being so stupid and making such a fucking mess of things. But he hated to waste the time on Myron now. Every second counted.

He wanted that smart-mouthed son of a bitch who thought he had done him a big favor by not killing him. Carl would rather he had slit his throat than extend him mercy. Like he needed mercy. Not him. Not Carl Herbold.

He crawled over the Jag-driving asshole. Next stop, the open door. But getting there was like trying to swim up Niagara Falls. Each second seemed like a millennium. He nearly blacked out several times. Only a murderous intent kept him going.

Until, finally, he was there.

Garnering all his strength, he climbed the jamb, hand over hand, pulling himself up, willing strength into his legs that already felt cold and lifeless. Once on his feet, he spotted the pistol. It seemed a mile away, although it lay on the porch not more than a few feet beyond the door.

He wouldn't have the time or the strength to reload. How many bullets had been fired? Three? Four? At least two remained, he thought. Maybe three. But bullets would be no damn use to him if he couldn't get to the pistol.

Moving only by a sheer act of will, he stepped across the threshold. Adrenaline alone allowed him to bend down and pick up the gun. Raising his arm took a thousand times more strength than he had, but he did it, by God, and aimed the pistol at the center of the hired hand's back.

In his peripheral vision he saw the woman pop up from behind the pickup.

"Jack!"

They had lied to him! Lied to Cecil. Like saps they had believed she was a deaf mute. Dumb fucking Cecil. He'd swallowed their phony story and fed it to Carl, and like a fool he'd bought it, too.

Jack. Is that what she'd said? Jack. Good name for a jokester.

Smiling because the last laugh was on them, Carl pulled the trigger.

The man went down. Carl angled his arm slightly to the right and pointed the pistol at the bitch who had tricked him.

Ezzy stood up, startling Carl and drawing his attention away from Anna Corbett. "Hey, Carl, remember me?"

Carl's mouth went slack with astonishment. He hadn't known anyone was there. He sure as hell hadn't figured on it being one of his sworn enemies.

"Drop the gun," Ezzy said calmly, hoping Carl wouldn't.

He didn't. He fired.

Simultaneously Ezzy pulled the trigger of his .357.

But his arm recoiled at the same instant, throwing his aim off, and sending the pistol flying out of his hand and into the flower bed.

The bullet smacked into the support column of the porch, splintering the wood, but doing Carl no damage whatsoever.

Carl laughed. Ezzy stared into the bore of his pistol.

* * *

Jack rolled to his side and looked behind him just as Ezzy Hardge and Carl Herbold fired simultaneously. He didn't think about it. Didn't hesitate. He didn't reckon with God or the devil, or ask why it was left to him, or consider the consequences. He acted on instinct. He threw his knife.

The knife struck as Carl fired.

It pierced his chest so deeply that only the handle was left sticking out and it quivered from the stunning impact.

For several seconds Ezzy didn't know why he wasn't dead.

Gauging by Carl's expression, he was bumfuddled too.

Ezzy gazed stupidly at the knife.

Carl tilted his head down and saw the carved handle protruding from his chest and opened his mouth to scream, but only blood bubbled out.

He staggered backward, but he was dead before he hit the porch.

Ezzy, jerked backward from the edge of his own grave, glanced into the yard, where Anna Corbett was kneeling beside Jack. She had his head cradled in her lap. The kid was beside her, crying. But the man's legs were moving. He was alive.

After retrieving his pistol from the bed of petunias, Ezzy climbed the front steps and paused to look down at Carl. He'd always had an ego big as Dallas. He would hate knowing that he hadn't died handsome. There was a real dumb expression on his face.

Ezzy moved past him and cautiously stepped inside the house. The entry hall of Anna Corbett's home looked and smelled like a slaughterhouse. Lomax lay supine, obviously dead from a gunshot wound in this chest.

Myron Hutts was lying against the wall in a fetal position, babbling in a low murmur.

Ezzy approached him with apprehension, but the man put up no resistance when Ezzy knelt beside him. "Give me your hands, Myron." Docilely, Hutts extended his hands, and Ezzy locked restraints on his wrists, then holstered his pistol.

"Is Carl mad at me?"

"Carl's dead."

"Oh."

"You're bleeding pretty bad, Myron."

"It hurts."

"Think you can stand up?"

"Okay." Ezzy assisted him to his feet and guided him past Lomax. He didn't give the body a second glance. Nor did he seem to notice Carl as he shuffled his big feet over the threshold and stepped outside. "Can I have a PayDay?"

"Sure, Myron."

"And a Popsicle?"

"Once we get you to the hospital I'll see what I can do."

Emergency vehicles and patrol cars were screaming up the drive. Ezzy was shocked to realize that it had been only a few minutes since he'd arrived at the gate. It wouldn't have surprised him to learn that a million years had elapsed since then. It seemed at least that long.

He turned Myron over to a pair of arresting officers who read him his rights even as a team of paramedics started working on him. He was telling them about the promised candy bar and Popsicle.

Another paramedic ordered Ezzy to lie down on the porch until the gurney arrived.

"What the hell for?" he asked querulously.

The young woman looked at him with perplexity. "Well, sir, you've been shot."

Only then did he become aware of the throbbing pain in his right arm. "Well I'll be damned." Actually he was glad to know Carl had shot him. He thought he had dropped his weapon out of carelessness or just plain old age.

He laughed, causing the young paramedic to regard him with alarm. "No, young lady, I'm not delirious," he told her. He also refused to be placed on a gurney for the short distance to the ambulance. "I can walk it."

"Hey, Ezzy!" Sheriff Ron Foster jogged toward him and fell into step. "Are you all right?"

"Can't complain."

"You did a hell of a job, Ezzy. A hell of a job."

Dismissing the compliment, he asked. "How's Steve Jones?"

"He'll need a lot of physical therapy once they rebuild his knee, but he'll make it."

"He's a good officer. Too bad about Jim."

"Yeah."

"How 'bout him?" He watched as the man who'd saved his life was loaded into an ambulance. Anna Corbett and her boy climbed in behind the gurney.

"Hanging on to consciousness. Could be internal injuries. He's a wait-and-see."

Ezzy nodded grimly and his throat felt thick. "I'd be dead, weren't for him."

"Soon as the doctors have patched your arm and you feel up to it, I need to know what happened."

"I don't know what went on inside," he told Foster. "But it must've been bad. It's a wonder they survived."

It wasn't much farther to the ambulance. He wouldn't humiliate himself now by asking for a gurney that he'd refused, but he was feeling a little woozy. He'd lost more blood than he thought. It took some concentration to get his legs to work right.

Foster was saying, "I can't question Mrs. Corbett until we get an interpreter, but when I asked the boy what happened he said that the mean man had shot Mr. Lomax and hit Jack, and that his mother had stabbed the mean man in the leg."

"Anna stabbed him?"

"With Jack's knife."

"The infamous knife," Ezzy muttered.

"Pardon?"

"Nothing." Ezzy saw no point in mentioning the incident between the hired hand and Emory Lomax. Their rivalry—if there ever had been one—was irrelevant now.

"Sheriff Foster?"

A deputy joined them. "Coroner said to give you this. It was plugged into Carl Herbold's chest tighter'n a cork." He handed Foster a plastic evidence bag with the bloody knife sealed inside.

"Thanks." Foster held up the bag and studied the weapon. "This son of a bitch would do a body harm, all right."

"Can I see it?"

The sheriff passed the bag to Ezzy. The knife was as unusual as Lomax's secretary had described it. Mrs. Presley had said it had a bone handle, although to Ezzy it looked more like stag antler. He had thought she was daft when she tried to describe the blade, but damned if it wasn't an iridescent dark blue, and rippled, like the surface of a deep glacier lake stirred by a high wind.

"Hmm. Isn't your run-of-the-mill hunting knife, is it?"

"I'd hate to be on the receiving end of it," Foster replied.

"I've only seen one other knife made like this," Ezzy said. "Years ago a guy here in town had one. Name of John—"

Suddenly Ezzy couldn't catch his breath and his footsteps faltered. He must've swayed dizzily, because Foster reached out to lend support. "Ma'am, I think he's gonna faint."

The paramedic slid her arm around Ezzy. "I knew he should've had a gurney."

Ezzy struggled to shake her off. "What do they call this?" he rasped, running his finger along the patterned blade of the knife inside the plastic bag.

"Come on, Ezzy. All aboard," the younger sheriff said in a patronizing tone that would have annoyed Ezzy at any time, but never more so than now.

Even with the two of them trying to move him along, he stiffened his legs and refused to budge. "There's a term for this among knife makers, isn't there? What is it?" He didn't want to get his hopes up if he wasn't right. He wanted someone else to confirm that he was right.

But he *knew* he was right.

"Ezzy—"

"Answer me, goddammit!"

"Uh, it's, uh . . ." Rapidly snapping his fingers, Foster groped for the word. "Flinting. It's called flinting. Because the Indians used to make knives like this out of flint."

Chapter Fifty

I don't think you're supposed to get up, Mr. Hardge."

The nurse trainee had entered his room to find him sitting on the edge of the hospital bed.

"I'm fairly sure I'm not supposed to, but I going to anyway."

"I'm calling the nurse."

"You're minding your own business," Ezzy snapped. "I got shot in the arm. Nothing to it. No reason I can't walk."

"But you had surgery. You're on an IV."

"I'm fine." He lowered his feet to the floor and stood. "See? Fine. I just want to take a walk down the hall. I'll be back before anybody misses me. So just keep quiet about it, okay?"

The rolling IV stand helped support him as he shuffled toward the door. The tile floor was cold on the soles of his feet. With his free hand, he reached behind him to hold together the flimsy hospital gown.

Leaving his room, he turned left down the corridor. He glanced behind him at the young nurse, who was wringing her hands with indecision. He gave her a reassuring thumbs-up.

By the time the ambulance had reached the hospital yesterday afternoon, he was high on whatever they'd put into the IV en route. Cora had always said he couldn't take half an aspirin tablet without catching a buzz. In the emergency room he vaguely remembered being probed and prodded, X-rayed and examined, and told that the bullet had passed through his arm without doing too much damage. Nevertheless, they had to operate to clear out debris and bone splinters, assess and repair any muscle damage, and so on. Ezzy lost interest and consciousness at approximately the same time.

This morning he had awakened with a bandage around his arm, all-over achiness, a muzziness in his head, and a fire in his belly to speak with the patient in a room down the hall. No LVN or RN or any other kind of N was going to keep him from it.

He made it down the corridor without being stopped. When he reached the door he sought, he pushed it open and went in. The only sound in the room came from his IV stand; one of the wheels was squeaky. The patient turned his head toward the sound. He looked like he'd been rode hard and put up wet, but Ezzy got the impression that he wasn't sleeping even though his eyes had been closed. Ezzy also got the impression that he wasn't surprised to see him.

He said, "Sheriff Hardge."

"Hello, Johnny."

Jack Sawyer smiled ruefully. "I haven't been called that in a while."

"When did you change your name from John Junior?"

He turned his eyes toward the ceiling, giving Ezzy his profile. The resemblance that had escaped Ezzy up till now was so apparent he wondered how he'd missed it. Of course he hadn't been looking for it.

Sawyer continued to stare at the ceiling for several moments. Finally he turned back to Ezzy. "I stopped going by Johnny after that night." Following a short pause, he added, "That night changed more than my name. It changed a lot of things."

The two men shared a long stare, each struck by the magnitude of that understatement.

The moment was interrupted when Anna Corbett came in carrying a cup of coffee. Unlike Jack Sawyer, she seemed shocked to see Ezzy. "Good morning, Anna."

She smiled at him and, after setting her coffee on the bed tray, wrote something on a tablet and extended it to him. "You don't have to thank me," he said after reading her note. "I'm just glad you and your boy made it out okay. That's the important thing. How's he this morning?"

"He's staying with Marjorie Baker," Jack told him. "She consulted a child psychologist on Anna's behalf. David'll likely need some counseling."

"After a time, he'll be all right. Kids are resilient."

Anna wrote another message for Ezzy on her tablet. "He's worried about Jack and angry at me for not letting him come to the hospital to see him."

Ezzy looked at Jack. "He likes you, huh?"

"And I like him. He's a great kid. I hate like hell he was there yesterday, seeing all that, hearing all the filthy things Carl said." His regret was obvious, and so was his concern for the boy. "Anna should be with him instead of hanging around here fussing over me." He looked up at her. "But she refuses to leave."

They gazed at each other with such blatant affection and desire that Ezzy felt himself blushing. Jack took her hand, lifted it to his mouth and kept it there a long time, his eyes tightly closed. When he opened them, Ezzy noticed tears. "I guess it's the anesthesia," he explained in a gruff, self-conscious voice. "The nurse told me it makes some people emotional. It's just . . . every time I think of how it might have turned out yesterday . . ."

He didn't have to say more. Anna bent down and kissed his lips softly, then dragged a chair forward and pressed Ezzy's shoulder. More light-headed than he had expected to be, he sat down gratefully. Anna draped a blanket across his shoulders.

"Thanks."

She motioned toward his arm, a question in her eyes.

"It's okay. Might throw off my horseshoe game a bit, but other than that . . ." He shrugged.

She sat down on the edge of the hospital bed and took Jack's hand.

Ezzy said, "I haven't asked about you yet. How's your wound?"

"Hurts like hell, but the doctor told me I was damned lucky. Bullet missed my spine and vital organs. Another fraction of an inch one way or the other, and I could have been paralyzed or dead."

"Ah, well, that's good."

That exchange was followed by an awkward silence. Anna began to sense it and divided a curious look between them. She wrote a note to Jack. He said, "No, you don't have to go. In fact, you might just as well hear this now. Then if you want to leave, I'll understand."

A vertical worry line appeared between her eyebrows as she wrote on her tablet. After showing the message to Jack, he said, "No, it's got nothing to do with the poisoned cows. It's more serious than that."

"Y'all've lost me. Poisoned cows?"

"It's insignificant," Jack told Ezzy.

Their dialogue only increased Anna's confusion and concern. Jack Sawyer squeezed her hand. "It'll be okay, Anna." He turned to Ezzy, locked eyes with him, hesitated a moment, then said, "That day you walked into the Dairy Queen and spoke to Delray, I nearly shit."

"I didn't recognize you, Johnny. You'd grown up, become a man. But even if I had known you on sight, it wouldn't have mattered. I didn't make the connection until yesterday."

"For all I knew, you had a twenty-two-year-old arrest warrant for me."

"No."

Jack looked at Anna, reached up and touched her cheek. "I took a real chance coming back to Blewer, but I . . . I had to. As long as Carl was in prison, my conscience stayed clear. He deserved the sentence he got for killing that off-duty cop during the convenience store holdup. But as soon as I heard he had escaped, I knew I had to be on hand in case he tried to make good his threat to kill Delray."

Anna made a quick sign.

"Why?" Jack said. "Because it's my fault that Carl issued that threat. Delray blamed Carl for something he didn't do. He thought his stepsons were connected to the death of a girl named Patsy McCorkle. They weren't. And I knew it."

Her lips parted in wordless surprise. She looked quickly at Ezzy. He lowered his eyes to his lap, where his hands were lying loosely clasped. The band of pressure he had felt around his chest for almost a quarter of a century began to shake loose.

"See, Anna," Jack was saying, "my mom raised me practically by herself. Occasionally my daddy would put in an appearance, but when he did there was always trouble. He'd get drunk. She'd whine. He'd get caught with another man's wife. There'd be a row. She'd cry. He'd flaunt his lovers. They'd have terrible fights."

He paused for a moment, and Ezzy could see the torment behind his eyes as he remembered unhappy times. "I won't bore you with the details. Bottom line, my old man was worthless. A lousy husband and a worse father. But don't feel too sorry for my mother. She put up with it. That was her choice. She loved her misery more than she loved either him or me.

"After she died, I was placed in foster care. My old man left me in the system for a while, then decided he wanted me to be with him. Not out of the goodness of his heart, or because he gave a damn what happened to me. He needed a playmate, an errand boy. He landed a job as a roughneck and was sent up here to Blewer. He made pretty good money. Things were all right.

"In fact, life got to be fun. Life with my mother had been drudgery. But with my old man, it was a constant party. More often as not, people thought we were brothers. He didn't look old enough to be my dad—he *wasn't* old enough to be my dad, except biologically.

"Discipline wasn't in his vocabulary. He let me do whatever I pleased, and after living with a couple of foster families where correction had been harsh, I loved the freedom. He never made me go to school. Once, when a truancy agent came by, he charmed her and they wound up in bed together that same afternoon.

"He took me out drinking with him nearly every night. For my fifteenth birthday he gave me a night with one of his girlfriends. After that, we shared women with no more regard than we'd split a candy bar. At sixteen I formally quit school and got a job with the same drilling outfit he worked for."

"I guess that's about the time I met y'all," Ezzy interjected.

Jack nodded. "Daddy hadn't cleaned up his act any. He still got drunk and disorderly sometimes. On more than one occasion you brought him home, Ezzy. Remember?"

Ezzy nodded.

"One night he got in a fight over a woman in a bar. You called me to come get him or else you were going to put him in jail."

"You had a lot of responsibility for a boy that age."

"As I said, it was fun. For a while. And then, I don't know what happened exactly. I can't recall a specific event that woke me up to what a sordid life we were living. I guess the realization crept up on me. Gradually our lifestyle no longer seemed so sweet. In fact it turned sour.

"The older Daddy got, the younger the women he chased. His sexual innuendos and seduction techniques didn't seem clever and naughty to me anymore, just distasteful. The harder he worked at satisfying his appetites, the more it took to satisfy them.

"One night we brought this girl home with us. Daddy got rough and she got scared. I said I wanted no part of that kinky stuff. He cussed me out, called me a wimp, a pussy, an embarrassment to him. While he was ranting and raving, the girl gathered her clothes and ran out. After he sobered up, I don't think he even remembered what he'd tried to do to her."

He paused and stared straight ahead. Ezzy figured he was too ashamed to look at either Anna or him.

"We met Pasty McCorkle at the Wagon Wheel. She ran around with a wild crowd, including the Herbold brothers. They hung out in the same taverns as Daddy and me, but they always meant trouble. Already they had spent time in reform school and in your jail, Ezzy, and were destined for bigger and better things. I steered clear of them.

"Patsy wasn't a pretty girl, but she had a spirit of adventure that appealed to my old man. He was way too old for her, but she was flattered by his attention. The first time they were together it was in the backseat of our car on the Wagon Wheel's parking lot. Later he described it to me in detail and told me that I shouldn't be put off by her looks, that I didn't know what I was missing, that if I closed my eyes it didn't matter what she looked like. Things like that, only in much cruder

language. Looking back, I think he favored women who were emotionally needy, like my mother, like Patsy, because they fed his ego."

"What happened that night, Johnny?"

"Daddy had forgot to make the payments, so our car had been repos-
sessed several days earlier. He was pissed and depressed, but he wanted
to go out and party, take his mind off his troubles. When we got to the
bar, it was already crowded. Daddy's mood didn't improve when he saw
Patsy carrying on with the Herbolds. He tried to woo her away, but she
had eyes only for them that night.

"Daddy drank steadily, until he had spent all the money in his pocket.
When he ran out, he offered to sell this guy his knife for cash. Everybody was familiar with that knife because it was so unusual. He liked to
brag about how it had been handed down through several generations of
Sawyers. Whether or not that was true, I don't know. He probably stole
it, but he'd had it for as long as I could remember.

"In any event, the guy wasn't interested in buying it, and Daddy took
that as an insult to his family. They got into a shouting match. The bartender—I think he owned the place—"

"He did. Parker Gee," Ezzy interjected.

"Before they could come to blows, he told me to take Daddy outside.
Try and cool him down. We were still out there when Patsy staggered
out with the Herbolds. She was drunk, but not so drunk that she didn't
realize they were dumping her. She expected to leave with them and
continue the party somewhere else. They said they had business to
attend to and she couldn't go."

"So their alibi was sound."

"I guess so, Ezzy. Because they left the Wagon Wheel without Patsy."

"She offered you and your daddy a ride."

"More or less. The details are foggy, but we left with her. To my
knowledge no one saw us getting into her car."

"But every last person I questioned testified that she had left with the
Herbolds. Including you."

"Yeah," he admitted, on an expulsion of breath. "I lied to you, Ezzy.
She walked out with Carl and Cecil. But she drove away with my old
man and me."

Ezzy remembered talking to Johnny Sawyer a couple days following
the incident. The boy had told him the same story he had heard from
other bar patrons. He'd had no reason to doubt him. "Go on. What happened after y'all left?"

It was as Ezzy had surmised the morning he saw her body. Patsy and
the two men went to the river and had a sex party.

Anna's face didn't reveal what she was thinking, although Sawyer appeared to be in pain when he admitted to his participation. "I took my turn with Patsy because I was a little drunk myself and didn't want to get Daddy riled again by saying no thanks. Then they went at it a couple of times while I just sat there drinking, getting drunker. I wasn't even alarmed when she got on her knees and he entered her from behind because he'd told me she liked it that way."

Ezzy's cheeks flamed, not because he was embarrassed, but because he was embarrassed for Anna. To her credit she sat stoically, her features composed. But Ezzy knew she was catching every word because tears shimmered in her eyes.

Jack stared into near space for a moment. "They were . . . involved in what they were doing. She as much as my dad. He had her by the hair, sort of whipping her head around. Then, just like that," he said, snapping his fingers, "her neck snapped. Like a twig. I heard it. I don't think Daddy did. In any event he didn't stop till . . . well, you know." After another short silence, he blinked Ezzy into focus. "I swear to you, he didn't intend to kill her."

"Then why in God's name didn't you tell me that?" Ezzy demanded angrily. "Goddamn it, Johnny, do you realize how many hours I have anguished—"

"I'm more aware of the cost than you," Jack said, raising his voice to match Ezzy's.

Ezzy tamped down his temper and took several deep breaths. "When I came to your house to question you, why in hell did you lie about leaving with her that night? Why didn't you clear up the matter then? If I recall, you covered for your daddy. You told me he was working out of town. God help me, I believed you and never even checked it out. I had no reason not to believe you. John Sawyer was a scoundrel, a drunk, and a womanizer, but he was no *killer*. If it was an accident, he would've been charged with involuntary manslaughter and probably gotten probation. No jury from Blewer County, Texas, would have sympathized with a reputed slut who engaged in anal sex with an older man while his underage son watched. Why didn't he come forward and explain what happened?"

"He couldn't."

"Nonsense. You said he didn't intentionally kill her."

"He didn't. But I intentionally killed him."

Chapter Fifty-One

*A*nna's quick intake of breath was audible. But she remained perfectly still and stared at Jack with the same stunned, unblinking dismay with which Ezzy was gaping at him.

Jack Sawyer's features worked emotionally. "I said to him everything you've just said to me, Ezzy. Patsy was beyond the age of consent. It wasn't rape. She was willing. She participated. It was an *accident*. I begged him to do the right thing.

"He wouldn't listen. Refused to even talk about it. Said he wasn't going to get tangled up in a legal mess over a piece of tail. Words to that effect. We got into an argument that turned violent.

"After exchanging several blows, I pushed him into the river in the hope of cooling him off, sobering him up, restoring his common sense. But he dragged me into the water with him and held me under. I fought and fought. He wouldn't let up. He held me under. His own son. I thought, *My daddy's killing me. He's going to drown me unless I do something to stop it.*

"My lungs were burning, ready to burst, and he wouldn't let me up," he said, his voice cracking. "I was clutching at anything. My hand connected with his scabbard. In seconds I had the knife in my hand and used it to cut his arm. He let go of me and I surfaced. But my cutting him only made him angrier. He called my mother and me every vile thing he could think of. Said he'd never wanted any part of either of us. Said we'd ruined his life and he was sick of being shackled to a sniveling little dick weed like me. Then he charged me again, put his hands around my throat, and pushed me under. So I killed him."

No one moved or spoke for a long time. Like strangers in an elevator, they avoided eye contact and conversation. Anything said now would have sounded banal, but perhaps the silence was even more uncomfortable.

It stretched on interminably until Jack finally spoke after loudly clearing his throat. "I was afraid to drop the knife in the river, afraid that it would be dragged for evidence. So I kept it. At first from fear of getting caught. Later as a talisman. It was a constant reminder of what I was capable of, and it frightened me. I couldn't number the times since that night that I wanted to throw it away, but, in a twisted sort of way, keeping it protected me from ever having to use it again. I couldn't even use it yesterday against Herbold until I absolutely had no choice."

"You had no choice that night, either, Johnny," Ezzy said quietly. "You acted in self-defense."

"Did I?" he asked on a bitter laugh. "I'd like to think so, but I'm not sure. I was younger and stronger than him. Maybe I could have eventually worn him down and talked sense into him. Or outrun him. Could I have done anything else? Honestly, I don't know.

"But not a day goes by that I don't ask myself if it was necessary to kill him. All I know with certainty is that when I drove that blade into him, I wanted him to die."

"So would anybody who was fighting for his life."

Jack looked at him a moment, then lowered his eyes noncommittally.

"What did you do with him?"

"Dragged him downstream. I waded for hours, towing him. When it was almost daylight, I pulled him ashore and dug a hole in the woods, using my bare hands. I covered it with boulders. I guess he's still there. It took me all the next day to make it back home. Then I slept for almost twenty-four hours. I was packing to leave when you showed up at our door asking questions about Patsy McCorkle. I was so scared I'm surprised you couldn't hear my knees knocking."

"You were only a boy, Johnny."

"I was old enough. Old enough to know I needed to get the hell out of Blewer before somebody started missing my daddy. I settled all our accounts in town, dropped off our rent with the landlord, told him we were moving and didn't know where, and hopped a freight train that night.

"I haven't stopped, not really, until now. Always looking over my shoulder. Never let myself stay in one place too long. Never formed any attachments I couldn't walk away from on short notice." He looked at Anna, then glanced away as though he dreaded seeing the effect his story had had on her. "When I heard Carl had escaped, I knew it was time to pay the piper. I risked my freedom coming back, but I wasn't really free, anyway."

Ezzy sat for a long time, contemplating the pattern in the linoleum, before painfully coming to his feet. "Well, you got Carl Herbold, and that's made you a hero. As for the other, I'm not a law officer anymore. This was strictly off the record. You've done more for me than you know, Johnny. Sorry . . . Jack. I'm satisfied just knowing what happened. It was a long time ago. In the grand scheme of things, I guess it doesn't matter how it happened."

"It matters to me," Jack declared, surprising him. "That night changed my life, but *not* forever. Not unless I choose to let it, and I no longer do. If I'd told the truth, neither you nor Delray would have held his stepsons responsible for that girl's death. Things might have been different between them."

"They were bad boys, Jack. Nothing would have made things right between them."

"In any case, he wouldn't have lived under Carl's death threat," he argued. "Anna and David's lives wouldn't have been in jeopardy yesterday." He shook his head stubbornly. "No, Ezzy, I caused a lot of people a great deal of pain—you included—because of what I did and didn't do.

"Any way you label it, I killed my father. I want the guilt off my back once and for all. This half-baked confession to you isn't going to do it. Put it into the system. Run it through all the proper legal channels, whatever that entails. Arrest. Jail. Grand jury. Trial. Whatever. I want it finished."

"What do you mean you don't know where he is? Are you in the habit of losing patients? Who's in charge? I want my husband found, and I want him found now."

Down the hall at the nurses' station, Cora was giving them hell. The timid young nurse who knew about Ezzy's escape from his room was pretending to be engrossed in a file.

"Cora?"

At the sound of his voice, she turned. Despite the blistering lecture she was giving the hospital staff, she looked on the verge of cracking. When she saw him, her chin began to tremble. She clamped her lips together to keep them still, although the tears standing in her eyes were a dead giveaway that she was about to cry, and not for the first time.

He rolled his squeaky IV stand along, wishing he looked and felt more like a man and less like a relic. Seeing her for the first time since she left, he would have preferred to be clean-shaven, fully dressed, and looking like a stud. Instead his legs looked like hairy, bleached toothpicks. His feet were pale and veiny and his toenails probably needed cutting. In this silly ass-baring gown he didn't cut a very dashing figure.

In spite of all that, she seemed damn glad to see him. She hurried down the hall toward him but pulled up just short of touching him. "They called me last night and told me what happened." That was all she could manage before she lost control of her lower lip again.

"You back?" he asked.

"If you want me."

"I always did."

He opened his arms and she stepped into them. She would learn all about the Herbolds from the media blitz the story was getting, especially since the bodies of Cecil and Connie had been discovered. There would be time later to fill her in on Jack Sawyer's story, and to impress upon her how different their life would be now that the mystery of that summer night had been solved for him.

He would file the confession as Sawyer had requested. But if he knew Cora, she would argue that John Sawyer, Jr., had been merely a boy in an extremely unfortunate situation, and that he deserved mercy, not punishment, especially since he had killed public enemy number one and saved Ezzy's life, and that if there was an inquest, Ezzy should testify on Sawyer's behalf, and that they should invite him and Anna Corbett to their house for dinner to demonstrate their unwavering support.

She would probably be surprised when he agreed with her.

But all that could wait. For now, he simply hugged her tightly, loving her, and loving the feeling of being whole again

With dread, Jack dragged his eyes up to Anna's face. He smiled sadly and raised one shoulder in a sheepish shrug. "You once asked me for my story. Now you know why I was reluctant to tell it. And I just want to say, well, that it meant a hell of a lot to me that my history didn't seem to matter to you when, you know . . . when we were together. That you were so accepting of me. That for a little while you loved me." He nodded toward the door. "But you're under no obligation to me, Anna. You walk out, I'll understand. You'll never see me again."

Anna responded in the language she was most comfortable with. She began to sign. *"I asked what your story was because I wanted to know you, Jack, not judge you. It's an unhappy story, and I hate that for you. But it doesn't change how I feel about you. In fact, it makes me love you more. It makes me want to give you unlimited happiness because you've had so little.*

"I don't believe that you'll be charged with the death of your father.

Not after saving all our lives yesterday. But if you are, I'll be right there with you every step of the way. I'll stand by you no matter what happens because . . . because you love me. Me," she repeated, pressing her chest.

"My parents' love was tinged with guilt. Two hearing people had a deaf child. They blamed themselves. They wondered what sin they had committed that was so bad their child was punished with deafness.

"I know Dean loved me. If he had lived we would have had a wonderful life together. But he looked upon my handicap as an enemy we must battle. He was willing to fight it, but because he felt it was something that needed to be fought, I knew he hated it.

"Delray loved me too. At least in his own mind he did. But his love was . . . was choking. No, not choking. A word like that. I couldn't breathe. Couldn't be what I wanted to be.

"My parents felt responsible for my deafness. Dean wanted to defeat it. Delray took advantage of it. But with you, Jack, it has made no difference. None. You accept it as part of me. That's why I love you.

"That's the main reason. There are others. I love you for caring about David. That's no small thing. I could never fall in love with a man who didn't also love my son. I know your affection for him is real and honest.

"I also desire you. Every hour of the day I think about making love to you. My fantasies make me hot. I had them before . . . but certainly now that I know what it's like to be with you. I tingle. Here." She touched her breasts, her lower tummy.

"I look at you, and my heart beats faster. I think about you, and I can't catch my breath. You touch me, and this . . . this wonderful feeling bubbles up inside me and I want to laugh and cry at the same time. I can't contain the feeling. I think it's joy. Joy. Because even though we're facing difficult times, I'm happier than I've ever been. You've made me happy because you love me.

"You'll try and talk me out of staying with you. I know you. You'll say that you've brought David and me nothing but trouble. You're wrong. I knew there was much missing from our lives, but I didn't know what it was until I saw you. And then I knew. We need you even more than you need us. Let us be your family, the one you never had.

"If you want us, we want you. If you want me, I want you. Flaws and all, if you take me, I take you. I love you, Jack."

Holding his eyes with hers, she lowered her hands to her lap and was still.

Jack hadn't taken his eyes off her face. He had read the words as her lips formed them, searched her eyes for meaning, evaluated inflections by her changing expressions.

To him her speech had looked like a graceful ballet, rife with emotion, conveying her innermost thoughts and emotions, her fingertips acting as an extension of her soul. He had no idea what she had said, but he knew what she had communicated.

He reached for her hands, kissed them in turn, then pressed them tightly between his.

He didn't speak.

After her eloquent profession of love, any spoken language would have been superfluous.